Praise for *Murder at Mallowan Hall*

"Two words describe this book: absolutely delicious . . . *Murder at Mallowan Hall* is a near-perfect traditional mystery." —*First Clue*

"Charmingly told, with a full upstairs-downstairs cast of guests and servants, *Murder at Mallowan Hall* is a wonderful mystery by Colleen Cambridge. . . . Fans of Agatha Christie, historical fiction and fierce female leads are all sure to enjoy." —*Shelf Awareness*

"Agatha Christie the person plays a very peripheral part in the proceedings, but Agatha Christie the writer haunts every page of this delightful book that both pays homage to the Queen of Crime, but also embroiders on her work with a fresh character and a fresh look at a part of her life. This is a wonderful series debut." —*Mystery Scene*

"[A] solid series launch from Cambridge. . . . Readers will want to see more of the clever Phyllida." —*Publishers Weekly*

"Finally it can be told: One of Agatha Christie's most popular novels was inspired by a murder at her (fictional) manor house solved by her (fictional) housekeeper. . . . Christie fans can expect a series."—*Kirkus Reviews*

"Colleen Cambridge has done her homework on English society and provides us with a clear picture of her characters, where they live, and how they act. She does well at capturing the era with all the right language and dialects. It's a good cozy to read with a cup of tea on the patio." —*New York Journal of Books*

"A delightful murder mystery! *Murder at Mallowan Hall* felt like a combination of Clue, *Upstairs Downstairs,* and of course Agatha Christie. I look forward to seeing what sleuthing Phyllida takes on next!" —Stefanie Lynn, The Kennett Bookhouse (Kennett Square, I

"An excellent beginning for a new *Magazi*

D1057593

Also by Colleen Cambridge

The Phyllida Bright mystery series

Murder at Mallowan Hall

A Trace of Poison

MURDER AT MALLOWAN HALL

Colleen Cambridge

KENSINGTON
PUBLISHING CORP.

www.kensingtonbooks.com

KENSINGTON BOOKS are published by

Kensington Publishing Corp.
119 West 40th Street
New York, NY 10018

All Kensington titles, imprints, and distributed lines are available at special quantity discounts for bulk purchases for sales promotion, premiums, fundraising, educational, or institutional use.

Special book excerpts or customized printings can also be created to fit specific needs. For details, write or phone the office of the Kensington Sales Manager: Attn.: Sales Department. Kensington Publishing Corp., 119 West 40th Street, New York, NY 10018. Phone: 1-800-221-2647.

The K with book logo Reg US Pat. & TM Off.

First Kensington Hardcover Edition: November 2021

ISBN: 978-1-4967-3246-0 (ebook)

ISBN: 978-1-4967-3245-3

First Kensington Trade Paperback Edition: October 2022

10 9 8 7 6 5 4 3 2 1

Printed in the United States of America

What I feel is that if one has got to have a murder actually happening in one's house, one might as well enjoy it, if you know what I mean.

—Agatha Christie
The Body in the Library

Author's Note

While Agatha Christie, her husband Max Mallowan, and their dog Peter actually existed, Mallowan Hall, its location, and the entire household staff are completely fictional, as are the murderous events portrayed in this story.

CHAPTER 1

*P*HYLLIDA BRIGHT HAD SEEN HER SHARE OF BODIES DURING THE Great War, so when she discovered the dead man sprawled on the floor, it didn't even occur to her to scream.

The unanticipated sight did elicit a quiet gasp of surprise and then a rush of concern, with exasperation following quickly on its heels. *As if I don't have enough to manage today,* she thought as her battlefield nurse's training kicked in and she knelt to ascertain whether the man was, in fact, actually dead.

He was quite dead—not to mention significantly bloodied due to the fountain pen protruding from the side of his neck. The stains in the library's rug would require an extra two hours of work, and then time to dry before it could be replaced. And she didn't even want to contemplate how long it would take to get the blood splatters off the books and wallpaper.

Nonetheless, Phyllida closed her eyes and wished a sincere Godspeed to the poor man's soul—then added a note of gratitude that she'd been the one to discover Mr. Waring instead of Ginny, the high-pitched parlourmaid who saw to the library each morning. That would have been just the icing on the cake.

Already mentally readjusting her staff's schedule in order to keep them clear of the library and its vicinity, as well as giving them as little opportunity as possible to gossip about the room's unexpected contents, she rose, the ring of keys at her waist jingling pleasantly, and went for the telephone on the desk.

As she waited for the operator to connect the call, Phyllida turned on the desk lamp, then straightened the carved mahogany tray where the fountain pen rested when it wasn't protruding from a dead man's artery. She also realigned the small vase always kept filled with flowers or greens (removing the single drooping leaf and tucking it into her dress pocket) and tsked when she noticed a dull streak at the edge of the desk's glossy surface. The scissors and the stack of stationery on the desk were untouched, as was the small agate paperweight.

At last, her call was connected, and even then, what should have been a simple task became tedious.

"Yes, Constable. It is in fact a real dead body." It was the third time she'd been required to give this information, and the reason for the repetition was not due to the crackling of the telephone line. "My name is Mrs. Bright. I'm Mrs. Mallowan's housekeeper here at Mallowan Hall."

"Mallowan Hall? D'ye mean the place where that detective book lady lives at?"

Phyllida gritted her teeth. "Yes, Constable."

"Yer sayin' there's a dead body in the library at Agatha Christie's house?"

"I am in fact saying precisely that, Constable. And I expect you'll attend to this posthaste. Mr. and Mrs. Mallowan have a houseful of guests." She wasn't certain he heard her over his guffaws of laughter.

"It's a good jest, it is, ma'am," he managed to say between hearty chuckles. "A dead body there at—"

"Constable Greensticks," she said in her most severe tone, "this is no laughing matter. A man has been murdered, and I suggest you attend to the matter immediately."

At last, she hung up the telephone, assured that the constable fully understood the gravity of the situation, while being well aware that the operator who'd connected them was probably beginning to make her own telephone calls to carry the news.

Her attention fell on poor Mr. Waring—she was confident but

not entirely certain that was his name; after all, his arrival last evening had not been anticipated, and he had most certainly not been on the guest list. That was only one of many problems with unexpected guests.

Phyllida was tempted to lay a blanket over the poor man but decided she'd best not disrupt the scene. Mr. Waring was young, in his late twenties, with light brown hair and a matching mustache. His attire was stylish—the premade trousers being the sort bought at a department store instead of having been tailored, but fine nonetheless. He wore a coat of excellent wool and fine cut that was only two years out of style. It was clean and, she noted with satisfaction, possessed a fully intact hem. In Phyllida's opinion, a sagging hemline was the first indication of a lack of attention to detail and appearance and was usually borne out in other ways.

Phyllida glanced at the clock and saw that it was just seven. Mrs. Agatha wouldn't normally be up for at least two hours, and even then, she would go into her office to write for a time before joining her husband and their guests. Phyllida was also reminded to schedule the men to come and oil the clocks next week, after the house guests had gone. It would be two weeks early, but she'd noticed the grandfather clock at the bottom of the main staircase was grinding a bit.

The more pressing task was to inform Mr. Dobble of the situation, and the very thought was enough to have her wishing for another very strong cup of Darjeeling.

One usually needed some type of fortification before interacting with the Mallowans' butler, and since it was hardly past seven in the morning, she would have to forgo the rye whisky.

Unwilling to leave the library unattended, Phyllida rang for Mr. Dobble. Admittedly, the idea of calling the butler to her rather than going to him, as one would normally do, made her smile.

Not that that was unusual. Phyllida, for all her exacting standards and regimental mind, was possessed of an optimistic, pragmatic, and sunny personality. Although she was most often required to act in a reserved manner as the individual who managed the majority of the household staff (not to mention its budget), she had been known to play whist with the parlourmaids, assist with fashion opinions for the maids during their days off, and give relationship advice to a chambermaid related to the former chauffeur. (He'd been a poor prospect due to his wandering eye—and hands.) And more than one of the kitchen maids had seen the very correct housekeeper go soft and gooey-eyed over a litter of fuzzy kittens.

Two of said kittens had subsequently found their way into a basket in Phyllida's sitting room, joining her collection of detective novels and books on nearly every topic under the sun, and were now full-grown, sleek cats who disdained the basket that had once been their bed. However, Stilton and Rye helped keep at bay any mice who might confuse the larder for their homestead. Holding one or the other in her lap—when the felines permitted, of course—also provided Phyllida moments of calm and restoration. Which was particularly appreciated after dealing with Mr. Dobble.

Phyllida had not come up working in domestic service, starting as a scullery maid or chambermaid when she was thirteen or fourteen and making her way to kitchen maid or parlourmaid and then through the hierarchy from there. That made her quite unusual. In fact, she hadn't worked in service at all until several years after the Great War and her work with the army had ended.

The reasons she'd chosen employment as the housekeeper of a large manor were excellent and no one's business but her own. That was part of why she and Mr. Dobble weren't particularly friendly. She suspected he was suspicious of a woman who had come into the coveted position of housekeeper without a long history of scrubbing floors (as far as he knew), and who was comparatively young (although certainly not *that* young and most definitely not inexperienced) to have such a prestigious role in a large gentrified household. And despite his best efforts, she did not deign to share with him the details of her background, marital status, or age, even when pressed.

But Phyllida was certain most of Mr. Dobble's dislike was due to the fact that she lived up to her name—not only in personality, but with her hair color. It was *bright*. Bright strawberry gold.

The first time she'd met him, the butler had eyed her up and down and suggested that she "subdue that fire upon your head."

She had refrained from suggesting that he remove the walking stick that appeared to have been inserted into his bottom, and had commenced with ensuring that whenever she was in Mr. Dobble's presence, her fiery hair was smooth, neat, and not the least bit subdued. Fortunately, housekeepers didn't wear caps, and so her uncovered head always shone like a beacon.

She'd just finished opening the curtains to allow the light to shine in when the library door opened.

Mr. Dobble stepped in silently, as the most excellent of servants did. He was approximately fifty years old (he was just as vague about his age as she was), with a clean-shaven face and an equally hairless scalp with a pronounced dent above his left ear (a characteristic that led some of the staff to call him Old Dent when safely out of his hearing). Everything about the butler was long—his ears, his fingers, his torso, the hair of his gray eyebrows—with the exception of his legs, which were, in relation to the rest of him, not long at all. It wasn't that he was short; it was simply that his height came equally from torso and lower limbs. He had dark eyes and pale, pale skin that was so smooth Phyllida could only assume he indulged in a very fine facial cream.

As most butlers did, he dressed in clothing as fine as that of the gentry. However, because no one in the upper class ever wanted their servants to be mistaken for someone of their status, there was always in a butler's attire some element that was "off"—a slightly out-of-date necktie, a too-old coat, a pair of trousers cut the wrong way. That minor anachronism assisted those of the upper class from assuming the butler was one of "theirs"—or vice versa, as when Lord Haldane had once been mistaken for being a butler by a chambermaid while traveling on a train.

Mr. Dobble took three steps into the library, his expression set and haughty and his eyes trained accusingly on Phyllida, his mouth open in what surely was about to be a crisp reprimand.

Then he saw Mr. Waring. Mr. Dobble stumbled to a halt with an inadvertent cry that strangled off whatever snappish comment he was about to make.

"As you can see, Mr. Dobble, we have a situation."

"I shall contact the constabulary at once." He'd recovered quickly, but Phyllida was delighted to note that he'd initially been far more discombobulated than she.

She hid a satisfied smile as she replied, "I've already spoken with Constable Greensticks. I expect he will arrive shortly, presumably with the doctor in attendance, so we have only a very short time to manage the staff and to inform Mr. Max and Mrs. Agatha." As one does, she prudently waited for the butler to seize control of the situation.

"*I* shall inform Mr. Max," he said. "And the footmen, of course. You'll attend to your own staff, Mrs. Bright. I do hope you'll be able to contain their squeals and shrieks. We do have guests, you know."

She gave him a frosty smile. "I shall endeavor to ensure the maids' histrionics are kept to a dull roar."

He paused, standing over the body. "Good heavens. A fountain pen?"

"Indeed." Phyllida moved closer. "Quite horrifying."

"That's the reporter, is it, then? To do the interview with Mrs. Agatha. Mr. Waring."

"To my recollection." Phyllida hadn't answered the door to welcome the guests as Mr. Dobble had, but she had made certain she caught glimpses of each of the arrivals as they came in, and at dinner, as well, for it would be her staff that attended to their chambers and general needs.

She supposed, if one could find a silver lining in the cloud of a murdered guest, it was that it would be less upsetting to Mr. and Mrs. Mallowan since the dead man wasn't known to them at all. Still. He obviously had been known to *someone.*

Mr. Dobble made a thoughtful noise. "Carbolic for the stains, I assume."

"Only after a salted water soak."

"And the wallpaper?"

"Milk and boiling water, of course. Lavender polish to finish."

"I'll have Stanley and Freddie remove the rug once the body . . . er, as soon as possible."

"I would appreciate that, Mr. Dobble." And so would Ginny, she thought dryly. Stanley, the head footman, was a particular favorite of the housemaids.

They looked down at the body, neither of them apparently willing to move.

Living in the house of a writer who penned popular detective novels meant that dead bodies were a constant source of discussion—including the finer points of the cleverest way to make them so. Poisoning and stabbing (but without so much blood) were particular favorites of Mrs. Agatha's, and occasionally, there was strangulation, of course. But to have an actual murder take place here . . . to see an actual dead body sprawled on the floor, with a writing implement projecting from an artery . . .

The bloodstains on the rug indicated that Mr. Waring hadn't died immediately and seemed to have crawled some distance, no doubt struggling to find help while bleeding profusely. Phyllida shivered, contemplating the horrifying last moments of the dead man's life. It must have happened late at night, or surely someone would have heard the disturbance.

"Who could have done such a thing?" Mr. Dobble's stiff demeanor slipped a bit as raw emotion crept into his voice.

"I cannot imagine," she replied in a likewise less formal tone. "But it must have been someone here."

The butler's breathing hitched a little, and he said a word under his breath that Phyllida hadn't heard since she was working with the troops. She was, however, inclined to agree with the sentiment.

All thoughts of carbolic acid, clock oiling, and managing the staff—tasks and thoughts she'd clung to as a shield against the reality—disintegrated as sensibility settled in.

There was a murderer here, at lovely, sedate Mallowan Hall.

CHAPTER 2

MALLOWAN HALL WAS A MODEST MANOR HOUSE WITH FIFTEEN guest rooms, an office each for master and mistress, and an array of sitting rooms and parlours. It was tucked in the rolling hills and lush forests of Devonshire, not far from Cornwall. Built at the turn of the century, it was surprisingly modern as country homes went, with running water, and indoor toilets, and electric lights in the kitchen, on the ground floor, and in all the bedchambers.

Phyllida wouldn't have accepted a position as housekeeper, even for Mrs. Agatha, if the country house hadn't had electric lights or hot running water. Constantly cleaning gas lamps—which gave off thick strings of soot that clung to the ceiling and walls—was a task she was disinclined to have her staff undertake in any household she managed.

Constructed of dark red brick and boasting seven chimneys, the four-story-plus-attic-and-cellar house presented an imposing front, with twenty windows and a grand front door that swept open into a well-lit three-story foyer featuring a large half-moon window. A curving drive split off to the recently renovated motor-car garage and was bordered by neat arborvitae hedges, spiral topiaries of boxwood, and massive pots of creeping ivy, sprawling red begonias, and springy pink gerberas.

Gracing the manor house and vehicle garage were terraces, more colorful gardens, a small apple orchard, riding trails, and, beyond, a dense forest. The near grounds were contained by a five-foot stone wall that rode up and down the gentle hillocks and even over the small creek at the north side of the property.

Mallowan Hall was a thirty-minute motorcar ride on the narrow, winding road from the village of Listleigh. The most popular
local establishment therein was the Screaming Magpie—a public
house known for dark, nutty ale and a testy publican. A post office, chemist's, physician's office, church, tea shop, and general
store were also situated in the village, along with a number of
other establishments such as a butcher, a cobbler, and a linen
shop.

It was hardly a quarter of an hour after Phyllida had discon-
nected her call that Constable Greensticks roared up the drive in
a motorcar. His enthusiastic navigation sent dust and gravel flying
through the air, and when the vehicle skidded to a halt, it left
deep marks in the drive. Phyllida was not surprised that the paint
on the conveyance was scarred and scraped and that it boasted a
small dent near the front passenger side.

A second vehicle rumbled up in the constable's wake in a far
more circumspect manner.

By now, the staff had heard the news. Phyllida had been firm
with Ginny and Mary—the front-of-house maids who normally
dealt with all "public" or common-area rooms on the main floor
and who kept designing excuses to walk by the library—and had
sent them to the music room in the other wing. Benita, the
scullery maid, was seen whiting the steps on the side of the house
closest to the front door, despite the fact she'd already done so at
dawn this morning and should have been in the kitchen, washing
eggs. And the gardener and footmen seemed to find a number of
urgent reasons to walk by the front of the house.

The lady's maid and the trio of valets who had accompanied
their mistress and masters to Mallowan Hall had surely also
heard the news, but they didn't have any excuse to wander
about and listen. They must wait impatiently for the gossip to
make its way to the belowstairs dining room, where they were
finishing breakfast—gossip that Phyllida knew wouldn't take long
in coming.

Mr. Max had been apprised of the situation by the butler, and
he had, in turn, taken it upon himself to break the news to his

wife upon her rising. The Mallowans would wait, Mr. Dobble told Phyllida, to inform their guests until they rose from what had been a relatively early night after a long day of travel. Mr. Max would speak with the constable and any other authorities in his study shortly. However, Phyllida decided she would take Mrs. Agatha her morning tea instead of having one of the chambermaids do so.

Mr. Dobble showed Constable Greensticks and the other gentleman, who carried what appeared to be a medical bag, to the library. Although the butler gave Phyllida a quelling look, she refused to budge from her position at the door to the chamber. Of course, the police would want to talk with *her*, as she'd been the one to discover the body. And aside from that, it was imperative she know what was happening if she were to maintain the smooth running of the household.

The constable had obviously managed to get his hilarity under control and was suitably sober as he greeted Phyllida. He was a short, pompous man with a full dark mustache who nonetheless did not remind her in the least of Hercule Poirot.

Phyllida considered herself an expert on Mrs. Agatha's most famous fictional detective, and part (only part) of the reason she was currently unwed was that she had yet to find a man who met the standards set by the proper Belgian detective. Despite the fact that he was a figment of her mistress's imagination, Phyllida had developed a sort of literary tendre for the clever little gentleman, his brilliant gray cells, and shared his appreciation for order and method.

Constable Greensticks might have characteristics similar to Mrs. Agatha's detective, with his pompous airs, short stature, and full mustache, but he was more of an Inspector Japp than an M. Poirot—a view which was borne out by the fact that said mustache badly needed trimming and his coat hung rather poorly, flapping awkwardly about his knees. His notebook was crinkled and stained, and he wore a pencil tucked behind an ear.

Still, he represented the authorities in Listleigh and, despite his name, was neither slender nor green in his experience. "I've called Scotland Yard, and the inspector will arrive anon. In the meanwhile, I'll examine the scene, take down some information, and assist the doctor here."

Dr. Bhatt was a man of forty with reddish-brown skin and true black hair. His mustache, though unwaxed, was shiny, luxurious, and combed perfectly straight. Not one stray hair was too long, too short, or curled out of place. Such a display would surely have garnered a sincere compliment from M. Poirot had he been present. The physician had a prominent nose with a hump in the bridge, that being the single physical characteristic that put him just on the wrong side of handsome.

"Mrs. Bright. Mr. Dobble. I'm very sorry to be here under these circumstances." His English was crisp, though the flavor of his homeland filtered through in a subtle accent. The doctor's manner was efficient and yet easy, and he gave the impression that even the most trying of situations would be met with calm and fortitude.

The four of them went into the library together, the soft clink of Phyllida's key ring the only sound, and the physician immediately knelt next to Mr. Waring.

Phyllida couldn't help but edge close to watch, closing her hand over the keys to keep them from jingling. As a devourer of detective novels and a nurse's aide who'd attended to terrible injuries, she was compelled by curiosity and uninhibited by the ugliness of death.

Dr. Bhatt didn't seem to mind her hovering. His movements were smooth and efficient, and when he rose to his feet moments later, he met her eyes in a moment of solidarity. "Dead from a single puncture to the carotid. Bled out; likely couldn't have been saved. Approximate time of death would have been between midnight and three in the morning. I see no reason for an inquest, as the cause of death is obvious, and I am confident in my conclusions."

"A fountain pen as weapon," said the constable, tsking as he shook his head and jotted notes on his crushed notebook. "Bloody ugly way to go." He looked up. "When the inspector arrives, he'll need to speak to everyone in the household. How many people are present?"

"There are seventeen staff—no, eighteen, with the new chauffeur, who arrived yesterday—in and outside the house, including the gardener, our man-of-all-work, and Mrs. Bright and myself," said Mr. Dobble as Phyllida sighed inwardly. She'd expected nothing less, but it meant only more disruption if each of her maids and the cooking staff were to be pulled from their work to speak to the authorities. "Mr. and Mrs. Mallowan are also having a house party, and there are eight other guests present. Mr. Waring was a ninth. And there are an additional lady's maid and three valets who accompanied the guests and are currently in the servants' hall, waiting to be summoned."

"Waring was a guest at this house party?" Constable Greensticks made a humming sound.

"In a manner of speaking," replied Mr. Dobble. "He was here to interview Mrs. Agatha Mallowan. She is—as you likely know—a famous detective novelist."

Dr. Bhatt stilled, and then his eyes widened. For the first time, his calm demeanor was disrupted. "Do you mean to say—no, no, it can't be true, can it?—that Mrs. Mallowan is Agatha Christie?"

Mr. Dobble inclined his head in an affectedly bored affirmation, but Phyllida knew for a fact that he was just as proud of their employer as she was. He had his own extensive collection of Christie novels and stories.

"That is remarkable!" Dr. Bhatt beamed, then seemed to remember he was, after all, at a murder scene, and his smile faded. But he couldn't resist adding the obvious: "I am a devoted fan of Mrs. Christie's novels and in particular the stories of Mr. Quin."

Whatever might have transpired next (possibly a discussion as to the origins of that mysterious literary character) was interrupted by a knock at the library door, which Mr. Dobble had prudently closed behind them. He went to it, and Phyllida noted that he managed to open the door only enough for a gentleman to step inside, but not wide enough for the gawping footman who'd delivered him to see within.

"Inspector." The constable immediately greeted the newcomer, then set about introducing him to those present.

Detective-Inspector Cork did not, at first appearance, elicit great confidence in his skill at investigation—at least in Phyllida's mind. He was younger than she, in his late thirties, and his blue eyes bulged slightly in their sockets, as if he were in a constant state of shock. He wore a buff-colored mustache the same way he wore his trilby of the same color: it was simply there to be correct, taking up space and requiring maintenance (which clearly hadn't been done to the hat, for it desperately needed a good brushing). But Phyllida's instant prejudice against his detecting abilities was mostly prompted by the smattering of freckles over the bridge of his nose and cheeks.

He seemed, quite simply, too young and boyish to be *good* at murder investigations.

The constable and the doctor filled in the man from Scotland Yard with the information they had. Then Inspector Cork turned to her with his fishlike eyes.

"Mrs. Bright, you were the one to discover the body. What time was that? Did you notice anything out of place in the room?" His voice did not match his youthful appearance, being deep and gravelly.

"It was a short while before seven. Normally, Ginny, one of the parlourmaids, sees to the library, but she hadn't come in here yet, and I wanted to open the windows right away since it stormed last night. Nothing better than the scent of morning after a good summer rain. Nothing was out of the ordinary in here except for poor Mr. Waring." Then, before he asked, she went on. "I didn't touch anything, except I knelt next to him to ascertain whether he was deceased—although I was quite certain that was the case— and then I telephoned Constable Greensticks."

She felt Mr. Dobble shift behind her and assumed he'd been reminded he was annoyed that she'd waited to notify him until after calling the authorities.

"The French doors were closed in here last night at what time, Mrs. Bright?"

She glanced at the double glassed doors. "It would have been about half ten. They were latched, as they always are. The Mallowans and their guests were playing bridge in the music room when the storm started. To my knowledge, no one else was in here after Stanley—the footman—closed the windows and locked the doors. I didn't touch anything in the room except to open the curtains—for the light, you know—and to straighten a few items on the desk."

Inspector Cork made some notes in a pristine notepad, then looked up suddenly. "Pardon me for asking, Mrs. Bright, but you don't seem terribly distraught over your discovery."

"If you're asking whether I screamed or otherwise audibly reacted, the answer is no—although I'm not certain whether that's relevant to the investigation. I was a nurse's aide on the front lines, Inspector. I've seen far worse than this."

He grunted and glanced toward the desk and then in Mr. Waring's direction. "And the fountain pen. Do you recognize it?"

"I'm not . . . I didn't get close enough to know for certain," she replied, annoyed that she'd stammered, "but the fountain pen is missing from its place on the desk. It could be the same one. They're both dark. The scissors and a heavy paperweight are still in place, however." She met his eyes meaningfully and recognized a flicker of acknowledgment therein.

Why hadn't the murderer used the scissors or coshed him on the head with the paperweight? A fountain pen seemed a far less exacting method than using a sharp pair of scissors or a hunk of agate.

Inspector Cork turned and strode to the body, then crouched next to it. When he rose, he was holding the murder weapon in a handkerchief.

Phyllida looked at the writing implement, which was slick with congealing blood and other fluids. "Yes, that is the fountain pen that belongs on the desk."

She realized Inspector Cork was pretending not to look at her as he wrote on his notepad, having given the kerchief-wrapped murder weapon to Constable Greensticks. Had the inspector been testing her mettle by thrusting the bloodied instrument toward her, wondering whether she'd react to the disgusting sight?

Phyllida Bright was made of far sterner stuff than that.

"You say Mr. Waring was here as a reporter." The inspector turned his attention to Mr. Dobble. "Not as a house guest of Mr. and Mrs. Mallowan."

"Yes, sir, that is correct. He arrived unexpectedly yesterday just as the others were arriving for the party. Instead of the normal Saturday to Monday, it's a Wednesday to Friday, as Mrs. Mallowan is required to be in London on Saturday."

Phyllida and Inspector Cork both straightened with interest. "Unexpectedly? Do you mean Mrs. Chri—I mean to say, Mrs. Mallowan—wasn't expecting Mr. Waring?"

"Not to my knowledge, sir, no. But that isn't terribly unusual for reporters to attempt to meet with her for interviews and such. Sometimes they telephone, and sometimes they simply appear on the doorstep and hope for the best."

"In this case, Mr. Waring was apparently only hoping for the best. And instead, the bloke ends up murdered." Inspector Cork looked at Mr. Dobble and then at Phyllida with a cool, skeptical expression. "Very interesting."

Those last words sounded more like a threat than an observation.

CHAPTER 3

WITH THAT UNHAPPY THOUGHT CLOUDING OVER HER HEAD, PHYL-lida excused herself from the library, leaving Mr. Dobble to finish with the gentlemen. It was after half seven, and surely Mrs. Agatha would have been awakened by her husband with the news. She'd likely need her tea, and Phyllida wanted to have it ready before she rang.

That necessitated a trip down to the kitchen, which Phyllida didn't mind, for she needed to ensure that Mrs. Puffley and her staff hadn't been distracted by the events of the morning (which, of course, they had). Breakfast, luncheon, tea, and dinner must go on.

She looked in on the guest servants, feeling a bit vexed that only one of the female guests had brought her own maid. That meant the two other female guests would need to be assisted in their toilettes by Violet, Mrs. Agatha's maid, as well as by Bess if necessary—and Phyllida's staff were already about to be stretched and distracted. It really was quite disruptive when women came to house parties without their own maids. It was much easier to feed extra mouths and provide for more sleeping arrangements than to require Violet and Bess to add to their daily tasks.

The four visitors were sitting at the long table in the servants' dining hall, just down from the kitchen. The remnants of their breakfast were still on the table but wouldn't be cleared away until breakfast was served upstairs. As visitors, they had nothing to do until their masters or mistress rang for them—which would likely be an hour or two from now.

"Is it true?" Fanny half rose from her seat when she saw Phyllida. Her face was pale, and her eyes wide.

"If you are referring to the fact that a man was found dead this morning, yes," Phyllida replied. "Your masters and mistress are still abed," she continued, speaking to the rest of the guest servants, "and the Scotland Yard inspector will interview each of you. So you'll need to remain here until someone rings for you and takes you to the sitting room upstairs." Obviously, being guests, they would have no understanding of the layout of the large house—especially the main floor—and Phyllida certainly didn't want any of them wandering about, distracting her own staff.

Having delivered that unpopular news, and having no reason to wait for their responses, Phyllida swept from the room and went on to see how her own people were doing.

"Molly, prepare the tray for Mrs. Agatha. I'll take it up," she said as she entered the kitchen. "And mind you, don't forget a biscuit for Peter."

The space was long, loud, and relatively cool for it was mostly underground. A great worktable stretched most of the length of the room, scarred from decades of knives and burns. The two kitchen maids worked on one side, and the cook on the other. A large gas stove, two ovens, and an array of cupboards lined one of the whitewashed brick walls. The scullery was adjacent to the kitchen, and just around the corner was the icebox next to the pantry. Beyond that was the storeroom where the household linens were kept. Farther down the corridor was the stillroom, where Phyllida oversaw the creation of household necessities, like tooth powder, pomades, and drawer sachets, as well as many of the cordials, syrups, and cleaning solutions used at Mallowan Hall.

The scents of sizzling bacon and toasting bread reminded her she'd had only one cup of tea this morning. And it appeared Mrs. Puffley had made apple cinnamon muffins with dried Granny Smiths—a personal favorite of hers. Pots and pans clanged, bowls spun, dishes clattered, knives tapped dully, and Mrs. Puffley was red faced, as usual.

"Is it true, Mrs. Bright?" the cook asked, looking up from where she was stirring something in a large silver bowl. She was a tall, solid woman, and her muscular arm moved faster than an aeroplane propeller.

"If you're speaking of the fact that Mr. Waring, the reporter, was found dead in the library, then yes, it is."

Something clanged behind her, and there was an ugly crash. Phyllida turned to see one of the kitchen maids staring down in horror at a shattered teapot, its contents seeping into the wooden plank floor.

Rebecca, the maid who'd dropped it, squeaked in dismay and shame at having been so clumsy in front of both her bosses. She dove for the broom as Mrs. Puffley shouted, the scullery maid, Benita, came running, and Phyllida looked on calmly.

She bent to pick up the largest pieces of the broken china. It was to be expected, this sort of disruption, when you had a murder in the house, now wasn't it? And there wasn't a whit to be done but see it through.

"And there now, Rebecca! Mrs. Bright shoulden be bending herself over, cleanin' up after *your* clumsiness!" Mrs. Puffley bellowed as she dropped her bowl onto the long table and reached for a dish of sugar. "See you move yerself and get that cleaned up."

"Never mind, Mrs. Puffley," Phyllida said, tossing the broken pieces into the rubbish bin. "Rebecca will sweep up the rest, and, Molly, you go off and find a different teapot for Mrs. Agatha."

"They're saying it was murder," said the cook as she went back to whipping up whatever was in the bowl. Likely meringue for the tea's lemon tarts. "Is it true?"

"It appears to be, as I don't expect one could fatally stab oneself with a fountain pen." There was no reason to hide the information, especially since everyone would be questioned by Inspector Cork. Phyllida preferred to make certain the staff had the facts, so that they wouldn't be gossiping about rumors—which, of course, usually turned out to be worse than the truth.

"A *fountain pen*? Land's! Why, I don't see why anyone would use a fountain pen to do something like that." Mrs. Puffley allowed her gaze to sweep the kitchen and its array of sharp knives, as if to say, *When there are so many other options.*

"Where was he stabbed, Mrs. Bright?" asked Molly, who was the senior kitchen maid and had known Phyllida since the beginning. She was the only one brave enough to address her directly.

"In the neck. It was, as one imagines, a gruesome sight. Which brings me to another important bit," she added in a carrying voice as Stanley, Freddie, Ginny, and Mary—all staff from the main floor and so-called public rooms—came into the kitchen. *Nosy ones*, she thought with an internal smile. But wouldn't she be doing the same herself, scuttling downstairs to get the news?

"Inspector Cork from Scotland Yard will be interviewing each of you. I expect you to be honest with him, to tell him everything you know without fabricating what you *don't* know, and then to return *immediately* to your tasks." She looked around at each of them, meeting their eyes one by one. "There will be no gossiping and standing about, gawping at doors, do you understand? Mr. Max and Mrs. Agatha still have guests here that must be attended to, and all of this will come as an utter shock to everyone." *Except the murderer*, a little voice reminded her.

Each of them nodded in turn, but Mrs. Puffley said, "I don't have the least bit of time to haul myself upstairs. That man wants to speak with me, he can bring himself right down and do his interview in my place. But I'm stayin' here. I got salmon mousse to mold, meats to roast, and a hare soup to make for lunch—and it ain't gonna debone itself. You know how tiny those rabbit bones are. Smaller'n fish bones, and then it's gotta be put through the strainer."

Phyllida stifled a sigh. Trust Puffley to wrinkle things up. The woman was an excellent cook and thus believed she was a law unto herself. "I shall suggest that to Inspector Cork, but if he's resistant, you'll have no choice but to abandon your domain temporarily. I suppose if I mention apple cinnamon muffins, he might be tempted to make his way down here. I know I would be. Molly, is that tray ready?"

"Yes, ma'am," she said, swiftly stepping forward with it. "Shall I carry it up for you, Mrs. Bright?"

Sympathizing with her curiosity—for the young woman had been stuck in the kitchen all morning, likely shredding hare meat (a horribly tedious job)—she replied, "Yes, that would be helpful, Molly." As the kitchen maid started to the stairs, the tray's contents clinking gently, Phyllida added to the room at large, "I intend to be present while each of you has your interview with the inspector. You'll go by order of seniority, and Mr. Dobble and I have agreed that the staff interviews will be conducted in my sitting room. I'll ring when we are to begin."

As the various responses of "Yes, Mrs. Bright" were satisfactory, she left the kitchen and proceeded up to the third floor using the back stairs. Although Mr. Max and Mrs. Agatha weren't strict about having their servants being neither seen nor heard as they went about their business—some households required that, for example, if a chambermaid was in a bedroom and a member of the family came in to retrieve a handkerchief or other sundry, the maid was required to interrupt her work and immediately and silently remove herself from the room while the item was retrieved so that she wouldn't be "seen"—Phyllida insisted that her staff be as unobtrusive as possible without being inefficient. Particularly when guests were present, as they were today.

Molly was waiting for her by the swinging door at the top of the back stairs, and so was Violet, the chambermaid who mostly attended to Mrs. Agatha.

"Is she up? Where shall I take her tea?" Phyllida asked.

"She's in her office, Mrs. Bright, although just now. She and Mr. Max were talking in the boudoir for some time about all of what's happened." Violet's eyes were wide with curiosity, and her broad brown cheeks flushed with interest.

"Thank you. I'll take the tray. You attend to Mrs. Agatha's chamber and clothing right away, as Inspector Cork will be interviewing the entire staff in my sitting room. And then I expect it'll soon be time to see to Mrs. Devine and Mrs. Hartford, since they didn't bring maids."

Leaving Molly and Violet to exchange what she hoped would

be very brief gossip, Phyllida pushed through the swinging door into a corridor. This put her on the "other" side—the family area of the house, where the Mallowans' bedchamber, private sitting rooms, and offices were. Guest rooms were above, on the second and third floors, and above that was the attic, where the servants slept.

Mrs. Agatha called her through as soon as she knocked, and when she caught sight of Phyllida carrying the tray, she smiled. "What a pleasant surprise to see you, Phyllie. And such awful news coming up from downstairs! You're the one who found Mr. Waring? I expect it's not quite the same finding a dead body in real life as I imagine when writing about it." Her smile turned rueful as she reached to pat Peter, who lay on the floor, panting. He rolled onto his back, tongue lolling, and she obliged, beginning to scratch his stomach. "Yes, yes . . . you're such a good boy, aren't you?" she crooned.

Phyllida—who did not particularly care for canines, even the mild-mannered Peter—set the tray on a table next to two arm-chairs. Mrs. Agatha's typewriter, a scattering of notebooks, and sheaves of papers were on a desk at the opposite side of the room—her working area. "It certainly wasn't what I expected when I went in to open the windows in the library."

"I don't know whether to laugh or to cry. A body in *my* library! Of all things!" A tall woman, Agatha had risen from her desk and moved to sit in one of the armchairs. Due to a recent illness while on an archaeological expedition with her husband, she'd lost over a stone of extra weight. Now she looked slender and healthy, and much happier than when Phyllida had first begun working for her. That was just after the unraveling of her marriage to Archie Christie—a time of which no one spoke.

"The constable in Listleigh got good a laugh out of it before he realized I was quite serious," Phyllida said as she poured tea.

"Oh dear. I can imagine." Agatha gave a pained chuckle. "Do sit, Phyllie. Surely you have a few moments to sit and have a cup of tea so you can tell me what you know! This detective writer is bursting with curiosity—while at the same time horrified that someone had the *temerity* to do such a thing in our house." The corners of her mouth were tight. "The poor man! I must have slept through it all. And Max, too."

"But apparently someone didn't," Phyllida said, settling onto the chair opposite her mistress.

Any other housekeeper would hardly have done such a thing, even at her mistress's invitation—except in extenuating circumstances. However, Phyllida and Agatha had an unusual relationship. They'd first met while Agatha was working at the medical dispensary during the war and Phyllida was a nurse's aide before being sent to the front lines. Of a similar age and both being single, they had become friends and had kept in contact through the years, until Phyllida—for reasons of her own—had desired such a position. Agatha had been delighted to hire her.

Since they'd met on equal footing, so to speak, long before Agatha Miller became the celebrated Agatha Christie and then Mrs. Max Mallowan, they had retained their friendship—but only in the privacy of these chambers. To the rest of the staff, and the world, the two were simply mistress and servant.

"I shan't stay long," Phyllida told her as she cut one of the apple cinnamon muffins in half. "Inspector Cork—who looks as if he's barely gone into long pants—will be doing interviews of the staff. I want to be there for them. Agatha . . . it has to be someone here."

"Oh dear . . . I was afraid you'd say that." She lifted her teacup and gestured for her companion to take half of the muffin. She sighed and settled back in her seat. "I can't imagine who would have done such a thing. Why, Max and I know everyone here! It's simply beyond comprehension."

"But you don't—didn't know Mr. Waring."

"Oh, yes, the reporter. I said all of three words to him yesterday. It was quite busy, of course, with the Hartfords and the Budgely-Rhodeses arriving one atop each other. One might have thought they planned it. And then right behind them Tuddy Sloup and Stan Grimson. Then the Devines—an hour late, as usual." Agatha smiled and shook her head. "But one always forgives them, doesn't one? They're just so . . . well, *divine* to look at, with their dark good looks and those lovely smiles. Max and I do enjoy them both, and the Hartfords, too. And then we all went into dinner and the parlour and so on, and I never even spoke to him—Mr. Waring, I mean to say. He claims he sent me a note to expect him, but I don't recall seeing one. And you know I am very careful with my correspondence, especially about interviews. I didn't see anything from the *Times*—of course I would have remembered *that.*"

"But you put him up for the night nonetheless."

"Well, of course I did. What else was I supposed to do? Send him out when the storm was coming in? Besides, Max and I have plenty of room." She looked around, as if she couldn't quite believe the expanse of her home. Then her attention fell on the silent typewriter. "And I've got to finish a chapter this morning, as I know I'll get nothing done in the evening. This is quite a nuisance, Phyllie—for you and for us. Are we *certain* it's murder?"

Phyllida knew her mistress's habit was to write at least one chapter in the morning, then another in the afternoon—or have a nap instead—but if she napped, then more pages must be written in the evening. With guests, however, that changed the entire schedule. "There was a fountain pen in Mr. Waring's neck," she said. "I'm certain he didn't put it there."

"A fountain pen . . . in his neck? Why, that's . . . Hmm. What an interesting way . . ." Agatha's eyes went blank as her words trailed off, and she reached for a pad of paper that wasn't there. Murmuring to herself, she rose and bustled over to her desk, where she took up a notebook that Phyllida recognized as one of her own household tally books

So that's where it got off to.

This wasn't new. Agatha was always "borrowing" notepads or notebooks from everyone—her daughter, Rosalind, who was currently away at school; her husband; her servants—to jot down ideas for books, both current and future.

"Yes, now, what were you saying, Phyllie?"

"It's just so curious . . . A man no one knows turns up out of the blue and then ends up dead."

"In *my* library."

"Yes, that is *quite* appalling."

"I can see the headlines now," Agatha said, pursing her lips. "I don't like it. I don't like it at all." She slapped the notebook vehemently onto the desk.

"No." Phyllida knew her friend was remembering the last time she'd been in headlines.

Several years ago, during the worst part of her dissolving first marriage, Agatha Christie had famously disappeared for eleven days. When she'd been found at a small inn, checked in under her husband's mistress's name, she'd appeared to be suffering from some sort of amnesia. Since then, the press had been fascinated by the strange event. That was part of the reason Agatha was at times reluctant to do interviews or radio appearances, for often her disappearance seemed of more interest than whatever book or story she had just published.

To this day, no one knew precisely what had happened and why—except for Phyllida. She knew more about the events of those eleven days than anyone else in the world (except perhaps Mr. Max), but she certainly never mentioned it, even to Mrs. Agatha.

"I'm certain it will all be resolved quickly, Agatha," Phyllida said, rising. She couldn't dally much longer, but there was one other thing she wanted to do first. "After all, you didn't know Mr. Waring, and neither did Mr. Max. It must have been . . . it must have been someone who broke in. Who . . . who followed him here and then broke in. Or . . . maybe Mr. Waring even *let* him into the library."

She said the words, even though she didn't believe them. No one had broken into Mallowan Hall. It had rained heavily last night, and there'd been no mud on the rug in the library—she certainly would have noticed.

"It's like being at Styles," Agatha said, looking up. "Or End House. Someone here is a killer. And we have no resident Poirot to find him."

"What about you?" Phyllida said suddenly. A spark of excitement shot through her. "You're a detective writer! I'll wager you could figure it out—"

"No, no, no." Agatha shook her head, glancing at the type-writer again. That was a clear sign Phyllida needed to leave. "It's difficult enough to write the dratted things. I'm not about to try and follow clues in real life—mainly because I can't put them where I want them!" She gave a little laugh, sounding more like herself. "But I do hope someone will set this all to rights. And soon."

All right, then, Phyllida thought suddenly as she excused herself. *If you won't be Poirot, then I will.*

She knew his methods. She had excellent little gray cells of her own. She adored order and method, and she noticed things.

The sooner this could be put to rest, the less unpleasant publicity Agatha would have—and the sooner Phyllida's life, and, more importantly, her staff, could get back to normal.

The first thing Hercule Poirot would do would be to examine the victim's belongings and find out everything he could about the man.

And a housekeeper had the perfect right to enter a guest's bed-chamber—assuming it wasn't occupied, of course. After all, it was her responsibility to ensure that it was made up properly and that her chambermaids had done their jobs.

So Phyllida had absolutely no qualms about making her way up one more flight to the second floor, where the Devines, the Hart-fords, Mr. Grimson, and Mr. Waring had been put up for the night. She knew that at least the chamber known as the Gray Room would be empty, for its former occupant was currently being swathed in sheets and loaded into an ambulance.

As it was barely past eight o'clock, there were no sounds from the other bedrooms on this floor or on the third, where the rest of the guests had been settled. Even the bath at the end of the corridor was silent, its door ajar to indicate vacancy. The cham-bermaids, Lizzie and Bess, would be up later to see to those rooms, once the guests had gone down for breakfast.

So Mrs. Agatha hadn't known the reporter was coming, and it was only by chance that he'd been given admission to the house—because of the impending storm, and because the house was already prepared to deal with guests. What would have happened if Mr. Waring had arrived on a different day? Would he still be alive?

Holding her ever present keys tightly so they didn't clink, Phyllida slipped inside the Gray Room. She had only to push a button to turn on the electric light overhead, and then switch on a table lamp. The smoke-colored curtains had been drawn for the evening while Mr. Waring and the others were down for dinner and cards, and so to add to the illumination, she pulled them open

The bed had not been slept in, although its silvery coverlet was mussed, as if he'd either lain on it or otherwise lightly disturbed it.

Everything else was as it should have been in the chamber: the water pitcher with its basin, the small candle in a holder in case he needed the toilet in the night, the soap and towels perfectly aligned on the small table near the door, a vase with fresh flowers, a covered plate with two small biscuits. She nodded approvingly. Her staff were quite excellent.

Mr. Waring had laid out his hairbrush and other grooming items, including a small bottle of hair oil (the scent of which Phyllida found unappealing) and a tin of tooth powder, on the dressing table.

His only other belongings appeared to be inside a small suitcase, which was open on a rack near one wall, and a briefcase. Phyllida had no qualms about flipping through the suitcase's contents, lifting them carefully to determine he had only one set of clothing (other than the one he was wearing, of course). It was haphazardly folded, and so was a nightshirt he hadn't utilized. The briefcase was locked, drat it, and she expected the key was on his person—which had just been driven off down the drive. She'd seen the rear of the ambulance as it eased away.

With a glance at the door, she removed a pin from her knot of hair and set to fudging open the briefcase lock. (She was a woman of many talents.) She'd just clicked it open when she heard voices at the door.

Phyllida bolted upright with a jingle from her key ring and shoved the briefcase under the bed. Folding her hands primly at her waist, she turned just as the door opened.

"Inspector Cork," she said, smiling calmly. "I expected you would want to see Mr. Waring's room. And you, Constable."

She gave no explanation for her presence and ignored the glower from Mr. Dobble, who'd delivered the inspector and the constable. Instead, she launched into a description of what items in the chamber belonged to the household and what did not. All the while, she was *very* aware of the briefcase stuck under the bed. She'd given it a good shove, so not even a corner stuck out to change the lay of the dust ruffle.

If Inspector Cork happened to check underneath (which she expected an excellent detective would do), he would likely see it but have no way of knowing she'd just opened the lock and shoved the briefcase out of the way.

If he didn't see the case, Phyllida would be able to examine its contents later and then produce it with the explanation that the maid had found it under the bed.

She strongly hoped that the latter would occur.

Inspector Cork eyed her with those protruding blue eyes but did what—in her opinion—was a surprisingly deft and thorough examination of the chamber. He was just approaching the bed when there was a knock at the chamber door.

Mr. Dobble answered it to find Ginny, the parlourmaid. "Mr. Dobble, sir, there was a telephone call when I was in the front parlour. For a Detective-Inspector Cork." Her eyes went to the two policemen, both of whom had ceased their examination at the knock at the door.

"Was there a message?" asked the detective.

Ginny, whose eyes hadn't stopped darting around the chamber, gave a little curtsy. Phyllida was pleased to hear the soft crinkle of crisp petticoat and to note that there wasn't a speck of dust on the maid's white smock. The girl's honey-colored hair was confined in a neat bun behind her lacy coronet cap. "Yes, sir, Inspector, sir. I wrote it down for you." She held out a slip of paper.

Inspector Cork took it from her, and Mr. Dobble closed the door, nearly on the maid's nose. Phyllida wondered how long it would take her to tell the others what she'd seen (nothing of import, but since when did that stop gossip?).

"Well, I'll be damned," said the inspector, looking at the paper. He curled his lips, and the mustache bristled out like a horsehair brush. "I had my office contact the *Times* to let them know about their reporter Charles Waring, and to obtain his family information. They've called back to say there is no Charles Waring who works for the *London Times*."

"But he said—" the constable began.

"Apparently, that man was not at all who he claimed to be," said the inspector.

Then why on earth had he come to Mallowan Hall?

CHAPTER 4

*T*HE UNEXPECTED NEWS ABOUT MR. WARING NOT BEING WHO HE claimed seemed to distract Inspector Cork enough that he didn't investigate under the bed and thus did not find the unlocked briefcase Phyllida had shoved there.

Despite that bit of luck, however, she felt obliged to follow the inspector, the constable, and Mr. Dobble as they left the bedchamber, which meant she would have to return as soon as possible. Her chambermaids were far too competent to leave the floor under the bed unswept, and she intended to intercept the discovery of the briefcase.

Phyllida, Mr. Dobble, and the policemen were going down the main staircase to the ground floor when they heard a loud, distressing crash from the vicinity of the library.

Phyllida and the butler exchanged horrified looks, and she hurried the rest of the way down with a swish of starched skirts, dancing keys, and gritted teeth. The raised voices of individuals of both sexes reached her ears as she rushed (Phyllida did not condone running in the house) down the corridor to the library, whose tall mahogany doors were flung wide.

The bloodstained carpet, now rolled into a heavy cylinder, lay like a downed tree crossing the threshold, and two footmen and one of the maids stood over it in heated discussion. The three-piece Baroque clock set that normally rested on the corridor's long side table was on the floor. The glitter of shattered glass sparkled on the rug, and the three pieces—a clock and two ornate side pieces depicting angels with long, flowing robes—had come apart as they tumbled to the floor. One of the tips of an angel wing was broken.

As soon as the staff saw her, they fell silent.

"There's no need to gawp," Phyllida said crisply. "Ginny, clean up the glass and take the clock pieces to Piero to see if they can be repaired. Don't miss that angel's wing tip, mind you. Stanley and Freddie, perhaps you'll take more care while maneuvering out of the doorway this time. I'm certain you're aware the Egyptian vase down the corridor is a particular favorite of Mr. Mallowan."

"Yes, ma'am," the three said in an unplanned chorus and immediately set about their tasks.

With Phyllida on watch, the footmen paid more attention to the angle of the heavy cylinder of carpet than the gossip they'd certainly been exchanging with Ginny, and the stained rug was successfully removed from the premises.

Despite the myriad of other items to which she must attend, Phyllida couldn't resist slipping into the library one more time. While Ginny cleaned up the damaged clock in the hall, Phyllida closed the door behind her and looked around.

The scene of the crime.

The thought hung in the air as she stood on the bare wood floor and observed the bloodstains that had seeped through the rug and the splatters on the wallpaper and bookshelves.

Sunlight streamed through the window, and Phyllida could hear voices from outside. Avoiding the dried, rust-colored blotches, where Mr. Waring had bled out, she moved across the room, her shoes clip-clopping efficiently over the polished oak planks.

"Inspector Cork," she said, looking out the open French doors. He and Constable Greensticks were crouched in the garden beyond the small terrace. Phyllida drew in a deep breath of air still moist from last night's rainstorm. It was fresh and laced with the scents of roses and lilies. "Are you looking for something?"

Cork looked up at her with his perennially surprised eyes and rose, politely replacing his hat as he did so. "Evidence for how the killer entered the room, of course. Footprints and the like."

Phyllida tsked and shook her head. "I already know you've found none—nor will you. There was neither a speck nor a scrape of mud in the library, Inspector, and certainly nothing by the doors. Or near any window or near any entrance on the ground floor. Whoever he was, the murderer was already inside the house before he encountered Mr. Waring."

Inspector Cork's jaw shifted, but he made no comment on the obvious truth of her statement. Instead, he said, "I'll continue my circuit of the building, then begin my questioning of the staff in approximately ten minutes."

"The interviews will be held in my sitting room," Phyllida replied. "With the exception of Mrs. Puffley, the cook, who offers you fresh and warm apple cinnamon muffins if you speak with her in the kitchen."

The idea of baked goods seemed to mollify the inspector, and he gave a brief nod. "Very well. Ten minutes in your sitting room, then, Mrs. Bright."

"I'll let Mr. Dobble know," she said, making the assumption— and leaving Inspector Cork no choice—that he would work his way from the top to the bottom of the staff hierarchy in his interviews. It was the most efficient and logical process. "I have several things to attend to, as the death of Mr. Waring has quite upended the morning schedule for us as well as for the poor man himself, and adjustments must be made."

She turned from the French doors and began to cross the room, eyeing the section of shelves that had blood spatters on the book spines and wondering if there was any help for some of those tomes. The leather-bound ones could be cleaned, but there were several with paper jackets—

She stopped suddenly.

Something was wrong (besides the blood, of course).

Phyllida frowned as she traced the rows of books with her eyes. After only a moment, she realized what it was: one of the books on the bloodiest shelf didn't have any blood on it, despite the co- pious amounts of splatters on its two neighbors.

The book was in its correct position on the shelf, for everything must be in its place in Phyllida's domain; therefore, she realized, it couldn't have been there when Mr. Waring was stabbed.

And whoever replaced it had done so after the killing, which meant that the murderer had to be the one who slid the book back into its rightful location on the shelf. Which, by logic, implied that he (or she, but Phyllida was leaning heavily toward a member of the male sex being the culprit, for several obvious reasons) had been reading or leafing through the book prior to the attack on Mr. Waring.

Or, she supposed, that Mr. Waring might have been looking at the book when his murderer approached him . . . but then how would the killer know to replace the book? And where?

And why bother to do so, anyway?

The book itself bore no obvious clue to the mystery of who'd been reading it and why it was related to the murder of Mr. Waring—for surely that went without saying. An old book about travel inns . . . One could only imagine what it had to do with murder.

What a fascinating clue!

CHAPTER 5

*H*ARVEY DOBBLE DIDN'T CARE FOR CHINTZ. AND IT WAS HIS OPINion that lace belonged on female attire or in the dining room, on napkins, and not adorning sofa pillows. But most of all, he despised cats.

Which was why he was not at all pleased that the interviews pertaining to the murder of Mr. Waring were being held in Mrs. Bright's sitting room—which contained all of the above nuisances.

He wondered briefly whether she'd purposely planned it that way—so that he'd be required to lower himself into a straight-backed chair upholstered in the abhorrent shiny material (the feeling of the glazed fabric against his palms and fingertips made the hair on the back of his neck and arms stand on end) and sit while two felines eyed him from where they lounged—the amber one on top of a bookshelf and the other, a white and bluish-gray creature, along the back of the sofa. He didn't know their names and didn't care to learn them. He certainly didn't expect to be so closely examined by the two beasts, but those unblinking stares, accompanied by skeptical chins and sneering whiskers, made him feel as if he were being judged . . . and found wanting.

Abominable creatures, cats. Sly and condescending, and they left hair *everywhere*, which made his eyes grow puffy and watery.

With regard to the lace, to be strictly fair, Mrs. Bright didn't have an *overabundance* of it in her sitting room. But even two pil-

lows spilling with the frothy trim was too much in Dobble's opinion. Why couldn't she just keep the furbelows to napkins and caps
on the maids? He moved one pillow from its place on the chintz
chair and sat reluctantly. Despite the chamber's sunny yellow and
blue decor and the comfortable overstuffed furnishings, he didn't
care for this room at all.

"Mr. Dobble, we'll need your full name, as well as date and
place of birth, for the record," said Inspector Cork. He glanced
pointedly at the constable, who was apparently supposed to be
making notes and instead was tapping his fingers (empty of any
writing implement) on the desk.

After Dobble reluctantly complied with the request—he decided at the last minute that it was inadvisable to succumb to vanity and underestimate his age in the response—Cork went on. "If
you'll tell us your whereabouts last evening, from the time of half
past nine until this morning."

"It was my weekly chess match with the vicar," Dobble replied
very smoothly, very steadily, even though inside, his stomach quiv-
ered a bit. His eyes were already watering due to the proximity of
the cats and the abundance of white hair one had deposited on
the chair. "I left here at just before nine o'clock and was at the vicarage until . . . well, it was half past midnight, I should say."

"How did you get to the vicarage?"

An absurd question. Butlers didn't own motorcars, and he
wouldn't be caught dead straddling a bicycle or, worse, a horse. "I
walked, of course."

"In the rain?" Cork was looking at him closely, and Dobble kept
his fingers relaxed, although they wanted to curl against the shiny
arm of the chair. "There was quite a blustery storm come in last
night."

"It wasn't pleasant, but I have wellies and a slicker. I rarely miss
our chess game." Dobble kept on a soft, easy smile as he shrugged.
He desperately wanted to pull out his handkerchief to dab at his
eyes. "Mr. Billdop is a challenging opponent. Chess keeps my
mind sharp."

Although Cork didn't react to that statement, the cat atop the back of the sofa curled its lip at Dobble. The beast with godless blue eyes seemed to look right through him.

"And you returned at half past twelve, on foot, in the rain," said the inspector. "Did you see anyone or anything upon your return?"

Dobble shook his head and blinked rapidly in an effort to relieve the sting of his eyes. Blooming cats. Blasted murder investigation.

"Not a soul," he said. "As I understood it, Mr. and Mrs. Mallowan and the others retired relatively early—just after ten—as it had been a travel day for the guests. I came in through the back, of course, and encountered no one. Although I did hear the maids in the kitchen, finishing up their work. Since I had no reason to check on them, I went on to my pantry, saw that Mrs. Bright had returned the key to the wine cellar, and then I retired to my rooms. I was in bed and asleep shortly after one o'clock."

"Your employers had guests here last night, and you took the night off?" Cork asked.

Dobble swallowed and saw Greensticks's eyes follow the bounce of his Adam's apple. "My weekly chess game is my only night off, and Mr. and Mrs. Mallowan rarely ask me to stay in. Mrs. Bright is very capable of managing the household in the late evening, even with guests."

"And you were with Mr. Billdop, the vicar, all evening? What time did you leave the vicarage?"

"We played chess and had a bit of sherry, and then I left to walk home well after midnight. As I do nearly every week." Thanks to the blooming cats, his voice squeaked a little.

"A rather long chess game, wasn't it, then?" Cork looked at him with pale blue eyes, and when Dobble made no reply—clearly, the inspector didn't play chess—Cork pursed his lips. "Very well. And what about this morning? What time did you rise, and did you go into the library?"

"I was up and dressed by half past six. I had no occasion to go into the library until Mrs. Bright rang for me. That was when I first saw the . . . Mr. Waring." Dobble was still put out by the fact that the housekeeper had summoned him to her, that she had discovered the body, *and* that she had made the calls to the authorities before notifying him.

She certainly thought well enough of herself to handle the situation without consulting him.

He was also irked that he hadn't heard her scream or otherwise react to such a surprise, for he'd been on the first floor most of the morning. By all rights, she should have shrieked to kingdom come.

At that moment, none other than the woman in question made an appearance, opening the door and stepping into her sitting room with the annoying, constant jangle of keys. The intense strawberry gold of her hair shone like a flame—something that was, in his opinion, unbecoming of a housekeeper (or, quite honestly, of anyone in service).

For how could one be discreet and melt into the background when one had a shiny, bright beacon for one's head? One could wear all the starched, correct frocks of gray, blue, or black one wanted—with a crisp collar and spotless cuffs—but the attention-seeking hair ruined the entire ensemble. Not that she was wearing a dress made of suitably drab material, either. This one was a far too happy bright blue with little flowers on it.

Mrs. Bright really had no business being a housekeeper. Especially at her relatively young age (Dobble had an ongoing argument with himself as to whether she had even breached the age of forty), and especially without any service background—at least, that she had deigned to make him aware of. And if she insisted on persisting in this role, she should consider wearing a cap to cover up that distraction.

But Dobble's flood of irritation was instantly superseded by a flash of relief that she hadn't made her appearance before he was required to divulge the date of his own birth; that would have simply given her too much leverage over him.

However, that relief disintegrated as Mrs. Bright, who had a small book tucked under her arm, took the armchair next to her desk where Constable Greensticks was making notes. Why, the blasted woman intended to sit in on the rest of his interview!

Blinking rapidly, he frowned at her effrontery but dared say nothing in the presence of the inspector and his constable. It would be unbecoming of his position to acknowledge such disgruntlement—either from the housekeeper or her infernal cats.

He and the two other men had risen upon her entrance, and now Dobble gave her the briefest of nods. "Mrs. Bright. Inspector, I trust there's nothing further you need from me?"

"Only one more thing," replied Cork, nodding for Dobble to sit back down. He did, reluctantly. "When Mr. Waring arrived yesterday, were you the one who answered the door?"

"I was."

"What time was that?"

"It was into the evening—not long before I left for the vicarage. Shortly after eight o'clock. Dinner had just begun, and I was required to interrupt my supervision of the serving staff to answer the door because the first footman was ladling the soup and the under-footman had gone to fetch another crock of butter. Mr. Hartford had placed his elbow in the first one, and we had to send off for his valet to bring a new jacket."

"And how did that go on, admitting Mr. Waring? I'm given to understand that he wasn't expected."

"No, he was not. I answered the door, and he gave his name as Mr. Waring. Of course, I knew the names of all the guests expected, as well as most everyone of the Mallowans' acquaintance, and as he wasn't known to me, I asked about his business. He informed me he was from the *Times* and that he had an appointment for an interview with Mrs. Mallowan."

"Did he offer any credentials to this claim?"

"No," Dobble replied, his lips firming as he tried to keep from sneezing. His eyes felt as if they were burning. And this extended interrogation—under the watchful eyes of Mrs. Bright—was far more than the "only one more thing" the inspector had indicated.

"Did he specify that he was from the *London Times*?"

Dobble thought for a moment. "No, he did not. I believe he merely said he was from the *Times*. I assumed he meant the *London*. Perhaps he was from a different paper."

When the inspector merely grunted, then lifted a brow at the constable, as if to indicate he should make a note that the butler had made an erroneous assumption, Dobble explained further—hating that he felt compelled to do so in the presence of Mrs. Bright. "I had no reason not to take Mr. Waring at his word, for reporters, photographer-journalists, and other curiosity seekers often make appearances in hopes of speaking to Mrs. Mallowan—or at least to some of her staff. Which, of course, I don't abide at all. Catch them sneaking around the grounds on occasion, as well. Sometimes wanting a book or one of the magazines signed. Once I apprehended a young woman attempting to pry away a piece of stone from the—"

"Yet you invited Waring in and went on to offer the man accommodations for the evening." Inspector Cork's eyes seemed to bulge even more, as if he were abjectly horrified by such a common courtesy.

"Mr. and Mrs. Mallowan are not in the habit of turning away travelers—particularly late in the day and certainly not when the weather is going bad. He assured me that his appointment was for the next day—today, that is—and that I needn't interrupt Mrs. Mallowan at dinner." Dobble shrugged. "It's not uncommon for unexpected travelers to need a place to stay out here in the country. Either they get lost or have motorcar trouble or bad weather might cause them to seek shelter."

"Was Mr. Waring driving his own motorcar, or did he get a ride from the train station?"

"He was in his own automobile."

"The constable will need to see it. Parked in the garage, I assume? The chauffeur will know?" When Dobble nodded, Cork went on. "Right, then. At what point did you tell Mrs. Mallowan about her unexpected guest?"

"Immediately, of course, while he waited in the parlour—despite his assurances to the contrary. I spoke to her quietly at dinner to confirm that he could stay. She was taken by surprise at his appearance but assumed there must have been a miscommunication—although I must say, Mrs. Mallowan does *not* make mistakes of that nature, and the facts have borne out that she was not in error, after all. 'Of course we won't send him out in this,' she said. 'The Gray Room, I think, don't you, Max? And you might just as well set another place for him, Dobble,' she told me. 'It's only just ending the soup course.' And that was how it happened that Mr. Waring came to be here."

Cork's expression didn't change. "Very well. So he ate dinner with the other guests and the Mallowans."

"That is correct." Dobble ignored Mrs. Bright, who'd leaned forward, as if preparing to interject. Fortunately, the inspector stymied her interruption with his own question.

"And you were there, supervising the serving staff, I assume. Did you notice whether anyone at the table seemed to know Mr. Waring—or vicey versy?"

"If anyone knew him, it wasn't evident. I introduced him, and he took a seat next to Mr. Grimson. What little of his conversation that I happened to overhear was superficial. I believe the conversation ranged from traveling about the countryside to the latest Cheltenham Cup to the new Fred Astaire film."

Cork glanced at the constable, as if to ensure he was finished making notes, then nodded. "Very well, then, Mr. Dobble. That will be all."

Dobble wasn't even out the door before he was rubbing his eyes and sneezing.

Blooming cats.

CHAPTER 6

"SEEMED A BIT NERVOUS, THAT BLOKE," SAID CONSTABLE GREEN-sticks as Mr. Dobble closed the door behind him. "See 'is shifty eyes, and the way they was all red in 'em? Looked nervous, like, as if he were blinkin' back tears."

The constable was speaking to Inspector Cork, but Phyllida took it upon herself to respond. "It's Stilton and Rye. Mr. Dobble is quite sensitive to cat hair."

"Stilton and Rye?" said Cork.

In response, Phyllida scooped up the soft, fluffy cat who'd been lazing on the back of the armchair, next to her. "May I introduce Stilton. As you can see, she is precisely the color of the cheese—white with gray, charcoal, and blueish markings. And the amber one up there on the bookshelf is Rye. He's prohibitively anti-social." As she pointed at the other cat, directing upward the attention of the two men, she took the opportunity to glance at the constable's notes. The scrawl was hardly legible, but she managed to make out the words *Harvey Dobble, butler.*

"Mrs. Bright, as part of our official investigation, we'll need your full legal name before and after marriage, as well as the date and place of birth," said Inspector Cork.

This initial request nearly took Phyllida by surprise, as such a banal bit of information was normally left out of the interviews conducted by the detectives in the fictional crime stories, like those written by Mrs. Agatha and her colleagues. But she immedi-

ately understood why the authorities should want that information for their records—regardless of whether she intended to
provide it. And the only reason a mystery writer would include
such information would be to offer a clue . . . or a red herring.
She might mention that bit of information to Mrs. Agatha. Her
mistress was always in need of good red herrings.

"Of course, Inspector," Phyllida replied demurely, having
formed this opinion and decided on her response to the request
in a matter of seconds. "I was born in London on—"

And she dropped Stilton onto the desk, precisely where Greensticks was writing and his notes were piled up.

Stilton, who always rose to the occasion no matter what Phyllida asked of her, scrambled wildly and scattered the papers into a
small cyclone, causing an utter uproar as Phyllida apologized profusely while managing to jumble the notes even more. (Later, she
would apologize to Stilton for the indignity by offering her a
piece of cheese.) "I'm so sorry, Constable! She simply launched
herself right out of my arms. Please, let me assist you . . ."

Once the last of the papers had been reassembled and an af-
fronted Stilton had taken refuge on the windowsill, Phyllida took
command of the conversation before it could return to dangerous territory. "Inspector, I was just in the library, supervising the
removal of the stained rug, and whilst therein, I noticed that this
book had been replaced on the shelf after the murder."

She set the volume on the desk. "What I haven't been able to
ascertain is why the killer would be so interested in a publication
about roadside inns in England."

Cork gave her a jaundiced look. "That's rather a stretch, Mrs.
Bright, to assume the killer cared at all about roadside inns." He
barely glanced at the book. "What makes you think it was put on
the shelf after the murder?"

"I don't think, Inspector Cork. I *know* it was *re*placed—not
merely *placed*—on the shelf after the murder, because there's no
blood on its spine. Unlike the books on either side of it, both of
which are decorated with splatters."

"Someone likely just shoved it back on the shelf without paying any attention to where they were putting it," Constable Green-sticks told her kindly. "A maid or—"

"Constable, I know where every book belongs on every shelf in that library. Aside from the fact that I've read most of them my-self, it's my *job* to know the proper place for every item in this house—and whether something is not in its place. I assure you, that book was returned to its normal location *after* the murder, and it must have been done by the killer—because it certainly wasn't done by poor Mr. Waring. And the fact that it was obviously *off* the shelf when the violence occurred, and then was put back after, indicates quite clearly that this book was somehow of inter-est to the perpetrator—and by replacing it in its proper location, the killer was making a vain attempt to keep anyone from realiz-ing its importance." She settled down into the chair, folding her hands primly in her lap.

Cork's mustache twitched irritably, but at least this time he picked up the book and flipped through it. "*Historic Travel Inns of England*, is it?"

"There aren't any notations inside, nor are there any pieces of paper tucked within," Phyllida told him helpfully. "I've already checked."

"I'm certain you have, Mrs. Bright," replied Cork.

"If you need lodging in the area, Inspector, I do recommend you take the notice about the Screaming Magpie in Listleigh under advisement," she went on.

"Very well. Thank you for this bit of information. We'll . . . keep it all in mind," replied Cork.

At that moment, someone rapped hesitantly on the door from in the corridor, and Phyllida rose, feeling quite pleased with the success of her machinations of distracting the authorities from her personal data. "That will be the first of the parlourmaids. I in-formed my staff that interviews will begin precisely at half eight and will go in order of rank every fifteen minutes thereafter so as not to waste time or infringe upon their responsibilities."

"And if one of the interviews should go longer than fifteen

minutes?" Cork asked with a bland look. "Would that not cause some havoc with their responsibilities?"

"Although it's unlikely that will happen, I have, of course, made arrangements to accommodate for such delays." Without waiting for permission, Phyllida opened the door to Ginny, the highest-ranking parlourmaid.

The young woman came in with understandable nervousness, but she didn't hesitate. Phyllida noted with approval that Ginny's gray muslin morning uniform was spotless and smooth, and the apron she wore over it, edged in eyelet lace, was straight and fairly gleamed bright white. Her matching eyelet lace collar and starched cuffs were likewise spotless. Black hose covered her legs without sagging, and Phyllida knew without looking that the seams up the back of Ginny's calves would be perfectly straight. The maid's cap, adorned with two rows of lace (as befitted her station), was tied in the back with a dark gray ribbon beneath her smooth knot of soft golden hair.

Ginny might be high pitched and prone to gossip (what servant wasn't?), but she was always neatly put together. That was why she was first parlourmaid.

"Good morning, miss. Please take a seat and provide Constable Greensticks with your full name and date and place of birth," said the inspector.

Before he remembered her lapse, Phyllida spoke up. "My goodness, I believe we got distracted earlier by poor Stilton—do give me a paper and I'll jot my information down, as well, Constable." Ignoring Stilton's miffed look, Phyllida gave Greensticks a very innocent smile as he slid a piece of paper toward her. She scrawled in utterly illegible writing a date and location while Ginny offered her personal data, the details of which were already known to Phyllida, of course.

"Now, miss, please tell me where you were and what you did from ten o'clock last night until this morning," said Inspector Cork.

"At ten o'clock I was finishing putting the library to rights. Mrs. Bright likes me to run a feather duster every evening—over the desk, mantel, and bookshelves, I mean—and to straighten the items on the desk. I'm to push the chairs into place and remove any dishes and use the carpet sweeper on the rug. I did all of that and drew the drapes, but then Stanley, the footman, came in to close the windows. Mrs. Bright sent him because it was going to rain."

"Was the fountain pen in place on the desk, Ginny?" asked Phyllida.

"Yes, ma'am, it was in its place. Right on the desk."

Cork glanced at Phyllida, as if to ensure she wasn't about to speak again, and she gave him her favorite demure smile while remaining silent. "After Stanley closed the windows and locked the doors, what happened?"

Ginny's cheeks turned slightly pink, and she avoided looking at Phyllida. "We left the library at—at the same time."

"And what time was that?"

The maid's cheeks pinkened a little more. "It was—I think—just a bit after half ten?"

Phyllida suspected that Ginny's hair might not have been quite as neatly confined when she and the footman vacated the room as when she'd entered it. She sighed inwardly. Stanley was quite the rogue.

"And did you see anyone when you left the library?"

"No, sir."

"Did you see Mr. Waring?"

"No, sir. Only when he first arrived, I mean. But not after that."

"And when you left the library, what did you do?"

The heightened color was back in Ginny's cheeks. "I . . . um . . . I stepped outside for some fresh air."

"Alone?"

"N-no, sir. Stanley walked out with me. He—he was going to make certain all the outside lamps were lit, since it was dark and was going to storm. One of them had been flickering out, he said. And then we—I—came back inside, and I put away all my supplies and finished folding the linens for the parlour. Then I went upstairs to my bedroom and washed up and went to sleep." These last words came out in a rush.

"What time was it that you went up to your bedroom?"

"It—it was nearly midnight." Ginny carefully kept her gaze from Phyllida, who was thoroughly enjoying her maid's attempts at subterfuge regarding the details of her evening, for it would have taken less than fifteen minutes for her to fold linens and put away her supplies.

But, quite frankly, someone ought to teach the poor girl how to dispel a blush as needed. Phyllida supposed that would be another task to add to her to-do list—along with a crisp lecture about making certain the young woman didn't get herself into "trouble."

"Did you see anyone else when you were outside or when you came out of the library?" Cork asked.

"No, sir. Only Molly, who was bringing a tea tray down on the back stairs. And the valets—they were playing cards in the servants' dining hall."

"Did you hear or see anything during the night?"

"No, sir. We're up on the attic floor, sir, and unless a bell rings, I sleep soundly and don't hear anything until the morning."

"Very well. Thank you, miss."

Thus dismissed, Ginny fled the room. Phyllida looked pointedly at the watch pinned to her bodice, then at Cork. Barely ten minutes had passed since the maid came in the room.

The inspector pretended not to notice. Instead, he began to peruse the papers Greensticks had been shuffling around. Before he could notice that Phyllida's writing was unreadable, she rose to open the door again. As anticipated, the second parlourmaid was waiting to be admitted.

Mary, who was lower in comparison to Ginny (in volume, in pitch, and in status), was startlingly slender and fair haired, which gave her an ethereal, blow-away-in-the-wind appearance. Her uniform was just as crisp and clean as Ginny's, but being a second maid, she had only a single ruffle of lace on her cap.

"Please have a seat, miss, and state your name, date, and location of birth," Cork said. Once that was accomplished and noted, he moved on to the expected questions about her activities last evening.

"At half nine, I had just finished putting the front parlour to rights, and then I waited for Mrs. Agatha and Mr. Max and their guests to leave the music room, where they were playing bridge. While I was waiting, I dusted up and swept the east corridor and the front foyer. I finished in the music room shortly before eleven o'clock, for they retired early." Mary spoke with the same manner as she did her duties: smoothly and efficiently, if a bit softly. She glanced at Phyllida several times during her speech and received encouraging nods in response.

"Did you see anyone near the library?"

"No, sir."

"Did you see Mr. Waring?"

"No, sir, I don't think so."

"What did you do after you finished in the music room?"

"I brought dishes down to the kitchen and gave them to the maids there. Then I went up to bed. It was nearly midnight by then."

"And after that, did you hear or see anything unusual?"

"No, sir."

Cork stroked his mustache. "Very well, then. Thank you."

Mary gave Phyllida one last glance before she left the room.

"Still on schedule, are we, Mrs. Bright?" the inspector said.

"Indeed, we are," she murmured, standing to open the door once again.

And so they remained on schedule, with each interview lasting for fewer than the prescribed fifteen minutes, usually far less. Next were the two footmen, including Stanley, who was far more matter of fact in his description of closing up the library than Ginny had been. His blithe narrative left Phyllida with the distinct impression she might have a heartbroken maid on her hands in the near future. She frowned inwardly. Dramatics between staff members were unavoidable, but she decried them, nonetheless.

After Cork finished with Freddie (the under-footman, and a far nicer young man than his counterpart), Piero, the man of all work, came in.

As expected, Piero, who was magnificently talented with re-

building things such as broken clocks, or repairing small mechanical items, had little of import to offer. He was a quiet man,
nearly fifty, with sparse gray hair and startlingly blue eyes, but with
the simple personality of an eight-year-old. Although he worked
at Mallowan Hall, his brother drove him to and from the estate
every day, and thus Piero, who had a small work area in the gardener's barn, had been gone by seven o'clock on the evening of
the murder.

Next, the first chambermaid, Bess, came into the sitting room.
She and her counterpart Lizzie had been on the third floor,
preparing some of the guests' rooms for the evening while said
guests were being entertained in the music room. Thus Bess was
in and out of the sitting room in under five minutes.

However, when the second chambermaid came in and took a
seat, Phyllida intervened in the questioning, having information
Inspector Cork did not. "Lizzie, you attended to Mr. Waring's
chamber, the Gray Room, once he was assigned to it. Did you see
him at all? Or did you notice anything unusual?"

Lizzie rubbed her nose with the side of her thumb—a habit
Phyllida was determined to help her break—and nodded. She
had a round, cheerful face liberally sprinkled with dark freckles.
"Yes, ma'am, I did the Gray Room, didn't I? Mr. Waring was in
there when I first knocked, and 'e poked 'is 'ead out and said as I
was to wait to do 'is room."

"What time was it that you first went there?" asked Cork.

"It wasn't ten o'clock, sir, as I heard the clock chime after, and
I was thinking how late it was and how much more I had to do,
didn't I?" She seemed to recall belatedly that her boss was sitting
in the next chair, and added, "The Wisteria Room—that's where
Mrs. Devine is assigned—took me longer than usual due to a broken coffee pot knocked all over the table, chair, and floor. Don't
know how anyone could make such a mess of it, broken china
and grounds everywhere—and then she wanted the coffee smell
out of the room! And she didn't even bring her own maid, didn't
she? So it was left to me to clean it up and see to the dress it spilt
on, too!"

"Have Violet attend to the frock," Phyllida said firmly. "She'll know what to do. Rosalind is always spilling on her clothing." Rosalind, who was away at school, was Mrs. Agatha's daughter from her first marriage.

"Yes, mum. Anyway, the Gray Room was my last one, wasn't it? And now I had to wait."

"How long did you wait there for Mr. Waring?" asked Cork.

Lizzie straightened in her chair, and her mouth flattened into a disapproving line. "Mrs. Bright don't like us to be standin' around, then, sir, just using up the oxygen, so she says"—she stole a quick glance at Phyllida—"so I went down the hall, didn't I? And I attended to the bathroom, even though I had just brought the clean towels. But someone had gone in and mussed it up, didn't they? And the rug was askew, and by the time I fixed that and was wiping off the sink, I heard the door down the hall open."

"The Gray Room door?" Phyllida prompted when Lizzie seemed to run out of steam.

"Yes, ma'am. Mr. Waring come out, and I heard him talking to someone, and then they went back downstairs."

At last, something that might be interesting. Phyllida remained still in her chair, but Cork shifted upright a bit. "Who was he talking to?"

"I couldn't see, sir. I was still cleaning in the bathroom, and the water was splashing."

"Was it a man or a woman? What were they talking about?"

"I think . . . It sounded like a woman's voice, but I couldn't 'ear what they was talking about."

The inspector drummed his fingers on the table. "How about impressions, then? Did they seem to know each other? Was it a lengthy conversation, or did it seem to be more like a casual passing in the hallway moment?"

"I don't know, sir." Lizzie gave Phyllida a nervous look. "I didn't really 'ear them, didn't I? And I wasn't paying attention, because I was trying to finish up the bathroom so I could get the Gray Room done up before 'alf nine."

"But you heard only one door open," Phyllida said.

Lizzie nodded as Cork shot Phyllida a sidewise look. His mustache rippled as he pursed his lips. The man could do with some pomade. And a trim. There were two bristly hairs that thrust out like minuscule arms from either side, making Phyllida want to take up—and put to use—the scissors stowed in her desk.

"Yes, ma'am, only one door." The maid shifted in her seat, but her hands remained primly folded in her lap.

"Any other impressions or idea of who might have been with Mr. Waring?" When Lizzie shook her head, the inspector moved on with his interrogation. "When you did up his room, did you notice anything unusual or out of place?"

"No, sir, not at all. 'E was a neatnik, 'e was, and I 'ardly knew 'e was there, didn't I? Course, 'e'd just got there, didn't 'e? Right during soup. Just a small suitcase and a briefcase and none was unpacked, and the bed warn't even mussed only a bit. It was good, that, as I didn't have much to do, and I finished it before 'alf ten, when Mrs. Bright likes us to be down to the main floor to 'elp getting the laundry sorted and—"

"A suitcase *and* a briefcase?" Cork mused.

Phyllida didn't bat an eyelash. "There wasn't a briefcase in the Gray Room just now, Inspector."

He made a low humphing sound and gave her a skeptical look. "Or so it seemed."

"Nor was there one found in the library," Phyllida added smoothly.

"Sir?" said Lizzie, getting even more antsy in her chair.

"Never mind that, miss. After you finished the Gray Room, what did you do?"

"Why, I went downstairs, didn't I? Like I always do. And did up the laundry sorting. And there was a bit of mending to attend to, as well."

"Did you see Mr. Waring after that?"

"No, sir."

"Did you go near the library last night at all?"

"No, *sir*."

"When did you go to bed?"

"'Alf eleven, it was, and not too soon. Slept like an old 'ound dog, didn't I?"

"Did you hear or see anything unusual last night, after you went to bed?"

"No, sir. I slept like the dead—" As soon as she said it, Lizzie winced and swallowed hard. "Sorry."

Cork's mustache twitched, but he otherwise kept his expression impassive. "Thank you, miss. That's all."

"Perhaps the briefcase was left in his motorcar," Phyllida suggested as she rose. "I'll have Stanley investigate."

"We've already looked in Mr. Waring's motorcar," Cork replied.

"And?"

Cork didn't deign to reply, but they both knew he didn't need to state the obvious: there was no briefcase in the auto. But he did give her a hard look, to which she responded with a bland smile.

"The first of the guest staff is next—that is, the servants that accompanied the Budgely-Rhodeses, Mr. Sloup, and Mr. Hartford. One lady's maid and three valets. As they have no other tasks until their masters and mistress ring for them, I thought it best that they speak with you before the kitchen maids. I suspect none of them will have much information to provide, as they're only guests and have no reason to be anywhere in the house but the servants' quarters belowstairs or their masters' and mistress's guest rooms."

"Oh, you suspect so, do you, Mrs. Bright?"

She gave him a cool smile but declined to answer his question. "I'll return shortly to escort you to the kitchen to meet Mrs. Puffley. I have several items to which I must attend."

"I'll bet you do," Cork murmured.

CHAPTER 7

*P*HYLLIDA CAUGHT UP TO LIZZIE AS THE MAID WAS CLIMBING THE last span of steps to the second floor. She carried a bucket with a feather duster, a carpet sweeper, and a clump of rags. In the other hand, she carried a pail with lemon-scented water.

"Mrs. Bright?" she said with a bit of trepidation. Her freckles stood out sharply in a face gone slack with nerves. "Did I do all right with the inspector?"

"Quite. You did just fine." Phyllida stopped at the top of the stairs before Lizzie opened the door to the "other" side from the servants' hall. "What rooms have you finished this morning?"

"Only the Meadows Room, Mrs. Bright, because it's vacant, and the bathroom, too, on account of none of the guests have left the bedrooms."

"You didn't go into the Gray Room?"

Lizzie's face turned pink. "Oh, ma'am, I was going to ask if I should do that, but I forgot. I didn't know if the inspector wanted to look in there first. For clues. That's 'ow they do it in Mrs. Agatha's stories, innit?"

"It is." Phyllida smiled. She really did have a superior staff at Mallowan Hall. "Before you do the Gray Room, I want you to go down and tell Amsi we need a fresh bouquet of gerberas for Mrs. Agatha's sitting room. Have Violet bring it up when she collects Mrs. Agatha's breakfast tray."

If Lizzie wondered why her boss was sending her on such an errand, she gave no indication. Instead, with the bob of a little curtsy, the maid turned and jogged quickly down the stairs.

That gave Phyllida the few moments she needed, and as she slipped into the Gray Room, she heard the sounds of activity behind the doors of the other bedchambers. The guests were stirring, and as soon as they learned about Mr. Waring's murder, there would be another wave of excitement and shock reverberating through the house. Nonetheless, meals and tidying must go on. And other fortification. Mr. Dobble had best put out more whisky and sherry.

She closed the door of the Gray Room and had Mr. Waring's briefcase on the bed and, thanks to her previous work on the lock, open within seconds.

The contents of the case were stingy. There were two notebooks—one completely blank and the other with some writing on a few pages—a collection of pencils held together by a rubber band, a road map of the county, and an appointment diary. Her ears attuned to the sound of anyone approaching (Phyllida didn't know whether Cork was going to wait for her to produce the briefcase, or send someone up to look for it), she opened the appointment diary.

Strangely—or perhaps not strange at all—neither today's nor yesterday's date had appointments written on it, and Phyllida was about to flip back a page when she heard a soft noise just outside the door. There was something about it . . . sly, hesitant, covert . . . that made the hair on the back of her neck stand on end. As the doorknob slowly turned, she reacted quickly and decisively, closing her hand over the jangling key ring and diving silently beneath the bed.

She immediately regretted this impulsive action for a number of reasons—even aside from the fact that she banged the sensitive part of her elbow and was trying not to moan as the sharp tingles raced up her arm.

First, she'd have an incredibly difficult time explaining her location should anyone find her. It would be humiliating in the least—especially if she was discovered by Mr. Dobble or Inspector Cork. Her face heated with the thought. And Lizzie would be returning at any moment. . . . She grimaced. Hercule Poirot would *never* be caught in such a mortifying situation. Captain Hastings, perhaps . . . definitely Tuppence . . . but not Poirot. And certainly not the very dignified Miss Marple.

Second, the direction in which she'd dived under the bed left her so she was facing the wall next to it, the precise opposite direction of the door and the chamber at large, so she couldn't see anything about the person once he or she entered the room. It would be difficult to rotate herself into a different position without giving away her presence.

Third, and arguably worst of all, she'd left the briefcase wide open on top of the bed.

Furious with herself for making such a cake of things, Phyllida could only lie there under the bed and listen to the activity, trying to interpret as much as she could from the movements. The door closed quietly, and the ensuing footsteps, which squeaked slightly, as if the shoes were new, hitched briefly as they came into the room, probably because the intruder wondered why someone had left the dratted briefcase wide open on the bed. Phyllida grimaced once again at her stupidity. Then, suddenly emboldened with determination, she began to slowly, carefully shift herself around to the opposite direction. She had to keep the blasted keys from scraping along the wood floor and lift herself up on her elbows (including the painful one) and her knees while making sure she didn't make a sound.

Above, the shuffling of papers in the briefcase indicated what she had sensed the moment she heard the sound at the door: whoever had entered was not there legitimately. For if someone had merely been sent up to look for the briefcase, that individual would not have closed the door behind them and would certainly not still be there, thumbing through the contents of the case.

Drat and *blast.*

She inched a little more in a counterclockwise direction, using her elbows and knees to lift herself so her clothing wouldn't rustle over the floor (which, incidentally, was devoid of dust bunnies, and she would commend Lizzie and Bess for that). She *had* to find out who was there, because . . . well, whoever it was wasn't supposed to be in there, obviously, and . . .

A chill wave rushed over her, and Phyllida paused her movements. Her throat went dry.

Could the person who was quite literally standing *over* her be the murderer?

It made terrible sense, for who else would be in there digging through Mr. Waring's possessions?

Phyllida became aware of the sudden hard thudding of her heart. Now it was more difficult to keep her breathing steady and soft, but she somehow managed to keep from allowing her emotions to get the best of her. Instead, she continued to maneuver herself gently around in an attempt to see *something* of the intruder—a glimpse of the softly squeaking shoes at the very least.

But just then, the presumptive murderer turned, and before Phyllida could get into a position to see, the creaking footsteps moved briskly away from the bed. The door opened, and there was a brief hesitation before the intruder left the room, as if he or she was looking into the corridor. Phyllida twisted sharply and pushed the bed's dust ruffle aside—and her keys clinked and scratched quietly along the floor. She froze at the sound and held her breath, heart thudding madly, as she waited to see whether she would be discovered . . . but then she heard the door open wider and the knob rattle as the footsteps went out. By the time she got turned all the way around, it was too late.

The door closed before she caught even a glimpse of clothing or shoe.

Cursing herself roundly for a variety of reasons, Phyllida clawed out from beneath the bed and stumbled to her feet. She dashed for the door and cracked it, panting a little, and peered out into the hall to see if she could catch a glimpse of whoever had just left the room. Unfortunately, it seemed that every one of the Mallowans' guests was venturing out of their bedchambers and congregating in the hall at the same moment, leaving Phyllida with no indication of who had just been digging around in Mr. Waring's briefcase.

There were Mr. and Mrs. Hartford, he being an old school chum of Mr. Max—or so she recalled. Mr. Hartford's blond hair gleamed damply, as if he'd just pomaded it, and his shoes (of course Phyllida looked at the shoes in an effort to determine whether they might have made the sound she'd heard from their movements) didn't appear to be new and squeaky. His wife was perhaps several years younger than he and was approximately in her late twenties. She had honey-colored hair and soft golden skin. Next to her husband, she stood tall and willowy, dressed in a lovely lean frock of sea-foam green trimmed in tasteful lace of which even Mr. Dobble would approve. Phyllida couldn't see their faces, as they were conversing with the Budgely-Rhodeses, but she recalled thinking that Mrs. Hartford was patrician and elegant and that her husband gave off a suave and sartorial look in both form and dress.

She knew less about Mr. and Mrs. Budgely-Rhodes, but she believed he was somehow related to Mrs. Agatha's writing business. Not from a publisher, she didn't think, but someone who had an interest in her work. Perhaps he was from the West End, about doing a stage play?

If there was talk about doing a motion picture with M. Poirot, Phyllida fervently hoped that would not happen. She feared absolutely no one would be able to portray the elegant Belgian in the way she saw him in her mind. She'd have to avoid seeing the film if it was ever made.

Mr. Budgely-Rhodes had sparse hair the color of faded carrots, and he was smoking a dark cigarette. She couldn't get a glimpse of his shoes, unfortunately. He looked about fifty, and his wife was within range of the same age. She had pudgy hands, with rings that appeared too tight, and wore her hair in a completely outmoded Gibson Girl style, which made Phyllida want to sit her down and have a frank discussion about the importance of staying up to date on fashion. It was an especial affront since Mrs. Budgely-Rhodes wore such expensive, well-made clothing. Modern hairstyles would flatter her round face much better than the mousy brown bun on top. Her shoes and feet were hidden by Mr. Hartford's legs.

The Devines weren't standing next to each other in the little cluster, and Phyllida considered whether that might indicate that one of them might have been a late joiner to the conversing crowd and therefore possibly have been the snoop in the Gray Room. Mrs. Devine had a delightful, infectious laugh, and she was very attractive, with bobbed ink-black hair fixed in little flat curls around her face. Her makeup was perfect—shiny red lips and penciled brows in slender arches—and she wore a long expanse of bangles on her elegant wrist.

Mr. Devine was handsome enough to make even the jaded Phyllida's heart skip a little, and his voice—low and velvet—matched his dark good looks. Together, the dark-haired couple looked like film stars or, if one were being fanciful, the god and goddess of human beauty. Phyllida couldn't recall precisely how they knew the Mallowans, but she thought he might be some distant relative of Mr. Max's. She'd have to find out.

The two single men, Mr. Sloup and Mr. Grimson, were also in the cluster of people. The group was standing just at the landing that joined the second and third floors—which was at the far end from Mr. Waring's chamber.

It was quite unfortunate that all eight of the guests happened to appear at the same time in the same place—even from different floors—when Phyllida needed to determine who'd just been sneaking about in the Gray Room.

Mr. Tuddy Sloup was a man with a slick look about him, in a way that reminded Phyllida of a sly fox. He was around thirty, and he combed his hair straight back with far too much shiny pomade. She'd felt an instant dislike of the man at first sight yesterday, and watching the way he held himself as he spoke to Mrs. Hartford—stepping too close to her, with his eyes heavily lidded in a condescending manner—only increased her antipathy. Phyllida knew better than to settle on him as the killer so soon, but she already *wanted* it to be Mr. Sloup. Even his given name—Tuddy—sounded superficial and fake. And though she tried to catch a glimpse of his shoes, it was in vain.

Mr. Grimson, who was a bit younger than Mr. Sloup, was soft spoken and dressed in clothing that appeared a bit shabby to Phyllida's discerning eye. He seemed more comfortable standing at the edge of the small crowd of people than conducting a conversation, but one could almost consider his actions furtive. He was tall and slender, and he needed a haircut, though Phyllida decided not to hold it against him. She did catch sight of his shoes—ones that had recently been polished—but was unable to determine whether they squeaked.

The tones of the guests' voices and their lack of excitement as they discussed how well they had slept, how comfortable their rooms were, and what would be for breakfast indicated that the news related to the murder had not yet reached their ears.

Except, of course, for the culprit himself . . . who clearly had to know the Gray Room was empty of Mr. Waring.

So whoever it was *had* to be the killer.

And whoever it was *might* have just heard her moving beneath the bed.

She eased back more from the slender opening, suddenly aware that any of them could notice that the bedchamber door was slightly ajar instead of closed. Only the killer would notice or care, and Phyllida was averse to the idea of having a murderer aware that he was being spied upon.

After observing for a few more moments to see whether she could tell who'd just joined the conversation (she couldn't), or if it was possible to discern whether someone's shoes were new enough to squeak, Phyllida drew back into the Gray Room. Brushing her skirt—which, to her edification, indicated a re-markable lack of dust—back into place and straightening her sleeves, she turned back to the bed and the open briefcase.

And then she gave a soft cry of dismay.

The notebook with writing in it was missing.

CHAPTER 8

REBECCA MCARDLE WAS THE SECOND KITCHEN MAID AND HAD been at Mallowan Hall for less than three months. She liked her boss's boss, Mrs. Bright, just fine; in fact, she thought the housekeeper was one of the handsomest women she'd ever laid her eyes on (not counting in photographs or talkies). Not that Mrs. Bright was movie star glamorous or fancy in her dress and manners like that cool blonde Mrs. Hartford, but she had a smile that always made you want to smile back and eyes that twinkled—except when you did something wrong.

Then Mrs. Bright laid down the hammer pretty hard. *And rightly so,* Rebecca thought.

On the other hand, Mrs. Puffley—Rebecca's actual boss—was a cyclone in the kitchen. She shouted, she stomped, she groused . . . and when she was really lit up mad, she pounded bread dough like she wanted to pound your head instead—or used a meat cleaver as if she were beheading a criminal on the cutting board.

Rebecca wasn't *exactly* afraid of the cook striking her or throwing anything (she had had to dodge pots and pans in her last position at Bunder House and once had got clobbered between the shoulder blades with a rolling pin). But she sure could get an earful enough from Mrs. Puffley to make her head ring, for the cook didn't abide anything less from her helpers than work done nonstop and at a brisk pace, and she wasn't shy about letting them know it.

If Mrs. Puffley caught you so much as pausing to stretch your back after you'd been bent over rolling out teacakes for an hour or peeling potatoes since eight in the morning, she'd start bellowing about what happened to lazy maids in her kitchen.

Which was why Rebecca was both relieved and agitated to have a few precious moments away from the kitchen. She was grateful to be able to move a trifle slower and catch her breath, and to be away from the constant banging, clanging, and chopping . . . but the fact that she had to be interviewed by the police tied her stomach in knots.

Of course, her stomach had been in knots ever since she heard the news this morning in the kitchen. That Charles Waring had been murdered in the library here at Mallowan Hall. How could that be true?

Thank St. Pete that her dropping the tea tray in the kitchen and sending china crashing all over had given her a few minutes to get herself under control, so to speak. It had even been worth the blistering reprimand from Mrs. Puffley after Mrs. Bright had left, and the promise that she—not the footman—would be polishing silver till midnight in payment for her clumsiness.

But now she was going to have to sit with the policemen and answer questions about it all.

Rebecca's fingers twisted together as she paused outside Mrs. Bright's sitting room door. The last time she'd been invited into the sunny, happy chamber was only last week, when she'd brought a tea tray to the housekeeper. Mrs. Bright had allowed her to come in and visit with Stilton and Rye for a few moments while she finished up approving a supply list for Mrs. Puffley.

But today would be far different.

Before she could decide whether to knock or to simply open the door, the knob turned and Molly, the senior kitchen maid, came out. The door closed behind her.

"How was it?" Rebecca whispered, looking with trepidation at the door.

"Not so bad," replied the other girl. Molly was nice enough, but she thought herself a little high and mighty sometimes—almost as if she were one of the housemaids or even an upper servant. Just because she'd known Mrs. Bright the longest.

Rebecca wanted to know more: Were they stern and ferocious, and how many policemen *were* there? Was Old Dent in the room, too? (Probably he was, because the man thought he was God.) Did they threaten to arrest her if she didn't talk . . . ?

But before she could ask, the door swung open, and there was a man who could only be the inspector. The first thing Rebecca noticed was his freckles, which made him seem a little less intimidating. But then she found herself caught by pale blue eyes that seemed to bulge a little from their sockets, as if they were scouring her for lies. That made her nervous all over again.

"Come in, miss," he said in a voice that seemed kind enough.

Rebecca stepped inside and immediately saw Rye, the fluffy cat who was the color of just-browned toast, and she scooped him up before he could dart away. For once, the cat was kind enough not to argue with her when she sat in the chair indicated by the inspector, and Rye even settled onto the lap of her uniform apron and skirt, where she stroked him so as to hide the trembling of her fingers. She could brush away the cat hair later. She didn't like policemen.

"I'm Inspector Cork, and this is Constable Greensticks," said the man who had freckles, even though he had to be in his thirties. "Mrs. Bright should return momentarily, but we needn't wait for her."

Oh, but could we, please?

"No, sir," she replied instead and then went on to give him her full name and place and date of birth, as requested. All the while, she kept her fingers buried in Rye's soft, silky hair. He was purring contentedly against her stomach, and it made her feel a bit less nervous. But only a bit.

"Now, miss, if you could tell me where you were last night, from nine o'clock, until this morning, when you woke."

"Yes, sir, yes, sir. I work in the kitchen, you see, and I don't hardly never get up from down there, you see," she said. "I was, at nine o'clock, I was—we were cleaning up from the first two din-

ner courses, see, and I was finishing up the dessert to go up with
Stanley, who's the only one Mrs. Puffley trusts to carry up a free-
standing trifle, on account of it being so delicate and all, and
Freddie, the under-footman, of course, the last time he bumped
into a wall coming out of the servants stairs and made it all slip to
the sides—ruined it all. Mrs. Puffley nearly had his ear twisted off
and red to boot—not that one can blame her, for it took us two
days to make it with the layers of meringue and cake, and it was
really Mrs. Puffley's finest creation ever, and it was for Mrs. Agatha's
birthday celebration." Rebecca was out of breath from the long
stream of words, which had tumbled out quite without her even
thinking about them. She wasn't even precisely certain what she'd
actually *said.*

Inspector Cork blinked at her. "So you were in the kitchen, and
then what did you do?"

"Yes, sir, you see, I was in the kitchen until nearly eleven because after the dinner we were cleaning up, and then I had to
make the dough for tomorrow's bread. Mrs. Agatha likes us to
make at least one loaf a week here instead of getting it from the
bakery, so the dough had to rise, you see, and then I had to put
together a tray for the guests and Mr. Max and Mrs. Agatha in the
music room for them for after dinner—it was just some slices of
cheese and strawberries, you see, but Mrs. Agatha likes there to
be something to nibble on with the after-dinner port or whisky,
you see. Sir."

"And did you deliver the tray with these foods to the guests in
the music room?"

"Oh, no, sir, no, sir. That's the footman or one of the parlourmaids. I don't never come upstairs here, because there's ever so
much to do in the kitchen all the time, Mrs. Puffley can't hardly
even spare me to go out to use the—" She stopped with a gasp
and felt her face go hot and red. She'd nearly mentioned *going to
the outhouse* to the inspector. She wanted to dive under the desk
and hide there until this was all over.

"Right, then, yes, miss, I think I understand." He didn't seem
offended or horrified by her remark. "And so is it true to say that
you didn't go into the library either last night or this morning?"

"No, sir. I—I mean, yes, sir, it's true that I didn't go to the library at all. We don't come upstairs much at all, sir, we kitchen maids, and when we do, it's only here, to Mrs. Bright's closet, you see, sir."

"Very well." He glanced at the constable, who'd been scratching notes on the notepad and been otherwise completely quiet. "Do you have any questions for the miss, Greensticks?"

The younger man seemed startled by the sudden, swift change of attention, and he dropped his pencil. "No, sir, Inspector. But only, miss, did you hear anything unusual last night? Or see anything?"

"No, sir, nothing unusual at all." Rebecca began to feel as if she might make it through this interview all right.

"Very well, then, miss, you're free to go," said the inspector after drumming his fingers on the table for an eternity.

Rebecca bolted from the chair, and Rye tumbled to the floor. He gave her a furious look before stalking away, tail held high and twitching just at the top. But she didn't take the time to apologize. For once, she couldn't wait to get back to the kitchen.

CHAPTER 9

*P*HYLLIDA DIDN'T NORMALLY SPEND MUCH TIME IN THE DINING room; that was Mr. Dobble's domain, his and the footmen's, for the serving and seeing to of the meals her staff prepared below-stairs.

But today was one of Extenuating Circumstances, and so she positioned herself discreetly outside the door of the dining room, which was open to allow the guests to flow in and find breakfast set up along the buffet. Phyllida was ostensibly adjusting a flower arrangement in the hallway, and then she was going to see to the way the curtains at the windows draped and whether they needed replacing, cleaning, or mending.

If one asked Mr. Dobble about that, he would inform her that it was not at all appropriate for even the housekeeper to be in the dining room while the guests were eating. But Phyllida had no intention of asking Mr. Dobble anything. These were Extenuating Circumstances, after all. And she knew he wouldn't lower himself to create any sort of conflict in the presence of their employers or their friends. Although later, he'd likely give her an earful—requiring Phyllida to consume yet another bracing cup of tea, with perhaps the addition of a titch of the rye whisky she kept in her bottom drawer.

Besides, Mr. Dobble must know that she, of all people, would want to be there when Mr. Max told their guests the news. And if the butler didn't realize this, Phyllida would be sorely disappointed in the man, for it was imperative that an excellent house-keeper be well informed about everything occurring in the household that was her domain.

"Good morning, everyone," said Mr. Max as he entered the room. "I trust you all slept well?"

Max Mallowan was a kind and relatively easygoing employer who spent a good portion of his time talking about archaeological digs in which he and Mrs. Agatha participated. In fact, Mrs. Agatha had met him while traveling in Mesopotamia, and she had set several of her detective stories in and around such digs. He was about the same height as his tall wife and was fourteen years younger than she. But unlike Mrs. Agatha's first husband, Archie Christie, Mr. Max was devoted to his writer spouse, and the two of them were quite happy together whether in England or when traveling on archaeological digs.

The murmurs of response and some hearty morning greetings filtered away as the Budgely-Rhodeses, Devines, Hartfords, and the two single men busied themselves filling their plates from the sideboard. No one seemed to notice that Mr. Waring was not in attendance.

Mr. Max didn't waste any time with further small talk, and Phyllida understood why when Inspector Cork appeared in the doorway adjacent to where she had moved so as to hear the conversations—and to listen for softly squeaking shoes. She had become busy rearranging the leaves belonging to a potted fern that stood just outside the entrance and saw no reason to interrupt this task to acknowledge the inspector's proximity.

"I'm sorry to disrupt your morning, but there is some news I must share with you," Mr. Max said from just inside the dining room doorway. "Agatha will be down momentarily to join us, but I shan't wait to fill you all in. Mr. Waring—whom you all met at dinner last evening—was found dead this morning. He . . . er . . . It was no accident. Charles Waring was murdered."

Phyllida couldn't watch the faces of everyone in the dining room at the same time—and neither, she noted with satisfaction, could Inspector Cork or, for that matter, Constable Greensticks, who was also standing there. Nonetheless, she did her best to observe the reactions of the eight visitors. Surely one of them had to be the killer and thus would have to manufacture whatever sort of shock or surprise he or she—most likely it was a he, a fact toward which she was leaning ever more strongly since her adventure in the Gray Room—would portray.

If she were writing the scene in one of Mrs. Agatha's detective stories, Phyllida would have Mrs. Budgely-Rhodes drop her cup onto the table with a loud gasp, sloshing tea everywhere and perhaps even shattering the china, and Mr. Devine freeze dramatically, then say something along the lines of "Good God!" Those two seemed the sort to be overly emotive, with Mr. Devine being the type to be fully aware of how handsome he'd look in an arrested moment of shock and horror.

Although there were murmurs and quiet gasps of surprise, no one dropped a teacup—although the quiet Mr. Grimson nearly upended the elevated tray of kippers when he blindly set down the tongs on its edge, and the coolly elegant Mrs. Hartford collapsed very suddenly into a chair, her face going slack with shock as she dug out a cigarette from a small handbag. The greasy-haired Mr. Sloup, whom Phyllida had chosen to watch most intently, frowned and looked around as if he, too, was attempting to identify the killer.

"Inspector Cork from Scotland Yard is here to investigate matters," Mr. Max went on smoothly, "and he's going to need to speak with everyone. Right, then?"

Cork stepped into the room, leaving Phyllida just outside the doorway. He made a brief speech about no one leaving Mallowan Hall until further notice—which elicited several annoyed harrumphs and one under-her-breath whine from Mrs. Budgely-Rhodes about missing an appointment with her seamstress—and then turned to Mr. Max. "I'll start with you, Mr. Mallowan, if you don't mind."

"Yes, of course. The front parlour will do. And you can speak with the others there, as well. Mrs. Bright will show them in."

Phyllida was delighted with this turn of events, for it would be much easier to lurk about near the parlour than the dining area, as there were no doors to that particular room and that chamber was smaller, which meant those conversing would be closer to the entrance. Additionally, and most serendipitously, the front parlour was immediately adjacent to her own sitting room, sharing an interior wall. Phyllida was not at all above holding a glass to said wall in order to listen in to the interviews or even putting her ear to the scrollwork air ducts that joined the chambers. This meant she could hear most of every discussion with everyone at Mallowan Hall and not just with her staff.

"Of course, Mr. Mallowan," she replied and managed—just barely—to keep from looking at Mr. Dobble, whose expression surely must be frozen with annoyance.

"Mrs. Bright, if you would please show the inspector and the constable to the parlour. I'll be there momentarily," said Mr. Max just as Mrs. Agatha stepped off the bottom stair and started toward the dining room. As she walked away with the inspector, Phyllida heard Mr. Max greet his wife. "Ah, there you are, darling. How was the writing this morning?"

Phyllida gestured for Cork to precede her into the parlour. "I suspect, Inspector, that you hadn't quite finished speaking with the staff before the guests came downstairs and interrupted you."

The parlour was a comfortable, welcoming room—as was most every chamber of the household, a fact that Phyllida took credit for and prided herself on—with two sofas facing each other in the center of the room. A low table between them held a squat vase of fresh white roses atop a delicate cream doily. Though it was summer, a fire danced merrily in its place on one wall to take the chill away from this shaded side of the house in the morning.

"I have yet to meet the esteemed Mrs. Puffley or the scullery maid . . . er . . . Benita I believe it was. Is it true that the kitchen maids never come up to this floor, Mrs. Bright?"

"It would be highly unusual, Inspector. They're extremely busy in the kitchen, and there's rarely ever a need for them to venture upstairs. Was there a problem with Molly or Rebecca?"

"Not at all. Only I found it curious that neither of them had ever seen the library but once." He sat on one of the sofas and gestured for the constable to take a seat at the writing table in the corner.

Phyllida didn't have the opportunity to reply, for at that moment she heard excited voices just outside the chamber. They were young and female and, she realized with exasperation, most likely belonged to two of her maids. Stifling a huff of annoyance, she said, "If you'll excuse me, Inspector . . ."

But before Phyllida could leave the room, Lizzie appeared in the entranceway. "Mrs. Bright," she said in a voice that carried too far and was too loud for a proper maid (which was why Lizzie was an upstairs maid and not a front-of-house maid), "I found something, didn't I!"

Phyllida saw the edge of another skirt as it disappeared around a corner—likely Ginny hightailing it out of there before *she* got reprimanded for high-spirited, loud conversation in the corridor—and then she noticed what Lizzie was holding. Ah. Perfect timing. "And what is it that's got your volume up and your productivity down, Lizzie?"

"I found it in the Gray Room, didn't I?" replied the excited maid, unperturbed by the mild rebuke. "It belonged to the dead m—to Mr. Waring, it did."

"Why don't you bring it over to the inspector, then, instead of announcing it to the entire household," Phyllida replied in firm tones. "So, what is it, then?"

It was, as she had known, Mr. Waring's briefcase.

"I found it wide open on the bed, didn't I? And there it was, just like this," Lizzie said, still babbling in a loud, excitable manner unbecoming of a servant. Phyllida would speak with her later about decorum and so on, but for now it would be an exercise in futility.

She suspected it would be thus with every member of her staff until this entire mess was attended to, a fact that did not sit well with her organized mind.

Which meant that the sooner this real-life murder mystery was solved, the sooner she and the servants could get back to a normal schedule. Yet another reason to give Inspector Cork an efficient helping hand with this case.

"Let's have it, then," said the man himself. Phyllida studiously avoided his eyes as Lizzie brought the briefcase over to the table. "Wide open on the bed, you say?"

"Yes, sir," replied Lizzie.

Cork looked up at Phyllida, who had plastered a mildly interested expression on her face. She didn't think he was fooled, however. After all, she had been in the bedchamber when Cork arrived to search it.

"So somehow someone got into the room and found the briefcase, opened it up"—the inspector paused to examine the case's lock, then pursed his lips—"and, from the looks of it, didn't have the key, so it was jimmied open. And then left it wide open—on the bed, you say?"

"Yes, sir."

"Imagine that," Phyllida said with perfect innocence as she handed the vase of flowers and the doily to Lizzie in order to make room on the table for the briefcase. Then she took a seat. "Perhaps he—or she—was interrupted in their perusal of the contents and left the room in a hurry so as not to be discovered."

"Perhaps." Cork's expression was none too pleased, and to her frustration, Phyllida felt the slight heat of a rising blush—something she hadn't allowed to occur for at *least* a decade.

But thanks to the fair skin that accompanied her strawberry hair, it was a reaction nearly impossible to hide once it got going. Still, she held her breath in an effort to dissipate the flush and hoped that the inspector hadn't noticed, for he'd returned his attention to Mr. Waring's satchel.

"And you just now discovered this, miss?" asked Cork implacably.

"Yes, sir. I brought the message down about the flowers for Mrs. Agatha's room like you asked me to, Mrs. Bright, didn't I, and then I came back up to see to the Gray Room—and there it was, wasn't it—plain as can be—right there on the bed."

Phyllida winced inwardly, for at the mention of her sending

Lizzie *down* with the message for the gardener, Cork had glanced up at her with an assessing look. "You were gone quite a while from your sitting room, Mrs. Bright," he said casually, flipping through the meager contents of the briefcase. "You missed several interviews."

"Unfortunately, my business called me away for longer than intended, Inspector. Surely you can appreciate when duty calls. That will be all, Lizzie," she said. "I'm certain the rest of the guest rooms need attending."

"Yes, ma'am," she said with a little bow and then was off with a flutter of apron and skirt.

"Note this down, Constable. The contents of the briefcase include an appointment diary," said Cork, "pencils, a road map of Devon, and . . . What's this? Some photographs, tucked here behind an inner flap."

"Photographs?" Phyllida had missed them during her cursory examination of the briefcase, drat it. "How curious." She wanted desperately to look at the pictures but was resigned to waiting until Cork set them down. If he ever did, for he seemed to be taking his time looking through them.

"What about a notebook?" she said. "Wouldn't one expect to find a notebook in a briefcase belonging to a journalist? Where would he keep his notes otherwise?"

Cork glanced at her again. "One certainly would, Mrs. Bright, if he were a journalist. Which remains to be proven. I wonder what could have happened to it—if there was such a thing."

"Perhaps whoever was digging through the briefcase might have removed it as possible evidence," she replied.

"I would say that's quite likely. If only we had some sort of idea *who* was in the Gray Room when they weren't supposed to be." His tone was frigid as he pierced her with those eyes, which somehow looked less fishlike and more feline at the moment. Even his freckles seemed less boyish.

Phyllida sighed inwardly. *Drat.* "Inspector, I have some information you might want."

"I'll just bet you have, Mrs. Bright."

"So sorry to keep you waiting, Inspector," said Mr. Max as he came into the parlour.

Phyllida rose quickly to her feet. She wasn't strictly out of line having seated herself in the parlour with the inspector, but she felt uncomfortable sitting in the presence of anyone other than Mrs. Agatha. "I'll just be waiting to hear when to fetch the next person with whom you want to speak, Inspector," she said.

"After that, I'll require you to convey me to the kitchen," replied Cork in a tone that sounded very much like a threat.

Oh, fiddle. Now she'd really put up the man's hackles.

"Shall I just take that and put it in my sitting room for now, Inspector?" she asked, reaching boldly for the briefcase. "Then you can examine it at your leisure."

He sighed a sigh of defeat. "I suppose so, Mrs. Bright. Now, Mr. Mallowan, if you could tell me what you know about Mr. Waring."

Phyllida had no reason to stay to hear Mr. Max's interview—and every reason to vacate the parlour so she could look at the photographs.

However, it was her turn to be thwarted, for the moment she stepped out into the foyer, just beyond the parlour entrance, Freddie was waiting there.

"Mrs. Bright, Mr. Tentley is waiting for you belowstairs."

Drat and *blast*. How could she have forgotten? It was Thursday, after all, and here was the butcher to meet with her.

Phyllida sighed and, regrettably, had to put the briefcase in her sitting room—with the unexamined photographs—for the time being.

Murder will out, but managing a household went on.

CHAPTER 10

"**N**OW, MR. TENTLEY, YOU KNOW I'M NOT ABOUT TO PAY THAT much for a beef rib roast—even from you," Phyllida said, looking up from the butcher's scrawl on the paper he'd given her.

They were sitting in the servants' dining room, across the hall from the kitchen and scullery. The heavy wooden table where they were meeting could seat as many as twenty at a time. The visiting servants had vacated the room for the time being, and Phyllida assumed they were in the guest rooms, attending to the belongings of their masters and mistress while the latter were down having breakfast.

"Mrs. Puffley told me the hams I purchased last week were smaller than they should have been. I looked at Mr. Barker's hams, and I must confess, they looked quite excellent for the price." Phyllida eyed him from over the pair of glasses she loathed but needed for reading—especially his writing.

Alton Tentley was wearing his uniform of a butcher's apron, but it was clean and unstained for his visit to Mallowan Hall. The hair combed over the top of a shiny scalp (he'd removed his cap and set it on his lap) put Phyllida in mind of the mist over morning fields—thin, insubstantial, and gray in color. "Aya, yes, Mrs. Bright, I ken, and that's why I come today to tell you I've got three hams I've put aside for your Mrs. Puffley. They're all larger 'an last week's, and the extra one's like to be a gift, too, to make up for the problem," he said. "And with that in mind, I'm hoping

you'll see your way to putting in your regular order again today."
With a flourish, he placed a slender bottle of dark glass on the
table right in front of her.

Mmm. Madeira.

Phyllida liked a good cup of tea and a finger of whisky, but she
had a particular fondness for Madeira. Even better, the label on
this one indicated it was of higher quality than the last bottle
she'd received—that one coming from the cheesemonger. Apparently, word of her preferences had gotten around.

Not only was it common, but it was also the accepted practice
for tradespeople to gift the housekeepers (and sometimes the
cooks) of large estates with tokens of appreciation for their business. After all, a customer like Mallowan Hall could make all the
difference for a butcher, dairy farmer, vegetable grower, seamstress, laundress, or the like. Thus, Phyllida had acquired a small
but respectable stock of whisky, Madeira, and wine for her pleasure, along with gifts of tea, samples of special cheese and beef
jerky, and fine fabric trimmings, such as lace or ribbons, which
she could use for her clothing or decor in her apartments. She'd
even been given a pair of soft kid gloves lined with silky rabbit fur
and stitched with red thread from the woman who supplied the
fine linens for Mallowan Hall.

"I'm happy to place an order with you, Mr. Tentley. Until now,
Mrs. Puffley and I have been pleased with the quality of your
meats as well as the prices, and thus I won't hold one error
against you." She frowned, adjusting her glasses. Then, looking
over the tops of the lenses, Phyllida fixed an inquiring look on
him as she pointed to the line item *Mutton*. "Is that a six there?"

"Oh, no, Mrs. Bright, not at all. S-sorry for my horrible writing," Tentley said, swiftly taking the paper and rewriting the number (it had of course, been a six) as a five—and therefore
bringing the price for seven pounds of mutton down 10 percent.

"Thank you for that," she replied and took back the order and
impaled it on the spindle mounted on a block of wood where she
kept such bills of sale until the bank draughts were written out.
The scraggly pile of bills offended her organized sensibilities, for

it was impossible to line them up neatly, as the papers were of varying sizes and often with raggedy edges and were crumpled or even stained and torn. And attempting to read the pencil scrawls from tradespeople with varying levels of literacy was an exercise in patience and, at times, cryptography—which made Phyllida feel even more untroubled about accepting the gifts from her suppliers.

"I ken there's a dead man found here this morning," said Tentley, leaning a bit closer from across the table, as if about to share a secret. "Murdered, was he? Scotland Yard come in for it, I hear."

It had been a full ten minutes of business discussion before he broached what had to be the biggest gossip in Listleigh in years. Still, it had taken rather far longer than she'd expected for the subject to arise. In fact, when Phyllida had come downstairs from the parlour (reluctantly abandoning the proximity of her sitting room to the interviews being conducted there) to meet with Tentley, she'd discovered a lineup of three other tradesmen eagerly waiting to speak with her—including the poultry farmer, who had just been in yesterday for an order of three geese, five ducklings, and seven roasting chickens. She wondered what excuse he'd give for another visit so soon.

"Apparently, the telephone exchange operator has been busy," she replied dryly.

"Ma'am," said the butcher apologetically—but his eyes still gleamed with interest, and he didn't ease back from his conspiratorial position of leaning across the table.

"Very well," Phyllida replied. She might as well put him out of his misery and make certain accurate facts were being disseminated. What happened to the veracity of the information after people left her presence was out of her control, but at least she could initiate the truth. "As it happens, I discovered the man this morning, dead in the library. He'd been stabbed in the neck." No need to go into any more detail than that.

"A guest of Mr. and Mrs. Mallowan's, then?" asked Tentley, his elbows on the table as he shifted a titch closer.

"An unexpected visitor, in fact," she replied. "Because of the bad weather, Mrs. Mallowan offered him accommodations for the night."

"And he stayed the night and had the bad luck to meet someone who sent him to his Maker, then? Might've been best he stayed away—or drove on. Or was he broughten from the station, then? Did Ol' Marcus drive him over?"

"He drove his own motorcar." A thought struck her, and she eyed the butcher speculatively. "He might have come through the village. If anyone happened to see him, Scotland Yard might be interested." *As would I.*

"What sort o' motor was he driving?"

Phyllida hesitated. She hadn't the foggiest notion of the model—all automobiles looked alike to her. "It was dark green . . . or maybe dark blue," was all she could offer. "With a black top."

"Don't remember seeing that," Tentley replied, scratching the foggy mist atop his head. He sounded disappointed. "I'd surely remember that."

"Very well, then. Thank you, Mr. Tentley. I believe we've concluded our business—all of it—for the day." Her chair scraped over the rough-hewn pine floor as she rose to usher him out of the dining room.

The cheesemonger, who was different from the dairy farmer, was her next visitor. Alicia Amaldi didn't even bother to wait ten minutes before broaching the subject. She shoved a hastily written bill of sale for five different cheeses (most of them in the style of her native Italy) toward Phyllida, then said, "I heard about the murder, Mrs. Bright. Right here at Mallowan Hall! Jesus, Mary, and Joseph! What is the world coming to?" She made the sign of the cross and fingered the crucifix she'd pulled out from behind her cotton bodice, even as her eyes gleamed with interest. "Who was he?"

Phyllida gave her the same information she'd provided to the butcher, and received the same disappointed response at the mention of the motorcar possibly having driven through the village. A similar conversation happened with the chicken man, Roger Winkle, with the same uninformative results, and again with the miller (who, in a surprising turn of events, had brought his wife with him). Phyllida assumed it was because Mrs. Miller (aptly named) wasn't about to wait for her husband to return home with all the details about the dead body at Mallowan Hall; she wanted to have the news as soon as possible. The woman's interest in gossip was profound, and her ability to spread information was as efficient as water flowing through a pipe.

But when Mrs. Miller offered her a lemon teacake glazed with sugar and candied violets, and a small tin of expensive Assam tea, Phyllida decided it was not at all a hardship to have the wife there. The teacake was still slightly warm and smelled of lemons and flowers.

"And 'e warn't expected, were 'e?" said Mrs. Miller. "A stranger showin' 'ere and then turnin' up dead . . . Why, Frankling, can you imagine that?" The miller opened his mouth to speak, but his wife barreled on. "And 'e druv 'is own motorcar and pulled up to the 'ouse 'ere as pretty as you please. Was 'e from London, did you say, Mrs. Bright?"

"I didn't say. We don't know for certain," Phyllida replied. "His credentials didn't come through when the inspector called on them, and so it's a bit of a mystery who he was and where he came from."

"Imagine that," Mrs. Miller said, her eyes wide with shock and greedy with interest. "But 'e must've known someone 'ere to come all the way in that motorcar. Why, 'e might even 'ave stopped in at the Screaming Magpie, mightn't 'e, then?"

Before Phyllida could interject, Molly poked her head around the corner of the servants' dining room. "Mrs. Bright, excuse me, but Mr. Dobble would like to speak with you. Right away."

Phyllida rose, grateful for the interruption that would bring her back to the main floor, where the more interesting things were happening. She scooped up the bottle of Madeira and the package with the lemony teacake and Assam, then tucked the former under her arm. "Mr. Miller, I'll need only our regular supply this week, as I indicated, although I do thank you for stopping in to make certain nothing has changed. Good day, and thank you again for the cake. Molly, please show the Millers out, and tell the others waiting that I'll not be meeting with anyone until tomorrow. We are, understandably, unexpectedly busy today. All previous orders will stand."

With the bottle of spirits wedged safely against her side, Phyllida took up the wooden block with its spindleful of bills and swept from the room. She glanced into the kitchen, where a red-faced Mrs. Puffley was sewing a large rolled roast into shape and Rebecca was scooping salmon mousse into a large copper form in the shape of a fish. Two other copper molds—smaller fish—sat on the counter, waiting to be filled, as well. Benita was just beyond, in the scullery, washing the dishes and cookware from the servants' breakfast and what had come down from the guests' meal.

Rebecca glanced up as her boss looked in, and although Phyllida didn't pause, she caught the flash of a strange expression—guilty, or perhaps merely wary—on the girl's face. Was Puffley on a tirade again? Had she been throwing pots and pans? Or was she still annoyed by the broken tea set this morning?

Nonetheless, Phyllida didn't have time to attend to that drama at the moment—and as none of the kitchen maids had red noses or swollen eyes from crying (the usual indicator of a Puffley outburst), she decided whatever the problem was, it could wait.

For Mr. Dobble rarely sent for her (possibly because he feared she might ignore his summons), and therefore it must be important. Possibly related to the murder.

When Phyllida pushed through the door covered in green baize and mounted into place with round brass tacks around the edges—this door on the ground floor being the literal divider between the world of servant and the master, the Upstairs and the Downstairs—she was startled to find the butler actually waiting for her. Dratted fool was hovering so close, if she hadn't been paying attention, he might have been skewered by her bill spindle.

"Yes, Mr. Dobble?" she said, tightening her arm against the Madeira. It wasn't that she needed to hide it from the butler; she simply thought it good practice not to flaunt her good fortune.

"Mrs. Bright, we have a situation." His lips were so tight with tension, they barely moved when he spoke.

"Several of them, in fact. To which in particular are you referring?" she replied.

He glanced at the dark bottle; then his attention slid to the aromatic package she held, and his mouth flattened even more. "Perhaps you should relieve yourself of your burdens and then we can attend to *that* particular one." With an unusually plebeian gesture, he jerked his head (led by its broad, prominent nose) toward the front door.

"I see what you mean," replied Phyllida when she caught sight of the small crowd clustered in front of the house. *Oh, fiddle.*

It wasn't difficult to construe the general intent of the individuals, for some of them held pads of paper and writing implements, while others brandished cameras.

"Has Mrs. Agatha seen them?"

"Not yet," Mr. Dobble replied, glancing furtively toward the parlour. "She's been in with Mr. Max and the inspector for some time. But surely they won't be in there much longer. Surely no one can suspect either of *them* of having done murder."

"Certainly not," Phyllida agreed firmly. "That would be ludicrous."

"But with all the talk of poisons and stabbings and death . . . and all the research Mrs. Agatha conducts," he said, again looking worriedly in the direction of the parlour. "And that strange disappearance of hers—"

"I'm surprised you haven't sent Stanley and Freddie out there to disperse them," Phyllida interrupted sharply. There was simply no reason for him to voice such terrible thoughts. And, incidentally, the exterior grounds weren't the purview of *her* staff, so why Dobble should interfere with her day to assist him in chasing off the press was mystifying.

"Freddie is engaged with serving breakfast at the moment, while I am forced to attend to more pressing matters. Incidentally, do tell Puffley the yolks in the boiled eggs were not centered. I noticed three of them that had sunk to the bottom."

Phyllida kept her mouth firmly closed, although she had several peppery thoughts she would like to share with the butler related to the waste of time it would be for a kitchen maid to stand at the stove, constantly turning boiling eggs so that the blasted yolks cooked in the middle of the whites instead of slipping to one end. Who in the world cared? Certainly not Mr. or Mrs. Mallowan.

"And Stanley is *nowhere* to be found," added the butler stiffly.

Phyllida frowned. Stanley might be quite the ladies' man, but he was a good worker and was responsible. It was mostly unheard of for a servant simply to go missing in action. Still musing over this unusual predicament, she answered the unspoken question. "I saw him last during his interview with Inspector Cork, just about an hour ago," she said, looking at the watch pinned to her bodice. "What's kept you from speaking to them yourself, Mr. Dobble? I should have thought *you'd* have run them off long before now."

"Right, Mrs. Bright. I was about to do so, but I decided it might be best if the two of us presented a united front to the rabble-rousers out there."

Phyllida had no intention of chasing off any rabble-rousers that might be part of the press corps and might snap her photo or obtain her name. She preferred to remain anonymous and inconspicuous here in her role as housekeeper, tucked away far from London, outside this lovely little town.

"I am certain you can manage a small handful of reporters without my feminine assistance, Mr. Dobble," she said blandly. "And as I hear Mrs. Agatha and Mr. Max taking their leave from Inspector Cork, might I suggest that time is of the essence? I cannot imagine what our mistress would think if she was to be hounded by the press again."

But Phyllida knew exactly what Agatha would think, and how she would feel if she knew there were reporters and photographers camped out on the grounds of her estate. She would be devastated and horrified, and it would bring back all the terrible memories from the disintegration of her marriage to Archie

Christie and the most talked-about event of her life. It was sad, Phyllida thought, that the press was more interested in those eleven days of Agatha's disappearance than in her creative works of detective fiction.

Mr. Dobble gave her a strange look that seemed to border on fear, but apparently, whatever made him nervous about facing the "rabble-rousers" was less of a threat than upsetting dear Mrs. Agatha, and he moved swiftly and stiffly to the front door, the tails of his coat fluttering.

Having attended to that problem, Phyllida moved just as efficiently to her sitting room, where she quickly dispensed with her burdens. Stilton was sitting in her normal spot in the blue chintz armchair where Phyllida liked to read, and she narrowed her steady blue eyes at her mistress's sudden invasion of the chamber. Rye was in his favorite place, draped over the top of her bookshelf, tail swinging like an agitated *J* in front of a collection of botanical, gardening, and herb-preserving volumes as he sneered down at her.

"Yes, I'll share, but not now," she told both felines when she caught them slyly lifting their noses to sniff the teacake. She saw no reason to keep her good fortune to herself, and the cats were well aware of her penchant for sharing. They'd made clear their preference for crumbles of carrot cake instead of lemon, but though they pretended to protest over anything citrusy, in the end both were practical enough to consume any offering Phyllida made. She reached over to give Stilton a firm stroke, eliciting a pleased ripple along her spine, accompanied by a rough purr, before the beast settled back into her nap.

Phyllida's attention slid over her desk and landed on her appointment diary, which was open to today, although she hadn't even looked at it since she turned the page last night. For obvious reasons.

But the list of items on it reminded her that she was woefully behind on today's tasks, which included making a new batch of tooth powder (or, rather, supervising while Bess and Lizzie did so) and distilling rosemary, orange, and rose waters. All that sort of work—which was the housekeeper's purview and not the cook's—happened in the stillroom, just next to the storeroom that was located adjacent to the kitchen. Far away from the interviews happening between Inspector Cork and the Mallowans' guests. She couldn't even spare a moment to look at those photos in Mr. Waring's briefcase.

How on earth was she going to investigate a murder when she had a household to run?

And now that Stanley had gone missing from action . . .

She tsked to herself. Strictly speaking, an AWOL footman was Mr. Dobble's concern and not hers . . . but in the end, it was the butler's and the housekeeper's joint responsibility to ensure the estate ran properly. Which meant Phyllida couldn't ignore this new turn of events, much as she would like to.

"Well," she said to Rye, who was still watching her with a jaundiced eye and flicking his tail, "I suppose I'd best see to finding out where Stanley has gone off to. I certainly hope it has nothing to do with Mr. Waring's untimely demise."

But it couldn't, could it? After all, the murderer had to be one of the guests, and they had all been asleep all morning and were now in the dining room.

Now would be the perfect time to do some snooping.

CHAPTER 11

*P*HYLLIDA DIDN'T WANT TO DRAW ATTENTION TO THE FACT THAT Stanley was missing—the staff had far too much to gossip about as it was—but she decided to make her rounds among the chambermaids earlier than usual in case they were any help in determining what had become of the head footman.

Normally, she would wait until after luncheon, just before it was time to prepare for tea, to do the inspections of the bedrooms while the girls were about their daily tasks, but today was different by all accounts. Aside from assessing the condition of the guest rooms, she could also take the opportunity to snoop around and see if there was anything interesting to be found.

As she climbed the steps from the ground floor, Phyllida glanced out the tiny window that overlooked the front of the estate. Most servants' stairways were dark, narrow columns, but here at Mallowan Hall, there were several unobtrusive openings that enabled one to survey the elegantly curving drive and the broad terraced porch. This was helpful—and was likely the intended purpose—to the likes of the butler, footman, and housekeeper—any of whom could need to be aware of arrivals and departures, which might otherwise go unseen whilst traversing through the hidden passages.

She noted with satisfaction that Mr. Dobble seemed to have dispersed the gossip-hungry press—at least temporarily. However, she was under no misconception that this desertion would last. In fact . . .

She paused in front of the little window at the first floor. No, her eyes hadn't fooled her. There was a shiver of movement among the boxwoods behind the hydrangeas at the south end of the brick-walled lawn. A glint of something metallic caught the sunlight for a moment, then was gone. Blasted photographers.

Incensed and frustrated by the invasion of privacy—for herself, as well as for the Mallowans—Phyllida continued up one more flight to the second floor. She passed through the doorway from the plain wooden servants' stairs to the thickly carpeted U-shaped hallway where most of the guest bedchambers were located. At least whoever was lurking outside was far enough away to get any good pictures. She'd advise Mr. Dobble about it soonest.

In the meantime, however, she intended to take a peek into the bedrooms being used by the Mallowans' guests.

Here on the second floor, where the Gray Room was and where Mr. Waring had been assigned, the Devines, Hartfords, and Mr. Grimson were also being lodged.

Phyllida wasted no time letting herself into the closest guest room. She had no fear of being discovered; should one of the visitors return, she had ample reasons for being there.

Darkly handsome Mr. Devine's chamber was first. She discovered that he was fairly neat and that his afternoon clothing had already been laid out, hanging on the valet stand. There was a pair of shoes against the wall, and she attempted to determine whether they squeaked when they were used, but she felt her experiment was inconclusive as she couldn't actually walk in them.

On the bureau was a jumble of cufflinks, tie studs, and two small rings that he would likely wear on his littlest finger. He had a jar of pomade, a small grooming kit, a pot of shaving cream, and nine crisp white shirts for a three-day house party. She flipped through the rest of the clothing folded in his trunk, but found nothing exceptional and nothing hidden beneath it.

His bed had been slept in, and it was obvious the maids hadn't come through yet. She peeked in the trash receptacle and found nothing but a crumpled piece of blank paper.

There was nothing on his bedside table except a handkerchief and a small appointment diary. Of course, she flipped through it, but she saw nothing that caught her attention. A lot of appoint-ments and meetings in London, it seemed. And he'd seen a den-tist last week—probably in order to help maintain his brilliant white smile. Phyllida grimaced in sympathy.

Mr. Grimson's room was next. It was extraordinarily pin neat; Phyllida had never seen a guest keep his or her chamber so undis-turbed. It was as if a ghost were staying there. If it weren't for the unemptied trash receptacle, she would have assumed the maids had already come through. Even the bed, though it had been slept in, had its coverings pulled up and the pillows plumped. It seemed that Mr. Grimson was one of those people who liked nothing out of place and even folded up his own used hand towels.

Even on the bureau, all his grooming items were lined up like perfect soldiers: pomade, a mustache brush and trimmer, a tiny pot of wax, shaving cream and brush. His accessories—rings and cufflinks—sat in neat rows on a small silver tray, which he must have brought with him.

His clothing remained neat and folded in sharp creases, and someone had also hung up his chosen afternoon attire. Phyllida was certain a man so particular as Mr. Grimson wouldn't wear shoes that squeaked, but once again, without being able to wear them and walk around, she couldn't make that determination.

There was a photograph of a beautiful young woman on his bedside table, along with a novel and a pair of reading glasses. There was also a book of matches from the Red Bar, somewhere in Yorkshire, it seemed.

Mrs. Devine's chamber was far more interesting—at least to Phyllida, as a female. There were pots and pots of rouge, face powder, cream, brightening lotions, lipsticks, and nail varnish, and there were a number of items the uses of which she wasn't even certain.

On the dressing table were tweezers, tiny scissors, a minuscule mirror that magnified one's face, and an elegant compact crusted with pearls and opals, which Phyllida examined a trifle longer than necessary. Mrs. Devine's jewelry was lined up, though not as neatly as Mr. Grimson's accessories, but without being the jumble that earrings, necklaces, and bracelets could often be. Phyllida admired the glittering hairpins, which would look stunning against Mrs. Devine's bobbed jet-black hair, and there was even a metal curling rod for making finger waves—and hundreds of hairpins in a small metal case for pin curls.

Mrs. Devine's clothing was just as spectacular. Mostly vivid tones (of which Phyllida approved, considering the woman's coloring), there were glittering frocks of sapphire, garnet, and emerald. A dressing gown thrown over a nearby chair was white silk embroidered with red and gold Chinese dragons.

Phyllida could have pored over the beautiful frocks for much longer, but she didn't have unlimited time, and she wanted to make certain she could investigate all the men's bedrooms, for obvious reasons.

However, she didn't stint on her examination and looked in the trash can, where she found several crumpled face tissues and cotton wool balls, and inside Mrs. Devine's clothing trunk and the wardrobe where her frocks had been hung.

Next to the bed was a pair of white slippers decorated with feathers—very impractical for keeping one's feet warm, but extremely fashionable. On the table was a small notebook with handwritten lines that appeared to be recipes for either food items or beauty treatments, and a teacup with a bit left over.

Phyllida moved on next to Mrs. Hartford's bedchamber and discovered that Lizzie or Bess had already come through.

Nonetheless, below the faint smell of lemon polish was the scent of Mrs. Hartford's perfume—something lightly floral with a bit of pine mixed in. It was pleasant without being cloying, and she thought it suited the suave and cool Amelia Hartford.

The same sort of array of feminine beauty accessories cluttered the top of her dressing table: creams, makeup pots of rouge, eyelash stain, kohl liner, lipsticks, powder, and more. Instead of being laid out on the table's surface, her jewelry and accessories were in a neat compartmentalized case: glittery necklaces and earrings, sparkling hairpins for her honey-gold hair, and stacks of bangle bracelets.

The wardrobe was filled with hanging dresses—day frocks, evening gowns, even a tennis costume. Soft, dense colors suited Mrs. Hartford: sea-foam green, aqua, cornflower blue, burnished gold, and rose-petal pink, and she had seven pairs of shoes, which matched these different ensembles, as well as flowing dinner robes and a sheer white sleeveless tunic with gold embroidered hems that appeared to be a covering for a bathing dress.

Phyllida was careful not to disturb anything left in the trunk, but she did find the bathing dress, as well as fine silk underthings and an excessive *eighth* pair of shoes.

A matching robe and set of slippers in pale blue silk lay on the neatly made bed, with its plumped pillows. The table next to it held a small tin of pills (of course Phyllida opened the tin and discovered they were all the same medications—likely for head-aches) and an empty, clean glass for water.

She nodded in approval that the rug had been straightened, the floor swept, and the hand linens by the wash basin folded neatly, with a small rose-scented soap on top. The maid had fresh-ened up the flowers in a small vase, as well.

Mr. Hartford's room was the last one on this floor, and she dis-covered that his traveling trunk matched that of his wife's. A sober brown and black waistcoat was hung on the clothes valet for the evening, along with a tasteful rust and brown necktie and a dark brown coat—all of which would look well with his fair hair and golden tanned skin.

She examined two pairs of shoes and was unable to ascertain whether they squeaked. There was nothing that seemed impor-tant in the waste can—an empty envelope, a used-up matchbook, and the receipt from a petrol station outside London.

Like his wife, Mr. Hartford kept his jewelry in a neat leather case with slots for each set of cufflinks and tiepins, as well as slots for several rings. There was also a small collection of fine ivory and tortoiseshell buttons—presumably to replace those on his fa-vorite clothing—in one of the slots.

Nothing but clothing in his trunk, and a hairbrush, comb, po-made, and shaving implements made up a small clutter on the top of the bureau.

She was just preparing to leave his room when there was a knock from the maid. She opened the door, and Bess started when she saw her boss.

"Oh, Mrs. Bright, I'm just getting to it, I am," said the maid nervously.

"Yes, yes, not to worry. Did you do the Lavender Room? It looks quite well."

"Yes, ma'am, and then I had to go down to get a new feather duster, as the last one was losing its feathers. I'll get to this one right away."

"Of course."

Confident in her maid's work, Phyllida made her way up to the third floor, reflecting that so far, there'd been nothing of interest in anyone's bedchamber—but, of course, what had she expected? The murderer wasn't about to leave anything incriminating lying about, now was he? But what her snooping was doing was giving her a sense of the individual: how he or she was organized and lived, and what sorts of things he or she thought were important enough to bring on a small holiday.

Pills, books, photographs, notes, the types (and array) of clothing (and shoes), and more.

Lizzie was on the third floor, and Phyllida found her in Mrs. Budgely-Rhodes's room straight off.

"My goodness," Phyllida said, looking at the disarray. Clothing was everywhere, along with cups and saucers from tea service and, apparently, some other snacks, as well. Crumbs, napkins, magazines were strewn all about.

Thank heavens Mrs. Budgely-Rhodes had brought her own maid!

"It's rather a dust-up, innit?" said Lizzie. "Gonna put me off my schedule, Mrs. Bright, ain't it now?"

"I'm sure you'll set it all to rights," said Phyllida, looking in the trash can. Lizzie had already emptied it, unfortunately.

Mrs. Budgely-Rhodes had the largest collection of jewelry and the smallest array of makeup and facial products of the female guests. Nail varnish had spilled all over a small tray on the bureau (thank goodness not on the bureau itself), and there were used brushes with rouge, powder, and lipstick scattered everywhere. Next to the bed was a pile of magazines about film stars and celebrities, along with a half-eaten biscuit and a cup of coffee that had long gone cold.

Phyllida did a quick scan of the clothing that was piled in jumbles everywhere, mentally threw up her hands, and left.

Mr. Budgely-Rhodes wasn't much neater than his wife. However, it appeared he'd brought fewer items in his wardrobe, and that at least gave the impression of less of a cyclone having come through.

His tiepins, cufflinks, and rings were a wild mess of silver, gold, and brass on a small wooden tray atop the bureau, and he apparently was of the same mind as Mr. Dobble, in that he employed an array of face creams and lotions, along with aftershave colognes and pomades.

He and his wife apparently felt it their duty to keep the health and beauty manufacturers in business.

Next to the bed was a sheaf of papers, which turned out to be the script of a play entitled *Fortnight at Hedgeberg*. Coffee stains and wrinkles indicated that Mr. Budgely-Rhodes had read approximately a third of it.

The waste can held an empty matchbook and a crinkled, torn road map spoiled with coffee stains, as well as used cotton wool balls and what appeared to be toenail clippings. At least he hadn't left them in a drawer, as Mr. Brevort had done last year. Phyllida shuddered as she left the room.

Mr. Sloup's chamber was well ordered since Lizzie had already come through. He had one large travel trunk that was still half-filled with clothing, despite the fact that the wardrobe was bursting with whatever his valet had chosen to hang.

Phyllida spent a little more time in this chamber simply because she didn't care for the man's smarmy personality. She was hoping to find something interesting.

She most certainly did.

In the bottom of one of his trunks was a magazine that had a certain sort of pictures in it. The sort that one would not want one's mother to see. There were bare breasts, round bottoms, and a large quantity of skin.

Well. If nothing else, she'd certainly had her impression of the man confirmed.

Phyllida tucked the magazine back beneath the clothing, careful to ensure it looked exactly as it had done when she pulled it out.

However, other than the magazine, there was little else to notice in the room since the waste can had been emptied and all the dishes had been taken out by the maid.

Nonetheless, Phyllida felt relieved when she left the chamber with the intention to return to her sitting room.

She paused in front of the large half-moon window situated in the center of the corridor's U and looked out over the front of the estate and then toward the southerly end once more.

The inspector's automobile was still parked behind that of the constable's, almost directly below the window. To the right was a stone walkway that led to the south gardens and around to the back of the house, where there was an expanse of lawn surrounded by shimmering willows and elegant oaks.

To the left was the large garage: the foundation was made of stone, but the structure boasted a wooden second floor like a hayloft. It had formerly been the stables but had been converted when the Mallowans bought Mallowan Hall. Neither of them hunted or rode horses—in fact, the first time Mr. Max had ever been on a horse was when he rode from an archaeological dig into Baghdad so he could hear his wife on a radio broadcast, and that was only last year. Thus, the Mallowans had seen no reason to keep the beasts—or pay for a groom—when they could employ a chauffeur and own several motorcars instead.

Seeing the garage reminded Phyllida that she wanted to examine Mr. Waring's automobile on her own—yet another item to add to her seemingly infinite task list—and she huffed to herself. There simply was not enough time in the day to manage a murder *and* a household. Still, if anyone was up for the task, it was Phyllida Bright.

Just as she stepped away from the window, she caught sight of a figure emerging from around the rear corner of the garage, near the edge of the enclosing brick walls. Phyllida stayed and watched as the man—too far away for her to see any details of his person other than dark hair and the lack of a proper coat and hat—paused, then swiveled in a different direction. He slipped into the side door of the garage whilst casting a furtive glance toward the house.

Into the garage.

Where Mr. Waring's motorcar was parked.

CHAPTER 12

*P*HYLLIDA DIDN'T HESITATE. SHE DARTED BACK THROUGH THE DIVID-
ing door to the dim, narrow stairwell and bounded down three
flights of steps without stopping, then one more half flight to the
downstairs servants' hall leading to the tradesmen's entrance at
the rear of the house. She was a bit out of breath and was therefore appreciative she didn't encounter anyone who might take
note of her harried condition. Swiftly she hurried past the
kitchen and through the back door out into the side yard.

The warm sun and fresh air were a welcome change from the
darker, more staid interior of the mansion, but Phyllida didn't
have the time or the inclination to take in the moment. She
rushed across the yard to the garage, noticing with satisfaction
that the back steps were freshly whitewashed, while paying no
mind to the small flock of chickens that scattered out of her path.

The side door to the garage was slightly ajar, and Phyllida hesitated before pushing through. Should she barge in and confront
the person—who was surely one of those bloody reporters snooping around—or do her own snooping and slip inside to see what
he was up to?

Unfortunately, any items of interest in Charles Waring's automobile would surely already have been found by Constable
Greensticks. At least, one would hope.

But Phyllida wasn't confident in either his or Inspector Cork's
ability to notice a clue when it was right in front of their noses.

Consider *Historic Travel Inns of England*, the book that surely was important to discovering the identity and motive of the murderer but had been pooh-poohed by the so-called experts.

But a journalist might also be interested in poking around the other vehicles parked there—perhaps in an effort to identify who else was in residence at Mallowan Hall and might be fodder for news, interviews, or even as suspects. If she were a journalist looking for a story, that was what she'd do.

She'd waffled long enough. It was time to confront him . . . unless . . .

She stilled, her hand outstretched to push at the door. She pulled it back.

What if it was the killer himself who had sneaked out of the house and was looking in or around Mr. Waring's motorcar for anything that might incriminate him?

Then Phyllida immediately rejected that possibility, for she was certain the man she'd seen darting into the garage—albeit from a height of three stories—was not one of the Mallowans' guests. Aside from the sin of being coatless as well as hatless, the intruder had curling dark hair that needed a decisive trim (far too disheveled and disordered to be any of the guests) and he had no facial hair.

No, surely not the killer.

Unless the murderer had some sort of accomplice—someone who was not a guest of the Mallowans . . . .

No. She could argue with herself all day, and that would accomplish nothing. She had no choice but to, paraphrasing the words of Shakespeare's Henry V, dive "unto the breach" once more.

Feeling as if she actually was girding herself for battle, Phyllida took a deep breath and stepped into the garage.

Since the spacious building had once been a barn for stabling horses and storing their feed, the ceiling loomed high above. All the stalls had been removed, leaving a large open space with a packed dirt floor, which was now stained with oil instead of animal debris. Although she couldn't see it from there, in the back corner was a storage room with a desk, and a small bedroom and sitting room. The scents of mechanical oil and grease, along with smells she couldn't identify but were not organic in nature, filled the air.

Due to the intricacies of automobile mechanics, clean, bright electric lighting had been installed since the days when horses had lived there. But since it was midday, the only illumination was a short string of bulbs in the far corner where an array of tools was located, along with a bit of light from two high windows at either end of the building. The two large swing-up doors were both closed, leaving the place dim and gloomy. Perfect for someone to sneak around unnoticed.

Six vehicles were parked in one long row, making bulky shadows inside the massive building—and there was room for at least one more. One of the autos belonged to the Mallowans (despite her ambivalence toward motor vehicles, Phyllida recognized it even in the shadowy light), and obviously, a second was Mr. Waring's, although it was difficult to make out the actual colors in the dim light. The remaining quartet must have arrived with the guests, and that meant either some of them had ridden together or had gotten a ride from Old Marcus from the train station.

The place was silent and still, and if Phyllida hadn't seen the man sneaking inside, she wouldn't have known anyone was there. Surely he hadn't slipped back out during her mad dash down the stairs. . . .

Leaving the door slightly ajar (a little more light wouldn't hurt), she stepped further past the entrance. Whoever had come in was making an effort not to be seen or heard, certainly indicating a nefarious purpose. Closing her hand tightly over the ever-present jingle of keys at her waist, she walked silently and purposely toward the row of cars.

Admittedly, her pulse was faster than normal, and her palms were a trifle—only a trifle—clammy. After all, there was a slight chance she was about to accost a killer or his accomplice. That reminder had her looking about for some sort of weapon with which to defend herself, and since it was a garage, it was no strange coincidence that her attention should light on a tire iron.

Brilliant.

She gripped its heavy comfort and continued walking along the row of cars, past the first, second, third. . . .

There was a soft thunk ahead—the sound of something bumping against metal—followed by the shift of a shadow near the sixth automobile. Of course. Charles Waring had been the last to arrive, and his dark green (or blue) vehicle would be parked on the farthest end.

And that meant the shadow probably belonged to the snooping journalist—or perhaps the killer, but she'd very nearly talked herself out of that possibility. She was no Tuppence Beresford to go charging into danger without thought.

Well, whoever it was, was doing precisely what Phyllida had intended to do: search the vehicle. Still brandishing the tire iron, she no longer worried about her jingling keys.

"Sir!" she said as soon as she caught sight of the dusty, unblackened boots and the denim-trousered legs protruding from the vehicle's open door. The feet and legs jolted at the sound of her peremptory voice, something thunked metallically, and the body began to withdraw from deep inside the automobile. "What do you think you're doing—"

He was up and out of the motorcar sleekly, faster than she'd expected, and Phyllida was so taken by surprise, she nearly stumbled backward.

The intruder was a tall man with large hands and muscular forearms, bared by rolled-up sleeves, immediately giving the unsettling impression that brandishing a tire iron would do little to discourage him. Yet Phyllida refused to take even the tiniest step backward, though her heart was now thudding wildly. She had faced down angry, desperate soldiers—ones wild with fever or engulfed in pain or shell shock (although perhaps none quite so large and intimidating)—and had stood her ground then. She wouldn't back away now.

"What in the he—blazes—are you thinking, sneaking up on a bloke like that?" The man glowered down at her as he rubbed the back of his head. He had dark eyes to match his unruly black hair and was either very tanned or had naturally light brown skin.

Shockingly, despite his too-long hair and clothing that hadn't made the acquaintance of an iron in recent history, he was clean shaven. "And who the devil are you?"

His expression lacked even a trace of apology or guilt, and Phyllida could almost appreciate the tactic of employing outraged braggadocio in the face of being discovered doing something untoward. That was precisely the strategy she'd be inclined to take if revealed in a similar situation (like being found under the bed in the Gray Room)—bluster her way through it. Yet his countenance was filled with suspicion, and his outrage seemed genuine, and he seemed to have a complete absence of anything remotely like civility.

"I saw you sneaking around," she replied in the clipped voice she used when giving a dressing-down to one of the maids. "This is private property, and you have no—"

"Good gad, woman, you're speaking nonsense," he snarled. His hand dropped from the back of his head, and he leaned closer, surely intending to intimidate. And just as he spoke, it occurred to her exactly what he was going to say (albeit not with such salty language): "I'm the bleeding chauffeur, and I have every dam—good gad, it's my *business* to be in here. Now, who the devil are you?"

In the instant she'd realized she'd accosted the newest member of Mallowan Hall's staff, Phyllida's knees had gone a little wobbly, like the mint jelly she'd made last week. For the second time today, her cheeks threatened to flush, but her own outrage at his boorishness held the heat at bay. "I am Mrs. Bright. The housekeeper. And—"

He grunted in a fashion that not only interrupted her but also gave the distinct impression that he had a preconceived opinion of her (probably from Mr. Dobble, the old goat). Putting his hands on his hips, the man glared down at her. "I was under the impression the housekeeper's domain was the *house*—not the bleeding garage." His attention dropped, seemingly for the first time, to the makeshift weapon she was holding. "Good gad, what are you going to do with that?"

Before she could react, he snatched it from her hands. He was able to wrest it easily from her grip, she told herself, only because she was so startled by his incredible rudeness. "I thought you were a newspaper reporter snooping around," she replied frostily.

"And you were going to . . . ?" He gestured with the tire iron, his brows lifting into arches of skepticism.

Phyllida declined to respond to that provocative statement. Instead, she replied, "There's been a murder up at the house—"

"Is that so?" He spoke with patently exaggerated surprise. Then, baring his teeth in a humorless smile, he tossed the tire iron into the corner by the other tools.

She gritted her own teeth and went on in a *most* calm manner. "And because of that, there have been reporters and photographers swarming the grounds, and when I saw you lurking about, creeping around the garage in a very suspicious manner—"

"Creeping about? Lurking?" His eyes were wide with incredulity. "Devil take it, I've been here less than a day, and already I've got a blasted busybody spying on me. Don't you have anything better to do up in that big house than bother a bloke going about his own business?"

Again, she declined to engage with what was clearly meant to be an inflammatory statement. And as she finally recalled the man's name (for Mr. Dobble had mentioned it only in passing, and that was several weeks ago), she felt more confident and responded crisply, "If you had deigned to dine in the servants' hall last evening or at breakfast this morning, *Mr. Bradford*, I would have made your acquaintance—and thus would have recognized you, lurking and creeping or not. And then you wouldn't have acquired that ugly knot on your head." She barely managed to hold back a smirk.

"Just Bradford, if you please, Mrs. Bright," he replied in something almost like a sneer. "And I did come in for breakfast, but you were obviously off putting your nose into someone else's business at that time."

Phyllida successfully hid her outrage. Did the man have *any* sense of civility? And why on earth had Dobble engaged such an uncouth creature to be on staff here? Thank Providence he was relegated to the garage, and she wouldn't have to interact with the lout. . . .

Until she needed a ride into Listleigh. Which happened regularly. Phyllida stifled a sigh.

"Very well, then, *Bradford*. In any event, there have been reporters swarming the grounds, and when I saw one of them—you—looking about furtively before you slipped into the garage, I thought it best to take matters into my own hands. Mr. Dobble has enough on his plate with serving breakfast, the murder investigation—and now the head footman has gone missing."

"Is that so?" This time, it wasn't sarcasm but surprise in his tone. Phyllida decided to be thankful for small favors.

"Yes. Stanley has gone missing since about an hour ago. As it's very unlike him, we are justifiably concerned."

"That's unfortunate." He actually seemed genuinely concerned, as well.

"Quite."

"One can hope he didn't decide to take matters into his own hands and sneak up on someone who didn't take too kindly to being accosted," Bradford said, destroying her moment of gratitude. "And who wasn't lurking suspiciously about but was doing his own bleeding work."

It took more than a little rudeness and incivility to vex Phyllida, but in light of the fact that she'd stumbled on a dead body only a few hours ago and a murderer was still lurking about—along with some nosy journalists—it was not surprising she was grinding her teeth.

"Thank you for your concern, Mr. Bradford," she said when she could trust herself to speak calmly. "I only hope Stanley hasn't met the same fate as poor Mr. Waring."

"Stabbed in the neck," he replied in a milder tone. "Not a pleasant way to go. Not easy to get it right into the carotid effectively. And takes a long while to bleed out."

"Especially with a fountain pen."

"A fountain pen? Someone used a fountain pen to stab a bloke?" He muttered something under his breath that sounded critical rather than horrified.

Phyllida decided she'd wasted her time long enough. He was a horribly rude, impatient, vexatious man, and speaking to him was like running in circles.

"While I'm here," she said crisply, "I should like to see Charles Waring's automobile. I presume this is the one?" She gestured to the vehicle where Bradford had been digging around as she approached.

"No, it's not." He stood with his hands on his hips, looking down at her. "Why?"

"Is it that one?" she said stubbornly, pointing at the next motorcar in the row. They really did all look the same to her.

"Why?" he asked implacably.

Her jaw was aching from clenching it. "I want to see Charles Waring's vehicle, Mr. Bradford. I'm not required to give my reasons for doing so."

"The Aston Martin ST18."

Phyllida looked around, hoping to see an *ST18* emblazoned on one of the vehicles.

"The one in the middle," he said flatly and jerked with his thumb in the direction of the Aston Martin. "With the top down."

As Phyllida stalked away to the car (which, she was relieved to note, was dark blue), he added, "You won't find anything there. The constable has already been all over it."

She turned to look back at him. He was still standing there with his hands on his hips, watching her with a surly expression on his face.

"I wouldn't trust Constable Greensticks to find his nose if it were sneezing," she snapped. "And even if he did, it's doubtful he or Inspector Cork would know what to do with it even if I handed them a handkerchief."

He made a strangled sound that could have been a laugh or a

snort, but Phyllida had already turned away, and quite frankly, she didn't care to know which it was. She just knew that if she continued speaking with that man, she was going to do something regrettable.

And that would simply not do. Phyllida Bright did not allow her emotions to rule her actions.

CHAPTER 13

*P*HYLLIDA DIDN'T FIND ANYTHING IN CHARLES WARING'S VEHICLE. Instead, when she withdrew from the depths of the motorcar, she had only a wrinkled skirt and far too many loose strands of hair to show for her determination to dig around in the vehicle.

Fortunately, Bradford was nowhere to be seen and therefore wasn't witness to the dishevelment unbecoming of a house-keeper. As she didn't intend for *anyone* to witness such dishevel-ment, Phyllida quickly removed the fasteners from her hair, smoothed it into place, and then expertly rolled it into a chignon. It took only three pins to anchor the thick twist into place, and she was set back to rights.

She was just about to quit the garage when another thought struck her—something she was certain had not occurred to Cork, and definitely not to the constable. She was confident the killer had to be one of the guests inside the manor. Perhaps there was something in a vehicle that might give him (she had settled on the gender of the villain) away. . . .

What, she didn't know. But she was here; she had the opportu-nity—

"You're still here?" Bradford's approach caught her off guard, and she jumped a little. How mortifying. "Good gad, woman, if I'd known how little a housekeeper had to do to keep busy, I'd take the job myself."

She resisted the urge to pat at her hair to ensure it was still smooth and in place. "I don't think donning a frock would suit you, Mr. Bradford. Now, if you could please turn more of the lights on, I would appreciate greater illumination as I continue my examination."

His eyes widened in something like incredulity, but to her surprise, he merely turned away. Moments later, ten bulbs fizzed to life, casting pure white electrical light over the center of the garage.

Phyllida opened the door of one of the vehicles that didn't belong to the Mallowans, and began to poke around between the seats and in the small storage console between them. It took her only a moment of observation to determine that the Budgely-Rhodeses had driven this motorcar, based on the receipt for a night at the Old Ivy Inn.

A little prickle skittered over her shoulders. The Budgely-Rhodeses had just stayed in a small country inn, and the killer had replaced a book about historic country inns on the shelf in the library. If one believed the tenets of Sherlock Holmes—whom Phyllida loyally found far less interesting than the dashing Poirot—there was no such thing as coincidences when investigating a crime.

"What are you looking for?" came a now-familiar annoyed voice from behind her. "And bloody hell, you've got grease on the back of your . . . uh, skirt, you daft—er, uh, Mrs. Bright. A garage is no place for a—a housekeeper."

Phyllida didn't even wince at his language. She'd been known to use a bit of salt in her verbiage at times—although certainly not in front of the staff. But the fact that he'd noticed a splotch of grease *on the back of her skirt* made her back out far too rapidly, and she bumped her head on the top of the blasted, dratted, *bloody* door opening.

When she looked up, Bradford wore an expression that could only be described as smug, and although she'd knocked herself bloody hard on the roof, she refused—absolutely refused—to rub at the throbbing bump.

"Thank you for your attention to the details of my attire," she replied crisply, wondering precisely *where* the grease spot was on the back of her skirt. This was one of her favorite frocks—made from a cornflower-blue fabric with tiny white flowers scattered over it. She resisted the urge to try to look or feel for it herself and clasped her hands at the front of her waist in order to keep from doing so as her head thrummed with pain. "And you needn't concern yourself with my activities, Mr. Bradford. I'm quite capable of conducting my business without supervision."

She turned away from him and, despite the unpleasant throb from the bump on her head, resumed her examination of the four motorcars brought by the Mallowans' guests. Unfortunately, her continued search yielded nothing more of interest—unless one considered that there weren't any other receipts for little country inns. She was able to identify which automobiles belonged to the Devines (thanks to a shiny strand of black hair) and the Hartfords (due to a pink-lipsticked cigarette butt on the floor), and was fairly certain the one without a speck of dust or debris on the floor had been driven by Mr. Grimson. That left the sly, smarmy Mr. Sloup, his valet, and his huge clothes trunk as likely having been driven from the train station by Old Marcus.

A glance at the watch pinned to her blouse made Phyllida gasp at the time. Heavens. She'd been out here for nearly an hour?

Not that anyone would miss her—the staff were far too busy with their own work. And even if they did, no one would have the temerity to mention it. Even Mr. Dobble. He'd make a snide comment, perhaps, but it was the privilege of the upper servants to have far more free time than any of those working under them. It wasn't as if *he* didn't disappear into his pantry under the guise of working, but instead read a detective novel or had a nip of beer in the middle of the day. Once, she'd heard him snoring from outside the door just before tea.

Still, she did have work to oversee, and being out there meant she was missing interviews between the guests and the authorities. But now she had something else of interest to show Cork, who had surely retrieved Mr. Waring's briefcase from her sitting room by now. Perhaps in exchange for this information—and that about the squeaking shoes—she'd be able to convince him she should look at the photographs that had been found in Mr. Waring's satchel.

However, she did have one more item to speak about with the chauffeur before she took her leave.

Phyllida located Bradford by the metallic sounds coming from a back corner of the garage. The smell of grease and oil became stronger as she made her way (carefully, so as not to add to the stains on her frock) toward him. He was doing something to a tire on a low table and glanced up as she approached.

"Don't you have anything to do up at the house?"

The man really was insufferably rude. "Mr. Bradford, when I saw you earlier today, you appeared to be sneaking around. Your actions were uncertain, and it was clear you didn't want to be seen—which I found quite suspicious."

"So I have been told. Multiple times." His arm muscles bulged and flexed, and he grunted a little as he tightened a bolt on the tire.

"Perhaps you can enlighten me as to why you were slinking about so suspiciously," she said. Her head was still throbbing from being bumped, and he was certainly not making it any better. But she would not give him the satisfaction of rubbing the knot.

"You want to know why I was sneaking—no, *slinking*—around suspiciously? If I tell you that, will you leave me in peace?"

"Of course."

"Because," he said, grunting again as he tightened a second bolt, "I'd forgotten in which direction the bloody outhouse was."

"But you—"

"And when I came back," he continued tightly, "I was turned around, coming in on the wrong side of the garage, and had to go all the way around to the side door." He looked up at her. "Does that satisfy your curiosity, Mrs. Bright?"

"Well, yes," she began. It did make sense—and he probably didn't want anyone to notice him wandering around, looking lost, so he was a little furtive with his movements. "But—"

"You said yes. Now stop talking."

She very nearly huffed with irritation but didn't want to demonstrate how he'd annoyed her, even though *he* was making his own feelings quite obvious. "Very well, then, Mr. Bradford—"

"Mrs. Bright," he said through teeth that were definitely clenched (although it wasn't clear whether the clenching was due to his exertions with the tire or some emotion), "go put some ice on the bump on your head and leave me the bloody—leave off bothering me."

Phyllida found Cork and Greensticks sitting in the servants' dining room. A plate of crumbs and two half-filled cups of coffee gave her all the information she needed: they'd finished their interview with Mrs. Puffley and enjoyed some of her apple cinnamon muffins.

"There you are, Inspector," Phyllida said as she came into the room. She'd changed her grease-stained frock and set it to soak with strong lye soap, checked that her hair was in place, and made a brief detour to the distilling room, where Lizzie was working on the rosemary water with the cold still.

Phyllida had even taken a few moments to do as Bradford suggested and put a cloth-wrapped piece of ice on her head.

"You were correct, Mrs. Bright," Cork said as she took a seat at the table. She noticed immediately that he had, indeed, retrieved the briefcase from her sitting room, for it was sitting on a chair next to him.

"Of course I was correct," she replied. "But to what specifically are you referring?"

His mustache twitched a little. "Mrs. Puffley makes the best apple cinnamon muffins I've ever had."

"Indeed. Now, shall I enlighten you regarding something else in which I'm also correct and is relevant to the murder investigation—which is rather more important than a full belly?"

"Why not?" replied the inspector. It seemed said full belly made him a more reasonable man.

She slid the receipt for the Budgely-Rhodeses' night at the Old Ivy Inn across the table to him. "I found this in their automobile."

Cork looked at it, then back up at her. "I suppose you believe this is relevant because of the book you claim was removed from the shelf by none other than the killer."

"Most certainly."

He looked at it briefly, then sighed. "Very well. I'll take it under advisement. Now, on to a more important concern of *mine*, Mrs. Bright . . . Why didn't you tell me there was a briefcase in Mr. Waring's bedroom, and when did you look through it? I've no doubt you were well aware that you were obstructing a police investigation." His eyes had become hard glints of blue gray, and for the first time, Phyllida had an inkling as to how he might have bumbled his way to chief inspector detective—freckles notwithstanding. "And, most importantly, what did you do with Waring's notebook? I'm assuming there was one, or you wouldn't have mentioned it."

"I always survey the bedchambers, Inspector, to ensure the maids are doing their job. I discovered the briefcase under Mr. Waring's bed. And, as I recall, you didn't look under there during your search of the chamber," she told him primly, then quickly went on when she saw the flash in his eyes. "I took the opportunity to glance through it. I fully admit to a base curiosity about the solving of murders. One cannot live under Agatha Christie's roof without acquiring that peculiarity." She gave him a sunny smile meant to ward off the storm that seemed to be gathering at his furrowed brows.

"The notebook, Mrs. Bright. Where is it?"

She hesitated, then plunged on. "Whilst I was looking through it, I heard someone at the door. I—uh—well, I thought it prudent not to be seen at that moment, so I hid myself from the newcomer. And—."

"You hid yourself where?" asked Cork, fixating on a detail she would have preferred to leave unmentioned. She swore this time the flash in his eyes was that of humor—as if he completely recognized her reluctance.

"Under the bed. Which is why I didn't see anything that might have enabled me—or you," she added sweetly, "to identify him.

I've come to the conclusion the culprit must be a man, given the strength it would have taken—not to mention the height required—to drive a fountain pen into Mr. Waring's neck."

When Cork gave no indication whether he agreed with her statement—or whether he'd even come to the same conclusion prior to her explaining her theory to him—Phyllida was forced to continue her story. "Whoever it was stood at the bed, looking through the briefcase—which, unfortunately, I'd left open and in plain sight in my haste—and he took the notebook with him when he left. So there must have been something in it he didn't want anyone to see."

Cork's only response was to comb two fingers down over his mustache. His cool blue eyes gave no indication that he was pleased or even grateful for her candidness, and after a moment of silence, even Phyllida felt the desire to shift in her seat. But she didn't, of course.

"There is one other thing of note, Inspector," she went on at last. "Although I didn't see him, I did notice his shoes squeaked when he moved. And there's no question whether it was the killer. Of course it had to be. Who else would have the temerity to go digging about in the room of a dead man and would then steal his notebook? Only someone who knew Mr. Waring wouldn't be in the chamber—because he was dead—and who feared some incriminating evidence might—"

"Thank you, Mrs. Bright," said Cork. "That is very helpful." He didn't sound as if he particularly meant it, but Phyllida didn't expect gratitude from the man for helping him to do his job. It was her experience that only the rarest of males didn't take offense at being guided by a woman, even when they were blundering about blindly.

She decided to proceed in a different direction. "I didn't see the photographs in the briefcase. It might be helpful if I looked at them now."

"Helpful for who, Mrs. Bright?" he replied.

She held back the urge to correct his grammar and counted that a personal victory in the face of a day with many trials and tribulations. "In light of the fact that I've brought two clues—no, three, for I consider the book and the receipt to be different items—to your attention, one would think you might accommodate my very simple request."

He frowned, but after a moment he sighed. "Constable, show Mrs. Bright the photographs."

The photographs were instantly recognizable as a series taken over the same day or consecutive days in the same location. The images were that of a sort of festival or outdoor fête being held at a large estate. The manor house up a small hill, overlooking a large expanse of lawn, looked familiar to Phyllida, but she couldn't immediately place it. But the estate was large, much larger than Mallowan Hall, and the event seemed to have well over a hundred people attending, if the photographs were anything to go by.

Phyllida peered at the blur of faces in the first picture, then capitulated to practicality over vanity and drew out the spectacles from the pocket of her dress. *Much better.* Now she could see the details of the festival attendees and even a banner that hung above a series of small booths selling baked goods; plants and flower arrangements; woven baskets; jams, jellies, and cordials; and other sundries one might find at a small fair. The banner proclaimed THE 20TH ANNUAL DUCK POND DERBY CHARITY FAIRE, and in smaller print SPONSORED BY SIR LAWRENCE AVERCROFT AND MRS. BIPPY AVERCROFT.

Ah, that was why the manor house looked familiar. Everyone knew about the Duck Pond Derby Faire, which was thrown at the gorgeous, sprawling Bunder House every year (weather permitting) in early May.

"Why, that looks like Mr. and Mrs. Hartford in this one," she said, wishing she had a magnifying glass to be certain. "She's putting a ticket into the raffle for a large ficus."

"I believe it is," Inspector Cork said. "They're all there, Mrs. Bright. They were all at the festival. Even Mr. and Mrs. Mallowan."

Well, that was quite curious.

She flipped through the photographs and saw that he was correct. The Budgely-Rhodeses were talking to Mr. Sloup in a picture. The stunning Devines were speaking to Mr. Budgely-Rhodes in another, while Mrs. Budgely-Rhodes appeared to be perusing a display of cream pies. Mr. Grimson was captured in one of the photographs, standing there with a young woman (not the one who was in the photograph on his bedside table), and further along were Mr. Max and Mrs. Agatha, standing about in conversation with Mr. Sloup and the Hartfords.

"I don't see Mr. Waring in any of the photographs," she said, lining the pictures up neatly.

She was just about to hand the stack of photographs to Constable Greensticks when something tickled the back of her mind. What was it about Bunder House . . . ?

Then she remembered. The kitchen maid Rebecca had been at Bunder House before she came to Mallowan Hall. In fact, she would have been there at the time the photographs were taken. "I'd like to borrow these, Inspector. There's someone to whom I'd like to show them."

Cork sat up straight and fixed her with those protruding eyes. "I've already shown them to all the guests here, Mrs. Bright. As well as to Mr. and Mrs. Mallowan . . ."

"One of the maids worked at Bunder House when this event occurred. Perhaps there's something about these photographs that she might notice. Surely it's not a coincidence that each of the pictures has at least one of the Mallowans' guests in it. Mr. Waring brought them for a reason. Perhaps he even took the photographs himself."

The inspector pursed his lips, then shrugged. "Right. Go ahead, then, Mrs. Bright. Take them. However, I don't expect you'll find anything important related to them, as the person who took the notebook didn't see fit to also take the pictures. Surely he would have done that if there was something incriminating."

Unless he, like Phyllida, hadn't seen the photos because they were tucked deep inside an inner flap and he was in a rush when looking through the briefcase. Instead of pointing that out, she merely smiled and slid the pictures into her pocket. "That's very kind of you, Inspector."

"You can show them to your maid," he said, leaning forward and speaking in a hard voice, "but let me warn you, Mrs. Bright, that if I find you've been tampering with evidence or otherwise interfering in this investigation again, I won't be as accommodating as I have been thus far."

Having achieved her desire, Phyllida decided it was best merely to smile and nod rather than quibble about precisely what he meant by *accommodating*. "I'll return them soonest, Inspector. But now I must be off to see that the arrangements for tea are coming along."

"You do that, Mrs. Bright. Stick with your job and I'll do mine."

She would be happy to do that—if only she believed he could do the same.

CHAPTER 14

"**T**HE PROBLEM IS, THERE HAS TO BE A CONNECTION BETWEEN Charles Waring and someone here at Mallowan Hall—someone who wanted him out of the way. But so far, there's been no indication that anyone even *knew* the dead man," Phyllida said to her employer. "And in order to kill someone, there must be a reason. A motive."

"Of course," replied Agatha Christie Mallowan. "As I said earlier, it's so much easier to create the situation. I often use the tactic that *everyone* should have a motive. It's far more interesting when simply everyone is a suspect, for that way there are so many options for who did the deed that *one* of them has to fit." She smiled wanly. "The more suspects, the better . . . but we don't have *any* at all, do we? It's very frustrating."

They were sitting in her office, Agatha having decided to attempt to finish writing the chapter she'd abandoned that morning in order to join her friends for breakfast—and not making much progress at all. At the moment, the guests were off to visit a nearby castle ruin, a small excursion led by her husband—who would be giving an archaeologist's perspective on the remains of the old motte-and-bailey keep—in order to give Agatha a chance to do some work whilst keeping their visitors entertained.

Phyllida had come up to the first floor while making her rounds over the maids' work and had found her old friend staring blankly at the typewriter. The fresh vase of orange gerberas sat next to it on the desk.

At Agatha's invitation, she'd closed the door and sat in the chair next to the desk where Agatha was working. They'd fallen into their old habit of sitting and chatting about death and murder—just as they had years ago, during the war. Somehow, back then, thinking about and plotting specific (fictional) killings had been an escape from the horror of mass murders as wave upon wave of men and women died—or were brutally injured—from motives that had very little to do with any of the victims personally.

But today, *now*, the actual concept of death and murder and motive had come home to roost, so to speak.

"No suspects, and so far, no one here even has a motive. We can't connect anyone to Charles Waring at all—who wasn't even who he claimed to be," Phyllida said. "Although, Inspector Cork did tell me that Charles Waring was his real name—they found identification in his motorcar, along with a camera. And there was a slew of photographs in his briefcase. Did you look at them? So Mr. Waring might not be from the *Times*, but I suppose he must have been some sort of journalist or photographer." She wished she'd brought Mr. Waring's photos up for her friend to see, but they were still in her sitting room. "It's as if a stranger was found murdered in someone's library, and no one in the house even knew who it was or how he got there—let alone had a reason to do away with him."

Agatha, who'd been about to speak, suddenly stilled. "Why, that's . . . quite an interesting idea, isn't it? Finding a dead body in a library is rather passé, but finding a *stranger* . . . dead . . . in one's library . . . Why, what a magnificent plot that would be!" Her eyes took on the faraway look that indicated she'd trundled off on a different path—a private adventure that might someday, if people were lucky, turn out to be a cleverly plotted detective story.

"It would be a case for Poirot, of course," said Phyllida, beaming at the thought and willing to be distracted from reality for the moment. "He'd—"

"No, no, no. Not Hercule." Agatha held up a hand, shaking her head. She was the only person Phyllida knew who felt comfortable referring to the Belgian detective by his familiar name. "No . . . it has to be Jane's. It'll be Jane's story. Yes, I *like* it.

"A stranger, found dead in someone's library. It'll be horribly incongruous—this shabby little library, well loved and oft used, and suddenly there's a tawdry, overused *stranger*, dead on the floor, whom no one in the household has ever seen. Before they can determine the why and the *who* of who did it, they have to ferret out who the victim even is! And in someone's home—which is quite different than if they found a dead body on the street and had to solve that murder. No, somehow the killer got a strange person into the house and murdered them. I *really* like that. Thank you so much, Phyllie! You always give me the best ideas."

Agatha smiled over her shoulder, for she had turned to scrawl notes on a pad of paper at her desk. "After all, it was you who suggested a story with a victim who everyone thought was an accidental murder, but turned out she was really the actual target and had been killed by the *supposed* victim as a way to hide her villainy. That is still one of my favorite twists."

"Right, yes, but, Agatha . . . we really must find a connection between Charles Waring and someone here at Mallowan Hall. Are you certain you never met Mr. Waring before?"

"I'm fairly certain . . . although perhaps he *did* seem a little familiar. But if I met him, it would only have been very briefly, otherwise I would remember. Yet someone here must know him . . . or . . ." Agatha's voice trailed off, and Phyllida wasn't certain whether she had gone off on a fictional trail or was still here in reality. But when she continued, the answer was obvious.

"Right. Well, there is the possibility that Mr. Waring wasn't murdered because he was *Charles Waring* . . . but because he was simply in the wrong place at the wrong time. What I mean to say is, perhaps he came upon someone doing something nefarious and had to be silenced before he could raise the alarm—or something of that nature. Don't you think, Phyllida?"

"Why . . . yes, that's certainly possible . . . but it still means that one of your guests is a killer—whether he meant to murder Charles Waring *because* he was Charles Waring or not."

"But that could certainly make the difference as to whether

there is a previous connection between the two, don't you think?" Agatha said. "And the motive."

"Yes, of course. But if Mr. Waring was simply in the wrong place at the wrong time and wasn't a targeted victim and didn't have any relationship with his murderer, then why would the killer sneak into his bedchamber and steal his notebook? What I mean to say," Phyllida mused, "is that if it was a—a random or un-planned killing, if they didn't have a history between them, then there wouldn't be anything incriminating in his effects that needed to be stolen. Don't you think?"

Agatha was nodding. "I see your point. Yes, I think you're cor-rect. And so that means someone here *must* have known who Charles Waring was. And wanted to kill him."

Phyllida smiled. "I thought you didn't want to be involved in the solving of a crime you didn't make up yourself."

Agatha gave a soft, affectionate laugh. "Right, then. Perhaps I was wrong. Perhaps I have a little bit of Hercule and Jane and Su-perintendent Battle in me, after all."

"I still can't get my mind off those photographs," Phyllida said thoughtfully. "I suppose if Mr. Waring was the one who took the pictures, perhaps he did meet all those people at the Duck Pond Derby."

She hadn't had the opportunity to show the pictures to Re-becca yet—she wanted to do it when she could talk to the kitchen maid privately and when the cook wasn't yelling about work to be done. As soon as she was finished here.

"Why . . . yes! The Duck Pond Derby. That could be it, Phyllida. That could be why Mr. Waring seemed a bit—only vaguely—familiar to me. If he was a journalist taking photographs at the Derby, I might have *seen* him about, but I wouldn't have necessar-ily met him or spoken to him. The same could be true about the others. That is where we invited everyone to our house party, you know. The Budgely-Rhodeses, the Devines, and the rest. We all sat near each other at the Bunder House dinner after the fête that night, and Max and I thought it would be a pleasure to extend the festivities a few months later."

"But you didn't invite Mr. Waring."

"Of course not. But I suppose if he was taking photographs of the event, he might have heard us speaking about it."

Phyllida nodded. Things were making a little more sense now. "The fact of the matter is Mr. Waring came here to Mallowan Hall under false pretenses—but possibly because he knew everyone who was at Bunder House was also going to be here. He lied about being from the *Times*. So what was the real reason he came? Did he come because he wanted to . . . what? To see one of your guests? To confront them? To spy on them? And then that person killed him?"

"That is an excellent point," said Agatha. "He did come here under false pretenses, so he had to have had a specific *reason* for making the trip in the first place. Perhaps he wanted to confront or spy on one of us . . . but he could just as easily have been a curiosity-seeker, perhaps, or as a freelance journalist, he was trying to gain access to my house in order to do a story on . . . on— oh, I don't know, 'The Intimate Life of Agatha Christie' or some rot like that."

"And then he encountered someone unexpectedly—someone whom he knew—who later murdered him. Why? Probably to keep some sort of secret, one supposes. What other motive would there be?"

Agatha shook her head. "I don't know." She sighed, looking at her typewriter. "I suppose I'd best get back to this chapter if I want to be able to enjoy the evening . . . though how much enjoyment we'll have, knowing a murder is hanging over our heads, I don't know. Phyllida, I simply *cannot* believe that someone in this house is a killer. How can that be?"

Phyllida closed gentle fingers over her friend's hand. Sympathy and concern flooded her, for she knew how much Agatha loathed her privacy being invaded and the insistence of the press. Not to mention the thought that one of her friends was a killer. "I don't know. But haven't you any idea at all who might have done it?"

Agatha squeezed Phyllida's fingers in gratitude and sat back in her chair. "Well, I suppose I ought to at least think about it, hadn't I? Max asked me the same. Why do people think that just because

I'm a detective writer, I know how to solve a crime?" She gave a rueful smile. "No, no, don't feel badly, Phyllie. I'm simply disgruntled and sick at heart that this could happen here."

She lifted her cup of tea—which Phyllida suspected had long gone cold—and sipped as if she needed something bracing. "All right, then. If I had to imagine any of my guests stabbing a man with a fountain pen, who would it be?"

"What about Tuddy Sloup?" asked Phyllida. "He seems rather . . . unpleasant."

"Tuddy? Oh, well . . . yes, he can be rather smarmy, can't he?" Agatha hunched her shoulders a bit, as if afraid of being overheard. "I'm certainly not terribly fond of him myself, but he helped Max with some funding for a dig a few years back, and my husband is nothing if not loyal. He felt obligated to include Tuddy in at least one of our house parties this season, and we decided on this one because poor Mr. Grimson was coming stag, as well, and so here we are. But I don't think he's the *violent* sort . . . just a bit . . . insistent. The sort one wouldn't want to be caught alone with in a shadowy room if one were a woman, if you know what I mean."

Phyllida knew exactly what she meant. "So Mr. Sloup has money, then? If he was helping Mr. Max with funding."

"Oh, yes, he's got an elderly aunt in Yorkshire, I believe, that's worth buckets, and he is very attentive to her. She takes quite good care of him is my understanding, and he dabbles a bit in art dealing to keep himself busy, as he puts it. Since his aunt happens to like Egyptian art, that's how he and Max got connected up. Now, there was some sort of scuffle a while back about a gallery piece that turned out not to be authentic after all . . . but I don't recall that he'd been implicated in anything untoward. I'll have to ask Max, but I don't think he's had any serious scandals.

"Still . . . I don't see him as the sort who would get himself all worked up over someone enough to kill them. Not to mention get blood all over himself. He is very particular about his clothing. I feel quite sympathetic toward his valet, considering the number of complaints he made about creases and cuffs and neckties and whatnot during bridge last night. We were partners for the first two rubbers," Agatha explained. "He's rather passable at bridge, in fact. The way one plays cards can certainly give one an idea of how someone approaches life as a whole, you know. Whether they take risks, think things through, and so on."

"What about the Budgely-Rhodeses? Mr. Budgely-Rhodes, I mean. I think it had to be a man," Phyllida said. "In order to be strong enough and tall enough to plunge the pen down into the carotid. Don't you agree?"

"Indeed. And on which side was Mr. Waring stabbed? That could indicate a left- or right-handed person."

"It would depend on whether the killer was facing him, I suppose. He was stabbed on the right side, so if it was from behind, it would likely be a right-handed person. But if he was attacked from the front, it would be someone left-handed." Phyllida decided that was another piece of information she needed to have—and that she should have asked Inspector Cork about it. Obviously, she was a bit of an amateur at crime investigation to have missed that important element.

"But for Odell Budgely-Rhodes to stab a man to death? He's just not the sort," Agatha said. "He's got soft, pudgy hands from all the typing he does. And I'm not certain he has the . . . uh . . . strength or stamina to go about stabbing someone. He seems more of a poison sort of killer, don't you think?" she said with a wry smile.

"He wants to adapt one of my stories into a full-length play, and he's written five shows already, and all have been produced quite successfully—so he's got loads of money. And so I'm inclined to go ahead and work with him, considering his experience in the West End.

"His wife, Dora, seems friendly enough. I've met her only once before, but aside from that horrific hairstyle from three decades ago, she's more than tolerable. No, I can't imagine why Odell would want to stab a man in my library. That would put quite a damper on any business arrangement we might consider, wouldn't it?" Agatha gave another little smile.

"Indeed, it would. Mr. Devine is quite nice to look at," Phyllida said, thinking again how the handsome brunet man (and his wife) looked as glamorous as film stars.

"Oh, yes. It's a sin how good looking he is. He's trying for the stage, you know—which is one of the reasons Max and I wanted to invite Odell Budgely-Rhodes while Geoffrey Devine was here. I think he'd be good in pictures, as well, but he has to start somewhere, and Odell knows everyone in London theater."

"He would look very nice on the large screen," Phyllida admitted with a smile. "Does he or Mrs. Devine have money?"

"Oh, it's his, all right. Very old family, lots of coal mining in the north, and they have pots of it. So he's devastatingly good looking and rolling in it to boot, and Tana is quite a good match for him, in my opinion. He and Max knew each other from summers when Max visited his cousin up there."

"Mr. Devine seemed very . . . erm . . . comfortable with Mrs. Hartford. One might wonder if he's gotten himself into a sort of philandering kind of trouble. That sort often does, don't they?"

"The dashing, good-looking ones usually do," Agatha said a little bitterly, and Phyllida kicked herself for bringing up the subject. Then Agatha pursed her lips. "Why, now that you mention it, I did wonder about him and Amelia—Mrs. Hartford, that is. She requested a separate room from her husband, as you know, and although that's quite common, with maids and valets being in and out of bedchambers, and the idea of being in one's toilette whilst the valet is standing there helping one's husband dress is simply not feasible . . . Well, it is something to think about. Of course, the Devines have separate bedchambers, as well, for the same reason. But not the Budgely-Rhodeses, I don't believe. She was the only one who brought her own maid. And he has his valet."

"Are you suggesting Mrs. Hartford and Mr. Devine might be carrying on?" Phyllida asked, circling from guest servants back around to infidelity.

"I have no grounds for such a thought, only that it wouldn't surprise me," Agatha replied. "The Hartfords and the Devines do run in the same circles often enough, I suppose. And I don't think Amelia is very happy being married to Paul—Mr. Hartford. She's such a lovely woman, I'd hate to think it of her . . . Perhaps she and Geoffrey—Mr. Devine, I mean . . . Well, this is just between you and me, isn't it?" Agatha smiled uncomfortably.

"Of course it is." *Unless it has to do with murder.*

"Right. Well, it's just that I came upon the two of them—Amelia Hartford and Geoffrey Devine—standing in the stairwell yesterday afternoon, before dinner, and they were standing *quite* close. Too close, if you understand me."

"I certainly do."

"I distinctly saw her hand on his chest when I came around the corner. And at dinner, they were sitting across from each other, and I noticed they seemed to be avoiding speaking to each other or even looking at the other." Agatha sighed. "And now I'm a gossip."

As someone who'd been on the receiving end of spousal infidelity, Agatha was very sensitive to such a topic. But this was a murder investigation, and there was nothing that could be discounted, in Phyllida's opinion, when it came to possible motive. She was certain Agatha would agree.

"I must confess," her friend went on, "that it makes me far more comfortable knowing you've taken an interest in this situation and that it isn't just the authorities. They really have no sense of . . . of sensitivity. All they've done so far is establish that everyone was in their rooms all night. Of *course* that's what everyone is going to say!"

"Thank you," Phyllida replied, then sighed. "Even if Mr. Devine and Mrs. Hartford are carrying on, I don't see how it would relate to Mr. Waring's death. What about Mr. Grimson?" Sometimes the quiet ones were the most dangerous, Phyllida thought.

"Oh, certainly not. The poor man's just lost his wife only six months ago, and he's been rather a wreck about it. She was run down by a motorcar, you know. Stepped into the road without looking, and the driver didn't even try to stop or avoid her."

Phyllida didn't know, of course, but she wasn't about to question Agatha's opinion. "How horrible."

There had been more and more instances of automobile deaths over the past few years, now that so many people were driving them. There was talk of putting in speed limit laws, but nothing had been finalized yet. Many drivers claimed the onus was on the pedestrians not to get run down. Their position was that since one wouldn't walk out in front of a team of horses or a spirited pair of fillies and expect not to get trampled, one should take care when stepping out into the street and should not place the blame on the motorcar driver.

Phyllida had her own opinions about the matter, but this was neither the time nor the place to air them.

"And I can't imagine Geoffrey Devine taking a fountain pen to a man if he wanted to kill him. It's far too . . . well, spur of the moment and unplanned. He's much too structured and careful to do something so haphazard as that," Agatha said. She sighed again. "If only it were a huge mistake and it wasn't a murder, after all."

But it was. And they both knew it.

CHAPTER 15

*R*EBECCA ALWAYS VOLUNTEERED WHEN MRS. PUFFLEY NEEDED someone to go outside for anything: to the small garden patch to collect herbs or vegetables for a particular dish at dinner, ice from the icehouse, or eggs from the coop. She didn't particularly like to confiscate the eggs from beneath the chickens—those hens were *mean*, and their flying feathers tickled her nose—but she was always eager to get out into the yard and away from the noise and steam in the kitchen, especially on a bright, mild day like today. Since it was so nice out and she was out of sight from the house, she'd taken off her cap and tied it to her apron strings. The sun beat warm on her uncovered hair, and a gentle breeze filtered over her face.

Days like today she didn't so much mind being a kitchen maid and relegated to the cellar level all the time. The upstairs maids didn't ever get to go outside, and she did, often multiple times a day—and not just to go to the outhouse.

With a large basket on her arm and a pair of scissors in her hand, she walked through the patch to where the herbs grew. Rosemary, thyme, sage, dill, lavender . . . Their fragrances mingled with the warm, sunny day, and it was easy for Rebecca to leave all thoughts of what had happened inside Mallowan Hall back in the house.

So horrible, it was. So awful and horrible and frightening. Her knees had felt wobbly all day, and she hadn't even had any breakfast. She'd just stayed in the kitchen while everyone else ate and spent her time deboning hare meat while trying not to think about it all.

But she had nothing to worry about, Rebecca told herself as she bent to snip several sturdy twigs of rosemary. *She* had done nothing wrong and certainly had never told anyone what she saw back at Bunder House, and no one—

From the corner of her eye, she caught a movement. A movement that shouldn't be there on this western side of the grounds. No, today there shouldn't be activity on this side of the lawn, for Amsi, the gardener, was working in the eastern gardens and would swing around the back to prune the boxwoods—but not until later. Rebecca knew this, for she often paused to chat with him for a moment—only a moment, lest Mrs. Puffley miss her— whenever she came out to use the outhouse or bring in ice from the icehouse Sometimes they were in the vegetable garden at the same time, and they were able to talk even longer then.

He wasn't all that handsome, and he was a lot older than she was, but he was kind, and he didn't leer at her like he wanted to take her clothes off, like so many of the other servants did. Even Stanley, who Ginny had a heat for, made Rebecca feel shy and strange sometimes when he flirted with her.

No, Amsi was kind and gentle, and he didn't even like to squash the beetles that got into his roses. He knew an awful lot about plants and gardening—

There it was again.

She straightened up and looked over across the lawn, where the trees sprang up behind a low stone wall that created a casual barrier. Yes, there was someone there—a silhouette moving in the shadows, coming near the apple trees. It was those reporters again.

Of course, the whole staff knew about the way Old Dent had chased off a gaggle of them out front a while ago. When she went back inside, she'd send word up to him that there were some of them sneaking around the west end of the grounds, by the orchard.

But she wasn't in a hurry to do that. It was too nice to be out here, away from the constant odors of onions, garlic, and grease.

She finished cutting rosemary and thyme, then went on over to snip garlic ramps and chives. The sun felt so good on her face, she wanted to stay outside forever . . . away from the dim, busy, loud kitchen, which was either cold and damp or hot and steamy, depending on the season and what was cooking.

After straightening from her task, Rebecca moved to the last row of the garden to pull up some carrots.

"Get small, tender ones, mind," Mrs. Puffley had said, wagging a long finger that glistened with grease. "I don't want any fat, tough ones. This is for the garnish on the roast, and they're meant to be sweet and young. And keep the tops on them, mind you, and don't crush the leaves—or I'll send you back out for more!"

She'd found three carrots that met the cook's requirements when she heard it: a soft feral cry.

Rebecca lifted her head and listened. It had sounded like an animal mewling in distress. She waited, but the noise didn't come again.

From around the front of the house, she heard male voices— maybe the constable and the inspector were finally leaving. Her stomach could unknot a little once they were gone. At least she hadn't had to lie to them, because they hadn't asked some of the questions she'd feared they would. Innocent questions, but she didn't want to answer them, anyway, for fear of where they might lead.

There was a metallic clanging from somewhere in the vicinity of the garage, a ways over there, and the low rumble of an engine. Had Mr. Max and his guests returned from their excursion? It must be nearly teatime, then. She'd best get back to the kitchen to help set up the trays before everyone came down after freshening up in their rooms.

But then that soft crying sound came again, a little louder this time, a little more urgent and distressed. Rebecca stood, holding her scissors and the basket, and started walking toward the noise.

It seemed to be coming from beyond the low north wall. The stone barrier was covered with ivy and bordered a small apple and pear orchard. Was it a cat caught in one of the trees? An injured rabbit or kitten?

She had to investigate. She couldn't leave it vulnerable or hurt where a predator could snatch it up. A quick look at the sun eased her worry—it wasn't even three o'clock. Another hour until she was needed for tea. If Mrs. Puffley sent someone looking for her and complained that she took too long, she'd say she'd been feeling sick and had had to use the outhouse. The sick part wouldn't be a lie, anyway.

Basket over her arm, still carrying her scissors, she hurried across the small expanse of lawn to the wall. The pained crying continued, sounding more urgent as she came closer.

When she got to the little wall, she set down the basket and scissors on top of it. The stone wall wasn't meant to be a barrier to anything but the grass into the orchard as well as a pleasant visual, so it was simple for Rebecca to climb over it even in her uniform. She didn't manage to do this without snagging her hose, however, for just as she brought her second leg over, a stubborn twig made a long rent in her stocking.

At least Mrs. Puffley didn't worry too much about that, since no one ever saw the kitchen maids. But Mrs. Bright wouldn't like it one bit, and Rebecca didn't want to mess up twice in the same day in front of Mrs. Bright—who would be down in the kitchen, overseeing the tea tray—because it was her dream to be promoted to chambermaid someday, so she could get out of the dungeon of the kitchen and away from the tyranny of every cook she'd ever worked for.

There was something about cooks and the way they shouted and complained and criticized—likely because it was all on their shoulders to make certain every meal was coordinated and prepared correctly and on schedule, and there was no one else who had to be on such a tight time—

A shadow—a man—emerged from behind one of the apple trees, right in front of her.

Rebecca stifled a cry of surprise and stepped back automatically. The sun was in her eyes when she looked up at him—it was definitely a he—and there was an instant where she couldn't see his face, because the sun was so bright right behind him.

But then she did see his face, and when she recognized who it was, she stumbled backward. Her body went hot and cold. "Wh-what are you doing h—"

She never finished the question, for the vicious blow to the side of her head stopped her cold . . . and dropped her to the ground.

CHAPTER 16

WHEN PHYLLIDA CAME DOWN TO THE KITCHEN TO SEE TO THE arrangements for tea—the only meal which she, instead of Mr. Dobble and the footmen, was responsible for serving—she found the place in an uproar.

Not that that was unusual for Puffley, but this time, instead of being ferocious and cantankerous in her mood, the woman was very nearly in tears. They filled her eyes and threatened to spill out into rivulets down her red cheeks.

"I'm going to quit, I am," cried the cook, even as she continued rolling out pie pastry with great violence. Phyllida had a rush of concern, worrying that salty tears might splatter on the dough and ruin it. "I'm going to walk out that bleeding door right now, Mrs. Bright, if things don't get back to the way they was! I just can't!"

"What is it this time?" asked Phyllida, looking around for some sort of clue as to what caused the woman's distress.

"It's that lazybones Rebecca! She's been out nattering in the garden for over an hour now, and I can't send Benita or Molly to fetch her, because we've too much work to do because we're bloody short a kitchen maid because she's *loitering about*! *And* there's been a murder *and* Stanley's gone missing and I am *going to quit*!" The tears were flowing now, and her rolling pin was trundling haphazardly over the delicate dough. "I *am*!"

Phyllida knew enough about pastry to know that too much

work ruined it, so she stepped over and plucked the rolling pin from the cook's grip. "I'll find Rebecca. You wash up your face and cease with the bawling, now, Puffley. There'll be time for that later, and you can go at it then. You can be assured I'll give Rebecca a good talking-to when I find her."

Feeling a bit discomposed herself, Phyllida set down the rolling pin at a safe distance from the distraught woman. With one last stern look at the cook—who seemed to be pulling herself together—and then a measured one filled with warning at a gawking Molly, she hurried from the kitchen.

Puffley was right. There was altogether too much going on here at Mallowan Hall. And Phyllida couldn't imagine where Rebecca had gotten herself off to—although she did like to talk to Amsi. Maybe she'd lost track of time—it was such a fine day. Still, maids could not lose track of time and expect to keep their positions.

And footmen couldn't go off and disappear and expect to keep theirs.

But for two of them in one day to go missing? It was so improbable—even ominous—that it worried her more than it should.

Phyllida didn't even glance in the direction of the garage as she marched up the steps, out of the house, and onto the back lawn. Mr. Max and the guests had returned from their afternoon excursion some time ago, and all the motorcars were back in the garage, giving that Bradford creature plenty to keep him busy.

She went directly to the vegetable patch, which was out of sight of the terrace and most of the windows of Mallowan Hall (and not necessarily convenient to the kitchen), in favor of the views for guests and residents to be traditional English landscaping. But even as she approached the garden, she could see that it was empty of any human.

The outhouse was the next obvious place to look for the absent kitchen maid. It wasn't unheard of for a servant to take a snooze in the privacy of the privy, although Phyllida had never caught one of her staff doing so. There were indoor bathrooms for the

Mallowans, for the guests on the second and third floors, and upper servants like herself, Mr. Dobble, and Mrs. Agatha's maid, of course, but the lower servants were relegated to using the outhouse.

The latches were loose on both doors of the outhouse, indicating that neither side was in use. But Phyllida knocked, then poked her head inside each stall to be certain. No. Empty.

Now beginning to feel even more anxious about Rebecca, Phyllida went to find Amsi, in case he'd seen or spoken to her.

The gardener was where she'd expected him to be, for it was Thursday, and he was always in the east-side gardens on this day.

"Mrs. Bright, ma'am," he said, looking up in surprise when she approached. He was holding large hedge clippers, and he gave a little bow as she approached.

The gardener was about forty and had a mild, calm manner about him. He was wearing clothing quite different from that of most gardeners she'd seen: a loose pullover linen shirt and matching loose pants that ended halfway down his calves, both articles of clothing dyed dark, and wellies. The wellies were British, of course, but the rest of his attire was more suited to his homeland.

Amsi had come back with Mr. Max after one of his expeditions years ago—from what Phyllida knew, there'd been some sort of political ruckus in Egypt, and it had been safer for him to be here in England—and he had taken to the British climate surprisingly well. Having been head gardener at one of the large tourist hotels in Cairo, Amsi was well suited to overseeing much smaller grounds in a much safer geographical locale. Not to mention, his English was better than that of half of Phyllida's maids.

"Have you seen Rebecca?" she asked.

He shook his head. "No, no, ma'am, not for a while. She was in the garden last I saw her. It was some time back, ma'am." He squinted at the sun. "Maybe it was an hour ago."

"You didn't speak with her?"

"No, no, ma'am. Not today. I only saw her when I went to get a load of peat in the wheelbarrow." His expression changed from reserve to tension as he realized something was wrong. "I'll help you find her, ma'am."

"Not at all, but thank you. You've got your own work to do. I shall find her." She started off, then turned back, suddenly feeling even more apprehensive. "Have you seen Stanley?"

"No, no, ma'am. I've been in the peonies and roses most all morning and just began here with the hedges. There was some newspaper people poking around, but I ran them off. A crazy dark man chasing them with loppers scared 'em away good." He flashed a smile that was quickly subdued. "I hope everything is all right. I would like to help you look for Rebecca, though, ma'am. With all the . . . happenings and strangers about . . . perhaps it would be best."

"All right, then." Phyllida couldn't deny her concern—and she knew Amsi and the kitchen maid had a close friendship. Perhaps even more. And two people searching were better than one.

Where would Rebecca have gone after the vegetable patch? She sent Amsi to look in the chicken coop and then in the garage (so she didn't have to bother attempting a conversation with Bradford) and the icehouse, and she went back to the garden to look from there. Maybe there were footprints.

What about the orchard? Maybe the girl had had a hankering for a pear. It seemed so unlike her, however, to have wandered off and lolled about. Despite Puffley's ranting, Rebecca had always been a hard and willing worker—or else she wouldn't be at Mallowan Hall.

As Phyllida approached the ivy-covered wall that ran along the orchard, she saw a basket sitting on top of it, with a few carrot tops spilling out. But there was no sign of the kitchen maid.

Still, it seemed she was going in the proper direction.

Could Rebecca have come across one of the newspaper reporters and got trapped in an interview? Those journalists were persistent and demanding and could easily have cowed the quiet maid into talking to them.

When she reached the wall, Phyllida saw scissors next to the basket and a bit of thread fluttering from a twig near the top of the wall.

So she went over the wall and left a bit of her stocking, did she? she thought.

Of course, Phyllida went over the wall without leaving *any* of her stocking, and once she was over it, she cupped her hands to her mouth. "Rebecca!"

The orchard was silent and still. The trees were thick with leaves, heavy pears, and apples still too small to be ripe yet. She looked around, turning in a fanlike direction, and saw no sign of the missing maid. But she'd definitely come over the wall, so—

Phyllida cocked her head and listened. A sort of buzzing sound caught her ears, faint but insistent. She looked over and saw something several trees away that made her chest tighten.

No.

Please, *no.*

But she was rushing toward the small swarm of flies that seemed to be hovering and diving over something on the ground, somehow *knowing* but at the same time not willing to allow herself to even *consider*—

"Dear heaven." Phyllida practically fell to her knees next to the bloody, beaten girl, swatting at the flies that had already gathered. *"Rebecca."*

She didn't need to feel for a pulse to know that it wasn't necessary. "Oh, you poor, poor dear," she said, blinking back the sting of tears as she pushed a bit of hair from where it clung to the girl's bloody face. Her eyes were open in blind terror. "You poor thing."

She closed Rebecca's eyes gently, then offered up a quick prayer of Godspeed—good gad, for the second time that day. Then she pulled herself slowly to her feet.

Phyllida wasn't ashamed to admit that her knees were trembling and her insides were painfully tight. Whatever was happening here at Mallowan Hall was awful, horrific, and incredibly sad. This was cold-blooded, evil *murder . . .* twice in one day.

Perhaps thrice—

No. Phyllida firmly removed the very idea from her thoughts. Stanley would show up any time now, and with a reasonable, logical—or, at least, nonviolent—explanation.

Instead, she focused her mind and gathered up her mental cloak of responsibility and action. Something must be done, and she, Phyllida Bright, must be—must *always* be—the one do to it, the one to get things done.

At the same time, she was loathe to leave the poor girl alone. But she must call for help.

Just as she turned to start back toward the orchard wall, she saw Amsi and Bradford coming across the lawn. She was too upset to mind that the rude chauffeur was going to be present.

When the two men saw her standing there, hands helplessly at her sides, they must have comprehended, for both started to run. Bradford leaped over the wall without hesitation, while Amsi clambered over a bit behind him. Thus, the chauffeur arrived at the scene a few moments before the gardener.

When he saw Rebecca, Bradford muttered something short and violent under his breath, then knelt next to the girl for a moment. Even Phyllida didn't feel the need to speak. There was nothing to say, even though inside she kept hearing her own voice saying, *Who would have done this? Who could have done this?*

And then all at once, the realization dropped into her head: she'd never got the chance to show Rebecca the photographs of the festival at Bunder House.

And now she never would.

A chill rushed over her body.

Just then Amsi loped up, panting, and he gave a soft moan as he, too, fell to his knees next to Rebecca. As neither of the men were wearing a coat, there was nothing with which to cover her, and Phyllida acutely felt the ignominy of the situation.

She drew in a deep breath, blinked back tears, and reminded herself who she was. The woman in charge. "I'll call the constable to come back."

"I'll stay with her," Amsi said, his voice gravelly. "I'll stay here."

"There's a sheet in the garage," Bradford said. "I'll be right back with it." He dashed off without having said a word to Phyllida, and she followed at a slower, yet brisk pace.

Grim, saddened, and suddenly exhausted, she returned to the house.

Tea was going to be very late.

CHAPTER 17

"**S**OMEONE BASHED HER HEAD IN?" DOBBLE FELT BLINDLY BEHIND him and settled his hand on a side table to steady himself. "Good God."

For the first time in his memory, Mrs. Bright looked less than luminous, and he was quite certain it wasn't because she was suddenly short a kitchen maid during a house party. Her face was more pale than usual, and although every strand of that shocking hair was in place, even it seemed subdued.

She'd come to find him in his pantry immediately after calling the constable, and Dobble didn't even have the heart to be irked that, for a second time, she'd notified him after the authorities.

"I'll have to take them out there when they arrive," she told him. "They'll have questions about how she was found and so on. I've already informed Mr. and Mrs. Mallowan that tea will be delayed, and, of course, they understand."

Dobble couldn't even summon up vexation that he—the butler!—was the *fourth* person she had notified about the second murder, mostly because it was simply inconceivable that there *had* been a second murder . . . in less than twenty-four hours. This sort of thing happened only in detective stories.

"In fact, Mrs. Agatha said we should just serve a cold tray and be done with it. Of course, we'll have hot tea and coffee, and chocolate, as well, but I am inclined to agree that a cold tray will do. Puffley will be utterly overset when she learns about it all—

she was already beating the beef's pastry dough into a blanket—and it'll be all I can do to ensure that dinner is ready on time."

"Of course. I'm confident that if anyone could do so, it would be you, Mrs. Bright," Dobble said, then realized he'd actually given the blasted woman a compliment. Just smashing. Now it would go to her head, and she'd become even more high and mighty.

"She might huff and rant like a madwoman," the housekeeper went on, "but she liked Rebecca—oh, everyone did—and the news will be quite a blow to her."

"Yes, of course." Dobble was well aware of the cook's volatile temperament (he'd never met a cook who didn't have one) as well as her well-buried sympathetic heart.

"I shall have to go into Listleigh tomorrow and see about engaging another kitchen maid. It may seem hasty and unfeeling," Mrs. Bright said in a subdued voice, "but it must be done. We do have guests, and they must be fed and cared for—particularly since the inspector has insisted no one take their leave from here." That reminded her: she would have to increase the order from the baker and the vegetable grower since the guests would be staying longer. And from Mr. Tentley, as well. And the laundry would need to be sent out soon, too. . . .

"Of course, one must be practical, even in the face of tragedy," Dobble agreed.

"I shall have to request Mr. Bradford drive me," she went on in a grim voice; then she frowned. "Really, Mr. Dobble, I don't care how excellent his references were. I find it quite inexplicable that you could engage such an uncivil man to the staff here at Mallowan Hall. Surely a good chauffeur isn't that difficult to find."

"As it happens, Mrs. Bright, Joshua Bradford was recommended to me by Mr. Mallowan himself. Apparently, he is an old school chum of Mr. Max's brother and is quite brilliant with engines. He worked on aeroplanes and lorries during the war."

"So he did." She nearly strangled on the syllables, then went on smoothly. "Well, that explains his lack of concern for the security of his position."

Dobble swallowed a smug comment. He'd already realized that Joshua Bradford was a law unto himself: leave him be to do his work—at which he was remarkably superior—and all would go on without incident. The man didn't even seem inclined to eat his meals with the rest of the staff, and he certainly hadn't made any egregious requests. He hadn't made any requests at all, despite the fact that the old groom's apartment in the barn turned garage was extremely spartan. The man simply wanted to be left alone.

"And then there's Stanley," said Mrs. Bright.

She said nothing more.

She didn't need to.

And Dobble certainly didn't want to put into words any of the whirlwind of thoughts in his head.

Before either of them could speak again, the roar of a motorcar and a spew of gravel in the drive indicated the return of Constable Greensticks. Dobble looked at Mrs. Bright, and they both rose from where they were sitting in her parlour.

"Once more unto the breach," she muttered and, squaring her shoulders, left the room.

As it turned out, Phyllida didn't need to show the constable and the inspector (who'd arrived in his own motorcar on the heels of Greensticks's vehement arrival—albeit far more sedately) to the orchard. Bradford took it upon himself to do so, and she was privately grateful enough that she put up only a token argument.

She could have dragged her feet going down to speak to Mrs. Puffley, but that would have been cowardice—a condition unbecoming to someone of her constitution and status. So she braced herself and entered the kitchen, prepared for any and all results—including flying rolling pins, wailing sobs, and the very real possibility of being left without a cook. The latter thought left her feeling mildly nauseated, for Phyllida did not do well in the kitchen.

"Oh, Mrs. Bright, did you find that Rebecca? Did you give her a good talking-to? I hope she's not crying in a corner over it, because we've got work to do." The cook's greeting was relatively calm, all things considered. Although she did have a cleaver in her hand and was using it with harsh, rapid strokes to behead a row of slender gray fish.

Molly was at a different side of the long worktable, and she was peeling potatoes and turnips. She looked up with interest and perhaps a little glee. There was always at least some rivalry between the maids—at least when it came to who was the current recipient of reprimand or criticism from the cook.

"I did find Rebecca." Phyllida had done this more than once during the war and knew it was best to get it over with quickly. "Mrs. Puffley, Molly . . . I'm sorry to bear such bad news, but Rebecca is . . . She's dead. I found her in the orchard."

"She's . . . *dead?*" Puffley froze and looked up at her, cleaver in midair. "She can't be dead. I need her in the kitchen. Why, there's the hare soup to finish, and . . . and . . . surely not, Mrs. Bright. Why . . . that's impossible." Her eyes were filled with hope and fear. "It can't be so."

"It's the truth, I'm sorry to say, Harriet." Phyllida thought it permissible to use the cook's familiar name in this situation. She pointed to a hardback chair in a corner of the kitchen. "Now, just sit for a moment, and then we'll decide how to proceed. A cup of tea"—with a splash of whisky perhaps—"will brace you up."

Just then, Ginny appeared in the doorway, responding to the bell Phyllida had rung for all the servants before stepping into the kitchen.

"I must speak to all of you," she told the parlourmaid. "But it'll wait until the others arrive. In the meantime, you can go into the stillroom and find the peach preserves, along with the cherry cordial." The latter would work just fine for Mrs. Puffley's tea.

Despite the fact that Ginny was head parlourmaid and such a request normally fell on someone far below her station, she didn't dare even flicker an eyelash.

In an effort to alleviate some of the cook's anxiousness while waiting for the others, Phyllida said to her, "Mrs. Agatha has de-

cided that a cold tray with tea and coffee and perhaps hot chocolate, if you're feeling up to it, will do for tea. A simple plough-
man's spread and whatever scone or biscuits you have on hand."
That put her in mind of the lovely lemon teacake the Millers had
brought her, and she decided to add that to the offering, as well.
She certainly didn't need to eat the dratted thing all herself . . .
though it would have been a welcome treat after such a harrow-
ing day.

Phyllida's resolve trembled a bit at the thought of how harrow-
ing the day had actually been—with it not even being five o'clock
yet and with far too many hours left in it—and she firmly shored
herself up. As she'd told Puffley, there would be time for weakness later. That time was not now.

At that moment, the thudding of footsteps down the stairs and
in the corridor indicated that the remainder of the staff was responding to her summons. She intended to give them all the information at once—unlike this morning—and to make some
recommendations as to how to proceed.

In the corner, Mrs. Puffley was nearly catatonic. Phyllida had
never seen the woman simply stop moving until now. She sat in the
chair, her normally flushed face ashen, her strong hands hanging
uselessly at her sides. Even her curling hair was drooping.

Thus, instead of asking the cook to move into the servants' dining room, Phyllida had all the staff crowd into the kitchen, despite the strong odor of fish. Freddie, the under-footman, was
missing (she had a moment of terror that perhaps another one
had gone AWOL), and, of course, Amsi and Bradford were outside, but at least all her own maids were present to hear the upsetting news. Mrs. Budgely-Rhodes's maid and the three visiting
valets weren't here, either—presumably, they were upstairs, helping their masters and mistress freshen up for tea. Violet was also
absent, but she would hear the news directly from Mrs. Agatha.

Just as Phyllida was about to speak, there was a disturbance in
the corridor near the outside door. Before she could remark, two
figures stumbled into the kitchen.

Stumble was the only word to describe the movement of two

young men, one leaning heavily against the slighter one, both dressed in the identical livery of Mallowan Hall footmen. As they made their way into the room, they were greeted with gasps and cries.

"Stanley!" Even Phyllida couldn't hold back an exclamation of shock and relief. "Whatever has happened to you?"

It was indeed the missing footman—no longer missing, but certainly not having completely avoided some violent mishap. Still, he was alive and upright with the help of Freddie, and that gave Phyllida a measure of relief.

He had cuts and scratches all over his face, and one of his hands was bloodied and already bruising. There were more blood-stains on his livery, and one of his boots was missing. Even from where she stood, Phyllida could see that this ankle was hugely swollen.

"Mrs. Bright," he said and immediately attempted to stand on his own—attempted being a valiant effort, for he swayed on his one good foot, and then his knee buckled. He collapsed, groaning with pain, against Freddie, who was nearly overset by the heavy weight.

"Where have you been, and what . . . ? Benita! Ice from the ice-house immediately, if you please, and, Mary, find the low stool from the dining room. Molly, fetch the wintergreen pomade from the stillroom." She turned back to Stanley, who was starting to speak. "No, no, save your story until Mr. Dobble arrives so you don't have to give it twice. Ginny, go upstairs and fetch Mr. Dobble immediately."

Within ten minutes, Stanley had his foot propped up on a stool, the twisted ankle bandaged tightly, and a package of crushed ice held against the worst of his facial injuries. Ginny eyed Molly darkly as the latter fussed over the footman, dabbing at cuts and scratches with rags and warm water she had fetched from the sink, until Phyllida interceded and took over the work herself. She absolutely did not have the time or energy to deal with competition between the maids.

Mr. Dobble arrived at that moment, and he took one look at

the scene, then met Phyllida's eyes. "I see you've told Mrs. Puffley. And what is the meaning of all this?" This last comment was directed to Stanley. "What have you done to your uniform—"

"One person at a time," Phyllida interrupted in a voice even she had to admit sounded ready to crack. "First, Mr. Dobble, if I may . . . the staff must be advised of the latest developments." She gave him a meaningful glance, and to her surprise, he quieted and gave her a deferential look.

"Yes, of course, Mrs. Bright. Do go on."

Phyllida told them about Rebecca, bluntly and calmly. The reactions were as suspected—gasps and cries, horrified wide eyes, and nervous looks about.

"Therefore," she went on as pragmatically as possible, "and especially in light of whatever has happened to Stanley—which we will get to in a moment," she said to forestall any questions or narratives that might derail the conversation. "Everyone will work in pairs for the time being. I don't believe anyone is in danger, but in order to ensure the safety of us all, no one is to go about any business or conduct any task alone until . . . until the situation has been resolved. Is that understood?"

Nine heads, all with their eyes fixed on her, bowed in acquiescence, then looked back up at her.

"But, Mrs. Bright," said Benita in a quavery voice, "how do we know no one is in danger? Who would have ever thought Rebecca was in danger?"

Phyllida glanced at Mr. Dobble, whose face was as implacable as that of a carved bust, and knew she was on her own. And before she knew it, she was speaking something that had only been in the back of her mind until now . . . but that somehow seemed to be the truth.

"It's my belief that Rebecca was murdered because she knew something that put the killer in danger. And I am fairly certain it has something to do with when she worked at Bunder House, before she came here three months ago. As none of you have worked at Bunder House, I feel confident in saying that you're not in any danger."

She studiously avoided looking at the battered, discomposed Stanley. She could only imagine his story, but that would come in a few moments.

"And there's one more thing," she said. "None of the maids are to be answering a call from Mr. Sloup in the Pines Room. Freddie, you'll have to see to anything he requires—or have his valet bring up the trays and whatnot. Is that understood?"

When Lizzie and Bess nodded vehemently, exchanging relieved glances, Phyllida knew her suspicions had been well founded. She hoped the arse hadn't badly accosted either of them before now. If she hadn't been distracted by the murders, she would have said something sooner, drat it.

"Now, everyone, back to work. Freddie, you'll be setting up tea in the music room immediately, as Mr. Dobble and I have other things to which we must attend. I shall serve, of course, but you see to it being ready. Are you quite all right?" The young man still seemed a bit out of breath from whatever he'd done to help Stanley, but he nodded stoutly.

"Yes, ma'am," he said.

"Mrs. Puffley," Phyllida said when the maids and the underfootman had been dismissed to do their chores, "I believe the fish requires your immediate attention."

The cook blinked, but Phyllida's words seemed to rouse her. "Yes . . . yes, I see. But how—"

"I'll procure another kitchen maid tomorrow," Phyllida said briskly. "But for now, you'll make do with Molly and Benita, and Lizzie and Bess can help with some of it, too, if necessary. I have the greatest of confidence that you'll sail through this tragic day, Mrs. Puffley."

The other woman blinked reddened eyes, but she nodded. "Poor mite," she said, obviously speaking of Rebecca. "I'd like to get my hands on the man who did such a horrible thing." She flexed her fingers as she reached for the cleaver, her voice strong and hard, and Phyllida knew that dinner would be ready on time, after all.

"I shall be back for the tea trays shortly. Molly, make certain everything is ready, and then you'll help Freddie bring them up-stairs for me. Mr. Dobble, shall we speak with Stanley in your closet?" Phyllida's logical suggestion did not invite argument from the butler, but she was mildly surprised that he didn't even give her a look for her presumption—or that he didn't question why she should even be present, with the footman being his charge and not hers. He must be even more agitated than he let on.

However, she prudently allowed Mr. Dobble to take the lead in the interview once the three of them were settled in the butler's pantry—which wasn't a pantry at all, but a surprisingly spacious office. Although it wasn't as comfortable as Phyllida's own sitting room (in her opinion, anyway), there was a handsome desk and several chairs, along with a worktable, where Mr. Dobble might do repairs to his master's clothing or buff and shine his shoes since Mr. Max didn't keep a valet. A thick crimson, navy, and cream rug, which Phyllida privately coveted, lay over the floor.

"Fighting, disappearing, your livery is an *abomination* . . . Tell me why I shouldn't dismiss you out of hand, Stanley," said Mr. Dobble in a cold, controlled voice that reminded Phyllida just how superior of a butler he was.

"I'm sorry, sir, ma'am—I'm so terribly sorry," Stanley said, speaking from behind the packet of ice he held to his eye. "I didn't mean to—I saw them reporters loitering about, they were, and the sneaky bas—a sneaky lot they were, trying to come close enough to peep in the window, and so I chased after 'em to get 'em to go away. I went after them—there was three of 'em—out past the far south wall, and just as I was turning to come back heres, another come out of the woods and shouted at me about how I din't know nothing about nothing."

Phyllida considered it yet another personal victory that she didn't even wince at the jumble of his grammar, although inside she couldn't help but count the double negatives and edit his poor syntax.

"O' course I couldn't let that go by—the dirty snake—and so I asked him whatever he meant by that, and he said that no one knew anything about Charles Waring but hisself, and he wanted to know what happened to the bloke when he was up to the big house. So he was baiting me, he was, Mr. Dobble, and I couldn't let that go by, and them reporters were trespassing all over Mallowan Hall, and—"

"And so what did you tell him about Mr. Waring?" Phyllida ventured into the shambles of his narrative.

"Why, I told him the bloke was a reporter from the *Times* and he was dead, stabbed in the throat—and then the man—I don't even know if he was a reporter, the one I was talking to—and he looked real shocked, like, and then he kinda laughed at me real strange—like he was shocked but trying not to show it, and he said Charles Waring warn't from the *Times*, but he was a lot smarter than that, and whoever killed him was gonna pay for it, he was. Crazy talk like that. I didn't really understand all what he was saying." Stanley adjusted the dripping packet so that it revealed his puffed-up eye, and covered the bruise on his cheek. "He got all worked up, he did, and was carrying on somethin' awful. Like it was *my* doing."

"This person knew Mr. Waring?" Phyllida said.

"Yes, ma'am. He said as how he was his mate and they druv up here together, they did."

Phyllida was on the trail. "Did he say *why* they came up here to Mallowan Hall? Where is this person now? And whom did you fight?"

"More importantly, where the devil have you been for three hours?" demanded Mr. Dobble, leaning forward with a hard glint in his eyes, his hands splayed on the desk, as if he were about to crawl across and seize the footman by his soiled livery. "Surely this conversation took less than half an hour."

And just as surely, Phyllida thought exasperatedly, Mr. Dobble didn't have the least bit of interest in investigating Mr. Waring's killer, even when there was highly relevant and interesting information coming out.

"But I run after those reporters far, sir, all the way to Beaming Berry Hill," Stanley protested—but not very stridently. He knew better than to counter the butler. Obviously deciding that it was prudent (and perhaps easier) to convince the female, he looked at Phyllida as he continued.

"I don't know where he is now, Mrs. Bright. And he didn't tell me his name, but he seemed like he warn't going to go anywheres until he found out who killed his friend." The battered footman spoke so earnestly, she got the distinct impression he was trying to get her on his side.

"Did you fight him, Stanley?"

"No, ma'am. We finished going at each other—shouting we were, and a little pushing but no fists—and then I went off to come back to the house before I lost my post, and then I found one of those other reporters I'd run off sneaking back up to the house again! Why, I'd had enough of that, and so I went at him pretty good. Pardon me, ma'am, but that was with my fists on that time."

"I didn't start it, though, Mr. Dobble, sir," Stanley said quickly. "I went after him to chase him off again, and he pushed me, and then I did the same, and next thing I knew, he took a swing! Right there, when he was trespassing all over Mr. Mallowan's property, the bloke took a swing at *me*. Well, I let 'im have it good, didn't I? And finally, he knew I meant business and he wasn't getting past me to the house again."

"Well, that all explains the blood on your livery," said the butler with a curl of his lip, "but it still doesn't explain your absence for three hours. If you'd been brawling for that long, you'd be . . . well, you'd be lying in a field somewhere."

"Yes, sir, of course. But when I finally run that sneak off the last time—he was bloodied up worse than me, he was," Stanley said in an echo of what every man said after a physical altercation. "I saw the sun and realized I had to get back before you missed me, sir, and then I started running, and that's when I did this." He gestured to his swollen ankle. "Stepped right in a rabbit hole, there, and went down flat on me face. Thought I broke it at first, sir, and then I knew I was in a fair sight of trouble, as a footman has to be able to walk, don't he?"

Stanley's attempt at humor didn't go over with Mr. Dobble.

Fortunately for him, he recognized this almost immediately and went on with his belabored tale. "But then I realized I just twisted it bad, and at least that'll heal in a bit. But, sir, I come back as quickly as I could, but it's like hel—uh, I mean, it's like burning flames trying to walk on it, and so I couldn't go very fast or very far without stopping to rest. I even found a walking stick, but that didn't help me none on the uneven ground and me not having me right foot to put any weight on.

"Finally, I got close enough to see Freddie, and I hollered for him, and he come and helped me the rest of the way, then, sir, and I'm so very sorry. I hope you'll see to not—not sacking me over this." His voice wavered a little.

"As you said, a footman who can't walk is of no bloody use to me," snapped Mr. Dobble. "And I don't see you putting a bit of weight on that foot for at least a fortnight."

Stanley's Adam's apple bobbed nervously, and he looked down. "Yes, sir."

"Go get yourself cleaned up. You can sit on a stool and polish silver, or do whatever it is Mrs. Puffley wants from you, until I figure out what to do with you. I want you in that kitchen in fifteen minutes. And there will be absolutely no flirting with the maids."

"Yes, sir," replied the young man morosely.

"There's a walking stick," added Mr. Dobble, jerking his thumb to a closet in the corner. "Use it."

Phyllida exchanged glances with the butler and saw that he didn't intend to send Stanley on his way—at least, not tonight. But she understood and appreciated his tactics and therefore said nothing. One had to be fair and yet firm with the staff, or they would take advantage. Instead, she went with the footman as he hobbled out, subdued and eyes downcast.

"What did Mr. Waring's mate look like?" she asked. "Did you notice anything about him?" She fully intended to pass the information along to the inspector or constable but wanted it for herself, as well.

"He had yellow hair, he did, and he warn't very tall. Maybe like you, ma'am," said the much taller footman. "He were dressed like a toff, but he didn't talk much like one, and he wore a green plaid Homburg."

"And how old would you say he was? Did he have a mustache?"

"He were maybe almost thirty, and he's a beard, too."

She nodded to herself. That should be enough. "All right, then, Stanley. You heard Mr. Dobble. Get yourself cleaned up and report to Mrs. Puffley."

CHAPTER 18

*P*HYLLIDA COULD EASILY HAVE ASSIGNED FREDDIE OR EVEN GINNY TO serve tea to the Mallowans and their guests in the music room, but she wasn't about to relinquish an opportunity to observe the array of her suspects. Most of them, anyway.

Especially now that there was a second murder and any of them could be the culprit. She'd already determined the group had returned from their excursion to the local castle ruins in plenty of time for one of them to slip away and cosh poor Rebecca in the orchard. (Although she was remaining objective, Phyllida was still hoping the facts would bear out that Tuddy Sloup was the villain.)

As she moved about the music room, pushing the rolling teacart, pouring tea, and offering the tray of cheese, cold slices of ham and beef, and triangles of thinly sliced bread, Phyllida listened and observed.

To her surprise and disappointment, there was very little discussion about the fact that a kitchen maid who had helped make the meals of which all of them had partaken was found brutally beaten to death. Although Phyllida supposed she shouldn't be surprised, for servants were meant to do and not to be seen, heard, or otherwise considered on a regular basis. This was how servants knew so much about the private goings-on in their employers' lives—the upper class often forgot they were around and rarely remembered to censor themselves, a fact that Phyllida intended to exploit as much as possible during this investigation.

And since the second death had happened not inside the house but out on the grounds, perhaps the lack of proximity contributed to their seemingly careless attitude.

"A kitchen maid?" said Mrs. Devine, patting her swath of shiny black hair. "Why, how horrendous."

And that was nearly all that was said on the subject matter.

"I simply don't understand why we must remain here," said Mrs. Budgely-Rhodes as she dumped four lumps of sugar into her tea. She stirred violently, her spoon clinking, cup vibrating, tea sloshing onto the saucer and table. It would leave watermarks for certain. "No one even knew that Charles Waring person. How could the authorities think one of us had something to do with his death? Odell, can't you make a call or something? Don't you know someone at Scotland Yard?"

"Now, darling, you know these things take time," replied her husband absently. He was applying himself most readily to a thick stack of ham and cheese, using most of the pot of spiced mustard to lubricate its way into his mouth. Apparently, touring a castle ruin gave stocky playwrights an appetite.

"I, for one, don't mind," said Mrs. Hartford in her low, throaty voice. She looked very elegant, sleek, and cool—rather a miracle, considering they'd all been traipsing and hiking about hillocks, crumbling staircases, and across a dry moat for much of the day. "It's absolutely lovely here at Mallowan Hall, Max and Agatha. You've found a most restful, beautiful estate."

Except when there are murders occurring daily, Phyllida thought. *But perhaps there's the added benefit of giving someone an opportunity to carry on with an affair . . . ?*

She glanced at Mr. Devine, whose sinfully good looks would certainly be enough for any woman to be interested in prolonging proximity to him, and noticed a little smile quirking his sensual lips . . . as if he were silently agreeing with Mrs. Hartford.

The two of them were sitting on separate sofas, back-to-back . . . and as Phyllida came around with the tray of cream, sugar, and thin slices of lemon, she noticed Mrs. Hartford tilt her head back just a little . . . just enough to gently brush against Mr. Devine's arm, which rested along the top of his sofa—once, twice—making it clear, at least to Phyllida, that the caress was intentional. As Mr. Devine didn't move his arm away, as one might politely do if one's personal space was accidentally encroached upon, she took that as confirmation that Agatha's instincts were correct.

So, that brought to bear the question, Did Mrs. Devine or Mr. Hartford know that their spouses were philandering together?

But more relevant to Phyllida's problem, Had Charles Waring known? Could he have tried to blackmail one of the four—and been silenced for his trouble?

For some marriages, particularly in the upper classes, cheating and infidelity were tolerated and even expected, since many unions were arranged in order to protect family lineage or to serve financial ends. But for just as many couples, philandering could be a horrific scandal—or reason for divorce, which in itself would be highly scandalous.

It was a shaky possibility but a motive nonetheless. People had killed for far less than to protect a reputation, Phyllida knew. Particularly if a divorce would mean a severe change in one's financial situation or social status . . .

She watched Mrs. Devine to see whether she seemed to take any notice of the interactions between her husband and Mrs. Hartford. Mr. Budgely-Rhodes was lighting a cigarette, and Mrs. Devine leaned forward with her own, asking for a light, as well—seemingly unaware that her husband was accepting quite public caresses from another woman. She settled back into her seat, gracefully exhaling a stream of smoke as she laughed over something Mrs. Budgely-Rhodes had said.

"Lemon teacake, Mr. Sloup?" Phyllida asked, offering a small platter with slices of the sweet bread the Millers had brought for her.

He looked up at her. His expression sharpened, and his eyes flared with interest. "Never say I'd pass up something so delectable," he replied, his gaze lingering on Phyllida. "Oh, and there's teacake, as well? How lucky can a chap be in one day?"

He gave a low chuckle and made certain to brush his fingers

over Phyllida's hand—despite the fact that it was nowhere near the slice of cake closest to him. "Now, where have you been hiding, you lovely thing? Been here more than a day and haven't set eyes on you till now, more's the pity." His voice was low, just for her ears, and he shifted so that his leg jutted out from the chair where he sat, effectively blocking her from moving past. It was a narrow space between his chair and the low table in front of him, and it would be difficult for her to turn around, encumbered as she was by the bulky tea cart.

"I've no need to hide," she replied smoothly, careful to keep her expression neutral, then looked over suddenly, as if noticing something. "Oh, yes, of course, Mrs. Mallowan. I'll fetch it right away," she said, pitching her voice to send it across the room. "Excuse me, Mr. Sloup."

"I think it's not quite so awful staying a few more days here with Max," said Mr. Sloup affably as Phyllida extricated herself from his vicinity—and not without difficulty, for he barely shifted his leg, and he made certain a hand skimmed up along the back of her calf, darting briefly up her skirt, as she moved past.

Mr. Sloup was fortunate that Phyllida was involved in a murder investigation and that he was her favored suspect (and therefore she felt it necessary to maintain at the very least civility between them), or she would have accidentally on purpose knocked the tea tray on his head. In any other household, that would be cause for serious reprimand or even dismissal, but Phyllida had no concerns over the security of her position at Mallowan Hall—even aside from the fact that Agatha would probably cheer her on if she put Mr. Sloup in his place.

However, it was more prudent to keep the peace, so to speak, with him in the event she needed to interview the lout in relation to the deaths of Mr. Waring and Rebecca. He seemed to be the sort of man who, given the chance, would brag about his villainous activities—thinking himself far too clever to get caught.

Her interactions with Tuddy Sloup had only confirmed the reason for her instant dislike of the man but sadly had given no motive for the murder of Charles Waring. Phyllida could think of several reasons *someone* might want to murder Tuddy Sloup, but, of course, that wasn't relevant to the current predicament.

Mrs. Agatha, who had obviously heard Phyllida's comment to her from across the room and had understood the reason for it, met her gaze . . . and then slid her look subtly toward Mr. Hartford.

Phyllida followed with her own eyes as she navigated the rolling tea cart around sofas, chairs, legs (both animate and inanimate) to the opposite side of the room. Poor Paul Hartford, the cuckolded husband, sat next to Mr. Grimson, the youngish recent widower, and appeared to be engrossed in conversation with him. But Mr. Hartford's hands were fisted tightly in his lap, and Phyllida saw the way his attention traveled to his animated wife, then to Mr. Devine, and then jittered back to his companion.

So it seemed Mr. Hartford knew—or at least strongly suspected— what his wife was doing with the theater-seeking Mr. Devine. Mr. Hartford's expression was one of pain and resignation, but Phyllida didn't recognize anger, violence, or even vengeance there . . . even when she rolled the cart closer and got a good look in his eyes.

"May I offer you more tea, Mr. Hartford? Or perhaps you'd prefer something a bit more bracing. Whisky or brandy? Mr. Grimson?"

Normally, spirits would be saved for predinner cocktails, but in light of the situation, Mr. Max had told Phyllida to be generous with the whisky, brandy, or sherry—whatever anyone cared for.

"Brandy for me—a large one," said Mr. Grimson in the same subdued manner he'd had every time Phyllida saw him. "And a match if you please." He certainly didn't seem to have the energy to be overcome by loathing or hatred for anyone, let alone have the grit to take up a pen and stab them or beat them to death.

"A whisky, neat, please. Thank you," replied Mr. Hartford as he fumbled a silver cigarette case from his coat pocket. "And a light for me, as well."

Hadn't Mrs. Agatha said that she believed Mrs. Hartford wasn't happy in her marriage? And that might be why she was finding affection and attention elsewhere? All indication from Mr. Hartford, however, was that he was unhappy and pained over his wife's infidelity. He didn't seem like a tyrant, just a bit worn down and resigned.

Phyllida shook her head as she poured the whisky from a heavy glass decanter. These interactions and relationships were interesting and enlightening in a psychological manner and in relation to the study of human nature—the sort of thing at which Poirot and Miss Marple excelled—but she didn't see how the affair between Mr. Devine and Mrs. Hartford was related to Mr. Waring's death. And Rebecca's demise made even less sense.

She served the spirits to Mr. Grimson and Mr. Hartford, then offered a tray of matches. Then she trundled the cart over to where Agatha, Mrs. Devine, and the Budgely-Rhodeses were sitting near the window.

". . . was such a lovely day," Mrs. Devine was saying to her hostess. "It was so very kind of Max to take us off and manage the lot of us all on his own." She smiled, and a glorious dimple appeared in her cheek, which made Phyllida want to smile, as well. "Of course, we couldn't all fit in one motorcar, but it was still a joyride to the castle. We made a sort of caravan."

"I'm so delighted you enjoyed yourself, considering everything else that has happened," Agatha said. "It's just so tragic. All of it." Her polite hostess smile faded, and she lifted her cup of tea to sip.

Phyllida could almost read her friend's mind: someone in this room was very likely a killer.

Someone who was genteelly sipping tea or swirling brandy or nibbling on biscuits or cheese had brutally murdered two people.

And neither Inspector Cork nor Phyllida Bright seemed any closer to determining who the culprit was.

CHAPTER 19

*P*HYLLIDA ADJUSTED HER HAT SO THAT IT SAT TILTED JUST SO OVER her right eye. It was a rakish, trilby-like confection dyed dark blue that looked quite well with her bright hair, if she did say so herself. Yellow daisies and thumbnail-size cornflowers made from silk were arranged in a cluster on one side, and there was a trio of airy blue feathers curling up next to them.

She caught up her handbag and gave a nod to Mr. Dobble. He looked as if he hadn't slept any better than she had—although Phyllida had made certain there was no physical evidence of her sleepless night, for bags under her eyes simply would not do. Then she marched out into the overcast morning.

The Mallowans' motorcar was waiting for her right at the base of the front steps—almost precisely where the gaggle of reporters had thronged yesterday. This morning there was no sign of any of them—at least not yet. But it was just half past eight, so there was plenty of time for them to congregate or, if Stanley were to be believed, lurk about in the wood.

Phyllida had almost hoped to see the reporters—and, among them, the blond, bearded man with the green plaid hat who claimed to be Charles Waring's friend. Instead, she would have to bear the company of Mr. Bradford as he drove her into Listleigh.

He was standing by the automobile, looking slightly smarter than he'd appeared yesterday—for today he seemed to have located a proper hat and coat. However, he wasn't wearing gloves, and she automatically adjusted her own spotless white ones, pulling them up over each wrist in turn, instead of making a comment about the lack of his hand coverings.

"Back seat all right, Mrs. Bright?" the chauffeur said in a pleasant, well-modulated tone as she approached. He had his hand on the rear door latch but hadn't opened the door yet.

Phyllida struggled internally for just a moment before responding, "Of course. Thank you, Mr. Bradford."

He opened the door, and she climbed in, then smoothed the lemon-colored skirt of one of her best frocks as she found her seat. It was a decidedly un-housekeeperish dress, for it was neither dark nor plain nor drab, but Phyllida didn't often dress as most housekeepers would. She certainly never wore an apron. And she particularly didn't dress like a matron when it was a day in the village or elsewhere away from her duties.

The dress was a soft, light calico of lemon yellow that should clash with the color of her hair—but not only did it not clash, it also looked quite well with her coloring. There were tiny white polka dots printed on it, and random ones had been enhanced with French knots, giving the fabric a bit of texture and interest. Over her shoulders she'd draped a dark blue sweater that matched her hat, and she was glad for it in the cool morning air.

Bradford was a good driver, she realized almost immediately— and with abject relief. Perhaps she would be all right sitting in the back seat of the vehicle, after all, even with the twists and turns down the narrow one-car road into Listleigh.

"Where to first, Mrs. Bright?"

"The Screaming Magpie, if you please," she told him.

He looked at her in the rearview mirror, lifting his single visible eyebrow. "A bit early for a pint, isn't it?"

She sneered at him. "Of course I'm not going for a pint. But I'm in need of a kitchen maid, as I'm certain you're aware, and it's the best place to sort one out on short notice. And aside from that, what I do in the village is not your concern, Mr. Bradford." It was only then that she recognized the silent laughter in the lone eye she could see in the mirror.

She looked away, tightening her hands over the top of her bag whilst imagining them going around his throat instead.

"No more dead bodies, then, Mrs. Bright?" he said after a moment of navigating around a horse-drawn wagon driven by the milkman.

"I should think two are plenty, don't you, Mr. Bradford?"

"They're two too many," he replied, and the expression in his eye was now sober. "And you've no idea who's done it?"

"Why would I have any idea?" she replied coolly. "I'm only the housekeeper. It's up to Scotland Yard to find the killer."

He scoffed. "Right. If you're not poking your nose around and telling those blokes what to do, I'm not driving a Daimler to a pub at nine in the morning."

Really, the man was abominably uncivil. How much longer until they got into the village and she could escape? She looked out the window. Through the tall hedges that made the road barely wide enough for one motorcar to pass through, she saw the sign for the crossroads at Merton Way.

Fiddle. Another ten or fifteen minutes until she could vacate the motorcar.

"For all I know, you could be the culprit," she replied waspishly, then immediately regretted showing her vexation. What was it about this man who made her speak without thinking?

"'S right," he said agreeably. "After all, I come on the scene at Mallowan Hall, and within hours, a man is stabbed and a woman is beaten to death. I'm tall enough and strong enough to do both. I'm brusque and rude, and I don't like to be bothered when I'm working."

It wasn't as if those very thoughts hadn't occurred to Phyllida. In fact, they had last night, whilst she tried to sleep—in vain—knowing that a killer must be somewhere in the house.

She had locked the door to her rooms for the first time since coming to Mallowan Hall and had informed Stilton and Rye that not only were they to rouse her immediately if anyone attempted to breach the doorway, but they should use their claws, teeth, and whatever other weapons were at their disposal to discourage the intruder, as well.

As she'd lain there, unable to sleep, all sorts of possibilities had rambled through her mind—including the very points Bradford had just made, along with another he'd neglected to mention: the fact that he knew some very specific details about the first death.

Stabbed in the neck, he'd said. *Not a pleasant way to go. Not easy to get it right into the carotid effectively. And takes a long while to bleed out.*

Not that it was a secret how Charles Waring had died . . . but the way he'd spoken so knowledgeably about the specifics stuck in her mind. And he *had* been acting strange, sneaking about, looking over his shoulder as he ducked into the garage. . . .

But in the end, Phyllida had reluctantly dismissed the idea that Bradford had done away with both Charles Waring and Rebecca McArdle. It was the expression on his face, the soft, anguished gasp he'd given when he saw the maid's body and knelt at her side.

His reaction had been genuine; she was certain of it.

Aside from that, there was another very practical reason he couldn't have done it. "All of that is certainly true," she said smoothly. "However, as disappointing as it might be, there's a simple reason you couldn't have done it."

"And what might that be?"

"Your shoes don't squeak, Mr. Bradford."

"My shoes?"

"That's correct. Aside from that, I'm fairly certain you haven't stepped foot inside Mallowan Hall—or at least, nowhere farther than the servants' dining room—since your arrival. Which would make it rather impossible for you to have wandered through the house and somehow stumbled upon the library where Charles Waring waited, unaware that he was about to meet his Maker."

"Unless he let me in and showed me to the library," the infuriating man pointed out. "And I stabbed him then. With a bloody fountain pen."

"Without your leaving a trace of mud or dirt on the floor?" she responded tartly. "Highly unlikely."

"I might have wiped my shoes. Or removed them."

She stifled a sigh. Now he was simply being contrary, and she knew the best way to respond to contrariness: ignore it.

They rode in silence for another few moments before he spoke again. "Squeaking shoes? Right, then, Mrs. Bright. Tell me again how you aren't poking your nose into this investigation. But first enlighten me on how you know the killer wears shoes that squeak."

She folded her lips closed. She did not want to get into details about how she knew that bit of information, for obvious reasons.

"You can leave me off at the Screaming Magpie, right there, Mr. Bradford," she said with relief as the car turned smoothly into the bottom of the main road that wove up through Listleigh. "I'll be only an hour here in town, I suspect, and I'm certain you have other things with which to occupy your time. Visiting a tailor perhaps? Or a barber?"

He made a noise that sounded very much like a snort, but Phyllida refused to acknowledge it.

Nonetheless, he did as she asked and eased the motorcar to a halt in front of the single pub in town. "An hour, you say?" he asked as he opened the door for her.

"Yes. I shall be back here by ten o'clock."

The first time she'd seen Listleigh, which was when she alighted from the train to take the position at Mallowan Hall, Phyllida had immediately felt at home. A stereotypical English village of the sort mentioned in *Historic Travel Inns of England,* Listleigh sported winding cobblestone streets, with many of the storefronts and other establishments built right up to the edge of the road. There were ivy-covered brick buildings, with splashes of color from flowerpots and from small gardens spilling with blooms contained only by spiked wrought-iron fences. Bicycle riders, horse-drawn wagons, pedestrians, delivery lorries, and motorcars shared the narrow streets, for there were few walkways. A tiny train station sat outside the little town, a half mile to the west

The Screaming Magpie was near the center of a village that barely stretched a square mile. There was an empty rectangular patch of lawn across from the public house, where the annual Beetroot and Chicken Foot Festival happened, and the bell tower of St. Wendreda's Church cast a long shadow over the green. Its red-brick rectory squatted behind it in the shade of elms and maples.

To the north were such establishments as the baker, a tea shop, and the chemist, and to the south was a haberdasher and a small general store, whose proprietor, Winnie Pankhurst, was in a constant battle with the chemist, Bartholomew Sprite, because he often carried items Miss Pankhurst claimed weren't pharmaceutical in nature and were encroaching on her general store business. Phyllida was always careful to purchase only medications and health and beauty aids from Mr. Sprite and other items from the general store. Word traveled quickly and thoroughly in small villages.

Not only was the Screaming Magpie the single pub in town, but it also had rooms to let for the few travelers who came in on holiday through Devonshire. That was the second reason Phyllida wanted to go inside the alehouse, for if Charles Waring's friend was staying in Listleigh, he'd surely be there.

The swinging painted sign hanging over the entrance was misleading, for the magpie wasn't screaming—it seemed to be sitting there quite calmly—and Phyllida wasn't convinced the creature even was a magpie.

The thick wooden door mounted with heavy black iron hinges had probably hung at the pub's entrance for more than a century—possibly two. Phyllida assumed that the long, scarred wooden bar counter had been present just as long—not to mention the smoke-blackened ceiling of plaster, the naked oak beams, and the dirt-covered wooden floor. At least, she assumed, there were planks beneath the dirt. If not, she didn't want to know.

Inside, the place was dim, and everything seemed limned with dark gold, for electric bulbs hadn't yet made their way to this particular establishment. It was probably just as well that the lighting wasn't bright and white, for Phyllida suspected she wouldn't want to actually see that many details.

A woman was behind the counter, and Phyllida was gratified to see that she appeared to be actually scrubbing its surface with what appeared to be a relatively clean cloth.

"Good morning, Guinevere," she said. It felt slightly odd to call the older woman by her familiar name, but no one in the village knew her by anything else.

Phyllida assumed the alewife was at least fifty, based on the deep grooves in her cheeks and the bit of sag to her jowls. She also had a square, masculine chin and surprisingly thin, dark eyebrows that arched over penetrating brown eyes. Over her curling gray hair, which was the color of iron and cut short so she didn't have to pin it up, she wore a poor excuse for a mobcap. It covered less than a cupped hand's worth of her head and sagged in the back like a sopping French beret.

Her apron was made from heavy cream linen striped with navy, and beneath she wore a man's work shirt and trousers. She had a lean, spare figure of average height, and her hands were slender and delicate in shape and form but had acquired numerous scars over the years. Phyllida didn't look too closely at the woman's fingers, for fear of observing the amount of dirt that might be living under their nails.

If Phyllida was a bit tentative in her greeting to the other woman, it was to be expected, for the wildly ranging, volatile temperament of the Screaming Magpie's owner was the stuff of legend in Listleigh.

She had even seen that fact noted in *Historic Travel Inns of England* (which she'd helpfully pointed out to Inspector Cork): *The Screaming Magpie in Listleigh is known for its brilliant nut-brown ale and rich dark brown bread, best served with a sharp cheddar made at the monger's shop down the street. But Traveler beware of the Magpie's proprietress, for if she doesn't take a liking to you, you'll just as likely be wearing the ale as drinking it.*

"Well, Mrs. Bright, you're here right early. Hope yourn't expectin' me to stand on ceremony for ye this morning—murders or no murders. Ain't got no bleedin' time for gossip. And I ain't ready to pull no ale yet, neither, because I ain't done cleaning the place."

"Of course not," Phyllida replied smartly. It didn't even occur to her to be amazed at how quickly the news of a second death had made its way here—it had, after all, been overnight, which was a fair eternity in village gossip. "No ceremony or ale necessary. I'm in search of two things—the loan of a kitchen maid and the identity of a visitor who might be staying here or who at least was likely in here yesterday."

Guinevere stopped what she was doing and planted a fist on her hip. "And you expect I know everyone who was in here yesterday? Was hopping all day meself and had to get me own help in here, with all them people filling me tables. Too many of 'em." She scowled. "Murder brings 'em in every time. No wonder that Mrs. Christie lady writes about killers and poisons and the lot."

"Right." Phyllida gave her a soothing smile. "I suppose you were terribly busy yesterday with all those reporters stopping in here for a pint and a meal."

"Didn't even have time for me afternoon rosary," Guinevere said, her dark brows snapping together. "Put me off, it did. Gonna have to say two of them today. And didn't even have time to use the outhouse until Kimmie got here to help pull the pints and slice the bread. Vernon in the kitchen was rowing with Teddy, and he couldn't help. Hadda roll two new casks in last night, I did."

Phyllida wasn't certain whether to sympathize or to congratulate the woman on the influx of customers. She suspected the latter option would be a mistake, but most business owners would be delighted with a huge rush of business. Instead, she opted to go down her own path.

"I'm in need of someone like Kimmie to help out up at Mallowan Hall until I can hire a new kitchen maid. Do—"

"You can't have Kimmie," snarled Guinevere. "Don't think you can waltz in here and take me help." She scowled again and began to scrub the counter once more.

"Of course not," Phyllida replied stoutly. "I wouldn't dream of it. But—"

"There ain't no one else looking for work, 'cept Mrs. Barkley's daughter, just come back from working for Lord Tatterling. Can't say whether she'd be worth her salt in the kitchen. Scrawny little thing, and that's why I ain't having her in here. Couldn't lift a cask o' ale if she tried. But you could ask. And then there's Miss

Pankhurst's sister, just come back from a visit to their auntie's lying-in. Mouthy thing, she is, but I wager Mrs. Puffley wouldn't take none of her guff."

"Thank you for the sug—"

"And then there's Opal Stamm. She's just turned thirteen, and her mama said as how she's looking for work, and she's wantin' to get her out from underfoot at home, where she won't have to feed her. Might not trust her wiv a knife, but she can do other things. That's Mrs. Stamm's girl, down the way, round the bend from the butcher, house with the blue shutters. You'll know it's the right one from all the brats squalling. She's got eight o' her own, and her oldest just had one more o' hers."

"Well," said Phyllida, "all of those sound very promising. Thank you very much." She hesitated; then, despite the possibility of setting Guinevere off into another rant, she plunged in again. "There's a man in town. Blond, about thirty, has a beard and wears a green plaid Homburg hat. I'd like to speak with him, and I know how busy you've been in here, but I thought perhaps if you happened to see him—"

She jumped a little when Guinevere slammed a palm down onto the counter and glared across at her. "And now, what you want the likes of *him* for? Uncivil prat, he is, and I'd toss him out on his arse if he weren't paying for two rooms upstairs." She jerked a thumb toward the steps that led to the rooms for let.

"I just need to ask him a question." *Or two*, Phyllida amended silently. "What's his name? Do you know where he might be at the moment?"

"Eugene Mustard's what he calls himself. Unlikely name, if you ask me," said the woman with one of her own. "Mustard. Who ever heard of a family named after the little seeds in the Bible?"

"I can't say I have," replied Phyllida, trying to keep the peace, because she needed answers to her questions. "Is he still abed?"

"How the blazes would I know? Think I go up there and poke around my customers' rooms every morning and evening?" Guinevere's curls vibrated with indignation.

"Certainly not," Phyllida said. "Well, I suppose I'll be on my way for now. I'd appreciate it if you wouldn't happen to mention to Mr. Mustard or anyone else that I was looking for him."

The other woman gave her a skeptical look. "You would, eh? Got secrets of your own, do you? No surprise there, with hair and a figure like *that*. Probably got lots o' secrets, you." She leaned across the counter, nodding. "I know your type."

"I'll stop in a bit later to see if Mr. Mustard has returned," Phyllida said and quickly made her escape before the alewife started asking more questions. She didn't want to spook Eugene Mustard away before she had the chance to talk to him—she suspected he wouldn't be terribly enthusiastic about submitting to her interrogations—and she certainly didn't want to risk having a conversation in which Guinevere started dissecting and surmising about her own background.

Despite the overcast day, it was refreshing to be outside the dim, smoky public house. It was mild enough that Phyllida could remove the sweater from her shoulders, and she tucked it into her handbag as she made her way to the Stamm household. Of the options Guinevere had listed, Opal Stamm seemed the most promising, for if she worked out, she could possibly become a permanent member of the staff. Benita would be delighted to move up to second kitchen maid, and the new girl could take over the scullery duties.

Less than thirty minutes later, Phyllida had satisfactorily concluded her business with Opal and her mother. She had to admit she was rather surprised that Mrs. Stamm didn't have the least bit of hesitation about sending her daughter off to work in a manor house that had had two murders in one day and where the mistress knew all about poisons.

Phyllida had made arrangements for the girl to ride back to Mallowan Hall with her and Bradford when they left from the pub at ten o'clock.

As she'd hoped, Phyllida had a short while before the meeting time—and even if she was later than the planned ten o'clock appointment, Bradford would have no choice but to wait for her.

For some reason, that made her feel less rushed and even a bit complacent.

She turned down a very narrow street that was hardly more than an alleyway and came out on the other side to a winding road and a sign that read DR. BHATT, GENERAL PHYSICIAN.

A little bell jangled above when the maid let her in. "Good morning, ma'am."

"Good morning. I'd like to speak with Dr. Bhatt if he's available. I'm Mrs. Bright, from up at Mallowan Hall."

The maid, dressed neatly in a crisp navy frock with a white muslin apron, of which Phyllida heartily approved, disappeared into a back chamber. Moments later, the door opened, and the maid gestured her through.

Dr. Bhatt rose from behind his desk. "Mrs. Bright, how nice to see you again. I hope you're feeling all right," he said in his precise accent and beamed at her. "Please, have a seat."

Phyllida was pleased to see that the physician's office was just as neat and organized as his personal grooming, and this gave her confidence in his efficacy as a man of medicine. As Poirot would say, order and method, and the doctor had both in spades when it came to his workspace, his clothing, and his lush mustache.

"Thank you," she said and took a seat on the upholstered chair across from his desk. His mustache really was a splendid bit of facial hair. If there was indeed a talkie made from a Poirot mystery, perhaps the producers could utilize Dr. Bhatt's mustache for inspiration.

"What can I do for you, Mrs. Bright? I hope you're not feeling ill or out of sorts."

"Not at all. I'm healthy as an ox and always have been. I'm here because I wanted to ask you a question about Mr. Waring."

"I see." Dr. Bhatt settled back in his chair, tenting his fingers together. A gleam in his eyes indicated he was more than happy to discuss the situation.

"You examined the body. Could you tell whether he'd been stabbed from the front or the back?"

His mustache stretched in a wide smile. "So that you can determine whether the killer was left-handed or right-handed, no, Mrs. Bright?"

She bowed her head modestly, but not before allowing him to see the gleam of appreciation in her eyes.

"The injury was from behind, which would leave one to believe the murderer used his right hand. Indeed, I mentioned that bit of information to the inspector late yesterday." Then the curve of his mustache flattened. "And I'm so sorry about the poor little maid. Rebecca was her name? You were the one to find her, as well?"

Phyllida nodded. She had seen the physician's motorcar parked in front of Mallowan Hall and was aware he'd been called in to file the death certificate, just as he'd been that morning for Mr. Waring. "Whoever did such a thing to her is a very evil person, and I'm asking these questions because I want to help find out who that person is."

"An ambition which I wholly support," replied Dr. Bhatt. "And if it helps, Mrs. Bright, it's my opinion that the person who bludgeoned Rebecca to death was also right-handed."

Unfortunately, that was not what she'd hoped to learn. There were far more right-handed people than left-handed, which meant it was possible there were two different killers lurking about Mallowan Hall.

"Do you have any idea what was used to . . . to do that to her?" she asked.

"It was a large stick—a branch, really. Mr. Bradford . . . Is that his name? The chauffeur? He found it flung not far from where the girl expired. Blood on it, of course."

"And so he just used whatever was convenient," she murmured. "A nearby branch. Just as in the library, he used the fountain pen. There were other, more lethal potential weapons in the room— an envelope cutter and a marble paperweight, both on the desk." She reached over and plucked up a fountain pen from its holder, then examined the sharp metal nib. It was dangerous looking, certainly, but not an item one would aspire to use as a murder weapon. "Such an imprecise way to kill someone. The killer must have been very fortunate to stab him in exactly the right spot with only one blow."

"Indeed," replied Dr. Bhatt. "I was thinking the very same thing. And that these appear to be killings that were unplanned, possibly made in a moment of rage or some other high emotion."

Poirot couldn't have said it any better. *It's about the psychology of the killer.*

"But it was only the one blow to Mr. Waring, was it not?" she asked. And when Dr. Bhatt nodded his assent, she went on. "While poor Rebecca was . . . was beaten."

"Yes, Mrs. Bright. She took several blows to her head. Three or four at least."

Phyllida straightened in her chair, for a thought had just occurred to her. Such an elementary consideration that she hadn't spent any time thinking over. "Blood . . . Of course, there would have been blood on the person who beat her, wouldn't there?"

"Most assuredly some," replied the doctor. "Little droplets, perhaps some streaks and splashes. But nothing like what would have sprayed onto whoever stabbed Charles Waring in the neck," he said almost cheerfully. "Once punctured, the carotid would have pumped everywhere."

"Of course. And so there would be blood on his clothing," she said.

"Undoubtedly."

"Was there anything else interesting or unusual that you noticed about Mr. Waring or Rebecca?"

"As it turned out, Mr. Waring seemed to have had quite a lot to drink before he was killed, which might have contributed to the relative ease with which the murderer was able to stab him. I could smell it on him, and a blood test agreed with my surmise. Thus, he would have been less able to defend himself against the attack, and since the killer came from behind, if Waring was very drunk—which he appeared to be—it would have been far less imprecise to puncture the carotid with one movement."

"All right, then. Thank you very much, Dr. Bhatt. I appreciate your forthrightness." Phyllida rose to take her leave.

He stood, as well. "There was one other thing I noticed. Perhaps it's relevant, perhaps not."

"What was that?"

"Mr. Waring had a bit of lipstick on his collar. Just here." Dr. Bhatt touched the left side of his neck.

"Well, that's quite interesting," Phyllida said, cocking her head. Who on earth would that be from? One of the Mallowans' guests? Surely not, but . . . why not? "What color was the lipstick?"

He blinked. "Er . . . red."

"What sort of red?"

"The . . . uh . . . Isn't red simply red?"

"Of course not. There are many different shades of red—and knowing which it was might assist in determining who was wearing the lipstick." When he continued to appear confused, she said, "Was it the sort of red like a claret or the red of a rose or like a poppy? Like a ruby or an apple or a dark plum?"

He smiled wanly. "I'm not certain, Mrs. Bright. It just looked red to me."

She hid her disappointment with his lack of order and method and smiled. "Very well, then, Dr. Bhatt. I think it's very important that Mr. Waring was apparently with a woman sometime after dinner and before he was killed."

"Precisely my thought. I wonder who it might have been." Now that they were past the question of shades of red, his eyes danced with interest once more.

"Thank you again for all the information."

"It was quite nice to see you again, Mrs. Bright. I do hope that you'll feel free to contact me for any future problems or questions," he said as he gestured for her to precede him through the doorway. "I only hope that it won't involve any more murders— and might, as a far more pleasant alternative, include a cup of tea at the café."

Phyllida smiled at him and was just about to reply in the affirmative when she heard a low squeak. She stopped, and he nearly bumped into her. There was another quiet, almost imperceptible creak with his movement.

"Your shoes," she said. "They squeak."

"Egh, yes. Well, one of them does." He appeared more than a

little embarrassed. "It's quite annoying and rather disconcerting to be accompanied by the noise. As quiet as it is, it's still not what one wants to hear when one is consulting with a physician. I've been meaning to take them over to Mr. Sanders to fix. The sole is coming just a bit loose from the upper."

"Right," Phyllida replied. "Mr. Sanders will fix it up, I'm certain."

"I promise I shall wear my other shoes when we meet at the tea shop," he said with a smile. "I rarely wear this pair, in fact, but the other ones got quite muddy the other day, and they're still wet from being cleaned up. So much rain in this country."

"Yes, of course," she said absently, her mind working rapidly. "I shall look forward to seeing you soon. Incidentally, my days off are Tuesday and Friday afternoon. Thank you again, Dr. Bhatt, for the information. You've given me quite a bit to think about."

CHAPTER 20

*P*HYLLIDA FOUND OPAL STAMM WAITING IN FRONT OF THE SCREAM-
ing Magpie. She was nervously eyeing the Mallowans' automobile, and Bradford was nowhere to be seen.

Tsking with annoyance, Phyllida checked the timepiece tucked
into her handbag and noted that he was more than five minutes
late for their meeting time.

"Opal, you may wait in the motorcar or just there next to it,"
she said. "It shan't be very much longer."

It very well better not be very much longer, she thought to herself,
then decided to take the opportunity to check inside the pub
once more for Mr. Mustard's whereabouts.

As soon as she stepped across the threshold, Phyllida discovered that Bradford was sitting at the bar counter . . . next to a
bearded blond man wearing a plaid green Homburg.

Of all the . . .

Was it merely coincidence, or had Bradford somehow anticipated her?

Phyllida shrugged off the moment of exasperation, for it would
be counterproductive to be annoyed about the very thing she'd
hoped for: to have the opportunity to talk to Mr. Mustard.

True to her word, Guinevere had not pulled any ale. (Phyllida
was privately pleased that the woman's poor service was extended
to the two men at the bar and not just to herself.) In fact, the proprietress seemed to be berating one or both of her customers.

". . . messing up my counter! Just cleaned it, and I ain't open for business . . ."

"But what about a piece of that delicious bread?" asked Eugene Mustard in a voice that sounded a bit like a whine. "Perhaps with a slab of cold roast? Or an egg, done up just right? Don't need to tap a keg to—"

"I *said* I ain't serving no one till eleven o'clock. No ale, no bread, no blasted roast beef. What do you think this place is? A bleeding café? Now, get your filthy elbows off'n my clean counter. And you, too, you big lug. Stop creaking around on that stool like you are. Tryin' to break it, are you?" This last was directed at Bradford, and Phyllida could hardly control a smile as she approached the melee.

"Mr. Mustard?" she said, having no reason to speak to the chauffeur, who—shockingly—had slid off the stool, as directed. Which, by the way, seemed perfectly capable of accommodating his solid, lean physique.

"Who's asking?" The stranger turned from the bar, a scowl on his face. But when he saw Phyllida in her pretty yellow dress, neat gloves, and rakishly coy hat, his expression changed to one of interest. "Well, now, you can ask me anything you want there, luv."

I do hope you remember saying that later. But instead of speaking aloud, Phyllida merely smiled, adding an extra layer of warmth to her expression. "How kind of you. Perhaps we could sit over here, so we don't upset Guinevere's cleaning." Still ignoring Bradford, she walked over to a round table as far from the counter as possible.

She pulled out a chair to sit, then thought better of it—she was, after all, wearing lemon-pulp yellow, and heaven knew when the last time the seat had been cleaned of sticky ale, gravy, and who knew what else. To her surprise, Bradford seemed to understand her hesitation, and he spread his coat over the chair so she could safely lower herself into it.

"Thank you, Mr. Bradford," she murmured, and hoping there were no grease stains on his coat that might transfer to her skirt, she took a seat.

Eugene Mustard glanced at Bradford, as if to measure his potential involvement in the conversation, but the chauffeur had stepped away. Bradford leaned against the wall of the pub, his arms crossed over his middle, his head nearly brushing the low ceiling, and proceeded to look bored.

Phyllida dismissed all thought of him and turned her attention to the man who'd taken a seat across from her. "You're a friend of Charles Waring's."

"Yeah. What of it?" His affability faded a little, but Phyllida gave him a sympathetic smile and pressed on.

"I'm sorry for your loss. Scotland Yard is working hard to find his killer," she said, trying not to sound skeptical about the possibility of that result actually coming to fruition. "I understand you had an altercation with and spoke to one of the footmen from Mallowan Hall yesterday."

"Yeah? What's it to you?" Mr. Mustard no longer appeared quite as eager to answer her questions. "Bloke tried to pop me one, he did, and I gave him something to think about. Nearly went a round with him, but it was the newspaper reporter really made him bleed." He smirked. "Saw them goin' at it after . . . fists flying, blood everywhere."

Phyllida felt a trickle of relief that Stanley's story had at least that element of truth to it. After all, he *had* had blood on his clothing, and she'd read enough murder stories to know never to dismiss anyone, no matter how unlikely or cherished, as a suspect. "I want to know why you and Charles Waring came to Mallowan Hall."

"Now, listen here, lady, I don't know why you think it's any your dam—"

A shadow fell over the table, broad and long and dark. Phyllida didn't have to look up to know that Bradford had moved to loom over them. Interfering lout.

"Wot?" said Eugene Mustard, though his voice was a trifle thready.

"You'll speak to Mrs. Bright with respect," said Bradford, completely ignoring the hypocrisy of his words. "And you'll answer her questions very politely."

The other man muttered something unflattering under his breath but obviously decided that complying was his best option. "Charlie rang me up about two weeks ago and said as how he wanted to . . . uh . . . to try something out for a story. It would be fun, because he was going to go undercover, and he wanted to borrow my Aston Martin."

"A story? Mr. Waring claimed to be from the *Times* when he arrived at Mallowan Hall, and we know that's not true. I suggest you keep to the truth, Mr. Mustard."

He exhaled a long breath, and Phyllida was forced to lean back in order to remove her nostrils from its not so fresh proximity. "Fine, then. But Charlie was a writer and a photographer—he did stories for magazines. That wasn't strictly a lie. He just wasn't exactly on an official job at the time." Mr. Mustard drummed his fingers on the table.

"Do go on, and let's keep *strictly* to the truth, now, shall we? With no embellishments."

"Right. Well, Charlie had a—what d'you call it?—a vendetta. Yeah, that's what it was. He had a vendetta against a bloke, and he'd found out he was coming here to Listleigh."

"What sort of vendetta?"

He sighed, rolled his eyes, took off his hat, and scratched his head. "Dunno really. Something about the bloke not treating his woman right or the like."

Phyllida abhorred ambiguous pronoun usage. "This . . . er . . . bloke was treating exactly whose woman poorly? Mr. Waring's or his own?"

"I think it was his wife—the bloke's, I mean to say," Mr. Mustard added quickly when Phyllida's face turned thunderous. "Dunno. Suppose Charlie took exception to the way the toff treated his wife—"

"It's certainly laudable—even obligatory—to be a champion of the female sex," Phyllida interrupted, "and one cannot fault a man for doing so, but it seems rather a weak excuse to travel to Listleigh and crash a house party under false pretenses."

"Don't know about that. Wanted to use my motorcar—seemed to think having his own car would give him . . . What's the word? *Credibility*, that's it. Credibility for joining a house party at a fancy place with a famous writer." He smiled and spread his hands in the picture of absolute innocent ignorance, even adding a shrug for punctuation. "I dunno. I didn't ask all the details. Just come along for the fun of it. Didn't have nothing better to do." His eyes danced, and his feckless expression put Phyllida in mind of the young men who'd signed up to fight in the war, thinking it would be an exciting adventure. "But now my motorcar's there, stuck at the big house, and I—"

"So you came along—just for the fun of it—with your friend so he could . . . do what precisely? Confront the man about his wife?" Despite her caustic words, a picture was beginning to form in her mind. After all, there was the lipstick on Mr. Waring's collar. . . . "Why did Mr. Waring care about the well-being of this man's wife? Was he in love with her or was she his sister or was there some other reason?"

"Told you, lady—*luv*." He glanced over at Bradford, who had gone back to holding up the wall in his boredom. "I just come along because he wanted to borrow my Aston."

"I find that quite difficult to believe," Phyllida said, adding a bit of menace to her voice. It worked with maids, footmen, and gardeners (though obviously not with chauffeurs). "Surely you know more than you are telling me."

"Told you, I *don't know*. Charlie didn't tell me all that much about it. Just wanted my car, and I wasn't going to let him take it on his own."

"You do understand that if Mr. Waring intended to injure—or worse—this husband who supposedly mistreated his wife, and you came along with him, providing his transportation, in fact, that would make you an accessory to the crime." Phyllida put on her most severe expression.

"Right, but it warn't the toff what was married to the woman up and died. It were *Charlie* who got dead," he sneered back. "So who's the accessory *now?*"

Well, fiddle. The man had a point, drat it. Nonetheless, Phyllida began to sympathize with Guinevere's opinion of Eugene Mustard being a prat.

"Clearly," Phyllida said in a firm voice, "if Mr. Waring intended to confront this man who mistreated a woman—presumably, the man's own wife—he must have loved her in order to be motivated to do so. What other explanation is there? I expect he intended to confront him at Mallowan Hall, and that is why he presented himself there under false pretenses."

Mr. Mustard grunted in a manner she took to be an assent, and so she continued. "So he must have accosted the husband and things went wrong and he ended up getting himself stabbed with a fountain pen. Therefore, you must tell me everything you know about this husband and his wife, and whatever you remember about Mr. Waring's plans."

"An' have you lock me up for accessory to a crime? No thank you, lady. I—" He pushed away from the table, but his attempt to flee was aborted when a strong hand clapped onto his shoulder and pressed him back down into his seat.

"I believe your exact words were, 'Well, now, you can ask me anything you want there, *luv,*'" Bradford said before baring his teeth in a cold smile. "The implication being that you'd gladly answer."

Eugene Mustard did not look happy. But he was at least self-preserving enough to comply. "I don't know the husband's name. I *don't.* All I know is he's a toff with a fancy motorcar and a pretty wife, is all."

"All right, then. How and when did Mr. Waring meet this mistreated woman—this 'pretty wife'?" Obviously, Charles Waring didn't move in the same circles as the guests staying at Mallowan Hall, which was why he'd felt the need to borrow Eugene Mustard's automobile. "Let me guess . . . It was when he was taking photographs at the Duck Pond Derby event, wasn't it? At Bunder House in May."

Mr. Mustard was clearly taken by surprise. His eyes widened, and it took him a bit too long to respond, as if he had to scrabble around for the words. But when he did, his explanation was smooth. "That's right. Charlie was a photographer come in for the weekend. He was doing a story for some feature in a magazine—mighta been *Life*. He's a right bloody good writer, he is . . . was, I mean," Mr. Mustard said. His face crumpled a little, as if he'd just realized he'd never see his friend again. "Won some awards and all even . . ." He shook his head.

"And so he must have met the woman whose honor he intended to defend—or more—whilst at the charity festival. But why wait until now to confront the husband?"

"Tell you, I don't *know*," Eugene Mustard said, his voice strident. "Just want to know *who* killed my mate."

"That is precisely why I'm asking you these questions, Mr. Mustard," she said sharply. "Now, if you could please cease with the hysterics and give me whatever details you have—no matter how small or insignificant—we will be closer to discovering what you want to know."

He glared at her but did as she asked and ceased his hysterics. "What else you want to know?"

She thought for a moment, then decided to plunge. "Do any of these names sound familiar? Devine, Budgely-Rhodes, Hartford, Sloup, Grimson?" She watched Mr. Mustard carefully, but he didn't make a visible reaction to any of them.

"No. Never heard of any of 'em before." Again, with the innocent smile and spread hands.

"What about the woman? Do you know anything at all about her? A first name? The way she looks? Where she lives?"

"Look, I didn't really care. The bloke wants to moon all over a married woman, that's his concern. I just came along for the ride and to make sure he didn't crash my motorcar."

She lifted a skeptical eyebrow, then went on. "And so what was your plan? You drove to Listleigh together, and then he took your motorcar to Mallowan Hall. What next?"

"We were supposed to meet that night—Wednesday, it was—so he could tell me how he got in and how it all went. I think . . . I think he was going to try and . . . and talk to the woman, maybe. Anyway, he was to drive into town and meet me here, but he never showed up. And now I know why. I heard about it next morning, but I couldn't believe it. That's why I was . . . well, watching around the grounds of the house. My Aston Martin is still there, you know."

"And Mr. Bradford is taking very good care of it, I'm certain," Phyllida said, pitching her voice in the man's direction. He didn't even flicker an eyelash.

"Is there anything else?" Eugene Mustard said in something very close to a whine.

"I believe I have exhausted my questions for now, but don't you even think of leaving Listleigh," she said firmly. "I'm certain the constable will want to speak with you."

He winced and glanced toward Guinevere. "Do I really have to stay here? She's a right mean old hag, she is, and there ain't nowheres else to stay in this town. Why, she wouldn't even let me take cocoa to my room last night. And . . . after Charlie's getting axed off like that, I needed it." That was definitely a whinge.

"Perhaps you would prefer to spend your nights in the Listleigh jail instead of the rooms at the Screaming Magpie," Phyllida said sweetly, although she knew it was a weak threat.

Eugene Mustard seemed to actually consider that possibility, then sagged in his seat. "Right, then. Fine. I'll stay here."

"First, however, you shall march yourself to the constable's office and tell him everything you've told me," she said, rising. "It's far better to offer information to the authorities than to have them drag it out of you. It tends to make them believe in your innocence if you come clean." She looked down at him with a stern expression. "I'll be phoning Constable Greensticks and Inspector Cork this afternoon to confirm that you've done so, so don't delay. Good day, Mr. Mustard."

Then, without further ado, she handed Mr. Bradford his coat and sailed out of the Screaming Magpie.

"Where to now, Mrs. Bright?" asked the chauffeur as he opened the motorcar door.

"Mallowan Hall of course," she replied. "This is Opal Stamm. She'll be returning with us. Opal, this is Mr. Bradford, the chauffeur."

"Fine to meet you, miss," he said with far more pleasantry than he'd ever shown to Phyllida. "And it's just Bradford."

Opal hesitated, then climbed in the back to sit beside Phyllida. The latter suspected the young girl hadn't been in very many motorcars, considering the way she was looking at it with a combination of trepidation and awe.

The new scullery maid was barely thirteen and had two very large front teeth, which one expected she'd grow into eventually. Though still gawky, she was quite pretty, with golden skin and soft walnut hair that was braided, then coiled into two knots on either side of the back of her neck. She'd been aptly named, for her eyes were luminous gray like the gem. Opal had a sturdy build, which made Phyllida quite optimistic of the girl's fortitude.

"Now," said Phyllida as the automobile pulled smoothly into the road, "when we arrive at Mallowan Hall, Benita—the scullery maid whose place you'll be taking—will show you where you can put your things. We don't have a uniform that would fit you at the moment, but I shall have that arranged by tomorrow. Until then, you can wear what you have on and put an apron over it. Benita will find you a cap, as well.

"You'll eat with the lower servants—that is, the cook, the kitchen maids, the chamber- and parlourmaids, the footmen, the gardener, and the chauffeur, if he deigns to dine—in the servants' dining hall. Dinner and tea are served to the upper servants—that includes myself, Mr. Dobble, the butler, Mrs. Mallowan's maid, Violet, and currently, the visiting lady's maid and three visiting valets, as well—in Mr. Dobble's pantry, and you may need to help with that if Molly is too busy.

"Mr. Dobble and the footmen will serve Mr. and Mrs. Mallowan and their guests, of course. Molly is the first kitchen maid, and she'll be telling you what to do when Mrs. Puffley is busy." She paused, then said, "Do you have any questions?"

"You give me a uniform?" Opal asked in a voice barely audible above the rumble of the motorcar. "Clothes?"

"Yes, of course. And Mr. and Mrs. Mallowan are quite generous and will gift you a pair of shoes and a new uniform, along with a coat, at Christmas. And then another pair of shoes and another uniform at midsummer."

"I might have two pair of shoes? At one time?" Her eyes were wide, and Phyllida, who'd noticed the frayed hem and bursting seams of a dress that had been oversewn and let out for several growing girls multiple times, felt a little pang of sympathy.

"You might very well have two or even three pairs of shoes at one time, if you don't grow too fast and don't wear them out too soon," she said with a smile.

They rode in silence for a moment as Opal digested this information, and then she said in a slightly louder voice that was still timid, "And what will you call me, Mrs. Bright?"

Phyllida looked at her and saw worry in those soft gray eyes, though the girl tried to hide it. And so she softened what would have been a more brisk reply in any other circumstance. "Why, your name is Opal—and a fine one it is. Shall we all call you Opal, then?"

"Yes, ma'am," replied the girl, and her hunched shoulders relaxed. She apparently had no further questions, for she fell into silence and looked out the window as Bradford smoothly negotiated the road. Her eyes were wide and her mouth was slightly open as she gripped the inside of the door.

Phyllida closed her eyes momentarily as the world swung one way, then the other when the motorcar swept around a series of curves rather faster than she would have preferred. She didn't like riding in the back of a vehicle, for oftentimes it made her head hurt and her stomach nauseated if the road was taken too quickly or if it was too bumpy. Fortunately, the throughway straightened out after that, and in a moment she was able to safely open her eyes.

When she did so, she saw Bradford's single eye watching her and realized he must have seen her moment of weakness. She looked away and was relieved that they were just about to turn into the grounds of Mallowan Hall. And none too soon.

"Now, Opal, you'll go in and present yourself to Mrs. Puffley in the kitchen. She'll be very glad to see you," said Phyllida as the car drew to a halt. "And if you prove to be a hard worker, why, I'm certain she'll want to keep you on here as long as you like."

"Thank you, Mrs. Bright," said the girl as Bradford opened the car door.

Phyllida showed Opal to the back servants' entrance and pointed down the five steps that descended from the side lawn to the downstairs area. "I'll be along shortly. Benita and Molly will be there to show you what you need."

"Yes, ma'am."

Phyllida turned and nearly bumped into Bradford, who was examining something on the side of the car.

"My goodness," she said involuntarily and reached up to adjust her hat, which had not actually gone askew, but this gave her something to do as the chauffeur looked down at her. He was quite close. She stepped back and was vexed with herself for doing so.

"Why did she ask you that about her name?" he said, pulling a rag from somewhere beneath his coat. He began to wipe away a bit of mud from the front wheel well.

A bit unsettled by such an unlikely question, Phyllida faltered. "Why . . . er . . . I suppose it's possible she knew of some other maid who'd been given a name by her employer. Some people can't be bothered to learn the names of all their servants, and so the parlourmaid is always Susan, the first footman is always John, and the cook is merely Cook, and so on. I believe Lord Sturgeon perpetually has a valet named Brutus."

Bradford, who straightened up at her explanation, seemed

taken aback. He made a disgusted sound, then went back to buff-
ing the tiniest specks of dirt off the Crossley.

Taking that as an end to their conversation, such as it was, Phyllida turned to go into the house.

"His shoes didn't squeak," Bradford said.

Phyllida halted and pivoted back to look at him. "I didn't antic-
ipate that they would. Eugene Mustard couldn't be the killer—"

"And why not? One must consider all possibilities, even the
most unlikely. He could tell us any story he wanted now that his
so-called friend is dead. Maybe they weren't mates at all, and he
followed him here just to murder him. What a plot twist that
would be in a detective story."

Phyllida sniffed. "I've already made that suggestion to Mrs.
Agatha, if that's what you're getting at—a stranger's body being
found in the library. But it would be impossible for Eugene Mustard to gain access to the house."

"Unless Charles Waring let him inside, and they had a row, and
things went bad," Bradford replied.

"Badly," she muttered.

"What did you say?"

She looked away. "Never mind. I suppose it's possible, but very
unlikely. After all, how would Mr. Waring get Mr. Mustard's motorcar if they weren't friends?"

"Right, then. I suppose you have a better suspect, do you, Mrs.
Bright?"

"Of course I do," she said, although she hadn't quite settled on
one particular suspect yet, for motives were still few and far between. Although she did have some ideas, especially since her interview with Eugene Mustard, and she certainly hadn't ruled him
out. His story had had so many holes in it, she was reminded of an
old pair of socks. The question was whether *he'd* made up the
story or whether Mr. Waring had done so.

Bradford gave her a satisfied look. "I knew you were trying to
investigate the murder."

Phyllida clamped her lips together. It was really best not even
to respond to the man. He always had *something* to say that would

irk her. "Good day, Mr. Bradford." Once again, she started back to the house.

"I could have two pairs of shoes," he called after her.

Phyllida ground her teeth but didn't stop walking.

She decided to move Bradford to the top of her suspect list—simply out of spite.

CHAPTER 21

*U*NFORTUNATELY FOR THE PROCEEDINGS OF HER CRIMINAL INVESTI-gation, Phyllida was hailed by Mrs. Puffley when she walked past the kitchen. She had no choice but to make a detour and venture into the loud, steamy, busy room. Benita was plucking feathers from one of a row of five ducks, and Molly was doing something at the far end of the long table that Phyllida couldn't discern, but it involved loud, vigorous chopping.

The temporarily banished Stanley had his injured foot propped on a stool whilst he churned butter. He appeared far less flirta-tious than usual, being required to work in the kitchen at tasks well below his status.

"She'll do, I think," said the cook, who was whipping a huge bowl of eggs with her powerful arm. "Seems to have a brain in her head."

"Excellent. Please keep me apprised," said Phyllida. It was her intention to go on and check in the stillroom to see whether Lizzie had finished the rosemary water, and then head to the laundry to look for bloody clothing, just in case someone had been foolish enough to send it down, but Puffley had more to say.

"Poor mite, that Rebecca," she went on. "Had 'orrible night-mares last night over her." She sniffled. "Locked my door, I did, and I'm not ashamed to say it. Better turn the eggs boiling there, Benita, or Old Dent will grouse about the yolks another day. What do you think about getting a dog for the yard, there, Mrs. Bright? To keep away intruders and the like?"

"A dog?" Phyllida didn't think at all about getting a dog. She didn't care to be jumped at, slathered over, or panted upon, and she was quite content with the company of Stilton and Rye, thank you very much—insofar as beasts went.

One of the reasons she liked working at Mallowan Hall was that the Mallowans didn't ride or hunt, and therefore, there were no canines to bark or whine or jump or lick or do any other unpleasant activities related to their species. Peter didn't count, because he was old and quiet and stayed with Mrs. Agatha most of the time. "Certainly not."

"But—"

"Mrs. Puffley, you're going to whip that bowl right off the table, and then we'll have a waste of good eggs—not to mention a scrub of the floor. I've things to which I must attend, and so I shall leave you to your business." And she marched out of the kitchen before the cook could drum up another complaint, suggestion, or argument.

A brief look into the scullery found Opal elbow deep in water, scrubbing the pots, pans, and serving dishes from the staff's breakfast. The fact that the girl was humming to herself made Phyllida smile.

As expected, Lizzie was in the stillroom, and to Phyllida's satisfaction, she'd already begun work on stuffing fresh perfumed bags for the bureau drawers. The balance of dried lavender and chamomile smelled just right.

"Right then, that looks very good," she told the maid. "Now, I want to ask you about when you cleaned up the bedchambers yesterday. Did you find any clothing with blood on it? Even a bit? Or perhaps a rag that might have been used to wash up?"

Lizzie's eyes went wide, and then her mouth opened a little. "Oh, Mrs. Bright, you're looking for clues, are you? Just like Mrs. Agatha's detectives, you are." Then her face fell a little. "I just can't believe it about Rebecca, I can't. I don't even want to go to the outhouse on my own, and so Bess and I are taking turns going together, aren't we, then? Standing watch and all."

"I'm relieved you're doing so, but quite honestly, I don't believe anyone is in any danger. Rebecca was a . . . target . . . because she used to work at Bunder House, I've come to conclude, and must have known something the . . . erm . . . killer wanted to keep quiet." Phyllida felt another pang of sadness over the loss of the young woman's life.

Lizzie looked around, as if to ensure they were alone, then said in a low voice, "Mrs. Bright, I should tell you something."

"And what is that?" Phyllida replied, moving to close the door . . . just in case.

"Rebecca . . . she was very upset about something that happened, she were. It was on the day everyone arrived. Wednesday, it was. I found her in the storeroom there, I did, and she was— well, she looked like she'd seen a ghost. Her face was dead white, it was, and I thought she were going to faint. I made her sit down. I afeared she was going to fall over," she said, emphasizing the last bit as if to excuse them for taking a break from their duties. "She were all shaking real bad, like leaves in the wind, she was . . ."

Phyllida made a soft, sympathetic sound but was loathe to speak until Lizzie was finished.

"She wouldn't tell me what was wrong at first. Just said over and over, 'He's here. Why is he here? How can he be here?'"

"And did she tell you who 'he' was?"

Lizzie shook her head. "I asked and asked and even asked what she was afraid of, and all she would say was, 'He won't see me down here. I'll stay in the kitchen.'"

Phyllida suppressed a sigh of frustration. She loathed it when important witnesses conveniently died in murder stories before they got to tell their secrets, and it appeared that this phenomenon was also true in life. "Can you remember exactly when this happened? What were you doing. What was she doing?"

"It was after dinner upstairs," Lizzie said, and this time, Phyllida couldn't fully suppress her sigh.

The maid looked at her as if fearful she'd done something wrong, but Phyllida waved a hand for her to continue and said, "No, no, I was simply hoping it was before all the guests had arrived, and that would help to narrow down who might have been the man who upset her."

"Right. I only wish she had told me more," Lizzie said.

"Well, I'm pleased that you told me about this," Phyllida said and decided when she was interviewing them about bloody clothes, she would also ask the other maids in case Rebecca had told one of them anything else. "And I hope that if you think of anything else she said or anything else you noticed, you'll tell me straightaway."

"Like blood on clothes," said Lizzie.

"Yes, or if you notice anyone wearing shoes that squeak a little."

"Oh." Lizzie's eyes widened. "Why is that important?"

Phyllida hesitated, then plunged on. "I happened to be nearby when I heard someone searching through Mr. Waring's bedchamber. I didn't see the culprit, but I heard him leave, and his shoes squeaked a little."

"Do you think it was the killer?" Lizzie said, her eyes going so wide, there was a large white ring around each dark iris.

"I am quite certain of it," Phyllida replied. "And therefore, if you hear someone wearing squeaking shoes, I suggest you remove yourself from the proximity immediately and inform me or Mr. Dobble at once."

Lizzie gulped so deeply, she seemed to be swallowing air, and it was a moment before she could form words. "Mrs. Bright, I did hear a squeaking sound only yesterday, I did, when I was up doing the second floor. Or was it the third floor? I don't remember, but I did hear it, because I said to myself, I said, 'Why didn't that person get their shoes fixed?' It's an annoying sound, ain't it? And it's only to have the cobbler fix it by tightening up the parts of the shoe. My pap was a cobbler, he was," she explained, "and people brought to him squeaking shoes all the time, they did. Not ones he made, though, of course, because he knew better than—"

"That's very helpful," Phyllida said, trying to keep the exasperation from her tone. Why couldn't other people notice things, observe closely, *remember* details? "Can you think very carefully and try to recall where you were when you heard that sound? What you were doing? It could be very important."

Lizzie's face twisted in what Phyllida took to be an expression of deep concentration, and she forced herself to remain silent as the girl went through her mental gyrations.

After what seemed like forever, she spoke slowly. "It were right after the Rosebud Room, because I had to wring out the mop in the bathroom, and I bumped my elbow on the corner of the sink, I did, when I was doing it, and it was prickling bad up and down my arm, it was, when I heard the sound, and that's why I noticed it, because I was already steaming, and I thought to myself, *Why didn't they see to those dratted squeaking shoes?*" She looked at Phyllida and smiled. "That sure did work, to remember just where I was! The second floor, ma'am, and I was in the bathroom right on the end."

That meant she was on the floor where the Devines, Mr. Grimson, and the Hartfords were staying. Phyllida made note of this, and also of the fact that it didn't relieve Mr. Sloup or Mr. Budgely-Rhodes of suspicion simply because their rooms were on the floor above.

"And did you see anyone when you were there? Either before or after you noticed the squeaking shoes?"

"No, ma'am, because when I heard the shoes, I kept myself out of the way so as not to bother whoever it was," Lizzie said proudly, as if it had been a sort of maidservant test as to whether she'd been seen or heard.

"Very well," Phyllida said without expressing her disappointment. "No one was speaking or talking? What time was this?"

"No, ma'am. It was very quiet, it was, but for the shoes. I'm glad now I didn't say anything, because then the killer would know I knew who he was, and then *I'd* be a . . . a target," she said in a rush as her face took on a sickly cast. "Oh, mercy me, Mrs. Bright! What if he knows I heard him and thinks I saw him, and he comes after me?"

"If you didn't see him, how could he have seen you?" Phyllida said soothingly. "And he hasn't any idea we know that his shoes have given him away. Nonetheless, you'll do as I said and work in pairs with Bess as you've been doing. I am confident this will be resolved very quickly."

Which reminded her that she needed to call the constable and make certain Eugene Mustard had come in to divulge his information. She also wanted to take a look at that lipstick on Mr. Waring's shirt.

She was just about to move on to the laundry when Mrs. Agatha's bell rang from her bedchamber. Phyllida hesitated, then strode back into the war room of the kitchen and said, "Molly, I need Mrs. Agatha's tray right away. Unless Violet has already taken it up?"

"No, ma'am. Violet is with Fanny and Lawrence, showing them the laundry and sewing room," replied Molly. "Fanny wanted to press Mrs. Budgely-Rhodes's dinner frock. And there was something about Mr. Budgely-Rhodes's trousers."

Fanny and Lawrence were the Budgely-Rhodeses' maid and valet, and it was their responsibility to see to any wardrobe mishaps for their master or mistress.

"Very well, then. I'll take the tea up for Mrs. Agatha. Has anyone else rung for a tray in their rooms?" Phyllida asked.

"Only Mr. Sloup, and Elton came down for it already," said Molly. She smiled, showing a perky dimple. "He's a right looker, too, that Elton. And what a charmer."

"Ain't he, though?" said Benita with a sigh. Until this morning, when she'd been promoted from scullion to kitchen maid, she would never have ventured into such a conversation. But apparently her new position had emboldened her.

"When did *you* get to see him?" asked Molly a trifle sharply.

"Why, I had to bring coffee and tea in for the uppers yesterday because Rebecca was too busy," replied the younger girl stoutly. "And I don't mind saying that Elton has the broadest shoulders I ever seen that don't make him look like an ogre. And his coat was off, and there's a nice look to him under that shirt o' his." She seemed to be making a point of speaking as much as she wanted in order to demonstrate her new position.

"He sneaked right up behind me and stole a kiss while I was folding linens yesterday," Molly said with a sly smile, sallying forth into the competition between the kitchen maids. "Took me all by surprise, it did, otherwise I wouldn'ta let him. But . . . it was so nice, I might even let him do it again tonight instead of him playing cards with the others."

If she were younger or less mature, she might even have stuck her tongue out at Benita, Phyllida thought wryly.

"The bloke creaks when he walks," Benita said, "so I don't see how he sneaked up on you without you knowing. He tried the same to me in the scullery, but I heard him coming in plenty of time." She gave Molly a skeptical look.

"Tray's ready, Mrs. Bright," said Molly—possibly in an attempt to forestall any further parries from her counterpart.

Phyllida saw that Agatha's tray was exactly as it should be— including Peter's morning biscuit—and took it from the room. She could have enlisted Freddie or Lizzie to help carry it up two flights of stairs, but Phyllida was of the opinion that a person should maintain a regular exercise regimen that included vigorous movement as well as some heavy lifting.

Therefore, she wasn't even out of breath when she reached the first floor and pushed through the door to the other side. The corridor was empty, as was to be expected, for Bess was up on the third floor, cleaning the bathrooms in readiness for the stirring guests and arranging tea and coffee pots on a hall table to be delivered to each room as requested.

"Come in," Agatha said at Phyllida's knock at her office door. "Oh, good, it's you." Although her eyes had dark circles beneath them and her face was drawn, she beamed. "I was hoping you'd be the one to come."

"I can't take much time," Phyllida said as she poured tea and brought the cup over to where Agatha was sitting and studiously ignoring (at least it seemed to Phyllida she was ignoring) the typewriter next to her.

"Of course not. I can't imagine how busy you must be with everything and now Rebecca gone . . ." Her voice trailed off.

"I was able to find a young girl to come in and help," Phyllida said and went on to explain about Opal Stamm.

"I certainly hope she works out," Agatha said; then her attention strayed to the window, which overlooked the south lawn. "I can hardly believe what happened to Rebecca—just out there. Why, if I had looked up from my work at just the right time, I might have seen something."

Phyllida's heart gave a disappointed lurch. "But you didn't, I suppose. That must mean the chapter was going well."

"It was. And no, I didn't see anything out of the ordinary." She sighed and passed a hand over her forehead, then straightened and smiled. "Now, Phyllie, tell me what you learned in town today and if you found out anything instructive about our guests whilst serving tea yesterday."

After giving a detailed description of her interview with Eugene Mustard (leaving out the unwanted interference by Bradford, of course), she concluded by saying, "I'm not certain what to believe of what he said, but there is one thing of interest. Eugene Mustard was at the Duck Pond Derby Faire. I thought he looked vaguely familiar, and when I looked at the photographs again after meeting him, I realized he was there in at least one of the pictures."

"Well, that's quite interesting."

"Indeed. I intend to confront him with that information now that I've confirmed it, but that will entail another trip into Listleigh."

"Of course. Bradford will take you, I'm sure."

Phyllida held her tongue on the subject of the recalcitrant chauffeur and embarked on a less vexing subject. "Incidentally, Agatha, after watching them during tea yesterday, I am in complete agreement with you that Mr. Devine and Mrs. Hartford are having an affair. And Paul Hartford is either aware or suspects and is quite aggrieved over it. Although I don't sense the sort of violence one must have in order to be willing to murder someone over it. He simply seemed sad and resigned."

Her friend was nodding. "And I wouldn't see how that relates to Mr. Waring, at any rate. I see you've also confirmed your dislike of Tuddy Sloup." She gave her a knowing look.

Phyllida shook her head in disgust. "I only hope he *is* the culprit, for I'd like nothing better than to see him incarcerated where he can't bother anyone. That reminds me, I should speak to the maids and make certain he hasn't been accosting them."

"I certainly hope not," Agatha said sharply. "If that's the case, I want to know, and Tuddy Sloup won't be welcome at Mallowan Hall again—funding for digs and rare artifacts or *not.*"

Phyllida smiled, grateful for her employer's support. "Very well. Now, I . . . What's this?" She picked up a notebook from Agatha's side table. It looked very familiar.

"I've got notes in there about a new idea I had . . . about someone committing murder whilst they're playing bridge—"

"This is Mr. Waring's notebook! The one that was taken from his briefcase!" She began to flip through it . . . but all she found were, as Agatha had said, notes in her handwriting about a card game that went wrong. "Where did you find this?"

Agatha was looking at the notebook in surprise. "Why, I'm not certain . . . I suppose I just picked it up somewhere when I needed something to write in. As I often do." She smiled ruefully. "But there wasn't any writing in it."

"Someone took it from the Gray Room and probably tore out all the relevant—or incriminating—pages. If you can remember where you found it, or when, perhaps we can narrow down who—"

A loud crash, followed by a woman's shriek, interrupted Phyllida.

CHAPTER 22

As PHYLLIDA RAN UP THE STAIRS TO THE SECOND FLOOR, SHE REAL-ized the sounds were from an altercation that was in progress.

Mr. Hartford was in the hallway and appeared to be attempting entrance to the chamber where his wife was staying. Just as Phyllida came on the scene, there was a shriek from within the bedroom, followed by something that flew out the doorway.

Mr. Hartford ducked, stepping back, and the water pitcher shattered against the opposite wall of the corridor. Lunging back toward the open door, he bellowed, "You don't know—"

"Leave me alone!" his wife cried, looking as far from her normal cool elegance as possible. "Go away! You and your—" Her words were lost under another crash, followed by a shriek of fury and a dull thud, which Phyllida imagined was the lovely olive-wood statuette that decorated a side table in the room. Or, at least, that had decorated a side table.

By now, the Devines and Mr. Grimson had emerged from their respective rooms and were peeking out into the hallway. Mrs. De-vine was two doors away from Mrs. Hartford, and her husband was across the hall from the altercation. The shattered pitcher had just missed hitting his door. Mr. Grimson had actually ventured into the corridor, but he was at the opposite end, near the Gray Room, and seemed more curious than upset by the battle raging on his floor.

"Now, see here, Amelia," Mr. Hartford said with a glance at the spectators. "Perhaps we could—"

"Get out!" she cried, and there was the flash of a slender arm bared by the full sleeve of her silky robe. "Don't you *dare*—"

"Paul, perhaps you might . . . uh . . . Well, she seems rather upset." Mr. Devine stepped into the hallway, reaching out a placating hand toward Mr. Hartford. "Perhaps you might, uh . . ."

Mr. Hartford stared at the hand, which came to rest on his arm, froze, then shook it violently away. His expression was dark with anguish, and for a moment, Phyllida thought he was going to strike Mr. Devine. "Don't," Mr. Hartford said, low and sharp, and stepped away. Mr. Devine did likewise, putting space between himself and the angry husband.

Amelia Hartford's bedchamber door slammed shut as everyone continued to stand there, gawking in silence.

The Budgely-Rhodeses and Mr. Sloup had come from the floor above to stand at the landing of the stairs. Bess, who'd been up on the third floor, had also come into view from the servants' entrance, carrying a feather duster and a small pail. She peeked around from behind Mr. Grimson.

Mrs. Agatha and Mr. Max, as well as Mr. Dobble and Freddie, had all appeared in the corridor, as well, having ascended from the ground and first floors.

Mr. Hartford looked at everyone; then without a word, he spun and went into his bedchamber. After the slam of his door, the only sound was that of a low sobbing from within Mrs. Hartford's room.

"Very well, then," Phyllida said briskly. "Bess, perhaps you could sweep up the broken porcelain. Freddie, we'll need a mop to get up the water on the floor there, if you please."

"I do believe breakfast is nearly ready downstairs," she added to the spectators at large—most of whom were still in robes and slippers, although it was nearly noon. "But if you would like tea or coffee in your chambers, please ring and we'll have it right to you."

"Perhaps I should try and talk to her," said Mrs. Devine. She stepped into the hallway, wearing the white dressing gown with Chinese dragons and the unpractical feathered slippers. Her dark hair, which was normally styled in flat curls, was covered by an exotic-looking red turban. Even recently risen from slumber, she still looked like a film star.

"Amelia, it's me . . . May I come in?" She knocked softly on Mrs. Hartford's door.

"I'll bring some tea, shall I?" said Phyllida. More than anything, she wanted to be in that room when Geoffrey Devine's wife spoke to his lover.

Mrs. Devine nodded in agreement, then carefully tried the door. It opened, and she poked her head in. "Amelia? May I come in?" The other woman must have given her assent, for Mrs. Devine slipped inside.

"What on earth was that all about?" exclaimed Mrs. Budgely-Rhodes. Her unfashionably long hair hung loosely to the middle of her back, and there were smudges on her face from makeup she hadn't completely removed before retiring last night. "How uncouth!"

"Have no idea," said her husband, taking her by the arm. "Back upstairs, shall we? I'm ready for breakfast. Where is that bleeding Lawrence when you need him?"

"He went down with Fanny to the laundry, dear, to crease your trousers," replied his wife as they started up the stairs. "Don't know what is taking so long."

"Madwoman, she is," muttered Tuddy Sloup, glancing at Mrs. Hartford's door. "No surprise. Seemed rather tense last night, she was. Fragile and all."

Phyllida had quickly put together a small tray with a pot and two teacups, along with lemon, sugar, and milk, from the table in the hall. She turned, started toward Mrs. Hartford's room, then halted when she realized Mr. Sloup was blocking her way.

"Some coffee to my room, as well," he said. "You'll bring it up, because I won't need any sugar, then, will I?" His leer couldn't have been any more blatant.

"Of course, Mr. Sloup," said Phyllida. "As soon as I deliver this to Mrs. Hartford and Mrs. Devine."

"Don't take long," he warned but moved out of the way for her to go past.

Phyllida sighed. Now she wouldn't be able to linger as long as she wanted in Mrs. Hartford's room. And she certainly wasn't about to send anyone—or at least any other female—to deliver the coffee to Mr. Sloup on the floor above.

Putting that concern out of her mind for the moment, she knocked on Mrs. Hartford's door and was bade enter.

The scene was even worse than she'd feared, and Phyllida sighed inwardly as she stepped around what was left of the porcelain basin that matched the shattered water pitcher. Two of the paintings on the wall were crooked. The bed was in shambles—all the blankets and coverings were rumpled and tossed. What appeared to be a teacup had spilled—or been upended—on the William and Mary dressing table. And the olive-wood statuette of a preening cat was on the floor, with its long, slender tail lying next to it.

Mrs. Devine barely looked up as Phyllida poured tea, and the latter suspected Mrs. Hartford was far too emotional even to notice she'd come into the room.

". . . such a boor," sobbed Mrs. Hartford. "Never takes into account h-how I f-feel. And how dare he ac-cuse m-me of . . ." Her tears covered whatever it was "he," presumably Mr. Hartford, was accusing her of, and she pounded a pillow—*thud, thud, thud*—for emphasis.

"Now, now, Amelia," said Mrs. Devine soothingly. "Men can be such unfeeling louts, can't they? I'm certain Paul didn't mean to upset you—the tea can go there, if you please—and he seemed quite overset himself. Perhaps you can speak with him and smooth things over."

"I w-wish we'd never c-come here," wailed Mrs. Hartford. "M-murders and n-now this! And we can't even leave!"

Phyllida remained as unobtrusive as possible, hoping not to be dismissed, as she quietly began to gather up the pieces of porcelain on the floor. Certainly no one wanted to step on one of them, and it gave her an excellent opportunity to be out of the line of sight should either of the women look up.

"Sometimes I even think I *h-hate* him," Mrs. Hartford went on, lifting a teary face.

"Of course you don't," said her companion, stroking the other woman's back, as if to ease her pain. "Have a sip of tea, dear. It'll make you feel better. But surely you don't truly feel that way. I'm certain you can talk to him about all of this. Once you're away from here, of course. Perhaps the inspector will let us leave today."

Phyllida wondered whether Mrs. Devine knew the truth about her husband and the woman she was comforting. If so, she was a far more tolerant and forgiving person than Phyllida would ever be.

Unless her goal was to encourage the Hartfords to leave as soon as possible, thereby removing the temptation of Mrs. Hartford from her husband.

The conversation between the two was more of the same, and eventually, Phyllida could no longer justify crawling about on the floor, looking for shards of porcelain—particularly since she had found one with the side of her hand and had a bit of an ooze of blood, which would surely drip on her yellow frock.

She rose, gingerly holding the pieces of the broken basin, and said, "Is there anything else, Mrs. Devine? Mrs. Hartford?"

"No," replied the former.

Back in the corridor, Phyllida was unpleasantly reminded of Mr. Sloup awaiting his "coffee" upstairs. She simply didn't have the time or patience to deal with the man. But Freddie was just finishing mopping up the water on the floor, and he would do just fine.

"Freddie, I'm taking a tray up to Mr. Sloup in the Pines Room. You are to watch the clock, and in precisely six minutes, you are to knock on that door and inform me that Mrs. Agatha needs to see me urgently."

"Yes, Mrs. Bright," he said.

"Precisely six minutes from the time I enter the room. Don't be late, if you please. And you are to come in even if you are not bade, do you understand?"

"Yes, *ma'am*." He gave her a little salute, but his expression indicated he knew exactly why she was making the request.

Bess emerged from the Gray Room at just that moment. "Oh,

Mrs. Bright! Thank goodness you're still up here. I've something to show you."

Something in Mr. Waring's chamber? How curious. Phyllida took two enthusiastic steps toward her, then stopped.

Drat and *blast*. And here she was, needing to go up . . . Well, why should she care, anyway, as long as the dratted man got his coffee? Even if he complained to Mrs. Agatha or Mr. Max, nothing would come of it—except perhaps the total banishment of Tuddy Sloup from the grounds of Mallowan Hall. She smiled a little.

"Freddie, you'll have to take this tray of coffee up to Mr. Sloup. If he asks, simply tell him that Mrs. Agatha summoned me and that I asked you to make certain he got his coffee." Phyllida looked at the tray, then, with a smug look, added an unusually large bowl of sugar.

"Now, what is it you need to show me?" she said to Bess.

"I don't know if it's important, Mrs. Bright, but I thought it was a bit strange because no one is staying in the Gray Room now that Mr. Waring's . . . well, gone . . . but someone has lit a fire in here."

Phyllida had followed her into the room, and upon those words, she went immediately to the fireplace. Sure enough, the remains of a small fire still smoldered. A little tendril of smoke curled up from a pile of ashes.

Not ashes from wood. From paper.

Someone had been trying to burn something.

She used a poker to shift some of the larger pieces around and saw the charred, partly ruined remains of whatever had been set ablaze. Some of it hadn't burned.

Phyllida snatched up the pitcher and dumped its contents over the small fire.

She didn't wait for the sizzling and the smoke to cease before snatching up the two pieces in the back.

Photographs.

"What is it, Mrs. Bright? Is that . . . ? My heavens, is that . . . is that . . . ?" Bess's face went bright red, and she gulped hard. "Why that's . . . that's obscene!" She dug behind her collar and pulled out a chain on which hung a small gold cross. "Saint Sebastian, pray for me!"

Phyllida rose to her feet, still looking at the photographs. She wasn't at all horrified by the images. Surprised and mildly intrigued, but not horrified like the maid. There was very little she hadn't seen or experienced—or at least didn't know about—in her lifetime, and as shocking things went, this was quite far from being obscene, at least in her mind.

There was enough left of one photograph to see the bare buttocks of a tall, lean man and the shadow of another person in front of him. This second person did not have the curves of a female but instead possessed a muscular forearm and a large hand, which was covering his companion's rear end.

The second image was even more explicit, with the two men—Phyllida wasn't even certain they were the same two as in the first photo—embracing and kissing. Both were naked, and their hands were strategically positioned to make it quite clear precisely what sort of activity was going on.

Unfortunately, the top part of the photograph—where the faces would have been—was the part that had burned.

"These pictures had to have been taken through a window," Phyllida murmured. "Or from a tree? Somehow, to get so close without being noticed . . ."

She peered at the photos more closely, paying more attention to the details of the chamber in which they were taken. There was something on the fireplace. . . . *Drat*, she needed the magnifying glass she used for close sewing work, which happened to be down in her sitting room.

"Thank you, Bess. This is extremely helpful," she said and snagged two pieces of Mallowan Hall stationery from the bedside table drawer. Carefully, she folded the damaged photos each into their own folder. "Please don't mention this to anyone."

"Of course not, Mrs. Bright." Although she still held her cross, Bess's eyes were lit with excitement. (Apparently, the horror from the so-called obscenity of the photographs had been replaced by fascinated interest.)

Phyllida straightened, holding the two makeshift folders. "Do you have any idea who might have been in here, lighting the fire? Did you see anyone?"

"No, ma'am. Not at all. I didn't see anyone or hear anyone, and I only came in here to take the bedding off for the laundry. I thought it was all right since Mr. Waring was gone and the policemen weren't here anymore."

"Quite right. Very well, proceed with your tasks." Phyllida took one careful look around the room, particularly in front of the fireplace, in an effort to see whether the culprit had conveniently left something that might help to identify him.

She could scarcely believe it when she saw the small book of matches on the hearth—just where someone might have crouched in order to light a small fire quickly. It certainly hadn't been there yesterday, when she, the constable, and the inspector had been searching the room.

When Phyllida scooped it up and looked at it, she would have crowed with delight if there wasn't a witness in the chambermaid.

The matchbook was from the Old Ivy Inn. The place Mr. and Mrs. Budgely-Rhodes had stayed only three nights before arriving at Mallowan Hall.

She couldn't wait to show Inspector Cork.

CHAPTER 23

*B*ESS KNEW SHE'D DONE THE RIGHT THING TELLING MRS. BRIGHT about the little fire in the Gray Room's fireplace, and it was never a bad thing when the boss was happy with you.

Still, happy as the housekeeper might be with her, it didn't take away the fact that there was a killer somewhere about and that Bess felt like she always had to be looking over her shoulder.

In fact, she'd had the sense someone was watching her just this morning, before the Hartfords got into their big row right there in front of everyone, like she was a fishwife screaming at her lug of a husband, who was bellowing back like a foghorn—just as happened all the time on the docks of the Thames. Bess hadn't seen anything like that since she'd left London (thank Jesus, Mary, and Joseph) and come to the country. She was never going back to that dirty, loud place.

But she had felt like, when she came out from cleaning the bathroom there on the second floor, someone had just been watching . . . though she couldn't tell from where. No one was around, and all the doors were closed.

Mrs. Bright had said to work together all the time, and Bess and Lizzie had started off that way (because neither of them wanted to get coshed in the head like poor, poor Rebecca) . . . but then they just fell into their old habits of going off to get a fresh feather duster or a new bucket of soap water or answering a call for tea, and pretty soon they weren't together anymore and were definitely alone.

Bess shivered, suddenly realizing that since one of the people in Mallowan Hall had to be a murderer, they could just as easily ring for tea or coffee, luring a girl into their chamber and then pushing her out the window or—or stabbing her with a pair of scissors or whatnot.

She felt a little sick as she gathered up the last of the sheets and pillowcases from where Mr. Waring hadn't even slept (but they had to be washed, anyway, of course, and folded up with lavender sprigs in the linen room). After bundling up a large armful of bed coverings and other linens, she poked her head out of the room to check instead of just walking out. Just in case.

No one was there, so she slipped into the hall and darted through the servants' door—which was just right next to the Gray Room—and, drawing in a relieved breath, trotted down three flights of stairs to the laundry.

Once down there, she separated the linens into those that stayed and those that were sent out. She tossed the sheets onto the pile that was to go out to the laundress in town, as most of the everyday bedclothes, napkins, and tablecloths did.

In the other pile was a small lace runner from the bureau in the Gray Room, along with a very old crocheted doily that went on a table in the hall and had got wet when Mrs. Hartford threw the pitcher. Those and other antique linens stayed in for gentle handwashing and any repairs that might be necessary.

Bess saw that the small washing sink was available, for the pearl-gray frock that had been soaking yesterday had finally been hung to dry. Most of the coffee stains were gone. Perhaps a bit of lye soap would help remove the rest—she'd mention it to Violet, who could always be counted on to appreciate suggestions. It was Bess's most cherished desire to be promoted to lady's maid some-day, and so she read everything she could in *Mrs. Beeton's* and else-where about attending to clothing and fabrics, along with all the news about updated hairstyles.

But those shirts really needed more starch, she thought, sniff-ing at the row of white garments that had been hung up by Mr. Grimson's valet.

Bess was bent over, digging deep into the supply trunk for a good brush, with her rear end high in the air, when she heard the soft squeak of a footfall behind her.

Startled at being caught in such an undignified position, she bolted upright so quickly, she bumped her head against the trunk top—hard enough to make her gasp in pain.

"Well, try not to sneak up on a girl like that, will you?" she said, holding the brush she'd managed to retrieve and rubbing her head with her other hand.

"Couldn't help it. Was such a pretty sight to be seen," replied the newcomer. Elton was one of the visiting valets and was far too easy on the eyes for her to be able to look away very quickly. It was just too nice of a view. He grinned in that way a bloke did when he wanted to let a girl know he was noticing her, and Bess felt her cheeks heat up.

"Now go off, you," she said, knowing she was nothing special to look at, with her pointy nose and pointy chin and the spots she couldn't ever completely get rid of on her forehead.

"I just say what I see," he said with a grin and went over to take down a set of neckties that had been hung up after being pressed. "Maybe I'll see more of you later, then?"

"And maybe you won't," she replied tartly, having already heard from Molly how he'd sneaked up behind her and stolen a kiss. But he was a fine-looking man, he was, with broad shoulders and berry-red lips that looked like they'd be just delicious to taste.

Elton just laughed, winked, and then was off with his handful of pressed and starched neckties.

Bess's cheeks were still warm at the memory when Lizzie came sailing in with her own armload of linens from upstairs a few moments later.

"You'll never guess what!" Bess said immediately. Lizzie was her closest friend here at Mallowan Hall, which was lucky because they worked together day in and day out, and it was no fun if the other maid was a priss or a meanie.

Mrs. Bright had told her not to say anything about the photographs, but it didn't count when you told your best friend, who might just as easily have found the pictures herself, now couldn't she?

"What's that?" Lizzie replied.

Bess told her about the fire in the Gray Room and how she called in Mrs. Bright right away (it was always good to let your coworker know when you'd made the boss happy). "And you'll never guess what was in those pictures!"

"I dunno. A naked girl?" Lizzie replied with a laugh.

"No! Two naked *men*, and they were . . . Well, you know!" Bess still couldn't get over what she'd seen. She touched her bodice and felt the shape of the cross behind it.

Lizzie dropped the rest of her pile of linens and stared at her. "Are you saying there were two men going at it? In a picture?"

Bess nodded smugly. "In *two* pictures. Those were some naughty photos someone took. Whoever woulda done that, I dunno. I wouldn't want to. It was bad enough, *bad* enough seeing it in a photograph, but to stand there and want to take pictures of it? Though the pictures were from outside the room—wherever they were—and so it wasn't all close and loud or smelly like it would be if'n you were there."

Lizzie's eyes were wide. "I couldn't imagine it!" She started picking through the pile of bedclothes she'd dropped. "It's like what Rebecca said when she walked in on those two men going at it. She saw it going on alive and all!"

"She said it was like she wanted to burn away her eyes or something, so she could forget she'd seen it! Two men humping like that would be a sight I'd never want to see in real life." Yet Bess sort of wanted to look at those pictures again. Because maybe it wasn't so obscene, after all. . . . One of those men reminded her a little bit of that big statue of David.

"That's why I always knock and *wait* to hear—" Lizzie stopped suddenly, her eyes going wide and her face settling tight. When Bess was about to say something, her friend held up a hand to keep her quiet. She tilted her head toward the doorway, as if listening.

Bess heard a low squeak, and just then, Elton, one of the visiting valets, came into the laundry room.

"Forgot the bleeding handkerchief for Himself, you know," he grumbled. "As if the bleeding toff doesn't have enough of them already folded up and packed, he wants the *polka-dotted* one. Not like we can bring his entire bleeding wardrobe to a house party, you know.

"Something's put him off this morning, I tell you. First, he wants the striped waistcoat, then the paisley one, and then he wants the polka dots, which means I have to come all the way down here to get them, but they're not the Swiss dotted ones, so he's not going to like it. Didn't bring those—couldn't fit them in the trunk, you know. And then the footman brings in the coffee, and it ain't good enough for Himself, and when he sees the sugar dish in the middle of the tray, he throws it across the room." He'd snatched up the handkerchief in question. "It's a right mess up there now, with sugar and china all over the floor."

Lizzie and Bess looked at each other and just barely managed not to roll their eyes. One of them would be cleaning up that mess.

"I'm off," he said and disappeared just as quickly as he'd come.

"Well, I—" Lizzie grabbed Bess's arm to shut her up.

Lizzie's eyes were wide, and her face was still tight with nerves. "He was listening to us out there in the hall," she whispered, looking at the door, as if afraid Elton would reappear. "I heard his shoes. They squeak when he walks, you know. I heard it, and then it stopped for a minute. And then he came in."

"Well, I don't suppose that really matters," Bess said, pulling her arm away from Lizzie. "Really, this murder thing had gotten everyone caught up and nervous."

"But Mrs. Bright told me to stay away from anyone with squeaky shoes!" Lizzie hissed, grabbing her arm again. "She says the killer's got shoes that creak when he walks!"

Bess's jaw dropped, and so did her stomach. Whatever Mrs. Bright said was gospel. She was always right and so very smart and mostly calm all the time, and if she said the murderer had squeaky shoes, then the murderer had squeaky shoes.

"Oh, Jesus, Mary, and Joseph," she breathed, hauling out the cross from behind her collar. "Oh, *lands*, I was just in here by myself with him only just before you came in! What if he'd coshed me on the head?"

Now that Lizzie had delivered the news, she seemed more at ease. "Well, there's nothing in here to cosh you on the head with besides a bar of soap, so you're probably safe, then, aren't you?"

"But he could hold my head under water in the sink, or—or strangle me with one of Mr. Max's neckties!" Bess was still clutching her cross, and she closed her eyes. "Saint Julian the Hospitaller, deliver me and pray for me!"

"Saint Julian the Hospitaller?" asked Lizzie, causing Bess to cease praying and look at her.

"He's the patron saint of murderers," Bess replied, then closed her eyes again, presumably to continue to ask for intercession.

"You're asking the patron saint of murderers to pray for your deliverance?" Lizzie said. She never did understand Catholics. And she certainly didn't know how her friend would even *know* there was a patron saint of murderers.

Bess's eyes popped back open. "Right, well, if he's all for murderers . . ."

"He'd want them to succeed in their work, then, wouldn't he?" Lizzie asked, barely resisting the urge to scratch her head in confusion.

"Right, but if Elton murdered me here in the laundry, he'd surely get caught, and Saint Julian wouldn't want that if he's his patron saint, now would he?"

Lizzie just blinked at her. There really was no understanding papists.

"Where to this time, Mrs. Bright?" Bradford didn't seem terribly pleased to be driving her into Listleigh a second day in a row.

But as he didn't have anything to say about it, Phyllida gave him a civil response. "To the constabulary, if you please."

He glanced at her with that single eye in the rearview mirror but said nothing more. She sat in the back seat and tried not to watch the winding, curving road as the motorcar skimmed right, left, up, and down. Although the drive was smooth and steady of speed, she commanded her insides to remain calm and still, regardless of how elaborate were the road's twists and turns.

It was her intention to meet with Constable Greensticks and Inspector Cork, if the latter was present, share her information as well as her theories, and return to Mallowan Hall in time to serve tea.

To Phyllida's surprise and vexation, Bradford insisted on accompanying her into the constable's office.

"Don't have anything better to do," he said when she protested. "Went to the barber and the tailor yesterday."

She swallowed her ire and sailed past him, then marched down the street and up the single step into Constable Greensticks's domain.

"Mrs. Bright," said the man in question when she stepped into the reception area from the outside. "What can I do for you?" He seemed apprehensive and even displeased regarding her appearance, but Phyllida elected not to take offense.

"Is the inspector in?"

Before the constable could respond, the Scotland Yard man stepped through the doorway from some back office. "Mrs. Bright. Please don't tell me you have another murder to report," said Cork.

Once again, she declined to be offended by the man's lackluster greeting. After all, in a few short moments she was about to hand him quite a few interesting clues, which she *hoped* he would use to put together the puzzle of who'd murdered Charles Waring and Rebecca McArdle and why. She'd certainly done so.

"Not at all. In fact, I have some very interesting pieces of information that might just assist you in solving the two murders that have already taken place—and hopefully prevent a third one."

Cork glanced at Bradford, who'd remained a silent, looming form just inside the doorway, and gave him an acknowledging nod. Then he bestowed a heavy sigh in Phyllida's direction. "Very well, then. What is it?"

"Someone burned these—most of them—in the bedchamber

where Mr. Waring had been staying." She handed him the photographs and waited.

"*Good gad,*" said the constable, looking over the shoulder of his superior. His face had gone dark red. "Why, that's . . . that's—"

"A motive for murder, Constable," Phyllida said crisply.

"It certainly is," replied Inspector Cork, and then, to her vexation, he handed the photographs to Bradford, who had come to stand closer and was peering toward them, as if actually interested in the proceedings. "And you say someone attempted to burn these?"

"Presumably, there were others of the same, but this was all that was left in the ashes. If you look closely—use a magnifying glass, if you please—you'll notice the coat of arms in the keystone on the fireplace in the chamber where at least one of these pictures was taken. Do you recognize it, Inspector?"

"I'm afraid I don't, Mrs. Bright," he replied resignedly. "But I can only assume you do."

"It's the Avercroft coat of arms, of course. These pictures were taken at Bunder House, and unless I'm greatly mistaken, they would have been done just in May, during the Duck Pond Derby Faire."

Bradford handed back the photographs. He stepped back, folding his arms over his middle, and remained uncharacteristically silent as Phyllida went on.

"One must conclude that at least one of the men in these pictures is currently present at Mallowan Hall and was trying to destroy this evidence. One could even make further assumptions as to whom it might be, based on the build and physique of the subjects, but only one of the figures is . . . er . . . fully visible. At least in these photographs. One could speculate there were other images that clearly identified the participants—or they wouldn't be very useful as blackmail devices, would they?

"I examined the figures in the pictures quite closely," she went on, ignoring a choked noise from the irritatingly nosy chauffeur, "for any identifying factors, such as birthmarks or tattoos, but came up short."

Cork harrumphed, and she noticed the tip of his nose was tinged red. "Thank you for your close attention to those . . . er . . . details, Mrs. Bright."

"Yes, of course. I was quite happy to do it," she said blandly, handing one of the pictures to him. "And if you notice on the back of that particular picture, one can see just a corner of the stamp of the photographer. Does *that* look familiar to you, Inspector?"

Without turning over the picture, he said, "I can only assume it is the same stamp as the one on those photographs that were in Charles Waring's briefcase."

"Quite right." Phyllida gave him a complacent smile. "That makes everything that much clearer, doesn't it?"

"I should say so."

"And now that you've spoken with Eugene Mustard, I can only assume everything has made quite a bit more sense," she said.

In truth, she hadn't completely put all the pieces together, but in her defense, she was rather new at this detecting business, and presumably, the inspector had been at it a lot longer than she had. There were only a few small questions left unanswered, and she was confident it would take only a bit more work on the part of her little gray cells to solve them. And then she would fully understand the situation.

"Eugene Mustard? Who the blazes is that?" said Cork, displaying his own vexation.

"Do you mean to say he didn't come down here and give you his story, Constable? I made it quite clear to him what he must do in order to keep himself above suspicion—and safe! And now what has he done? Thrown himself *right* into the fire, now that these photographs have been rescued from one!"

"Mrs. Bright, if you could please enlighten me as to who this Eugene Mustard is," pressed Cork, making free with proper grammar.

Studiously ignoring Bradford, who'd made a sort of snorting sound during her exclamations about Mr. Mustard shirking his duty (really, the man should just *say* what he was thinking rather than making all sorts of ambiguous noises), Phyllida said, "Eugene Mustard is Charles Waring's friend, and he is staying at the Screaming Magpie."

"Poor sot," said Greensticks.

"He claims he came down with Mr. Waring, allowing the latter to use his motorcar in order to make a good impression on Mr. and Mrs. Mallowan when he arrived at Mallowan Hall under the false pretense of interviewing her for the *London Times*. According to Mr. Mustard, Mr. Waring had a more compelling purpose for coming to Mallowan Hall. He intended to speak to a neglectful husband and indicate his displeasure in the way said neglectful husband treated his wife, for whom, one can conclude, Mr. Waring had a tendre."

"There was very little of Mr. Mustard's story that I found plausible"—here there was such an audible snort from Bradford that she was forced to cease speaking and fix him with a very dark glare before continuing—"other than the fact that he and Mr. Waring were friends, and that they'd come down to Devonshire together. Also, the fact that Mr. Waring was a photographer-journalist. That has, by now I'm certain, become quite clear to even yourself, Inspector."

"Quite so," replied Cork weakly.

"However, one item I wasn't certain of when I interviewed Mr. Mustard yesterday was only confirmed after I returned to Mallowan Hall and was able to look once again at the photographs of the Duck Pond Derby at Bunder House—which I am herewith returning to your custody, Constable." She flipped through the stack of photographs before handing it over to Greensticks, extracted one and placed it on top. "That gentleman there standing next to the pie-shooting booth is none other than Eugene Mustard."

"I see." Cork took the top photo from the constable and examined the picture, then returned it to the stack. "But he has not come here to make his statement."

"Then we shall have to go to him," Phyllida informed him.

"But Guinevere—" said Greensticks, his Adam's apple bobbing violently.

"Nonsense," she snapped. "This is a police matter, and she wouldn't dare stand in the way of the authorities."

Phyllida didn't wait for a consensus from the three males standing about, looking uncertain. She marched out of the constabulary and down the street to the Screaming Magpie.

CHAPTER 24

*E*UGENE MUSTARD WAS NOT AT THE SCREAMING MAGPIE. HE WASN'T in the dining area, nor was he in the room he'd let abovestairs—to which Guinevere had reluctantly allowed the authorities access.

"Flew the coop, did he?" she cried, peering around Inspector Cork's shoulder as he looked around the room. Her voice rose to a screech. "Knew he wasn't to be trusted, I did. Don't know why I—"

"If you all could go back downstairs," said the inspector firmly. "We need a few minutes to look around."

Whilst Cork was speaking to Guinevere, Phyllida edged around and behind him into the room and thereby avoided making eye contact with the inspector. She was well aware that she had no real business poking around Eugene Mustard's room, and that the inspector's command had included her, as well as Guinevere and Bradford. But even if she had a bare moment to search the room, it was better than having none at all.

Her first impression was that Mr. Mustard had left for good—there were no personal effects in the room. The bed appeared to have been slept in, likely last night, but possibly only Wednesday night—the day he and Mr. Waring had arrived in Listleigh and the night of the first murder. She highly doubted Guinevere's hospitality included daily cleaning and bed making.

However, whether Mr. Mustard had left only the Screaming

Magpie or the entire vicinity of Listleigh and Mallowan Hall was unclear. She suspected it was the former, not the latter, for Eugene Mustard had made it very clear that he wanted his motorcar back.

"Nothing, Inspector," said Constable Greensticks after looking under the bed (apparently, Cork had learned something about searching a room after missing the briefcase in the Gray Room) and through each of the bureau drawers.

Inspector Cork muttered something under his breath, and then his eyes lit on Phyllida. "I told you to go downstairs," he said from between clenched teeth.

"Oh, dear," she said with wide, ingenuous eyes. "I thought you were speaking to Guinevere."

"Mrs. Bright," he said even more tightly. "Despite whatever impression you might have about my requiring your assistance in this investigation, it is police business, and you are *not* invited."

Phyllida gave him a measured look. How quickly one forgot benefactions that had been given.

"Very well." She lifted her chin proudly and was about to vacate the room when she noticed the mattress. It was slightly crooked on its stand, as if it had been moved in haste. Obviously, that had happened after someone slept in it, for the weight of a somnolent individual would have pressed the mattress back into its proper place.

She went over and lifted the mattress by the corner that was off-kilter. "And what have we here?"

It was a partial photograph, but it was clearly another of the same series that had been burned in the Gray Room's fireplace. The fact that Eugene Mustard had copies of those pictures was not the least bit surprising to her.

"He stowed the photographs under the mattress—a patently obvious hiding place—and when he removed them, this one must have caught on the bedspring below and ripped. He likely didn't even notice," Phyllida said, looking at the torn picture with interest. There were naked arms, legs, and buttocks in this one, as well as a face she recognized.

Although she was mildly surprised to see Eugene Mustard, it didn't affect her theory about the identity of the killer at Mallowan Hall.

Not much, anyway.

She looked closely at Mr. Mustard's companion in the photograph.

"And herewith at last we have an identifying factor of another of our subjects," she added with satisfaction—fully aware that she'd selfishly held the scrap out of the inspector's view as she examined it. There was a signet ring on the hand that was brushing the hair away from Eugene Mustard's face during an extremely intimate activity.

And that ring, she was certain, would unequivocally identify Eugene Mustard's lover—and, undoubtedly, one of the guests at Mallowan Hall. If only she could remember if she'd seen a signet ring like that in one of the bedchambers at Mallowan Hall . . .

Holding the picture like a hostage, Phyllida said to the inspector, "I should like to see the shirt Mr. Waring was wearing when he was killed. I think it only fair that you should reciprocate the assistance I've provided to you during this investigation. I assume the authorities are in possession of Charles Waring's personal effects."

Inspector Cork's jaw creaked a little as he looked at her. "Very well," he said without moving said jaw.

Phyllida smiled, then handed over her hostage.

With Inspector Cork having paid the required ransom by allowing her to examine Mr. Waring's shirt, Phyllida was just about to open the back door of the Mallowans' Crossley when Bradford stepped up, blocking her from doing so.

"Here you are, Mrs. Bright." With a pointed look, he opened the front passenger door instead.

"Thank you, Mr. Bradford." Mildly chagrined, Phyllida climbed inside and settled in her seat.

No sooner had he navigated the automobile onto the road than the driver asked, "Why did you want to see Waring's shirt?"

Phyllida gave him a sidewise glance. She'd considered it a minor achievement that he'd not followed her in to look at the dead man's personal effects. "I wanted to see the color of the lipstick on it."

"And what color was it?"

"Red."

He looked over at her. "What sort of red?"

Surprised by the question, she hesitated before answering in more detail than necessary. "It was a bold crimson color. Blood-red." Not just any woman could wear such a color successfully, but Phyllida saw no need to mention that to the man sitting next to her.

Bradford nodded and lapsed into silence as his gloved hands smoothly managed the wheel around a series of curves. "Better in the front, is it, then?" he asked.

"Yes. Thank you," she replied stiffly. She didn't think it had been *that* obvious how uncomfortable she'd been sitting in the back. Best to change the subject. "You didn't seem terribly shocked at the content of those photographs, Mr. Bradford."

"Nor did you, Mrs. Bright."

She lifted her chin. "It takes quite a lot to shock me, Mr. Bradford. While those pictures were very explicit, I didn't find them the least bit obscene, and I certainly don't find the content unlawful—despite what others might think."

"That is certainly an evenhanded opinion," he replied.

"It's my own, and quite frankly, I feel that if two consenting adults wish to engage in any sort of . . . personal interactions . . . that is their business."

"I see."

"If Mr. Waring took those photographs, which it appears he did, and endeavored to use them as blackmail tools—which one must surmise was his reason for coming to Mallowan Hall—then one cannot be terribly surprised that he is no longer with us. People do not take kindly to being blackmailed over something that can, regrettably, ruin their social standing and, even more seriously, land them in jail. Unfortunately, society—including the legal authorities—do not share my . . . What did you call it? Even-handed opinion."

Bradford made a noncommittal noise that sounded like an as-sent, but one never really could tell with him. Not that Phyllida cared what the brusque man thought.

"And so now what, Mrs. Bright?" he said after a moment. "Have you solved the murders, then?"

If she hadn't heard a bit of mockery in his tone, she might have responded more honestly. But as it was, she sensed he was making fun of her, and Phyllida Bright did *not* take kindly to being nee-dled. "Of course I have. If only the authorities would make the same headway! I find it terribly off-putting that I have had to pro-vide them with every worthwhile clue to help solve these cases. I do fear for Mr. Mustard's safety," she concluded candidly. "I hope he is somewhere safe."

"You think he's in danger?"

"He is in the same compromising photographs. Of course he's in danger."

He grunted, and her interpretation of that pedestrian commu-nication was skepticism.

Very well, then. The boor could draw his own conclusions.

"I do hope you've advised your maids not to be alone while car-rying out their duties," he said, turning the automobile into Mal-lowan Hall's long, tree-lined drive.

"Of course I have."

"And presumably you're following the same advice, Mrs. Bright."

She looked at him. "Why, Mr. Bradford, you sound concerned for my safety."

There was that scoffing snort again. "Not as much as the desire to avoid having another corpse bringing the authorities and the press running all over the bloody grounds," he said. "I came to the country to get away from people, not to be overrun by them every day."

Phyllida clamped her lips closed as the motorcar rolled to

a halt, then felt she had to respond. "Very well, then, Mr. Bradford. I shall endeavor to keep from causing you any further bother."

She opened the door to let herself out of the vehicle and heard him say something that sounded like, "Not bloody likely."

As planned, Phyllida returned in ample time to serve tea to all the guests. It was a task which she looked forward to even more now that she had a signet ring to identify.

Between the small signet ring and the shape of the mystery man's hand, Phyllida felt certain she would soon confirm the identity of the man who was in the pictures with Mr. Mustard. Especially since she had a strong suspicion she already knew who it was.

She hadn't, however, counted on Mr. Sloup's persistence. He kept calling her over to where he sat in the corner—conveniently away from everyone so no one would see what his hands were doing as they swept up and down her legs—asking for a match and then a whisky and then the plate of scones and so on. He was subtle enough about requiring her attention that she doubted the other guests noticed, for they were too busy grousing about when they could leave Mallowan Hall, at the same time as being highly complimentary to the Mallowans about the comfort and beauty of the place. Nonetheless, Phyllida had to dance about quite deftly in order to keep those nosy fingers from making their way up past her knees.

Finally, she decided the only way to stop the nonsense was to respond with her own subtle dodge, parry, and thrust. "My goodness, those sweet peas smell lovely, don't they, Mrs. Budgely-Rhodes? When they're in season, I simply cannot get enough of them in every room—the bright colors and the scent just make everything seem happy. I made certain the maid put some in your chamber. I hope you're enjoying them."

"Why, yes, Mrs. Bright, I am. The fragrance is just lovely." Mrs. Budgely-Rhodes, who sat angled slightly away from Mr. Sloup in his corner, smiled at her. "It was very kind of you to ask."

"The flower garden is so quiet, since it's on the far side of the house. I often take a walk there just before dinner," Phyllida went on, and Mr. Sloup's ears literally twitched in her direction. She kept a smug smile to herself. "While everyone is gathering for sherry, of course, for I know I won't be needed, as Mr. Dobble is handling drinks. It's so lovely with the gardenias and phlox blooming everywhere, and very private and quiet."

After that, Tuddy Sloup no longer seemed to require as much of her attention, which left Phyllida free to examine the hands of every man in the room—except for Mr. Budgely-Rhodes, whose fingers were far too pudgy, and Mr. Max—both of whom she'd already eliminated from the list of potentials.

Of course, having experienced Mr. Sloup's hands far too closely and personally, she'd also had to remove him from her list of potential photograph subjects. His fingers were simply too short to belong to the elegant hand that was wrapped around Mr. Mustard's—

"Mrs. Bright, do you have the clotted cream?" asked Mrs. Hartford. "Paul and I simply can't get enough of the cook's scones. I do hope you'll send our regards down to her."

Unsurprisingly, Amelia Hartford seemed very subdued after the blazing scene earlier in the corridor. The skin around her eyes was a bit puffy, and she wasn't quite as smoothly elegant in her movements as she normally was.

She and her husband were sitting next to each other on one of the settees, obviously to give the impression they'd made up or at least settled their differences. Their gilt heads tilted toward each other—hers dark honey and his like burnished gold—as they spoke privately and quietly. Phyllida even noticed Mr. Hartford taking his wife's hand and holding it, as if to comfort her.

His was a golden-skinned hand that had slender, well-formed fingers but no sign of any rings. His appendage resembled the hand in the photograph, but she wasn't prepared to conclude whether it was his or not.

Mr. Grimson's hands were busy with a handkerchief, dabbing

at some dust or dirt on his coat, when Phyllida brought him a cup of coffee, and to her vexation, she wasn't able to get a proper look at them with all the movement going on.

Mr. and Mrs. Devine were sitting together, as well, which Phyllida realized was unusual. While the gorgeous couple didn't seem estranged—in fact, they interacted quite easily and warmly with each other—she'd never seen them sitting or standing next to each other. She wondered if this development had anything to do with the scene this morning and was somehow the result of Tana Devine comforting her husband's presumed mistress.

Geoffrey Devine's hands were just as handsome as the rest of him, and Phyllida couldn't eliminate him from being in the running as the photograph's second subject, either. It was difficult to tell from the picture whether the hands were as tanned as they appeared, or were simply in shadow. If only there were such things as colored photographs!

She sighed. No signet rings on any hand (which wasn't a surprise to her, as that would have been far too easy, and aside from that, she certainly would have noticed a ring before now) and three inconclusive opinions.

If she had the photograph with her and could compare it with reality, things would be different. Drat. Why didn't she ask to keep the picture? For that matter, why didn't the constable or inspector come here and do it himself?

Perhaps they meant to do so, but they certainly hadn't mentioned it to her, and if so, why weren't they at Mallowan Hall?

Phyllida no longer even pretended to understand the process the law enforcement personnel were using to solve these crimes. It was fortunate that she had taken it upon herself to investigate, or it was likely they wouldn't know anything about the racy photographs.

And then where would they be?

She was beginning to understand the frustration of Poirot and even Sherlock Holmes when it came to dealing with law enforcement.

With a sigh, she began to clear away the tea dishes. She was so close to understanding everything . . . and yet, despite her easy boast to Bradford, was still too far from a solution.

And now, in a few hours, she was going to have to contend with Tuddy Sloup in the flower garden.

CHAPTER 25

"NASTY BUSINESS, ALL OF IT," SAID DOBBLE, LOOKING UP FROM the notes in front of him. He resisted the urge to smooth down a tuft of hair that no longer existed on his bald head. "Two deaths—murders, no less—in fewer than twenty-four hours."

"Not at all what I expected coming to the country," replied Bradford dryly.

"It's certainly not like this all the time," said the butler stiffly.

"I should hope not."

"Have a seat, if you please," said Dobble, feeling as though the very tall, very large man was just a bit too tall and too large to be looming over the desk, above him. The chap could certainly use a haircut, although admittedly the unruly dark hair did suit his gruff personality.

The two were in Dobble's pantry—his private office and work-space—reviewing the list of proposed purchases and the mainte-nance schedule for the Mallowans' automobiles. The window was open, allowing the gentle summer breeze to waft in—along with the fragrance of sweet peas and gardenias from the flower garden sprawling outside.

Beyond the potted gardenias and tangle of sweet peas, on just the other side of a small lip of ground bursting with low-growing moss and creeping myrtle, was the quiet splash of a small goldfish pond studded with waterlilies. Dobble considered the view and the quiet rhythm of water offered by his domain well worth the fact that it was placed on the cellar level rather than on the ground floor, where Mrs. Bright's rooms were.

When Bradford had requested a meeting only two days after arriving at his new job, Dobble hadn't known what to expect. He knew next to nothing about these newfangled motorcars and their upkeep, which was why he had been secretly relieved when Mr. Max proposed his brother's mate Joshua Bradford for the position of chauffeur and garageman.

"He's gruff and broody—doesn't like people much at all—but a hard worker and brilliant with a motor engine," Mr. Max had said. And that was that.

And, of course, as Dobble wouldn't decline the request for a meeting from one of his people, now he was looking at a list of supplies and costs that *sounded* reasonable, but he was so out of his purview that, for the first time in literally decades, Harvey Dobble felt inadequate.

He did not like the feeling, did not like having this very large, very male, very dark man in his office. Yet he was the man's superior, and thus he had no reason to feel intimidated.

"I shall have to review the budget. However, I see no problems with anything you've proposed," Dobble said after staring uncomprehendingly at the list in the dark block-letter scrawl for far too long. "As long as it remains within the budget and the vehicles are maintained to Mr. Mallowan's specifications, I foresee no problems, Mr. Bradford."

"It's just Bradford," replied the other man.

"Very well, then, Bradford. I am certain I will be able to approve these expenses. I'll get back with you tomorrow." He sighed. "I do hope the authorities will allow everyone to leave by then. With us being short a footman and having extra people in the house, it's been quite a challenge." He wasn't certain why he'd allowed himself to be so frank—especially with a subordinate—but he simply felt as if he needed to speak to fill the void of the room. It was a strange sentiment, and he became annoyed with himself for feeling that way.

"Mrs. Bright was speaking with the constabulary today," said

Bradford. "If she has anything to say about it, things will be wrapped up soon." His tone was dry and skeptical.

"It was she who found those . . . those photographs," said Dobble, then immediately regretted bringing them up.

Of course, the news had run rampant through the downstairs at Mallowan Hall: there were sordid photographs of two naked men found half-burned in the fireplace in the Gray Room.

"Right."

"I'm certain she was . . . Surely she was horrified by them. After all, considering what they *were*," Dobble said, speaking around a strange lump in his throat. "Absolutely obscene, I understand."

Bradford shrugged, his large shoulders shifting beneath the shirt and work apron he wore. It appeared the man didn't care for coats, caps, or gloves. "Mrs. Bright wasn't the least bit overset by the photographs. Apparently, she examined them so closely, she used a magnifying glass to identify the coat of arms on the hearthstone of the room where the pictures were taken."

Dobble was taken aback. "She didn't. She did?"

Bradford's mouth flattened into something that could be a grimace or a suppressed smile. "There doesn't seem to be much that oversets Mrs. Bright."

At that moment, they both heard the sound of voices from outside the window.

To Dobble's surprise, none other than Mrs. Bright herself came into view—with her damnably blazing hair even more of a flamboyant beacon in the late afternoon sun.

She was wearing a different frock than she'd had on that morning—this one a pale green sprigged thing that was, thankfully, devoid of lace other than a dash of it over the top edge of a breast pocket. The woman had more dresses than Lady Marjorie Stirling—the daughter of an earl. Mrs. Bright simply had no business being a housekeeper with that sort of wardrobe and such a flashy, youthful style at her age. Whatever it was.

He huffed under his breath, causing Bradford to glance at him curiously.

"That woman should wear a bleeding cap," grumbled Dobble.

Bradford lifted a brow, and they both looked back at the window when the voices—a male one joining with Mrs. Bright's—became more intelligible.

"Why, what on earth is she doing out there with Mr. Sloup?" The words came out of Dobble's mouth before he could stop them.

It was quite unseemly for staff to consort with the gentrified guests. He would never have expected it of Mrs. Bright . . . or perhaps he shouldn't be surprised. After all, the woman certainly thought herself above her station.

He gritted his teeth and felt no shame as he listened to the conversation.

". . . how kind of you to think so, Mr. Sloup," she said in a tone that was very nearly simpering. ". . . the staff are seeing to your . . . whatever you need . . ."

". . . never get a cup of coffee . . ."

"I'm so sorry . . . I'll speak to . . ."

Their voices came in and out, as it seemed they were walking through the garden. Dobble couldn't see what was happening, but he could hear enough to catch snatches of the conversation.

". . . blasted woman sent my own valet off on an errand . . ."

". . . imagine how trying that must be . . ." Her voice was matter of fact.

". . . policemen crawling all over . . . not a whit of privacy . . ." He stopped speaking all of a sudden.

"Oh, Mr. Sloup, I don't think—" Mrs. Bright's voice suddenly sounded tense and annoyed.

"Perhaps you could find a way . . . make it up . . ." Sloup's voice had dropped to something oily and suggestive, and that had Dobble coming out of his seat to go to the window.

"Mr. Sloup, remove your hand this instant." Mrs. Bright's tone had gone frosty and clipped.

Bradford beat Dobble to the window, and they stood there, nearly shoulder to shoulder, looking out into the garden.

"Oh, come now, little lady," said the gentleman (Dobble used the term *gentleman* quite loosely in his mind). "No need to be coy . . . No one will see us . . ."

Sloup was standing nearly on top of Mrs. Bright, and he was holding her by the arm, whilst his other hand had slid around to the back of her skirt. Dobble gasped with shock and was about to shout out through the window when Bradford put up a silencing hand.

"Wait." The driver's single word was low and tight.

"I'll not say it again," said the housekeeper. Her voice was still crisp and calm, but it was evident she was in quite the pickle. Even from where he was, Dobble could see that her hand was turning paler above the man's tight grip on her wrist. "Release me immediately."

Despite Mrs. Bright's warning, Sloup did not release her. Instead, he moved in closer and was pulling her up against his body in an attempt to kiss her when she stumbled and twisted a bit, jerking in his hold.

This movement set Sloup off-balance, and she was able to move away . . . but he followed and grabbed at her once more as they did a sort of awkward dance up along the mossy, myrtle-covered berm at the edge of the garden.

Dobble could take it no longer, and he couldn't understand how Bradford could simply stand there and watch a woman being assaulted. His estimation of the other man plummeted as he hurried out of the pantry, intent on getting himself out through the servants' entrance and into the flower garden in moments. Giving no thought to the possibility of losing his position by assaulting a member of the gentry, he rushed down the corridor, up the stairs, and burst out into the garden. . . .

Just in time to see, in one smooth series of movements, Mrs. Bright give a sudden, sharp twist of her arm, breaking Sloup's hold, hook a foot behind one of his, and then follow through with an abrupt shove against his chest.

Sloup stumbled backward, arms flailing, and fell with an ugly splash into the goldfish pond behind him, just as, Dobble realized with reluctant admiration, Mrs. Bright had choreographed and planned.

He heard the low bark of a laugh and turned to see Bradford standing among sweet peas just outside the window watching as well.

"Figured she didn't need us," said the other man as Dobble walked over toward him, feeling slightly foolish over his aborted heroism.

If Mrs. Bright noticed either of her would-be saviors surrounded by a tangle of yellow and pink flowers near the butler's pantry window, she gave no indication.

She simply turned from the bellowing, accusing, threatening, and very, very wet and algae-covered Tuddy Sloup, smoothed her pale green dress, patted her hair into place, and walked back toward the house.

She was wearing a very satisfied smirk.

Phyllida didn't know whether Tuddy Sloup had dared to complain to her employers about the incident in the garden, but she did know he'd had to slog back into the house through the front door (he wasn't about to use the servants' entry!) covered in slimy green algae and smelling of fishy water.

He would have been forced to walk past the parlour where everyone was just gathering for drinks in order to go upstairs and freshen up, and surely he'd been seen by his peers.

She hid a grin. He'd gotten precisely what he deserved. Even after she'd given him a number of clear verbal and physical rejections, he had not only ignored her but had also doubled down on his efforts. He'd been warned.

Phyllida had no fears about any sort of dressing-down from either of the Mallowans. She knew she was fortunate in this situation, for that would not be the case for many—if not most—servants at the majority of gentrified households across the country.

In fact, she remembered that had been part of the reason Rebecca McArdle had come here to Mallowan Hall, leaving the much larger and prestigious Bunder House. There'd been some sort of incident there that caused her to leave. . . . She'd never told Phyllida exactly what it was, but Phyllida knew how to read between the lines, so to speak, and had understood what hadn't actually been said: It hadn't been a performance problem or dissatisfaction on the part of her employer. It had been something unpleasant that happened to Rebecca.

That, in turn, reminded her of what Lizzie had told her about Rebecca being very upset after the guests arrived at Mallowan Hall.

He's here. I can't believe he's here. Something like that, she'd said.

There were lurid photographs taken at Bunder House, Rebecca had left there after something unpleasant happened, many of the guests from Bunder House were now at Mallowan Hall, and Rebecca was dead.

It was patently obvious to Phyllida that none of that was a coincidence and that Rebecca's murder certainly had been carried out by one of the people involved in the Bunder House incident. But she still wasn't certain how a few pieces fit together . . . which was the only reason she hadn't called the constable and filled him in on everything else she'd concluded. She liked everything to be neat and tidy, and it wasn't . . . quite yet.

After the incident among the sweet peas and creeping myrtle, the rest of the afternoon and evening passed quickly. Yet something continued to nag at the back of her mind. Something she knew she was missing, something she'd forgotten, something that someone had said or that she'd seen . . .

Something that would confirm all her suspicions and allow those last pieces of the puzzle to fall into place.

It was after half eleven when Phyllida finally settled in her cozy bedroom, accessed via the sitting room where the police had met with the staff. She sat in her cushioned rocking chair next to a lamp and a reading table, with a small cup of tea and half a lemon biscuit. A vase of spilling sweet peas offered their sweet perfume, acting as a trophy for her victory over lechery earlier today.

Stilton and Rye had expressed their indignation over her lack of attention during her murder investigation, and she'd had to coax them out of their pout by offering cuttings of catnip Amsi had given her from the garden. Now Stilton was sitting in Phyllida's lap, purring like a well-run motor as she idly stroked her fur. True to form, Rye was perched on the highest flat surface in her bedroom—over the top of the rectangular mirror at her dressing table.

She didn't know how he managed such a feat of physics—not only sprawling up there on the narrow ledge but managing not to knock over the mirror as he leapt up or off. On occasion, he even catnapped there, with one half of his body, including two legs and a tail, hanging over and obstructing the glass.

"If only I could remember what I'm forgetting," she said aloud. "There's something . . ."

There was no one around to hear her musings. Mr. Dobble and the footmen, the visiting valets, and the gardener had lodging downstairs, near the kitchen. The maids, including the visiting Fanny, were up in the attic. The Mallowans were on the first floor; the guests were on the second and third floors. And of course, Bradford was in the chauffeur's apartment in the garage.

And so Phyllida went on speaking to her cats. They were quite intelligent. Perhaps they'd help her plug the holes in her theories.

"I've got naked men in photos, two dead people—one being a blackmailer and one, sadly, an innocent—lipstick on a collar, squeaky shoes, and almost certain blackmail. Someone is interested in historic country inns—presumably, the murderer—and two of our guests have recently been to one, obtaining a matchbook whilst there. We also have a missing motorcar owner, two different methods of killing, and a vexatious chauffeur."

She didn't know why Bradford had come up in her list. Probably because he'd been wildly unhelpful with his dry, mocking comments. "In addition, we have cheating spouses and a fiery row earlier today, which seems to have been resolved, and I did find it quite curious that—"

She stopped suddenly.

Had that been a noise?

Phyllida waited in silence for a moment. The only sound was the thud of her own heartbeat, deep in her ears.

When she didn't hear anything else other than the normal low creaks and shifts of an old house, she began to breathe a trifle easier. Still, she didn't feel like talking aloud anymore.

And then she wondered if she'd locked the door to her sitting room.

After putting Stilton down and gathering her Chinese silk robe about her, Phyllida padded silently from the bedroom through to the sitting room.

Just as she reached the knob and was about to check it, she heard a definite creak in the floor, followed by a quiet footfall.

And the squeak of a shoe.

Phyllida's breath caught, and she froze, listening over the roaring in her ears and the thudding of her heart. Surely she'd been mistaken—

There it was again. Just beyond her door.

Squeak. Creak. Squeak.

Then it stopped.

Outside her door.

Just on the other side of the flimsy wooden barricade.

Later, Phyllida would remember how cold terror had flitted through her, but for the moment, she had only thoughts of self-preservation.

Somehow the killer had realized she'd discovered his identity (which wasn't precisely true, as she was waffling between two individuals) and had come to silence her—just as had been done to Rebecca.

Squeak.

She looked around for something to be used as a weapon, considered a heavy book, a china teapot, her letter opener (in that instant of adrenaline-forced clarity, she passed over the fountain pen as an option), and settled on her steel-ribbed umbrella leaning in the corner. It had a sharp point at the top and was extremely sturdy. She'd found it useful once in chasing off a curious garden snake.

Just as she snatched up the umbrella, the sitting room door moved slightly in its frame, giving a soft rattle. Her heart shot into her throat, and she stepped back so as to have more room to use her weapon.

Then someone knocked.

CHAPTER 26

"*M*RS. BRIGHT?"

She didn't immediately recognize the voice coming through the door and waited to see what would happen next.

"Mrs. Bright, are you awake? It's Elton, ma'am, and I need some help."

A suspicious excuse if she'd ever heard one.

He knocked again, still softly—though there was no one else around to disturb. "Mrs. Bright, are you in there? I'm sorry to bother you, but I saw the light under the door."

Still hesitant, Phyllida considered the situation logically. Would a murderer announce his presence, knock, and wait for her to answer—while apologizing and asking for assistance?

He might.

If he were clever, he might.

But if he meant her harm, why did he not simply open the door and come inside—or attempt to? For she had already determined she had indeed locked the door.

He hadn't even tried the knob.

"What is it?" she replied, deciding it was best to do so, thus advising him that she was awake and aware and could certainly shout—for Phyllida never screamed—the house down should things go wrong.

"Oh, thank goodness you're awake." His relief sounded genuine. "It's rather silly, really, but not to Mr. Sloup, you know."

"What is it?" she asked again.

"It's just that . . . I don't know where the music room is, and Mr. Sloup believes he lost a cufflink in there. And, well, he's very particular about his clothing, and if I don't have it for him when he wakes up tomorrow, I'll . . . well, he might sack me."

Considering the situation, she found it comforting that he had neither tried to open the door nor asked her to do so, despite the awkwardness of speaking through the wooden barrier.

"What does the cufflink look like? Did he say where he was sitting in the music room?" The more information she had, the easier it would be to determine whether he was lying or was truly in distress. Tuddy Sloup's demands were certainly believable, and it made complete sense that the visiting valet had no idea of the layout of the huge house.

"It's jade and silver, ma'am, and he says he was sitting in a tall blue chair and then was near the piano for a while. But I'm to look until I find it." He sounded weary.

Still gripping the umbrella, her stomach a little tight, Phyllida unlocked the door. When she opened it, the valet stepped back from the threshold, and that made her feel even more confident about her decision.

"I'll show you where the music room is, and how to turn on the lights. None of the staff have mentioned anything about finding a cufflink, however." And then a thought struck her. "Was he wearing the cufflink when he came down for drinks before dinner?"

"Why, yes, he was. That was before he . . . oh." The valet's eyes widened comically, and she swore his mouth twitched a bit.

"Indeed. It's very possible that cufflink is either among the sweet peas or at the bottom of the goldfish pond."

They looked at each other in complete solidarity for a moment, and Phyllida decided she concurred with all the maids who'd been atwitter over the handsome valet. Elton was a rather fine specimen of masculinity.

"Very well, then, Mrs. Bright. I'm terribly sorry to have bothered you."

"Not at all," she replied. "I do hope you have a good rest of your night."

She stood in the hallway for a few moments just to make certain he did indeed go back down to the servants' quarters. And then she decided, quite suddenly, that she wanted another lemon biscuit.

Having the life scared out of one—and then finding out the catalyst thereof was completely innocent—apparently stimulated the appetite.

She was making her way down to the kitchen, still prudently armed with her umbrella, when she glanced habitually toward the single window in the stairwell.

What was that? She stopped. There'd been something out there. A bit of illumination, a glint, a flash. A lightning bug? Was her mind playing tricks on her?

Phyllida waited for a moment and saw nothing. She continued down the stairs to the kitchen, but before she went in to find a biscuit, she detoured to the five steps leading to the outside door. There was a window, and she looked out onto the grounds, peering closely into the darkness.

And there it was again—a flash. Definitely not a lightning bug. It was more like an electric torch someone was trying to keep unnoticed whilst moving about.

Whoever it was, was moving toward the garage.

Phyllida hesitated, but only for a second. It could be Bradford, but if it wasn't, things could be far worse than another terse exchange about her interfering with his work.

The telephone was upstairs; there wasn't time for her to run up and call over to the garage and try to awaken him. Whoever was sneaking around out there could do whatever nefarious thing they intended or, worse, could run away.

Nor did she have time to run down the corridor to awaken any of the footmen or valets. It would take too long, and she might lose the intruder.

Brandishing the umbrella, she opened the door and stepped out into the mild summer night. Fortunately, she was wearing her slippers; unfortunately, they were made from the same sapphire silk as her Chinese embroidered dressing robe, and the damp grass was going to ruin them.

Muttering a curse under her breath, she gathered up the robe in her free hand so as to keep as much of the hem from dragging across the grass and becoming soiled as possible. Umbrella in one hand, wad of silk in the other, she crept out into the yard and looked in the direction of the garage.

Yes. There he was. In the moonlight, she could see the shadowy figure of the intruder making his way to the side door of the garage. He seemed to be cupping his hand over the torch, then moving it away for a brief moment in order to illuminate his path.

And now that she saw the figure more clearly, she recognized that it definitely wasn't Bradford. In fact, she was fairly certain she knew who it was.

Sticking to the shadows and wincing mentally every time she stepped onto the soft, damp grass, Phyllida eased her way along the path of the intruder. Once he opened the garage door and slipped inside, she felt safe enough to dash toward the building and still remain unseen.

She was only slightly out of breath from bolting across the lawn when she reached the garage, so she waited for a moment. Didn't want the intruder to hear her breathing when she came up behind him in surprise.

However, before she even had the chance to duck into the garage, she heard a low, dull rumbling. It wasn't a car engine, and it took her a moment to realize it was the large door at the front of the building being rolled open.

Her suspicions were confirmed, and Phyllida sprang into action.

"Stop right there, young man!" she shouted and pushed the light switch near the door.

Only one string of lights fizzed to life, but it was enough to recognize Eugene Mustard's blond beard and green plaid hat. He jolted in shock and dashed toward his car.

But Phyllida was on his heels.

"Get out of my way!" he cried, fumbling with the motorcar's door.

She ran toward him, wielding her umbrella like a broadsword with the intent of chasing him away from the vehicle and further back inside the garage, where he might be cornered.

"Not so fast," she panted, struggling a little to keep from tripping over her robe whilst using two hands to swing her umbrella. "You—"

Suddenly, every light in the garage popped to life, and there was Bradford, bolting out from the shadows.

"Stop him!" Phyllida cried needlessly as Mr. Mustard shoved past her and yanked at the door of his car.

He fumbled the latch free and dove inside, then slammed the door just as she jammed her umbrella into the opening. The metal crunched a little but kept the door from closing all the way. Phyllida held on, trying to pry the door open.

"Bradford, hurry!" she shouted.

The car roared to life, and as it leapt forward, she was thrown violently off her grip of the umbrella. She stumbled backward and landed on the dirty floor of the garage. In her fine blue silk dressing robe.

Bradford tore past her after the automobile, which barely made it through the half-opened garage door as the driver's side door flapped open due to her umbrella. She struggled to her feet in time to see Bradford launch himself at the passenger side of the car and grab it by the door handle.

To her amazement, with the vehicle barreling away from the garage, picking up speed as it went, he held on, riding with his feet on the running board and somehow managing to stay upright and on.

Phyllida ran out of the garage after them in time to see Bradford disappear inside the moving motorcar. . . . And then, moments later, the vehicle swerved once, twice . . . and then on a third swerve, it went off the drive into a small ditch, where it halted, nose-deep into the depression. The driver's side door, which had never latched and had likely contributed to the vehicle's haphazard skittering, hung open. Eugene Mustard tumbled out and collapsed on the ground.

She didn't realize until after the fact that she'd had her hands over her mouth, and now she removed them as she ran toward the stopped vehicle—stopping to pick up her umbrella on the way.

She didn't ever remember running so fast in her life, and she was rewarded for her efforts by arriving at Eugene Mustard's side before he struggled to his feet.

"You're not going anywhere, sir." She used the tip of her bedraggled umbrella to poke him in the belly and keep him prone, leaning on the handle as she tried to catch her breath. "Mr. Bradford . . . are you quite all right?" she called, still panting a little, just as his shadow fell over her and her captive.

"That was a blazingly foolish thing to do, Mrs. Bright," he said.

She jolted upright. "Why, I—" Bradford was *reprimanding* her? And the lout wasn't even a bit out of breath!

"I had everything well in hand until you threw it all into the muck." He had his hands on his hips, which drew Phyllida's attention to the fact that the chauffeur was fully clothed . . . and was not wearing nightclothes, as one would expect, for it was well after midnight. "I'd been waiting for him to show up." He stepped forward, then set a heavy boot on Mr. Mustard's chest.

"You had?" Phyllida said, then realized how vacuous she sounded. And that her silk dressing robe was slipping open. She prudently pulled it closed. "Well, it was quite obvious, wasn't it? He wanted his car back so he could abscond in the night and never be seen in Devon again."

Bradford glanced at her, and if it wasn't so dark, she might think he rolled his eyes. But she couldn't tell for certain, and it didn't really matter.

"All right, on your feet, Mustard," he said, yanking the younger man upright.

"It's my car," whinged the captive. "I can take it if I want to."

"You may eventually get your vehicle returned," Phyllida told him smartly. "But not until after—"

She stopped cold right there. Literally and figuratively.

She didn't know why, but all at once, everything fell into place. It was like the sounds of coal dropping down the chute—*plop, plop, plop*—until the scuttle was full.

"Keep a tight grip on him, if you please, Mr. Bradford. The fact is, Mr. Mustard," she said, giving the chauffeur a meaningful look, "I don't believe you'll be getting your automobile back anytime soon."

"But I—"

"Because you're going to spend the rest of your life in jail. For murder."

CHAPTER 27

"*I*'VE ALWAYS THOUGHT IT WOULD BE QUITE SATISFYING TO DO THE denouement talk that Poirot does at the end of the book," Phyllida said to Agatha. "Standing in a room full of all the suspects, playing out the entire story bit by suspenseful bit . . . But I don't see how I could ever get Inspector Cork to allow it."

Agatha nodded. She seemed far more rested this morning than she had for the past two days—likely because she and Phyllida knew the end of these horrible events was in sight. "The denouement device really is quite convenient for explaining everything—at least in the book. In real life, I suppose it's not all that realistic . . ."

"If Phyllida wants to do a denouement speech and explain how she figured everything out, then she should," said Max Mallowan. "I'll speak to Cork. It's not as if *he* put it all together, did he?"

Agatha smiled at her husband. "Quite. That would be lovely, Max."

It was the morning after Phyllida (with the help of Bradford) had apprehended Eugene Mustard. The latter had been taken into custody, proclaiming his innocence the entire time and whinging about getting his car back.

"Mr. Mustard should be present for the speech, too, Mr. Mallowan," said Phyllida as he picked up the telephone. "Because it's not quite as simple as all that. There's more to the story than Eugene Mustard being a killer." She managed not to clench her fingers too tightly. What if she were wrong about the last bit? That was why she hadn't yet said anything about it. . . .

He nodded gravely. "I shall convey that information to the constable and the inspector. When would you like to do your speech, then?"

"As soon as possible, I should say. All the guests are ready to leave, and I, for one, would like the household to get back to normal." *And get everyone safely into custody as soon as possible,* she thought.

"Very well."

And so it was arranged. Phyllida wasn't present during the conversation between Mr. Max and the inspector, so she didn't know how hard he'd had to influence Cork to make it happen, but she did know that the constabulary and the other authorities more often than not bowed to pressure from the gentry.

And since this was a case of not one, but two murders, and the authorities had fumbled their way through it, she suspected Cork simply couldn't refuse the request of the gentry.

It was just noon when everyone gathered in the library—a fitting location, Phyllida thought, and the only room large enough to hold everyone comfortably.

The rug stained with Mr. Waring's blood was still being treated, but Freddie and Dobble had found a replacement, and it had been wrested into place with the help of Amsi and Bradford. There were extra chairs arranged, along with several settees brought in temporarily.

Inspector Cork had approached her on his arrival, and Phyllida had told him what to expect, but without giving the details. She wanted him to hear how it all had worked out step-by-step— so he could understand her brilliance and realize where he and Greensticks had gone wrong. Perhaps they would learn something about investigating murders.

She'd insisted the entire household be present: the parlourmaids (Ginny and Mary), the chambermaids (Lizzie, Bess, and Violet), the footmen (Stanley and Freddie), Mrs. Puffley, the kitchen maids (Molly, Benita, and Opal), Mr. Dobble, Amsi, and, of course, Bradford.

Due to his heroic assistance in capturing Eugene Mustard last night, she'd asked the chauffeur to join Amsi and stand at the French doors that led to the patio. Just in case someone tried to make an unexpected exit.

The visiting servants were in the room, as well: Fanny, Elton, and the two other valets, Leon and Tom.

And, of course, the guests were all present. The Devines, the Hartfords, the Budgely-Rhodeses, Mr. Grimson, and Mr. Sloup—who fixed Phyllida with a most unpleasant look when he came in to take his seat. Many of them had poured whisky, brandy, or sherry upon entering the room and now sipped and swilled. Phyllida fancied they were all attempting not to appear nervous.

Mr. and Mrs. Mallowan, Cork, and Greensticks, with Eugene Mustard in cuffs and sitting next to the constable, made up the rest of the audience. As Phyllida faced the room of expectant listeners, she admittedly had a pang of nerves.

Not about speaking to a group, but about whether somewhere, somehow, she'd made a mistake.

But no. Her conclusions made so much sense.

And so she began.

"As you are all aware, it was in this room two days ago that I discovered Charles Waring's body, stabbed with a fountain pen."

"Why is *she* talking?" demanded Mr. Sloup, standing in outrage. "I thought we were here to listen to the police inspector."

"Have a seat, Tuddy," said Mr. Max.

Mr. Sloup grumbled, but after seeing the forbidding expression on Cork's face, as well as the indomitable one on that of his host, he sat back down—but not without shooting another dark look at Phyllida.

She was just about to begin speaking again when the bell at the front door rang, reverberating through the house. Mr. Dobble looked surprised. They weren't expecting anyone else. Who was there left to arrive?

The butler swept from the room, and whilst he was gone, Phyllida suggested that Freddie refresh drinks and offer lights for cigarettes. She didn't want Dobble to miss *any* of her brilliance.

Moments later, the butler returned. "Dr. Bhatt has arrived," he said in a statement that sounded rather like a question.

"I do hope I'm not intruding," said the physician as he stepped into the room. "I heard there was to be a denouement!"

Phyllida smiled and very nearly blushed, for he was looking at her with admiration and unabashed enthusiasm in his dark eyes. "Of course. Please, have a seat. We've just begun."

Once Dr. Bhatt had his own drink of whisky and soda, Phyllida gathered her thoughts and went on. "At first, the mystery of who would kill Charles Waring was compounded by the fact that he was not who he'd presented himself to be—that is, a reporter from the *London Times* here to do a story on Mrs. Mallowan. He *was* a journalist—a photographer-journalist, as we soon found out—but he wasn't here to do a story. He *was* here to share some photographs he'd taken only a few months ago at the Duck Pond Derby Faire at Bunder House."

"I knew it," whispered someone. "Blackmail!"

Phyllida gave the room at large a quelling look. "Yes, but . . . not quite." Then, feeling more comfortable as she pulled her thoughts together, she began to move a little bit about the room as she spoke.

"And thus Mr. Waring's true identity and purpose for being here at Mallowan Hall stymied the investigation for some time. How could a motive be determined and a killer identified if we didn't truly know who Mr. Waring was and why he was here? It wasn't until his briefcase was found and its contents examined that we began to understand it all." Phyllida paused because she was certain she'd heard Constable Greensticks mutter, "*We?*" from where he sat near the door. She chose not to comment, but to plunge onward.

"Someone went into Mr. Waring's bedchamber and removed a notebook from the briefcase the morning after his death. I'll get to that particular event in a moment. The notebook was discarded, then later found by Mrs. Mallowan, who has a propensity for . . . er . . . collecting and using notebooks or notepads from wherever she finds them. Although any incriminating pages were torn out, the impressions made by Mr. Waring's pencil went through to a page beneath, and we were able to decipher those notes earlier this morning. The most recent page that had been removed had a note that read, 'There are more where these came from.' A rather threatening statement indeed." Phyllida looked around at her audience but gave no further information.

"Not long after that, we learned from Lizzie, one of the chambermaids, that Mr. Waring had been speaking to what sounded like a female in his chamber. No one saw her or heard anything to confirm this, but later, when I learned that there was a lipstick stain on Mr. Waring's collar when he was found here in the library, I realized that had to be true. But who was the female with whom he'd been talking . . . and obviously in conducting other business—likely in the library—at half past midnight? That is a question I shall also answer momentarily.

"Now, moving on to the scene itself. There were no footprints or mud stains anywhere in this room or on the first floor, which indicated that the killer *had* to have been in the house already when he killed Mr. Waring, considering the great rainstorm that occurred that night. That left out Eugene Mustard, Mr. Waring's supposed friend, as the possible killer—"

"I told you I was innocent!" cried Mr. Mustard. "Now release me!"

Phyllida looked at Inspector Cork. "You might be innocent of the murder of Charles Waring, that is true, but you aren't innocent of murder. You killed Rebecca McArdle."

Mr. Mustard's eyes widened, and he sagged back into his chair. "How the bloody hell do you know that?"

"We'll get to that, as well," Phyllida said with a smile. She was beginning to enjoy herself.

It was rather heady having a roomful of thirty people all waiting with bated breath for her next words . . . and knowing that one of them was sitting there, either squirming mentally from the fear that she would soon expose them, or sitting there confident and smug that she would never figure out what they'd done.

She couldn't wait to surprise the villain with her astuteness.

"Later, when the inspector examined Mr. Waring's briefcase, he discovered a packet of photographs tucked into an inner flap. It has always bothered me as to why the thief would take a notebook with what turned out to be rather banal notes in it but leave the photographs of the Duck Pond Derby. Certainly, those photographs weren't of a sordid nature, but they did prove that Mr. Waring was in the same location as every one of the people here at Mallowan Hall had been at one time, which also meant that someone here *did* know him—a fact which everyone denied. Therefore, someone was lying." She looked around the room, careful not to allow her gaze to rest on anyone for too long.

"Later that day, poor Rebecca was in the garden, picking vegetables for dinner. She must have been lured or otherwise drawn to the orchard—out of sight of the house—where Mr. Mustard beat her to death with a large stick. Why would he do this? Because Rebecca would have recognized him from an incident at Bunder House."

For the first time, Phyllida allowed herself to display the full and intense loathing she had for the man who'd killed her maid in cold blood. She gave him a cold, disgusted look. "Isn't that right, Mr. Mustard?"

Tight lipped, he looked away, refusing to meet her eyes.

"There'd been newspaper journalists lurking about the house and grounds since word got out that a dead body had been found at Agatha Christie's home, and even after Mr. Dobble chased them away from the house, they remained on the grounds, trying to get a glimpse of what was happening. Mr. Mustard simply joined the crowd. He had likely caught sight of Rebecca when she went out to use the outhouse or collect ice from the icehouse or did some other task and had recognized her then and known he had to silence her. Isn't that correct, Mr. Mustard?"

Again, the man sat silent and sullen.

"But it wasn't only Eugene Mustard that Rebecca McArdle recognized from Bunder House. She was quite overset on Wednesday night when she caught a glimpse of everyone at dinner—probably when she was helping the footmen to clear the table at the end. She recognized two other people at the table, one whose presence greatly worried her. So much so that she intended to remain cloistered in the kitchen for the rest of the house party in hopes of not being seen. It wasn't difficult for her to do that, of course, being a kitchen maid. They don't leave the kitchen area most of the time. She had no idea that she wouldn't even be safe in the garden, though, did she?"

There were quiet murmurs, mostly from the other maids, and Phyllida saw Lizzie reach over and grasp Bess's hand tightly.

"At the time, I didn't know anything about Rebecca's concerns, but her friends knew. And they also remembered what she'd said about her time at Bunder House—about how she'd walked into a bedchamber that was supposed to be empty, only to find it occupied by two men in a very compromising position.

"I wasn't aware of any of that until after the half-burned photographs were found in the fireplace in the Gray Room. It was clever of whomever Charles Waring had threatened with those pictures to use the fireplace in a vacant room to dispose of them. Unfortunately for that individual, the maids here at Mallowan Hall are so stellar that they noticed a fire in the middle of July and saw that the hearth needed to be cleaned—in a room that was supposed to be empty.

"The pictures, as I'm certain you have all learned before now, are of an explicit nature. The subjects of the photographs were not identifiable, due to the destruction of most of the images. However, I was able to ascertain that the pictures were taken at Bunder House and that they were taken by Charles Waring.

"And then, yesterday, I found the greater part of one more photograph under the mattress in the room at the Screaming Magpie where Eugene Mustard was staying. Unfortunately for him, that portion clearly showed his face, revealing him as one of the men in those intimate pictures. The other man is someone in this room."

Phyllida paused here, as she'd expected the low gasps and shocked looks that took place. She had been watching a particular person's countenance and was pleased to see a subtle confirmation of her conclusions reflected therein. Once the reactions subsided (and even more drinks were refilled, and more cigarettes lit), she continued.

"Now, let us back up a bit, shall we? Let us uncover the real reason Mr. Waring—and Mr. Mustard—came to Listleigh and Mallowan Hall. During my interview with Eugene Mustard, he said many things that were half-truths. For example, he claimed that Charles Waring had come to Mallowan Hall to confront a man about the way he treated his wife. That was partially true. He did want to speak to a man, but he more desperately wanted to speak to a woman with whom he had become infatuated—and likely had an affair—during the Duck Pond Derby at Bunder House.

"Charles Waring also came to Mallowan Hall because he was in possession of those compromising photographs. That was where Mr. Mustard came in. I wondered how someone could take such intimate photographs without being noticed or exposed, and I realized it was because Eugene Mustard was a willing participant in the setup.

"I suspect, although I cannot prove, that Mr. Mustard and Mr. Waring made a partnership wherein they took turns creating compromising situations—Charles Waring with women, and Eugene Mustard with men—and creating an opportunity for the other partner to take photographs of them in those intimate situations. And then the photographs would be used to blackmail the participants." She turned to Eugene Mustard. "Am I correct in that surmise?"

To her surprise, he lifted his chin and scoffed. "Been doing it for two years now. Going to big festivals and fairs and finding a mark and getting the pictures. Not difficult at all. Charlie was very

attractive to women, and I . . . well . . ." He shrugged. "Men aren't
quite as discriminating."

"That's how you bought such an expensive automobile, isn't it?
And wear such fine clothing? How else would you have had the
money to do so?"

"Made a lot o' blunt," he replied smugly.

"In this case, at Bunder House, however, Charles Waring actually fell in love with a woman, and that rather mucked up the
plans a bit, didn't it, Mr. Mustard?"

"He was moonin' all the time, talking about getting her to run
away with him. It would have ruined all our plans," said Eugene
Mustard.

"Quite so," said Phyllida.

"But I didn't kill him!"

"No, you didn't kill Charles Waring. Someone else did that. But
you did kill Rebecca McArdle . . . because when you were at Bunder House, *she* walked in on you and one of your—what did you
call them? Marks? She clearly saw you and could easily have exposed either of you.

"Poor Rebecca was quite overset by the sight and felt rather un-
safe at Bunder House after that. Perhaps you even lurked about
there, trying to get to her then, didn't you? If she exposed you, it
could ruin your entire blackmail scheme. She knew what she'd
seen was dangerous, and so she left the employ of Sir Avercroft
and came here to Mallowan Hall where she took a position as a
kitchen maid, which would keep her out of bedchambers, and
out of sight of any visitors."

Phyllida paused. Her voice was becoming rough from overuse,
and she needed a moment to recollect her thoughts. This was
quite a complicated matter. "Freddie, if you could pour me a cup
of tea?"

"Do you want I should put anything in it, mum?"

For an instant she considered whisky but supposed it was a bit
early—and she still had a killer to expose. "One lump and a
splash of milk, if you please."

"How much longer do we have to sit here?" grumped Mr. Budgely-Rhodes. "Said we could leave this morning, you did. Can't see how you can keep us here!"

"That's right," said Mr. Hartford, tucking away a handkerchief he'd used on his forehead. He made to rise. "Amelia, let's go—"

"You'll all stay here as long as Mrs. Bright is speaking," said Cork, with a sigh. "Which I do hope won't be much longer."

Mr. Hartford muttered something but sat back down, then took his wife's hand in his and grumbled over his shoulder to Mr. Devine.

"I shall endeavor to be as brief as possible," she said and heard a derisive sort of snort from over near the French doors. She ignored it and went on. "I had always suspected Mr. Mustard as being involved more than he let on." There was another, even more obvious snort from over near the French doors, and this time she did send a sharp look toward Bradford. "And once I identified him as being in the photographs, I realized he was the only person with a motive who could have killed Rebecca without being seen.

"Anyone else would surely have been noticed leaving the house and walking across the grounds to the orchard. And additionally, shall we be practical? None of the guests in this room would have enough knowledge of the grounds, of where to go and how to get there, to find a place where they could bash a woman to death without being observed. Not to mention getting back to the house unnoticed and with blood on their clothing. None of you had left the house since arriving on Wednesday, except to go together to the castle ruin. Nor did anyone have the *time* to do it, even though everyone had returned from the excursion. It simply didn't make sense relative to the timing.

"And when I considered the murder of Rebecca McArdle—a slapdash, hasty, violent one that required a number of blows to do the job—and compared it to the single, masterful stroke of a fountain pen into the carotid, I suspected we were dealing with two different killers. Once I drew that conclusion, all the other details began to fall into place." She smiled ruefully. "Not that I was the least bit pleased, knowing that we had not one, but two murderers here, but it was the truth, and one must accept the truth and plunge into correcting the problem without hesitation.

"Now, let us move on from the killing of Rebecca McArdle and examine what happened with Charles Waring. One of the things that nagged at me was the fact that whoever killed Charles Waring would have been sprayed with quite a lot of blood. Isn't that correct, Dr. Bhatt?"

"Yes, indeed. Even though one punctures the carotid, the heart continues to pump, and thus it would shoot blood all over the place. It would be quite fantastic to see . . ."

"Er, yes," Phyllida said quickly. She was still aggrieved over the amount of blood that had splattered the lovely books. "Thank you. So whoever stabbed Charles Waring would have certainly gotten a significant amount of blood on their clothing. But nothing showed up in the laundry—which isn't surprising, for who would be so foolish as to send their bloody clothing down to be washed? Nor were there any signs of bloody clothing being burned or otherwise discarded. Again, the staff here would certainly have seen or noticed anything unusual. And so I surmised that the bloody clothing would have been stored or packed away in the individual's trunk of clothing. Hopefully to be kept out of sight from valets and maids.

"Another concern I had was how difficult it would be to actually stab a man in the precise place one needed to in order to kill him with a single stroke. Now, I learned later that Mr. Waring had been quite inebriated at the time of his death, and so that would certainly have made him slow, sluggish, and perhaps not quite as aware of his surroundings. But those facts made me think differently about his killing, especially when it became clear the murderer had come up from behind him to fatally stab him.

"I had already determined that the murderer had to be a man—for who else would have the height and the strength to drive the fountain pen into his neck? Part of the reason for that conclusion was that I happened to be a witness to the individual who took the notebook from the briefcase. Whoever it was, was clearly removing incriminating evidence. Although I didn't see who it was, I did hear the way they moved and walked. The heavier footfalls clearly indicated a man, but there was something else that would give me the ability to identify him. Squeaky shoes."

She looked around the room, and her eyes stopped on a specific individual. "Just like yours, Elton."

CHAPTER 28

*T*HE HANDSOME YOUNG VALET SHOT TO HIS FEET. "NO! I DIDN'T DO it! I didn't kill *anyone!*"

After the briefest moment of suspense, Phyllida shook her head. "No, I don't believe you did. You may sit down, please, and allow me to continue to explain."

She looked at her audience and saw more interest reflected there now, as well as some tension around the mouth of a particular individual's countenance. *Excellent.*

"As I mentioned previously, I never understood why the person who stole the notebook from the briefcase didn't also snatch the pictures of everyone that were taken at Bunder House. It took me some time to realize why. Because that person—Elton—didn't know what he was supposed to be retrieving or why. He had just been told to take the notebook, and he did what he was told—as any proper servant would do."

The visiting valet relaxed visibly, and when he started to speak, she held up a hand to stop him. She didn't want Elton getting ahead of anything and ruining her story.

"And so who would ask a servant to do such a thing? Whoever did so was very clever about it, I must say. First, the individual asked a visiting servant, who wouldn't know his way around the house—as was demonstrated last night, when Elton was looking for the music room at midnight in order to retrieve his master's cufflink—or even know who was staying in which bedchamber, to do the job. Elton's master, Mr. Sloup, was on the third floor, and therefore Elton wouldn't know whose room was whose on the second floor, and so when he was asked to retrieve a notebook from the briefcase in the Gray Room, he simply assumed he was being asked to do so by someone who had the right to access the room. Am I correct, Elton?"

"Yes, ma'am," he replied, his eyes gleaming with gratitude. "That's exactly how it was when—"

"Please. I'd like to tell them all who it was at the proper time, shall I, Elton?" Phyllida said as Freddie brought her cup of tea.

"Yes, ma'am." Only Phyllida saw Elton's eyes flicker in a certain direction, and once again, she was pleased to have her conclusions confirmed.

"So let us step back once again and look at Mr. Waring's activities when he arrived here at Mallowan Hall." She took a bracing sip of tea. "Charles Waring arrived late. He joined everyone for dinner, where he presumably had his first contact with the woman he'd come to care about. Shortly afterward, everyone met in the music room for drinks and bridge, although apparently, Mr. Waring took a detour to his bedchamber to freshen up after his travels. Whilst he was up there, his—shall we say *paramour?*— met him, and they had a brief conversation. Or more. That might have been when she deposited the lipstick on his collar—at least, that was what I originally thought.

"So now we come to the crux of the matter—why Charles Waring was killed. It's very obvious. Surely you've all drawn your own conclusions by now. He was killed in order to keep those certain photographs from becoming public. Eugene Mustard's companion in those pictures would stand to lose everything if the images became public—his social standing, his wealth, and quite possibly his liberty." That saddened Phyllida quite a bit—the thought that a person could be imprisoned for what they did in the privacy of their own bedchamber.

"Well, are you going to tell us who it was so the bloody chap can be arrested, then?" snapped Mr. Budgely-Rhodes.

"I certainly am. But once again, it's not quite that simple," she said, fixing her most severe look on the room at large. "We are talking about murder here, ladies and gentlemen. Cold-blooded killing."

Phyllida gave Inspector Cork a significant look. Her hands felt a little damp; her belly a little queasy. This was it. If she was wrong, if she'd somehow missed something, some fact, some conclusion . . .

But no. She hadn't. She knew she hadn't.

"As it turns out, I was wrong about the murderer being the subject of the photographs. Although he would have everything to lose should they become public, he wasn't the only one whose lifestyle would be jeopardized. His wife would lose everything, as well, wouldn't she?"

There was a general "sitting up" of everyone in her audience then. Now they were really engaged. A murderess was far more interesting than a male killer.

"What I believe happened is that Charles Waring met up with the woman he'd fallen for at Bunder House—the woman whose husband 'mistreated' her by having affairs not with other women, but with other *men*. She would have been shocked when he showed up unexpectedly at dinner. For whatever their affair had been back at Bunder House, it had certainly never meant anything to her. And so as soon as she could, she met him upstairs to try and find out what he was doing here.

"He wanted to convince her to run away with him—a ridiculous notion, of course, that she, a woman of the gentry, would run off with a journalist—but Mr. Waring had been presenting himself as someone with a good amount of money, thanks in part to his ongoing blackmail scheme, and, well . . . love can be supremely blinding and cause one to take quite silly actions. I'm referring to his actions, not hers. There was never any chance that she would run off with Charles Waring. She was certainly shocked and dismayed by his arrival, but she is nothing short of a sharp, calm, cunning individual, and so she made arrangements to meet him in the library after midnight.

"I'm not certain when he told her about—or showed her. He

probably even trustingly *gave* them to her—that is, the photographs of her husband with Eugene Mustard—and it doesn't really matter. Poor Charles Waring thought that the pictures would shock her enough to make her want to leave her husband and run off with him . . . but in reality, I believe that she was already quite aware of her husband's propensities and didn't care about them at all. It might even have been part of their marital arrangements. After all, she obviously had her own affairs."

Here Phyllida looked at Elton again. "One can only assume she . . . er . . . showed her gratitude for your 'running an errand' for her up to the Gray Room, didn't she?"

His face was bright red, and he gulped. "She said it was her husband's notebook and that I was to retrieve it for him but not mention it to anyone, because he was sensitive about forgetting things."

"Of course she did. She really didn't leave any stone unturned, did she? The blood on her dress . . . Oh, yes, she was indeed the killer. She had to make certain those photographs never saw the light of day.

"It became so patently obvious to me once I saw the placement of the lipstick on Mr. Waring's collar. It was on the inside of the collar on his *left* side, and he'd been stabbed from behind on his *right* side. How easy it would have been to be standing behind him, looking over his shoulder, as he perused a book about historical country inns"—here she glanced meaningfully at Cork—"which they no doubt were discussing visiting after their escape . . . a logical continuation after the conversation at dinner. He wasn't a terribly tall man, and she would have been wearing heels . . . or perhaps he was even sitting in a chair she'd pulled into place for him.

"She was very possibly kissing him along the neck as he paged through the travel book, lulling him into complacency—as I've mentioned, he was quite inebriated, likely by design on her part—and then *kuh!*" Phyllida made a stabbing motion. "Right in his neck. She wasn't rushed, wasn't hurried, had plenty of time to make certain it was a single blow in the proper location, which would mean certain death."

The room was utterly silent. Everyone was looking Mrs. Budgely-Rhodes, Mrs. Devine, and Mrs. Hartford in turn.

Phyllida didn't need to look at them. She was, in fact, watching the husband. Because until now, she hadn't known whether he was complicit and aware of his wife's actions or not.

The expression on his face told her that he had *not* been aware . . . and for that, she felt supremely sorry for him. He'd done nothing wrong, but now his entire life would be shattered.

"How did I determine which of the married women was the murderer? It couldn't be Mrs. Budgely-Rhodes, because it was obviously not her husband in the photographs. The . . . er . . . shape of the . . . er . . . his limbs made that clear. And so that left me with Tana Devine and Amelia Hartford.

"Ultimately, it was the lipstick and the dress that helped me determine who the villainess was. The lipstick was a crimson red—a hue with cool blue undertones, one that only certain women can wear without it clashing with their coloring. But, of course, women do wear lipstick that doesn't suit their complexion or their hair, so I couldn't rely on that fact alone. But the dress . . . the dress that must have had blood all over it from the spraying carotid . . . where was the dress? There was no sign of ruined clothing anywhere. But . . . then again, yes there was. There'd been an accident with a coffee pot early Thursday morning, where the pot had spilled everywhere, Bess told me and Inspector Cork. On the table, the chair, the frock that had been lying over the chair . . .

"What better way to hide bloodstains than to create new stains over the top of them . . . isn't that correct, Mrs. Devine?"

CHAPTER 29

As the room exploded with gasps, Tana Devine merely looked at Phyllida with her cool, dark eyes. "You think you're clever, do you?"

"Well, I—"

"But not quite as clever as I am." She stood, holding a very small pearl-handled gun that, despite its size, appeared quite lethal.

"Tana!" cried her husband in a low, agonized moan. He reached toward her blindly. "*No* . . . you didn't. You *couldn't* . . ."

His wife looked at him, and in that moment, Phyllida saw not a cold-blooded murderess but a sad, exhausted woman with love and true regret in her eyes. "I'm sorry, Geoffrey. So sorry. But I couldn't let that little weasel do that to you—and to me. But really, to you. I just couldn't allow him to drag you through the muck . . . I really do love you, you know."

"I know . . . Tana, please, don't do anything else—"

"It's too late, darling. It's really too late. It's all over and done. Everyone here knows about it all. What more is left for us?" Still holding the gun, she swiveled and pointed it at Mrs. Hartford, who'd been sitting frozen and openmouthed since Mrs. Devine's name had been announced.

"And *you.* You thought you could get him into bed, didn't you?" Tana Devine sneered. "Not a chance, my dear. Not a chance. Which is why it didn't matter to me whatsoever that you flirted and teased and caressed Geoffrey. Although your poor husband . . . he didn't realize, did he?"

Mr. Hartford had gone very pale, and there was a faint green-ish cast under his skin. Phyllida thought she understood why—and it wasn't because of his wife's actions. But she decided to keep that bit of information to herself; there was really no reason to destroy the life of another person here today.

"Now, Mrs. Devine, let's not make another—"

"Hush up there, Inspector. I've got the floor now, and I must say, I wasn't worried at all when I saw you and the constable here bumbling around, trying to determine what happened. It wasn't until *she* began to get involved that I became a bit nervous. Still, I didn't expect you to put it all together, Mrs. Bright. I thought I had covered my tracks very well."

"Leaving the matchbook from the Old Ivy Inn by the fireplace in the Gray Room was a nice touch," Phyllida said. "It did make me think . . . but in the end, it was the lipstick and the missing bloodstained clothing that filled it all in for me."

Tana Devine sighed regretfully. "It always takes a woman to get things done properly, doesn't it? Now, if you'll just get out of my—"

Everything happened so quickly, Phyllida was never precisely certain what actually occurred. There was a flurry of movement from near the French doors, a loud crash, and then something flew through the air, just missed the top of Mrs. Budgely-Rhodes's head (she shrieked, of course), and then suddenly Mrs. Devine was crying out in pain and outrage.

When Phyllida looked over, she saw that Bradford had grabbed Mrs. Devine by the waist from behind and had closed his large, dark hand over her pale wrist. He had forced her hand—the one holding the firearm—down and was obviously squeezing her in order to force her fingers to open and drop the weapon.

Everyone was still. Even Mrs. Budgely-Rhodes, whose Gibson girl knot had been bumped akilter by a small pillow flying through the air during the moment of struggle, was frozen. Other than Mrs. Devine's soft, gasping breaths as she struggled to keep hold of her weapon—and, surely, to attempt to utilize it—the room was perfectly silent.

At last, with a low cry of fury, Tana Devine released the gun, and it fell harmlessly to the floor.

Constable Greensticks sprang into action, going immediately to relieve Bradford of his prisoner, while everyone else exploded into shocked and excited chatter.

Dr. Bhatt went over to Phyllida right away. He was beaming beneath his glorious mustache, and taking one of her hands in his, he said, "Very well done, Mrs. Bright. You had me hanging on every single word! It was like living in a detective novel."

Phyllida smothered a wry comment. He'd had *no* idea.

"Yes, indeed," said Mr. Dobble, who'd unbent enough to *almost* give her a smile. "It was a very instructive speech. A trifle long, perhaps, but I suppose it *was* a complicated matter."

But it was Agatha who was the most grateful. She pulled Phyllida away from the throng of people whose conversation had filled the room with a dull roar, and eased her off to the side. "Indeed, you were quite brilliant, Phyllie. I cannot thank you enough for helping to put this whole affair to rest. Hercule couldn't have done any better."

And that, in Phyllida's estimation, was the greatest of all compliments.

It was the day after the arrest of Mrs. Devine, and the household (thankfully) was getting back to normal. The last of the guests had left this morning (Phyllida found it ironic that after complaining about not being able to leave, the Budgely-Rhodeses and Mr. Sloup had stayed on for an extra day), and it felt as if the house itself had given a great, deep sigh of relief.

Mrs. Puffley was happy with a full staff in the kitchen, and so far, Opal had been working out to her satisfaction. The cook had even taken the girl under her wing, it seemed, and begun to show how to make some of her specialty items.

Mr. Dobble was back to being his stiff, condescending self, and although Stanley was still at least a fortnight away from being fully recovered, the butler had agreed to allow the footman to stay on.

Not that Phyllida thought he'd ever truly considered sacking him, but one never could tell with Harvey Dobble.

The maids were still gossiping wildly, of course, about everything that had happened, and Phyllida was still supervising the painstaking process of cleaning all the blood spatters off the spines of the library books.

She'd also had a brief conversation with Agatha early this morning, when she'd taken her tea.

"I hope your writing is going to pick up speed, now that all of this is over," Phyllida had said. She had set down the tea tray, then had offered Peter his biscuit.

"I truly cannot thank you enough for getting involved," Agatha had said. "I never imagined how awful it would be to actually live through such an ordeal—a murder in the household. Although, I suppose if one is going to have a murder in one's house, one should make the best of it. Even have a little bit of fun with it?"

"I wouldn't say I had fun with it," Phyllida replied. "It was more that I felt I couldn't trust the inspector to do a good enough job. Perhaps he would have come to the same conclusions I did, but not living here, not understanding how the household works . . . I'm not confident he would have done that."

"Quite. Well, everything made perfect sense the way you described it. I even made a few notes for my next book about the way you delivered the speech." Agatha smiled. "There was one thing, however, that remains confusing to me . . ." She shook her head. "No, perhaps I should just let it be."

"It's only me," replied Phyllida. "I shan't say anything to anyone."

"I know you won't. I only . . . Well, it's about Amelia and Paul Hartford. It just seems . . . He seemed so terribly hurt when she was going after Geoffrey Devine. I do hope . . ." She trailed off when she saw Phyllida's expression. "What is it?"

Phyllida sighed, struggling with her conscience. One man's life had already been ruined, possibly irreparably, thanks to Charles Waring and Tana Devine. But she knew Agatha wouldn't say anything to anyone, and after all, Paul Hartford was an old chum of Mr. Max's. "I don't believe Mr. Hartford was upset about Mrs.

Hartford's feelings for Mr. Devine. I believe he was upset about his *own* feelings for Mr. Devine."

She might never have realized that if she hadn't witnessed Paul Hartford's reaction the morning of the row with his wife. When Geoffrey Devine had reached out and touched his arm as if to pull him back and calm him over the argument with his wife, Mr. Hartford had looked pained and filled with anguish because the man he cared for (a man who, for all Phyllida knew, cared for him in return) was touching him . . . and he simply couldn't bear the emotion of the moment.

"I see," said Agatha slowly. "Well." She smiled wanly. "I do hope everything works out all right with them."

Phyllida hoped so, as well.

She had also taken the opportunity for a few pointed words with Inspector Cork on a related subject early this morning.

"In exchange for my assistance in bringing not one, but two murderers to justice," she had said firmly, "I expect that you'll forget about the identity of the other man in the photographs and simply allow things to go on as they have done. I'm certain you can come up with a reasonable explanation for why Tana Devine killed Charles Waring that won't involve her husband's . . . activities."

"But everyone in that room already knows about it," Cork had protested.

"That may be so, but if it comes from them, it'll be only gossip—*if* anything comes from them. It's only the authorities that could truly upset his life. And Geoffrey Devine is innocent of everything related to either of the two murders. Do I have your agreement, Inspector Cork?"

Phyllida Bright wasn't of the gentry and therefore didn't have the same influence on the authorities as a titled person would, but she did have many years of experience in dealing with recalcitrant boys, stubborn males, and irascible men.

And while Inspector Cork didn't precisely agree to keep quiet, he didn't make any move to arrest Geoffrey Devine for indecency, and that told Phyllida all she needed to know.

* * *

A little while later, as he was loading up to leave Mallowan Hall, Elton asked to speak to Phyllida privately.

Of course she agreed, for she hadn't had the opportunity to hear whether he had anything else to say on the matter related to Mrs. Devine and the way she'd used him to protect herself.

"Mrs. Bright, I just wanted to say to you . . . thank you for it all. I could . . . Well, it could have turned out worse for me, being fingered for taking that notebook, and if it hadn't been for you, I might have been sent up the river m'self."

"Not at all," she replied. "Anyone who looked closely at the situation would have known you had no motive and even less opportunity. After all, you were playing cards with the other servants during the time Mr. Waring was killed, weren't you?"

He nodded. "Yes, I was." He grimaced, shuffled his feet (a rather endearing activity, she thought, coming from such a masculine young man), then said, "I . . . wanted to say also . . . that I know my shoe squeaks a little. I could have it fixed, but I haven't done it. It's because . . . Well, if I'm going to sneak up on a maid to try and steal a kiss from her . . . I want her to know I'm coming. So . . . uh . . . she can run me off instead if she wants."

This caught Phyllida by surprise, and she was so charmed by this admission that she laughed uproariously. "Why, Elton, that is one of the most delightful things I've heard from a young man. I must confess, I was a trifle concerned that you might have . . . erm . . . picked up a few of your master's unpleasant habits."

"Oh, no, ma'am, not at all. In fact . . ." He hesitated, then went on, speaking in a lower voice. "I'm about looking for another position right now. But Mr. Sloup won't give me a recommendation, and so I fear I may be—"

"I believe Mr. Mallowan might be in need of a valet," she said— then instantly regretted it. As pleasant as Elton was, she could only imagine what sort of effect having a thoughtful, good-looking young man like him on the staff would have on her maids and their productivity.

It would wreak havoc, she was certain.

But the damage had been done, and Elton was already looking at her with shining eyes. He really was a very attractive young man. She could see why Tana Devine had—

"Thank you so much, Mrs. Bright," he said effusively. "I wouldn't presume, but it would be an honor to work here at Mallowan Hall with all of you."

Oh dear.

Later in the afternoon, Phyllida left her sitting room and descended the steps to the kitchen.

She'd been putting off this conversation long enough, and since Phyllida Bright was no shrinking violet, no coward, and not one to shirk her duty, she gritted her teeth and marched across the lawn to the garage.

She hadn't reached the building when Bradford came into view from around the back of it. As usual, he was coatless, hatless, and gloveless. The dark gray shirt he wore had the sleeves rolled up but no sign of grease or oil stains. There were some strange marks that looked like scrapes of mud on his lower legs.

When he saw her, he stopped short and settled his hands on his hips. His entire demeanor was uninviting, but he said nothing as she approached.

"Mr. Bradford," she said, speaking quickly before she could change her mind and stalk back to the house, "I wanted to thank you for your assistance yesterday."

He grunted an acknowledgment, then nodded, as if expecting her to go on.

For some reason, she did. She didn't even know why the words kept coming, but they did. "Things might have gone quite wrong if you hadn't stopped Mrs. Devine when you did. Because quite obviously, Constable Greensticks and Inspector Cork weren't precisely prepared to spring into action."

"Wasn't that why you stood me and Amsi at the French doors in the first place? I was only doing my duty," he replied.

"Well, it was much appreciated." She turned, ready to find solace in the house, away from the vexatious man.

"What about Eugene Mustard?"

She spun back. "What about him, Mr. Bradford?"

"You scoffed when I suggested he might be a suspect—"

The man was *infuriating.* "I was speaking of the murder of Charles Waring. Mr. Mustard was not a suspect in the murder of Charles Waring."

"But he is a killer, nonetheless, and during your very detailed speech, you claimed you suspected him all along," Bradford pointed out in what he likely thought was a reasonable tone.

"And I suppose *you* suspected him?"

"*I* wasn't sticking my nose into other people's business and trying to solve a murder, and so I wasn't suspecting anyone."

She felt her nostrils flare, and she managed to keep her tone steady. "Very well, then, Mr. Bradford. You've made your point."

Never say that Phyllida Bright wasn't reasonable.

But apparently, the chauffeur had more to say on the subject. "You nearly let him get away."

"Who? Mr. Mustard? I . . . *what? I* was the one who happened to see him lurking about the grounds, gaining access to the garage. If I hadn't accosted him, he—"

"You nearly let him get away. I was waiting for him in the garage. I—"

"What do you mean, you were waiting for him?"

"Obviously, he was going to attempt to steal his motorcar back and flee that night. He'd already abandoned his room at the Screaming Magpie. Oh . . . did you not draw that conclusion, Mrs. Bright?" His smile was filled with genuine humor, and the corners of his eyes were crinkling with delight at her consternation.

"Well, of course I suspected he was going to be trying to retrieve his vehicle—"

"But you nearly ruined the whole thing. I was lying in wait and was going to stop him after I was certain he didn't intend to make any other mischief—like disabling another automobile or stealing anything else. But you had to start shrieking and turning on lights. And what on *earth* did you think you were going to do with that measly umbrella?"

Phyllida was nearly speechless. She simply couldn't carry on a conversation with that man any longer.

"Very well, then, Mr. Bradford. Once again, you've made your point. I see that it's time for me to return to my—"

"It was very clever of you to figure out about the dress," he said, stopping her in her tracks.

She turned. "It was utterly simple logic. If there was no blood-stained clothing, what had happened to it?"

"It was clever," he said again. "I'm certain Mrs. Devine would have gotten away with her crime if you hadn't been interfering in a police investigation."

She supposed, as compliments went, that was about the best she was going to get from Mr. Bradford. "I read quite a lot of detective novels. I could see that the authorities weren't . . . What on earth is *that?*"

All at once, a black bundle of *something* came tearing around from the back of the garage. It was *barking.*

Phyllida looked down in horror at the wild mass of unruly black fur. Goodness, it was as if Bradford's mop of hair had duplicated itself into a living creature with beady black eyes, a maniacally wagging tail, and a long, pink, *wet* tongue.

"It's a dog," replied the chauffeur, who'd crouched to greet the feral beast, which seemed intent upon washing over every bit of the man's face with that slathering tongue. "Actually, she's just a puppy."

Phyllida shuddered and stepped back. Fortunately, the creature hadn't seemed to notice her yet. "I can see that it's a *dog,*" she replied, looking at the thing skeptically. It was far too large to be a puppy. "But what is it doing *here?*"

"Mrs. Puffley suggested we might want to have one—to keep intruders away and to help chase the foxes from the chicken coop. I concurred it would be an excellent idea to have a companion in the garage," said Bradford. He was actually *laughing* as he attempted to remove his face from the enthusiastic washing it was receiving.

If the foolish man really wanted to avoid the slathering, all he had to do was stand up, didn't he?

"Mrs. Puffley mentioned something to me about a dog, but we already have Peter and—"

"I put it on my list to Mr. Dobble," Bradford said, standing up at last. He had an idiotic grin on his face as he did so, and Phyllida blinked because she had never imagined he might look so . . . ungruff. "And he approved it."

"*Mr. Dobble* approved a *dog*?" Surely the world was being turned upside down as she spoke. "But he loathes animals—cats, dogs, horses, especially rats and mice, even birds—so I cannot imagine . . ."

"Well, it was on my list, and she's here now. And here she's going to stay, aren't you, little miss?" Bradford said, leaning down once again to pet the squirming, leaping, wagging creature. "We just have to come up with a name for you, don't we?"

And then the unthinkable happened.

The beast discovered that Phyllida was standing there.

With a joyous yelp, she (apparently, the canine was of the female sort) launched herself at Phyllida.

"No! No! Off! Away!" she said, stepping back so quickly, she nearly tripped over her own feet. To her utter mortification, Bradford caught her by the arm as she staggered backward.

The furry beast—who was the size of *two* Stiltons—didn't seem to understand and leaped at her again. Phyllida felt the brush of a wet tongue *through her stockings*, and the creature jumped so high in an effort to gain her attention that her fur brushed over the back of Phyllida's hand. It was cloud soft, not at all wiry, as she'd expected, but that still didn't mean Phyllida was going to allow it to touch her.

"Get it—*her*—away," she said from between clenched teeth as Bradford watched with unconcealed humor.

"All right, all right. You don't need to get in a lather over it," he said, and still chuckling, he bent down to pick up the twisting, writhing mess of dark fur.

"This is the second time in three days I've been accosted by unwanted attentions," Phyllida said primly.

"Ah, yes. The obnoxious Mr. Sloup," replied Bradford.

"How did you know about him?" Phyllida said, surprised.

"Mr. Dobble and I were witness to you knocking him over the berm of moss and myrtle into the goldfish pond. It was a battle plan well executed, I must say, Mrs. Bright."

Taken by surprise, she lifted her chin. "Thank you." She looked at the still-wriggling beast in his arms, who seemed almost rabid in her desire to be set free. "If you insist upon keeping that . . . thing, please don't let it come near me."

"Might I remind you that *you* came out here into *her* domain, Mrs. Bright?" said Bradford smartly, turning his face away to avoid a bright pink tongue. "She lives in the garage now."

"Very well. I shall keep myself as far from the garage as I possibly can," she said.

"One can only hope," he muttered.

"Mr. Bradford, I really think . . ." She barely caught herself from stomping her foot. *So* vexing.

"Aha. I have the perfect name for her," he said suddenly.

Phyllida, who'd once again spun around to stalk to the house, turned back. "And what is that?" she asked suspiciously.

"Myrtle. I believe I'll call her Myrtle. In honor of a well-executed battle plan."

Phyllida Bright's Orange-Sage Syrup

Oranges are dear to come by in England in the 1930s, so when they do make their way to Devonshire, Phyllida Bright ensures that no part of the orange goes to waste!

Mrs. Bright oversees the making of this autumn-inspired syrup in the distilling room, so as not to get in the way of Mrs. Puffley and her kitchen maids, although she does use the ovens for the roasting. (In return for invading her space, Mrs. Bright promises Mrs. Puffley her own quantity of the syrup once finished.)

Mrs. Bright recommends adding a generous amount of syrup to hot tea instead of lumps of sugar, and if one is in the mood for a hot toddy, a dollop of whisky should also be added to the tea and syrup. However, Mrs. Bright's favorite use for Orange-Sage Syrup is to simply mix it into straight whisky, brandy, or cognac for a cozy, bracing autumn drink. One can imagine that Mrs. Bright might employ this libation after a long day dealing with Mr. Dobble.

The syrup may also be drizzled over scones, vanilla cake, or pancakes if one desires as well.

INGREDIENTS

- Peels from 2-4 *washed* oranges
- 1-1½ cups of honey
- ¼ cup brown sugar (or regular sugar)
- 10-15 large, fresh sage leaves; include the stems if you like

DIRECTIONS

- Mrs. Bright roasts the orange peels in the kitchen oven by putting them on a cookie sheet at 400° F for approximately a quarter of an hour, until they turn a little brown and become fragrant. She suggests watching them closely so they don't burn.
- Add all ingredients, plus 1.5 cups of water, to a saucepan.

- Bring to a boil, stirring occasionally.
- Once boiling, turn heat down to simmer. Stir occasionally. Mrs. Bright is not concerned if the syrup foams up a little; she merely stirs the foam back into the concoction.
- After about 20-30 minutes, the syrup is finished. It won't be very thick, Mrs. Bright warns, but taste it. It should be very, very sweet, and the orange and sage flavoring should be delightfully noticeable.
- Remove the orange peels and sage, and strain the rest of the syrup into a container (glass is best). Mrs. Bright often saves some of the orange peels and cuts them into long strips to be used as garnish for whisky or cognac.
- The syrup can be refrigerated in a covered container for two weeks . . . although at Mallowan Hall, it doesn't last more than a few days.
- Makes about 1.5 cups of syrup.
- Add to hot tea or whisky (or both!) to taste. Drizzle over lemon sponge cake. Pour over vanilla cupcakes, pancakes, or scones.

DISCUSSION QUESTIONS FOR MURDER AT MALLOWAN HALL

1. In managing the household of the large estate at Mallowan Hall, Phyllida Bright has a lot of responsibility. What do you think would be the biggest challenge she faces on a regular basis—when there isn't a murder!—and how does her personality help or hinder her?

2. Phyllida acts as both a sort of drill sergeant and mother hen to her staff. How does this dual approach help her success as a housekeeper?

3. Phyllida and Dobble have a competitive relationship, yet they both have the same end goals: a smoothly run household that keeps the master and mistress happy. Do you think their competition is an asset or a detraction for their positions?

4. Phyllida does her best to ensure that the authorities don't have her real age. Do you think this is merely a vanity, or is she hiding something else? If so, what? And why?

5. Phyllida and Agatha Christie Mallowan have an unusual relationship between housekeeper and employer. What do you think about this? Why do you think Phyllida would have taken a job working for her friend?

6. The shade of red lipstick was instrumental in helping Phyllida identify the murderer. Are you more like Dr. Bhatt, who thinks "red is red" or more like Bradford, who seems to understand the nuances of shade?

7. Phyllida is most certainly not a "dog person." Do you think her preference for cats—and Bradford's for dogs—indicates a personality type? If so, why and how? Do you think Phyllida will ever warm up to Myrtle?

8. There are parlourmaids, chambermaids, kitchen maids, footmen, a gardener, a chauffeur, and more at Mallowan Hall. If you were starting off in "service," which position would you want to have?

9. What surprised you most to learn about the way large households like Mallowan Hall were run during the 1930s?

10. There are many references to Agatha Christie novels in Murder at Mallowan Hall, especially during conversations between Agatha and Phyllida. Which ones did you catch?

11. What did you think about Phyllida's decision—and her influence on Inspector Cork—to keep Mr. Hartford's personal life private, and to protect Mr. Devine from being charged for "indecency"?

Don't miss Phyllida Bright's next case . . .

A TRACE OF POISON
by
Colleen Cambridge

In this sparkling new historical mystery, Phyllida Bright, house-keeper to the grand dame of murder mysteries, Agatha Christie, must uncover the killer among a throng of crime writers . . .

In England's stately manor houses, murder is not generally a topic for polite conversation. Mallowan Hall, home to Agatha Christie and her husband, Max, is the exception. And housekeeper Phyllida Bright delights in discussing gory plot details with her friend and employer . . .

The neighboring village of Listleigh has also become a hub of grisly goings-on, thanks to a Murder Fête organized to benefit a local orphanage. Members of The Detection Club—a group of celebrated authors such as G. K. Chesterton, Dorothy L. Sayers, and Agatha herself—will congregate for charitable events, including a writing contest for aspiring authors. The winner gets an international publishing contract, and entrants have gathered for a cocktail party—managed by the inimitable Phyllida—when murder strikes too close even for her comfort.

It seems the victim imbibed a poisoned cocktail intended for Alastair Whittlesby, president of the local writers' club. The insufferable Whittlesby is thought to be a shoo-in for the prize, and ambition is certainly a worthy motive. But narrowing down these suspects could leave even Phyllida's favorite fictional detective, M. Poirot, twirling his mustache in frustration.

It's a mystery too intriguing for Phyllida to resist, but one fraught with duplicity and danger, for every guest is an expert in murder—and how to get away with it . . .

Coming soon from Kensington Publishing Corp.

Read on for a preview.

CHAPTER 1

Friday morning

"*I* JUST DON'T SEE ANY WAY AROUND IT. HE'S SIMPLY *GOT* TO BE done away with," said a hushed voice.

"Right. The problem is . . . *how* to do it," replied another voice. ". . . soon . . ."

While anyone else overhearing such an exchange would surely be alarmed, Phyllida Bright merely smiled to herself and went about the business of counting tablecloths for the welcome luncheon at the Listleigh Murder Fête.

Being the housekeeper at the vast and elegant Mallowan Hall, the home of the famous novelist Agatha Christie and her husband, Max Mallowan, Phyllida was quite used to overhearing—and participating in—discussions about murder and the finer points of how to permanently do away with an inconvenient person.

Whether abovestairs or belowstairs, there was always some conversation going on about which poison to use, whether a knife or a gun would be more or less bloody when employed than the other, and if a blow to the head would actually do the deed or whether a spike shoved into the back of the neck would need to be added to complete the task before stuffing the body of a maid into a downstairs cupboard.

"Poison . . ." replied the first person, whose words were becoming less audible. Perhaps they were walking away. " . . . coffee. Or a drink. . . ?"

"There is . . . that," replied the other. ". . . his new car, eh?"

Phyllida was fairly certain the first was a man speaking, but it was difficult to be certain as she was inside the social hall at St. Wendreda's Catholic Church and the voices were coming through an open window. Regardless, surely it was one of the detective fiction writers who were here for the Murder Fête. There were dozens of them milling about—both published and unpublished writers—many hoping to get a glimpse of some of the popular and well-known authors such as Mr. Chesterton or Miss Sayers.

"Yes, poison . . . wouldn't it? . . . something . . . done," replied the companion, whose sex was indistinguishable due to its hushed tone. "And soon . . . cannot *bear* his boastful, overbearing nastiness any longer." These last phrases became stronger and more distinct, clearly indicating the frustration of the speaker, whose voice was low and crusty enough to be either male or female.

Phyllida *tsk*ed to herself, wondering how writers could come to dislike characters they'd created. Of course, not being a writer herself, she couldn't imagine such an occasion.

However, there was a time only recently when Agatha had become weary of and annoyed by her most popular fictional detective, Hercule Poirot. Like Sir Arthur Conan Doyle, whose Sherlock Holmes had so become the bane of his existence that he actually killed off the character—only to be required to revive him in order to silence his fans—Agatha had become fed up with Poirot and his persnickety, bombastic ways.

Fortunately, Agatha hadn't actually plotted to kill the little Belgian detective—an event that would have prompted Phyllida to have a pointed and impassioned conversation with her employer. For Phyllida had what one might term a literary *tendre* for the brilliant, mustachioed detective.

Of course, the discussion to which she was currently privy might very well be about a villain rather than a meddlesome crime fiction detective, but she quite doubted it. The tone of voice implied a person very much at the end of their rope in dealing with the individual, which implied someone well-known to the speaker such as a recurring character.

She hoped it wasn't Miss Sayers speaking about Peter Wimsey. Not that Lord Peter could hold a candle to Poirot, but Phyllida certainly enjoyed his detective work—and, having recently solved a real-life murder herself, she highly approved of the intrepid Harriet Vane as his partner (although she was no comparison to the spunky Tuppence Beresford).

"Mrs. Bright, ma'am, the flowers for the tables are here. The vases are on their way."

Phyllida turned from her stack of tablecloths to speak to Ginny, the first parlourmaid from Mallowan Hall. Presumably, the person standing next to her was Amsi, the gardener from the manor house, but it was impossible to tell for certain as the figure was completely obliterated by the mountains of roses, Michaelmas daisies, and gladioli in the cart he was pushing.

"Excellent. When they arrive, line up the vases on the table there and you may arrange them—five roses, six daisies, and two gladioli for each. Make certain the glads are in the center, mind, and mix the colors," Phyllida told her, even as she scrutinized the fresh apron and uniform her maid was wearing.

Not one straggle of honey-gold hair escaped Ginny's cap, and her stockings were sleek and smooth—as they should be. Phyllida had extremely high expectations of her staff at all times, but she was particularly exacting when they were to be interacting with the public.

She turned to the second of the maids she'd brought with her from home. Despite being a kitchen maid and not usually seen by guests or even the family, Molly was just as clean and pressed and starched as Ginny was—and could be counted on not to gossip quite as much. Phyllida mentally nodded approval. "Molly, you can put out the tablecloths—there's a rectangular one for the head table and the rest are circular—and then help Ginny place the flowers. Directly in the center of the tables, if you please, with three spaced out across the head table."

Phyllida gestured to the tablecloths she'd just finished counting. As anticipated, there were sixteen round ones, which left two extra since there were fourteen luncheon tables. Phyllida always had an extra of everything.

Except a strand of patience when it came to Myrtle, who'd just made her appearance.

"What is that beast doing in here?" she demanded as the dark, curly-haired mop of a puppy barreled into the hall.

Bradford, the Mallowans' chauffeur and Myrtle's master (Phyllida used the term loosely, for she wasn't quite certain who was the master of whom when it came to the two of them), came strolling into the room as if he had not just unleashed a hell-hound in a church hall. He was carrying a large crate that presumably held the vases. "She wanted to come with me," he replied, as if it were the least bit permissible to allow a puppy to run rampant through a luncheon hall if it wished to do so—unwittingly confirming Phyllida's opinion about who mastered whom. "Where do you want these, Mrs. Bright?"

Every time he said her name in that drawling, ironic tone, Phyllida's hackles went up. She couldn't help it. The man was impossible, and simply *filled* with arrogant criticisms and unwanted observations. "On the table there," she replied frostily. "Dogs are *not* allowed in the luncheon hall."

Myrtle was tearing about the space, her tail flying behind her like a banner, barking, bouncing, skittering, and generally making a nuisance of itself. Phyllida removed herself quickly from the beast's path as it streaked past her. Since Myrtle's invasion of the grounds at Mallowan Hall, Phyllida had had to retire three pairs of silk stockings due to rents from the creature's paws as, for some reason, the beast seemed particularly enamored with her.

Needless to say, Myrtle was not welcome inside Phyllida's domain of the manor house.

"Of course not, Mrs. Bright," replied Bradford as he set down the crate. Was he chuckling at her quick footwork to avoid the beast? "But the luncheon isn't for four hours. She'll be long gone by then."

Phyllida was interrupted from a tart reply about the remnants of Myrtle's hair being everywhere by the arrival of Mrs. Agatha, Miss Sayers, Mr. Chesterton, and Mr. Berkeley.

"Good morning, Phyllida. I see you have everything well under control here," said the lady of Mallowan Hall. There was a hint of laughter in Agatha's voice, for upon her entrance, Myrtle had come charging up to her, tail wagging wildly. "Yes, you *are* quite adorable, aren't you?" As she bent to scratch the wriggling four-legged bundle of curls, Phyllida smothered an acerbic comment.

She and Agatha had become friends during the Great War when women were eagerly conscripted for all sorts of jobs. At the time, both were single women, and since they were about the same age, their rapport was natural. Agatha had worked in the dispensary at the hospital—which was how she'd learned so much about the poisons she used in her books—and Phyllida had worked as a nurse at the same hospital before going to the frontlines. They were great friends and had got along tremendously for more than ten years. The fact that Phyllida had chosen to take the position as housekeeper at Mallowan Hall had not altered their relationship in the least, although they did take pains to keep from being too familiar around each other in front of the other servants or guests.

One thing housekeeper and mistress did not agree upon was an affection for dogs. Mrs. Agatha had a wire terrier named Peter, and when Bradford had brought Myrtle to live with him in the garage apartment, both of the Mallowans had taken to the beast with rapturous affection.

Phyllida had not.

"Mr. Bradford promises to remove it well before the food arrives," she told Agatha primly, knowing he was listening. "But of course we will have to sweep again due to the dog hair." She shot the chauffeur a dark look and was rewarded by him ignoring her.

"I have no doubt everything will be in strict shipshape with you at the helm, Phyllida." Agatha straightened, leaving Myrtle to find another victim.

Phyllida quickly sidestepped the slathering, drooling, panting beast once more, and so the mop transferred its attentions to Miss Sayers.

"You'll be sitting at the head table there, G.K.," said Agatha. She was speaking to Mr. Chesterton, who had agreed to be the

Grand Master for the Murder Fête, as it was a charitable event being sponsored by the Detection Club.

The Detection Club was a group of detective fiction writers, including Agatha Christie, G. K. Chesterton, Dorothy L. Sayers, Anthony Berkeley, Hugh Walpole, Freeman Wills Crofts, and a dozen or so other popular authors. They met regularly in London to discuss the techniques and travails of crime fiction writing, and to provide each other support. Each had taken an oath to be fair to their readers in creating and presenting the solutions in their stories. Whether the oath was anything more than an inside joke, Phyllida wasn't certain.

The Murder Fête in Listleigh was a weekend event that had been arranged to allow aspiring writers of detective stories the opportunity to meet successful writers of such works, as well as for the public to come and listen to the authors speak and to buy their books.

The aspiring writers paid a fee for the first day, which included the private Welcome Luncheon at half past one with the Detection Club attendees who were present—Sayers, Chesterton, Berkeley, and Christie—along with short classes taught by some of the published writers. The highlight of the first day was an outdoor cocktail party in the evening, giving the aspiring writers another chance to hobnob with the author celebrities. Along with their entrance fee, each amateur author had been offered the opportunity (for an additional fee) to submit a short story for a contest to be judged by the professionals. Tomorrow, Saturday, the fair on the grounds of St. Wendreda's would be open to the public for book sales and a general festival. On Sunday at tea time would be the awarding of the Murder Fête Grand Prize.

As Grand Master, Mr. Chesterton would speak at the luncheon today, and on Sunday he would give out the prize for best short story to one of the aspiring authors. The prize was a publishing contract for the story in both England and the United States. Phyllida was privately rooting for Dr. Bhatt to win, for she'd read some of his work about a physician turned amateur detective. She thought it was quite, quite good.

Listleigh had been chosen as the site for the Murder Fête because of the local writers' club. After John Bhatt, the town's doctor and a member of the local club, heard about a fundraiser the Detection Club had participated in in London, he conceived the idea of a local fundraising event. This one was for the nearby orphanage and school for wayward children sponsored by St. Wendreda's, which needed a new roof. Dr. Bhatt had sent a very compelling proposal to the Detection Club president, Mr. Chesterton, by way of Mrs. Agatha. The publicity such an event would afford the writers, the money it would raise for children in need, and the opportunity to get out of London during the hottest part of the summer prompted the Club to accept the Listleigh writers' club's proposal.

Because of Agatha's involvement, Phyllida had readily taken charge of the planning and execution of the event. Not only was this sort of activity exactly what she loved to manage—and was exceptional at doing—being at St. Wendreda's for several days during the setup and event meant she was *not* at Mallowan Hall, and therefore did not have to interact with Mr. Dobble, the butler. That was always a reason to be particularly chipper.

"Very well," Mr. Chesterton replied after he looked at the table. Well into his sixties, the writer of the popular Father Brown stories had masses of thick dark hair and habitually wore a pince-nez. He was a bulky, imposing man in his sixties whose dark clothing merely added to his commanding persona. "How many aspiring writers will be here?"

"There are fifteen of them who have registered, and paid, of course," Agatha told him. "They aren't all from Listleigh. Some are coming from as far away as Wales." She had declined the local club's request to be the Grand Master, for she was quite shy and preferred not to speak in public or even in small groups unless she knew them well. It was a monumental decision for her to agree to participate at all, for Agatha disliked publicity and the press—but she could hardly decline with the event being such a local undertaking.

Being instrumental in the planning and executing of the event afforded Phyllida the opportunity to help keep her reclusive friend out of the public eye as much as possible, and the only public event was tomorrow's book fair and the announcement of the grand prize winner.

"I trust you all received your copies of their short stories—there were only ten submitted—for the judging?" Agatha asked her colleagues.

"Yes indeed," replied Miss Sayers. "I received my packet a fortnight ago, which gave me ample opportunity to read them—although I had to finish the last on the train here." She was a large, boisterous woman who tended to wear long black frocks that ebbed and flowed around her. Her dark hair was cut short in a style called the Eton crop, giving her a mannish appearance despite her draping clothing. "Some of them were actually quite good."

"Quite. I thought so myself. Might there be some competition with publishers for us?" said Mr. Chesterton with a chuckle.

As she watched Ginny make up the vases and Molly finish the tablecloths, Phyllida couldn't help but listen in hopes of overhearing any hint about who might be awarded the prize.

"Father Tooley has had all of the rankings since Monday of this week," said Agatha. "So no one can accuse us of falling to any undue influence once we begin mingling with the writers." She smiled.

"Indeed," replied Mr. Chesterton. "A holy man counting the tallies would be above suspicion."

"Have you decided on a favorite yourself?" asked Miss Sayers.

"Oh, yes," replied Agatha. "There was one tale that particularly stood out to me. I found it quite entertaining, as well as clever. But there were several others with great merit. It should be quite interesting to see where we all stand with our preferences."

Unfortunately, before she could get any indication of which story that was, Phyllida was required to move out of earshot when Myrtle discovered the swaying tail of a tablecloth that had just been placed.

"Leave that be, you little recalcitrant, annoying, hairy, beastly thing," Phyllida said as she marched over to stop the nonsense. "Mr. Bradford, if you would remove this nuisance at *once*."

Looking not the least bit abashed—and, in fact, appearing almost as if he were enjoying himself—the chauffeur swooped up the motley beast. As Myrtle began to slather his face with what passed for affection, Phyllida couldn't help but notice that the beast's thick curls were indistinguishable from her master's unruly mop of hair. *Two of a kind,* she thought irritably. *Both lacking any sort of decorum or respect.*

"All right, then, Mrs. Bright," said Bradford. The bridge of his arrogant, blade-like nose was shiny where the dog had been licking him. Phyllida suppressed a shudder. "We'll take ourselves off, then. What time shall we return to bring you back?"

It was Phyllida's current private, most fervent desire that the Mallowans would either hire a second chauffeur, or that Bradford would leave—and take his dog with him—for some greener pastures or greasier garages. Having to ride in the Daimler with him whenever she wanted to go into town or anywhere else was nearly as trying as dealing with Mr. Dobble.

Nonetheless, she was the consummate professional and she had learned over the years that she could get along with anyone, regardless of how irritating or sardonic they might be as long as they did their job. Unfortunately, Bradford was more than adequate at his job.

"I should like to be picked up at three o'clock, and then I'll need to return here at half five in order to see to final preparations for the cocktail party, if you please, Mr. Bradford."

He looked at her from over the top of the panting puppy's head. The beast's little pink tongue was lolling from the side of its mouth like an unfurled ribbon. "Right, then. Myrtle and I will be here to collect you just before three o'clock." He gave her a cheeky grin, obviously knowing how much she loathed the idea of being trapped in a vehicle with that slathering menace.

She gritted her teeth and smiled. "Thank you, Mr. Bradford."

A loud thud followed by an ominous crash had her spinning from further repartee with the driver.

One of the tables had somehow been upended—and she couldn't blame it on Myrtle, as she'd been safely in her master's arms, drat it. Flowers, water, and a shattered vase were all over the floor.

It was a good thing Phyllida had extras . . . of everything.

"I'm so very anxious about meeting them!" said Digby Billdop.

He was the vicar at St. Thurston's Church, C.O.E.. His parish was located across the village green from St. Wendreda's, the papist church in Listleigh and the bane of his existence due to competition for flock members. He was still annoyed that the Catholic parish had landed the distinction of being the location for the Murder Fête instead of his own St. Thurston's, which didn't have the convenience of an orphanage with a bad roof.

As if that should have made a difference.

Both churchyards were shaded by many maples and oaks and had colorful gardens, as well as residences for the vicar and priest respectively. Digby grudgingly admitted that even though St. Thurston's yard was larger, St. Wendreda's had the nicer lawn, for it was bordered by the small river that ran through the village. Tomorrow it would be filled with tents and festival-goers.

"I'm certain it will be far less taxing than you imagine," said Harvey Dobble, the butler at Mallowan Hall. "Meeting all of them."

They were sitting at the same table at which they played their weekly chess game at the vicarage. Dobble had risen unusually early and slipped away from his duties at Mallowan Hall this morning in order to buck up his friend before the Murder Fête luncheon—and to make certain the vicar didn't back out of going at the last minute. Digby was prone to anxiousness and he had delicate nerves, but in Dobble's opinion, the vicar was a gifted writer as well as a worthy chess opponent.

Digby clasped his pudgy fingers together on the table in front of him as if to keep them from fluttering. "To meet Mr. Chesterton in particular is quite upsetting my insides, because he's simply . . . but you know how he's my *idol.* Oh dear . . . what if none of them liked my story?"

Dobble shook his head. "Not at all, Digs," he said. "I've read your stories and they're eminently publishable. Why—and don't repeat this—I find your Father Veritas to be far more compelling than Mr. Chesterton's Father Brown. He overdoes the umbrella bit, Mr. Chesterton does, and *'little'* Father Brown—as he continues to describe him—is far too doddering for my taste. Gives the clergy a bad name when he's so rumpled and vacant-eyed."

"Do you really think so?" replied the vicar, his eyes hopeful.

"I certainly do." Dobble gave him a warm smile—something that would never be seen by any of the staff at Mallowan Hall. "Don't I always insist on reading your new pages the moment I arrive, even before dinner? Father Veritas has become my favorite detective—after M. Poirot, of course."

"Oh, thank you for saying so," replied Digby, clasping his hands even tighter together. His eyes glittered with raw emotion. "That is quite a compliment, as M. Poirot is simply . . . well, *parfait*—as he would say—as is Madame Christie." He gave a little chuckle that trailed off into a sigh. "I know I must sound silly, but Alistair is always picking at every little detail in my stories, and sometimes I simply can't help but wish *he'd* run out of ideas, or that his words would dry up, or-or that his pages would get accidentally dropped in the fire and destroyed. Or-or that *something* would happen to him. Even though it's not very Christian of me," he added ruefully.

"Alastair Whittlesby is an unmitigated arse, and *I* have no qualms about wishing his papers would go up in flames—or worse," Dobble said stoutly, for there had been more than one occasion when Digby had been near tears after a Listleigh Murder Club meeting. Mr. Whittlesby reigned as president of the group and, in his mind, as the as-yet-undiscovered Shakespeare of Detective Fiction. "From what Drewson—his butler, of course—has told me, the man is no more civil at home than he is at the writers' club meetings. Drewson claims the rows between him and his brother are something to behold."

Mr. Whittlesby was meddlesome, opinionated—and blunt about it—and oftentimes rude and cruel. But he was the only solicitor in the village, and his father had had a baronetcy and a bit

of money so the man thought himself above most everyone he encountered even though he was barely considered a gentleman.

"Even Wednesday, when we were all there at his house for tea,
he was simply insufferable. He's so very certain he will win the
story contest and the publishing prize—I'm certain that's why he
had us all there. To gloat in advance," said Digby.

"Was everyone there?" asked Dobble. His attention slid—not
for the first time—to the cake sitting on the counter, and he was
quite regretful that his friend hadn't cut into it yet. A piece of
whatever it was—a luscious white confection—would be an excellent partner to the tea he'd been sipping. Digby's housekeeper
was a formidable baker, a fact which Dobble would never even
think of acknowledging in the hearing of Mrs. Puffley, who
reigned in the kitchen at Mallowan Hall.

"All of the members of the Murder Club were there," replied
the vicar, seemingly oblivious to Dobble's interest in an early
morning dessert. "Even Miss Crowley, who refused to touch even
a glass of sherry." Digby sighed. "I'm rather afraid Mr. Whittlesby
will be the winner of the prize—and then he'll be utterly intolera-
ble. I might have to quit the club if he wins. I just wish something
would *happen* to him, to-to put him out of the way."

"Now, now, Digs, let's not put the cart before the horse. You've
as good a chance of winning as anyone—save Vera Rollingbroke."

They chuckled, and Dobble was relieved that his friend seemed
to relax a little. He very much hoped that Digby would win, but
more than that, he desperately hoped that Alastair Whittlesby
would *not*. Even if Dr. Bhatt won instead of Digby, it would be far
better—though in that event, Dobble would have to contend with
Mrs. Bright's subtle, but smug, satisfaction.

Dobble glanced at the clock, and saw with a start that it was past
time for him to return to the manor house to see that breakfast
had been cleared, and tea and dinner were being prepared. For
the last few days during the preparations for the Murder Fête, the
residence had been unusually quiet. This was mainly due to the
long absences of Mrs. Bright. She'd taken her impudently bright
hair and her righteous temperament to St. Wendreda's—along

with some of her staff, which had actually left Dobble in a rather trying position, keeping the meals coming and tea on time. But that inconvenience had been balanced by the fact that Mrs. Bright had been blissfully and regularly *not present* at the manor house.

"I'd best be off, then, Digs," said Dobble, once again looking regretfully at the cake as he stood. "Mrs. Bright has left the household in quite the straits as of late, and there's no one to set it right but myself."

"Why, that's not very sporting of her, is it?" said Digby, rising as well.

"Not in the least," Dobble replied as he settled his hat in place. "But it does afford me the opportunity to ensure the maids are doing their work to *my* standards. There's simply so much *lace* and *chintz* everywhere, I've taken the opportunity to decrease its presence." And he'd made certain those blasted cats of Mrs. Bright's hadn't so much as poked a whisker from outside of her sitting room. Their frustrated yowling at the door had brought a smile to his face.

"I do know how indispensable Mrs. Bright is up at Mallowan Hall," Digby said earnestly. "She's quite a wonder, isn't she? So clever and well turned out, and so very civil too, if a bit intimidating. It must be very trying with her being absent so much this weekend."

Dobble stiffened a little. "Wonder is hardly a word I would use to describe that woman, Digby. She's . . . well, she's slightly more than adequate at her position—which, incidentally, I cannot begin to understand how she acquired, with her surely never having been in service until Mrs. Agatha brought her on."

"Oh!" replied Digby with a conspiratorial smile. "I didn't realize you'd finally ferreted out that information! What *did* she do before she came to work for the Mallowans? I've been simply *dying* of curiosity."

Dobble's mood soured even further. "Well, I haven't actually determined for certain that Mrs. Bright hasn't been in service before. The woman is extraordinarily tight-lipped about her past!

Why, I don't know much of anything about her other than she knew Mrs. Agatha during the war and it seems she was a nurse at the frontlines. And whatever happened to her husband is a mystery as well. For all I know, Mr. Bright might arrive at Mallowan Hall someday and murder us all in our sleep!"

"Oh." The vicar's eyes widened into perfect circles behind his round glasses. "So you did find out that she was married, then?"

"Well, not precisely," Dobble was forced to admit. Why *did* Digby have to be so interested? Couldn't he just allow Dobble to grumble without asking questions? "And quite honestly, I'm not certain *who* would marry someone like her anyway—so perhaps she never *has* been married after all. One absolutely doesn't know a thing about her past. The problem with Phyllida Bright is that she is simply *not* suited to being a housekeeper."

"Quite. At least you'll be able to get things done properly with her out of the way," replied Digby soothingly.

"Thank fortune for that," Dobble replied. "Although of course she has taken all of the better maids with her to St. Wendreda's and left the lesser ones for me to contend with, along with some extra ones—and you know that managing *maids* is simply not done by a butler!" Dobble frowned. Had he remembered to tell the extra maids about the damper in the sitting room?

"Perhaps one of the footmen could manage the maids for you," said Digby, patting him on the arm.

Dobble sighed and shook his head. "And that is why you are a vicar and have no servants to speak of, other than an old day maid-cook, Diggy," he said. "One does not put footmen in charge of maids if one does not want little ones running amok nine months later."

After a quick glance to be certain no one was walking past the vicarage, he bent to give Digby a quick kiss. "That's for luck today," he said, and then slipped out the door.